THE INVISIBLE BRIGHT

MINDI BRIAR

CITY OWL
PRESS

This book is a work of fiction. Names, characters, places, and incidents either are products of the author's imagination or are used fictitiously. Any resemblance to actual events or locales or persons, living or dead, is entirely coincidental and not intended by the author.

THE INVISIBLE BRIGHT
The Halcyon Universe, Book 3

CITY OWL PRESS
www.cityowlpress.com

Cover Design by MiblArt. All stock photos licensed appropriately.

Edited by Lisa Green.

For information on subsidiary rights, please contact the publisher at info@cityowlpress.com.

Print Edition ISBN: 978-1-64898-391-7

Digital Edition ISBN: 978-1-64898-392-4

Printed in the United States of America

This book is dedicated to myself at age fourteen.
Hey, kiddo. It gets so much better. See? We're published now!

AUTHOR'S NOTE

In my ideal future, there is space for everyone to find their happy ending. As part of my commitment to promoting diversity, I want to take the opportunity to uplift diverse voices when I can. Please check out the recommendations list in the acknowledgements section for books by asexual and aromantic authors that I've enjoyed reading recently.

Additionally, I want you to feel secure while reading my book, so please note the content information below.

- Strong language
- Character death (off-page)
- Adoption trauma
- Open-door sex scene

BEFORE

Phoenix Refuge, Halcyon

Year 3730, Week 3,

Dayfour

BEFORE

Miri, Age 8

THE REPORTER TURNS TO FACE THE CAMBOT FLOATING AT HIS shoulder. It captures a wide shot of the scene: crashing waves on an idyllic tropical beach, a Refuge's thatched roof huts in the background. And in the foreground, twenty children between the ages of four and seventeen, arranged in rows, most of us wishing he'd get on with it so we can go eat lunch.

"I'm here with the Ediya Experiments for another interview," he announces. "These twenty children were conceived of stolen DNA, fertilized in test tubes, and birthed from incubators. Just four weeks ago they were rescued, thanks to young biology student Amy Ediya, niece to the mad scientists who were performing illegal tests on these poor innocent souls. Now, weeks after their miracle rescue, how are they feeling? How are the youngsters integrating into Halcyon society? And what's next for the Ediya Experiments?"

"If he calls us 'experiments' one more time, I'm going to kick him in the shins," my best friend Clara whispers behind her hand.

I hold in the giggle that's bubbling up in my throat. The cutesy nickname the newsies gave us is annoying, but if I ruin the shot, the reporter will only keep us here longer. Last week he made us redo a whole section of the interview because Harris kept loudly repeating a curse word he heard the reporter mutter under his breath.

"Let's start with the oldest." The cambot zooms in on Raoul's face. His expression looks a bit constipated underneath his pasted-on smile. "Raoul, at age seventeen, you're the big brother of the group. Do you think you'll be sad to say goodbye to the younger ones when they get adopted?"

We all look at Raoul as he opens his mouth to answer. The reporter is only repeating what we've told him in previous interviews. We consider each other siblings, and skinny, brown-haired Raoul has always been our protector. But he does get annoyed with us a lot. Sometimes he uses mind control to put us to sleep just so he can have some peace and quiet. It doesn't work on me very well, but that's fine—I'm not noisy.

From the conflicted churning of the energy aura around him, which displays his emotions as colors, I can tell that part of him is glad to shed the weight of his responsibilities. Lightning flashes of yellow tell me he's even a little excited.

But he can't say that to the newsies. So he mumbles something about how we'll all miss each other, which is true. He *will* miss us. There's dark gray sadness mixed in with the excitement in his aura.

I blink, focusing hard on Raoul's solemn face instead of the colorful energy radiating from him in a halo. I have to remember that the newsies can't see auras the way I see them. No one can—just me.

The reporter goes down the line, asking a variety of questions. Some are about our upcoming adoptions. Obviously, twenty kids can't go to the same home, so we've been split into singles and pairs, and we'll be scattered across a dozen different households. Losing each other is maybe the scariest thing that's happened to us so far, and that's counting the space battle during our rescue.

Some of his questions are about adapting to life here on Halcyon. That's been hard too. We were raised by nannybots and a skeleton crew of scientists who failed to teach us how to exist in a world we'd never seen. Every day is a new surprise, and often a new embarrassment. New rules stacking up on each other. Saray went outside in a thunderstorm and got scolded, but she didn't know what lightning *was*, let alone that it could have killed her. Table manners continue to elude the youngest kids; Ian keeps asking why spaghetti and pizza are made with the same sauce, but one requires utensils and one is for eating with hands. Not to mention the strange new array of flavors and textures that take getting used to after a lifetime of tasteless, nutrient-dense space station food.

When the reporter comes to me, he locks me in with an intense stare. I freeze. My siblings and I look human like everybody else, but sometimes our catlike golden, reflective eyes make people do a double take. It's the only outward mark of the genetic modifications that make us who we are—the reason why we were born at all.

"Miri. Our shy little sweetheart. I heard a rumor, and I wonder if you can tell me if it's true."

I stare at him, trying not to see the voracious spikes in his energy. Trying to notice only the stray beard hair on his chin that's a centimeter longer than the rest.

"I heard," he says, his voice hushed but plenty loud for the cambot at his shoulder to pick up, "that you kids have some kind of superpowers. I heard the Ediyas were trying to push human evolution farther than it's ever gone. Tell me, is it true?"

Fear washes through me. He's leaning too close, and I wasn't prepared to answer this question—I expected him to ask about adoption. *He did this on purpose,* I realize, watching the way his aura quests greedily outward like grasping fingers. *He thinks by surprising me, he can get me to tell secrets.*

My instinct is to shove him away. My energy butts up against his, and he rears back in surprise. I don't know what it feels like for him—maybe he thinks it's the intense glare on my "sweet" face that makes him recoil—but I can see the interplay of the aether between us. With the pure force of my will, I'm making him back down. If I poke at just the right spot in his aura, I can even make him apologize...

"Cut the cam!" a sharp voice interrupts, and the reporter turns away, his face scrunching in a flash of frustration.

Amy Ediya strides toward us across the beach. She's wearing nothing but a waterproof black underlayer, which covers her from shoulders to upper thighs but leaves her arms and legs bare. Her bouncy curls are soaking wet. Sand sticks to her legs as, with each furious step, she kicks it up. She looks like she's just crawled out of the ocean. Knowing her, she probably has.

"Do you mind?" the reporter snaps. "There's an interview in progress."

"Oh, I heard." Amy's expression is as dark as thunderstorm clouds. Her aura billows out from her body in a brilliant shifting rainbow. Her injury leached the life out of her, making her aura weak and colorless, but she's almost back to her full force-of-nature self.

She marches right up to stand between me and Clara, a hand on each of our shoulders. "I thought we agreed there were topics these children will not be asked about. They need to integrate into this society, and they can't do that if you're exposing them to constant scrutiny, or even putting them in danger, by revealing more than is necessary."

"It's a simple question," the reporter replies. "All she needs to say is *no*, and the rumors will die out."

"But a *no* isn't what you were fishing for, is it?" Amy glares him down, her golden eyes intense as twin suns. "I noticed you didn't ask the older kids. You asked one of the little ones. Why is that?"

The reporter waves his hand. "Fine, fine. If you'll back away from the shot, I'll retake the scene."

"No." Amy moves to stand in front of me, arms akimbo. "This interview is over, and it's your last. You'll wrap up this segment with some speech about how it's best to leave these kids alone to adjust to their new lives now. They don't want celebrity. They want to be normal. And you're going to let them, because as we all know, Halcyonite newsies are deeply committed to ethical journalism."

I don't really get what "ethical journalism" means, but that line makes the reporter's face go bright red. He clicks the remote in his hand, and the cambot's "eyes" shutter, its green lights blinking orange. He catches it as it sinks toward the ground, then tucks the skull-sized globe under his arm and storms away without another word.

As soon as Amy is sure that he's gone, she turns to face us. We're all grinning. It was fun watching her tell off the man who kept calling us "experiments."

But our smiles melt when we see how dead serious she looks.

"I need to tell you something really important right now," she says. "If you kids remember nothing else I've told you, remember this: *Don't ever tell anyone about your powers.*"

"No one?" Clara pipes up. "Not even our adoptive parents?"

"Not until you're older," Amy amends. "When you're a grown-up, you'll learn how to tell if people can be trusted. But for now, don't tell anyone, ever. Got it?"

We all nod. Then Raoul says, "Would it be so bad if the newsies found out? They don't experiment on kids here. That's what you told us. You said we can be safe on this planet."

"On Halcyon, yes. There are laws to keep you safe, and the dragons will protect you." Amy lets out a breath. "But the newsies broadcast all over this galaxy. Lots of people on other worlds might want to capture and study you or use you and your powers to do bad things. Also...you should all know that my aunt and uncle didn't die when their station blew. They survived. They're going to prison, but that doesn't mean they're gone."

I gasp, and I'm not the only one. After four weeks living on a planet, learning about the outside world, I'm just beginning to understand how cruel the Ediyas were to keep us locked away. And how truly dangerous our powers might be.

Amy's been gently explaining to us that those special abilities are why we were born. Her aunt and uncle, Melanie and Oberon Ediya, were trying to make kids who had the same powers as the alien "dragons" who protect this planet: teleporting, invisibility, mind reading, maybe other things we don't know about.

It worked.

But it worked differently with each one of us. Raoul can put suggestions in people's minds, while Clara can read thoughts like a book. Talia has visions of the future. Saray tastes words like they're candy. Fatima can go invisible if she's frightened. None of us have figured out how to teleport yet, but Amy thinks we will someday.

When we first landed, it was hard to know which abilities we needed to keep secret and which were normal-people things that everyone could do. We scared a couple of Devotes by accidentally reading their thoughts or appearing out of thin air in front of them. But Amy's been coaching us, and I think we've done a pretty good job learning what to keep secret.

"Having these abilities...it doesn't make life easy," she tells us. "From the time I was little, I knew I had to hide my ability to see flashes of the past. People got scared when I did it, or they wanted to study me, or they told my mum I needed medication. I learned that it's better to never, ever tell anybody. Not unless you're *sure* how they're going to react."

She looks each one of us in the eye, one after the other. "You kids are more or less my family, so anytime you need to talk to someone...call me first. I promise I will always do what I can to protect you." She sighs. "But you have to understand that not everyone will be like that. So keep your powers secret. Understand?"

I nod.

Then I look around at the crowd of kids around me, each exuding watercolor rainbows of aether energy...and I blink twice, focusing my vision on the sharp outlines of the physical, tangible world. The colors recede, leaving only newly sunburnt noses and sandy feet.

I can be normal.

I *will* be normal.

PART ONE

Evergreen Refuge, Halcyon

Year 3745, Week 12,

Dayone

CHAPTER ONE

Miri, Age 23

DRAGONS FLOAT ABOVE ME IN AN AURORA SWIRL OF EMOTIVE COLOR. I can see them with my eyes closed, invisible brightness glowing against the back of my eyelids. To be honest, it's a bit distracting.

My meditative trance breaks. I blink, and the world comes into focus. Nebulous energy auras resolve into bodies at rest, legs crossed, hands on knees. My powder-blue robe drapes in soft folds around me, wordlessly conveying my status as a Devote—a combination of spiritual guide and social worker. The two supplicants across from me both wear the earth-tone trousers and tunic common among rural farming communities.

Their appointment was first thing this morning. They're a married couple, mid-thirties. They're seeking counseling because they can't agree on a solution to their infertility issues. But their auras tell a deeper story. The husband's energy has questing feelers out, seeking his partner's attention and reciprocation. The partner's energy is in turmoil, roiling and surging in shades of bitterness and frustration. The dragons can sense it—that's why their pastel-iridescent soap-bubble forms are clustered on my side of the room. They're drawn to calm, peaceful energy and repelled by discord.

I begin to lead my supplicants out of the guided meditation. "Open your eyes and take a moment to be aware of the present," I murmur. My Devote voice is on full blast: low and smooth, syllables drawn out and fully enunciated, every word deliberate. My friend Clara accuses me of speaking like a Devote all the time, though I swear I don't. When I'm off duty, my voice sounds much chirpier and faster-paced. I also stumble over words more because I'm thinking about them less.

I take a moment to ground myself. Dim lights, harsh after ten minutes with my eyelids shut, glowing softly against the dark wood grain of the walls. Piney, fresh air, sharp with the chill that leaks through the crack under the door. The counseling room is an intimately small space modeled after our larger meetinghouse. Whereas the circular log-cabin building hosts group meditations, these private spaces are meant to give people a safe place to talk about their deepest concerns. As a young Devote-in-training, I rarely entered them except for counseling sessions with my own mentor, Sister Tierza. But I've finished my training, and now I'm expected to be the one giving advice.

It's not always easy.

"Mx Perino," I say. "Tell me again about the difficulty that brought you here." They've barely spoken a word to me all morning. I suspect their husband put them up to this counseling session, as they seem closed off to the idea of participating. They eye me warily, arms crossed, lips sealed.

It would be so, so easy to reach out into their aura...to just nudge their anger brighter and suppress their pride a little. To just get them *talking*. I know if they let their husband know the true source of their frustration, they'd be able to work it out...but the dragons hate it when I interfere. Even if my intentions are good.

Even if, sometimes, I can't help it.

"It bothers me that you won't even consider moving offworld to raise our kids!" Mx Perino blurts. "You always talk about your childhood here like it was *sooo* perfect, but I miss the city."

Oh fuck. I slipped.

Mas Perino looks at them in shock. "I thought you agreed with me that this planet is the perfect place to raise a family!"

"I *did*," Mx Perino wails. "But the thought of spending the next twenty years here... I'm so *bored*, Luca. I don't even know if I *want* to have kids anymore, if it means I'm stuck here forever."

Mas Perino's aura is taking on some of his partner's chaos as anger filters in. "You probably should have said something about this before we sold the townhouse. Or maybe before we got married! We committed to a shared future, Kay. This was the plan we both agreed on."

Mx Perino is sobbing now. "I know! I had this romantic idea about what Halcyon would be like, and I thought it would be what I wanted! I just don't know anymore. I can't stay here. And if you want to stay... maybe I should leave, and let you do what you want."

Oh shit. I don't want them breaking up right in front of me because I pushed them too far. The wave of released pent-up frustration is washing over them, making them feel it all at once. Panicking a little, I search for the affection that binds these two together and pull it to the forefront, tamping down the anger.

Why does one little mistake always turn into a whole mess I have to untangle?

Mas Perino gathers his partner into a careful hug, stroking their hair. "I'm not leaving. You're my person, Kay. I wish you'd told me all of this stuff months ago...but it's not too late. We don't have kids on the way yet. We can talk it over, make a new plan."

Mx Perino burrows into his shoulder, their shaking sobs beginning to subside.

I clear my throat. "Do—do you two want a moment alone?"

They both nod wordlessly. I let myself out of the room, shut the door, and collapse back against it, breathing out a shaky sigh as guilt washes over me.

I shouldn't have done that.

Digging the heels of my hands into my eyes, I struggle to refocus on the world as everyone else sees it. Muted colors and sharp outlines. No glowing swirls of energy. Safe and tangible and *normal*.

The dragons followed me out. One of them hovers just behind my head, tasting the bitter shame rolling through my gut. Usually, such a negative emotion would repel dragons. But this one has something to say.

::We have warned you before about manipulating people's emotions without their consent,:: ze says. *::This is our final judgment. We cannot allow you to be a Devote anymore.::*

Dragons speak in feelings and images, not words, but zir meaning is quite clear. Ze shows me handing over my powder-blue robe, taking my meager belongings, and leaving the Refuge. I'm no longer welcome in the only home I've known since I was eight years old.

Ze's right. This wasn't my first warning. I know better. But I just can't seem to control myself.

Stars, what am I supposed to tell Sister Tierza? The other Devotes have no idea this has been happening. They think I'm a gifted young trainee, empathetic and deft at navigating people's problems to reach a solution.

They have no idea I've been cheating all along.

I've kept my secret carefully, as I promised Amy so long ago. None of the Devotes know I have gen-mod abilities. And even before the Refuge, my siblings and the Ediyas only knew I had aura sight. The fact that I could manipulate energy to meddle with people's emotions and make them do things, just like Raoul used to do...I never told anybody. Not Melanie Ediya, not Clara, not even Amy. I was too ashamed, even then. I knew that to mess with someone's mind without permission was a bad thing to do.

And yet, once I began giving a nudge here, a suggestion there, tweaking someone's mood brighter and muting their sadness...it's so hard to stop. How could I not help people when it's as easy as breathing?

The aura sight never goes away for long, even when I'm making a concentrated effort to ignore it. Already, faint outlines of color are reappearing around me. A healing glow emanates from the room I've just vacated—the Perinos are back to mending their relationship without me.

Guilt weighs heavy on my shoulders. I can't bring myself to talk to Sister Tierza yet. Leaving the gravel path that winds through the Refuge's cluster of buildings, I forge my way into the woods.

There's a snap of cold in the air this morning. A blanket of fog lies over the mountain, hazing out all but the closest trees. I pull my hands into the sleeves of my robe to keep warm, wishing I'd put on something cozier than a gray tunic and black leggings. A tantalizing whiff of coffee mingling with something savory floats up the hill from the dining hall. Breakfast is starting soon, as is the morning meditation. In an hour, I'm supposed to be in the kitchen helping Sister Tierza chop vegetables for the midday meal.

As a resident of the Refuge, I'm accustomed to early mornings and hard work. Half the job is the physical labor that comes with a tech-free environment: weeding, harvesting, cooking, dishwashing, spinning, sewing. While most communities on Halcyon employ an army of bots to labor for them, the Refuges work to keep the old ways alive.

I've spent most of the past fifteen years here at Evergreen. All the other Ediya Experiments went to adoptive parents, but I was claimed by the group of Devotes who've dedicated their lives to this mountain valley paradise. They promised me it'd be like having a dozen parents and a rotating army of siblings.

At first, I believed them.

But as time went on, the loneliness crept in. I started to miss the family and community I could have had. Sister Tierza genuinely cares for me, but Devotes are, by nature, detached from the rest of the world. Their job is to guide Halcyonites as impartial counselors. They rarely form long-term bonds, and they're discouraged from marrying or having children of their own. There's plenty of fondness among them—the Refuge is like one big extended family—but I share their affection with every new visitor.

Maybe it's selfish, but I've never quite let go of that childish dream of a family who puts me first.

I'm getting a little too deep into the forest, so I veer toward the mountainside path that leads along the riverbank. The packed dirt is damp with morning dew, the air full of the clean, fresh scent of water and fallen pine needles. As I climb higher, the roar of the waterfall that powers hydro generators for three neighboring communities drowns out the quiet.

I hike all the way to the lookout point, a wooden platform at the edge of a cliff. I lean against the railing to watch the shimmering sheets of water in free fall, the noise of it filling my ears. The spray of mist arcs rainbows in the afternoon sun.

The dragons want me gone. I don't know where I'm going to go. Some local community might take me in, sure—but they might kick me out, too, the next time my aethersight gets away from me. And it will. Because I don't have the faintest idea how to control it.

I reach for the inner pocket of my robe that hides my scroll-tablet. I'm lucky it still connects to the uniweb up here in the mountains. Some Devotes are purists who insist on no tech at all, but my tablet is my connection to the outside world. I always carry it with me.

I flip through my contacts until I find the one person I know will help me, no questions asked.

<Amy Ediya.>

I'M HALF-SURPRISED WHEN A DRAGON AGREES TO TELEPORT ME TO Avalon Community. I thought I might get a snippy refusal after angering them this morning. But the dragon deposits me right where I asked: the driftwoody, rocky beach right outside Avalon, where Amy waits clad in a sleek green wetsuit.

"Miri!" she exclaims. "Stars, it's good to see you." She sounds relieved. Why? I didn't tell her anything in my message. Just said I needed to talk.

I feel vulnerable, keenly aware that everything I own is in the satchel over my shoulder. I'm still wearing the Devote robe, but it feels like a lie now, claiming a rank I've proven myself unworthy to hold.

Amy peels her wetsuit halfway off, revealing a sleeveless black shirt underneath. She's not wearing her usual navy blue Knight uniform today —it must be her day off. Spiraling vine tattoos snake down from her shoulders, bright green glow-ink against her dark skin. It's a tribute to her wife, who's an agriculture technician for their community. Her braids brush her shoulders, tipped with gold charms that match her reflective gen-mod eyes.

Today those eyes have bags under them. It might be my imagination, but does she have more wrinkles than she used to?

"Amy," I say, wishing it didn't come out sounding so plaintive, "I think I messed up."

"Come here, sit down." She indicates a dried-out log of driftwood further up the shore. "What's wrong?"

It's not the most comfortable seat ever, but I perch on the log anyway. Amy straddles it, facing me with her hands braced on her knees.

"Whenever I try to do a counseling session with people..." I suck in air. My chest feels too small for my lungs. "I keep changing their feelings. I do it on purpose sometimes, but a lot of the time I don't even mean to. And today the dragons...they..."

Amy glances up, but there aren't any dragons lurking. At least, none that I can sense. They know how to make themselves invisible even to me. "They what?"

"I can't be a Devote anymore. They told me to leave." My eyes sting. "Amy, I need to know how to hold back my powers from changing people. How do I do that?"

Amy's aura pinkens with sympathy. "I wish I knew. My abilities are weaker now, but when I was young, I couldn't stop myself from seeing visions no matter how hard I tried. It's like if you tried to stop seeing or smelling, but you don't have the option to pinch your nose or close your eyes. Basically impossible."

Tears overflow, dripping down my nose. "So I can't ever go back to the Refuge?"

"I didn't say that." She sighs. "All I'm saying is I don't know how to help you. But there's got to be a way. I almost wish..."

"What?"

"It's horrible to say. I don't really wish—but if Melanie and Oberon had only had more time to observe you all as children, maybe they would have been able to figure out—" She shudders. "No way. It wouldn't have been worth it."

"Have any of my other siblings learned to control their abilities?" I ask. "You talk to them all, don't you?"

"Funny you should say that." She picks at a loose splinter on the log. "I was glad to see your message. I've been trying to get in contact with Ian all week. I can't reach him. I'm worried he's...missing like the others."

My pulse starts to race. "Another one?"

Back when we were young teens, we had a group chat, all of us collectively adjusting to life on Halcyon and recovering from trauma. It dwindled as the years wore on. We were all growing up to have different interests, personalities, coping mechanisms...after a certain point, our shared youth wasn't enough to keep us bonded.

And lately, some of my Ediya Experiment siblings have been disappearing altogether. Saray, Harris, Rosa, Fatima...no one's been able to get in contact with them for more than a standard year.

And now, Ian may be added to that list.

Amy rubs her forehead. "You don't know how fucking relieved I am every time I hear from one of you. Um, 'scuse my language. Clara hasn't been answering my messages either, but I saw on her uniweb profile that she's back on Halcyon to visit Mercy. So at least she's not missing. She's just ignoring me."

"Where do you think they're all going?" I know Amy doesn't know. But I have to ask.

She presses her lips together. "Whether someone's kidnapping them or...*murdering* them, or if they're just too busy to answer messages or post on the uniweb...I really can't say. But I wanted to tell you to please be careful. I'm afraid whatever happened to the others is going to keep happening."

That puts a prickly feeling at the back of my shoulders, like I'm being watched. "What can I do to protect myself?"

"I wish I knew." She throws a hand in the air, a helpless gesture. "The only common thread, as far as I can tell, is that all of them were offworld when they disappeared. Makes sense. If they were snatched or killed, nobody could do it while they were on Halcyon. The dragons would be able to protect them here." She sighs. "That's all I've got. It's not much. Sorry."

"I wasn't planning to go offworld...not unless the dragons force me to," I say. Then my stomach lurches, remembering that Clara's back home only for a short visit. She'll be headed back to her acting school soon. It's on Monroe, a planet famous galaxy-wide for its high concentration of holo-stars, stage actors, and pop singers. Not exactly low profile.

I have to warn her.

Amy groans. "Here I am dumping all my worries on you, like I'm a supplicant, and you're the one who just got kicked out of your Refuge. How can I help? Do you need a place to sleep? Avalon has plenty of spare guest beds. You're welcome to stay as long as you need."

"Actually...I'm going to try to call Clara really quick. If she doesn't answer, then I may take you up on that."

Amy pushes herself to her feet. "I'll give you some space. I'll be over in the community garden if you need me. It's my turn to pull weeds."

I wave goodbye as she retreats, then dig in the pocket of my robe for my scroll again. Clara's call code is still in my favorites, even though I haven't messaged her for months.

The call connects almost instantly. "Miriiii!" Clara squeals. She centers the vid-capture on her face, tossing her long, platinum blonde hair over one shoulder. My freckly, tanned face and wispy brown braid seem dull next to her vibrant presence. "Did you know I'm back on Halcyon? I was just thinking about calling you. How's nun life?"

Despite the pit of shame that boils in my gut, I can't help laughing a little at her phrasing. "You know we don't use that archaic term for—"

"You should come over! Raoul's home for a visit too. And there's this big wedding the whole community's invited to."

"Raoul's home?" I raise my eyebrows. "I haven't seen him in, what, six years?" He doesn't visit Halcyon very often, if at all.

Clara's expression falters. "I guess you haven't heard," she says, her tone losing some of its sparkle. "Mercy isn't...she isn't doing very well."

"Oh, Clara..."

Mercy Seranath adopted both Clara and Raoul when we first arrived on Halcyon. I visited their community often when I was younger, because Sister Tierza and Mercy both thought it was healthy for me and

Clara to remain close friends. The weeks of my childhood that I spent at Newcastle Community are my fondest memories.

"How bad is it?" I ask. Mercy has had cancer for years, but modern nanite treatments can keep it at bay indefinitely, allowing a patient to live a perfectly normal life into old age. Only rare, very aggressive cancers are beyond the abilities of nanites to control.

"The healers think she has a few weeks left. A month, if she's lucky." Clara pastes on a smile, grasping for her former cheer. "But you know Mercy! I bet she'll kick its ass after all. She's not that easy to get rid of."

Her golden eyes betray her by tearing up.

I clear my throat against the sudden lump rising. "You know what? I've, um, just gotten some time off, so I think I'll take you up on that invitation. It's been too long since I was at Newcastle."

Clara brightens. "Yay! I can't wait! Bring something nice to wear for the wedding!"

"I don't want to invite myself," I say hastily. "Who's getting married anyway?"

Clara's eyes crinkle mischievously. "You remember Christo Galway?"

My heart thuds painfully in my chest. "Of course," I say. My lungs can't seem to expand properly. "Who could forget the Galway boys?"

"Not you!" *Oh, she's really going in for the kill, isn't she?* "I seem to remember you had a thing with his brother. What's his name—Leo?"

Flatly, I say, "There was no *thing*."

"Oh, wasn't there?" She winks. "If you say so. He'll be there, you know. Him and his whole family."

"On second thought, I'm really busy at the Refuge, and I—"

"Uh-uh." She giggles. "You already said you'd come. No backing out now. Message me what time you're going to arrive."

It's only after she clicks off the call that I realize I completely forgot to tell her what Amy said. I guess it can wait until I see her in person.

I thought I was going to spend the rest of the day contemplating Amy's warning—my siblings going missing—not to mention my failure as a Devote and the dragon's censure. But now the name *Leo Galway* has taken up residence in my head, and I can't think about anyone else.

Leo Galway, the goofy, blond string bean of a kid who used to play with me and Clara.

Who puberty unexpectedly took on a journey from bad skin and cracking voice to muscles and sweet brown eyes.

Whose kisses almost made me forget my own name.

Leo Galway, whose heart I broke into a million pieces.

PART TWO

Newcastle Community, Halcyon

Year 3745, Week 12,

Daytwo

CHAPTER TWO

Leo

MY BROTHER, CHRISTO DOUBLES OVER LAUGHING, BRACING ONE HAND against the wall of the flyball court. "You did *not* ride a dinosaur," he chokes.

"He totally did," says Wes, also chuckling. "My buddy was there. Saw the whole thing. He said Leo was...how did he put it? *The baddest buckaroo this side of the galaxy.*"

"Please shut up," I groan. "I already got the lecture from Chief Knight Jostlin."

Robbie, my oldest brother, shakes his head. "Stars, Leo, have you got a magnet for accidents strapped to your ass?"

"Maybe." I rub my bruised buttocks. "That'd explain why it hurts so much."

"Uh, I think that might have to do with the buckin' bronto you decided to ride."

"It wasn't a brontosaurus," I groan. "It looked more like a fat alligator with spikes. Are we gonna play flyball or what?" My brothers' spouses are standing across the court from us, geared up and ready to play. When we give the ready signal, they'll flip the switch that activates the antigrav field and the game will begin.

"Hold on, hold on, not yet," Christo says, gasping for breath. "I wanna hear the whole story."

I groan and roll my eyes, but my brothers aren't letting me change the subject.

"All right, fine. FINE. It all started on our last aid run to Susannah..."

WORKING FROM THE HALCYON KNIGHTS' OFFWORLD STATION, WE never quite know what to expect. One day we're handing out nutrient bars to starving miners whose Imperial bosses skimp on worker rations to line their own pockets. The day after that we're rescuing prisoners from a planet on fire with civil unrest. Then we barely get a chance to recover from getting shot at before we're on our way to ferry an alien species offplanet before their sun expands and wipes them out.

Halcyon's Knights aren't really an army, even though that's how everybody thinks of us. We could act as one, hypothetically, if someone tried to attack Halcyon...but the dragons are so good at keeping malevolent forces away that we've never needed to.

That's the deal the Knights have kept with them for over three millennia. Dragons owned this planet first. Halcyonites settled here with their blessing and agreed to abide by the dragons' conditions. Settlers must respect the land as if they're visitors rather than owners, keeping Halcyon's natural resources safe. We agreed to exile anyone who threatens the peace. We've kept our society equal and free, so that all citizens can flourish and have a chance to find happiness.

In return, the dragons promised to protect Halcyon's inhabitants. And they've more than kept their side of the bargain.

Their ability to teleport is the most efficient method of transportation available. It allows people to travel between planets in a blink. Because humans rely so heavily on dragons for interplanetary travel, their power to refuse someone transport is as close to exile as it comes. If a dragon perceives ill intention in someone's mind—if they think that person will cause a disturbance to their carefully balanced order—they simply don't allow that person to teleport anywhere near

Halcyon. Sure, any person could get aboard a starship and fly there, but the highest-speed ships would take them several hundred years to get here from the nearest neighboring system. The dragons would see them coming lightyears away.

That means we Knights spend most of our time on philanthropic missions to other planets: feeding the hungry, medicating the sick, and rescuing the threatened and oppressed. So as not to break Halcyon's declared neutrality, we aren't supposed to interfere in planetary wars or political disputes; we focus our attention on the civilians affected. Funded by a pool of donations from Halcyonite communities' surplus and guided by the ever-present collective consciousness of the dragons, Knights are known around the galaxy as saviors, angels of mercy.

Obviously, the Imperial Authorities hate our guts. The Empire controls almost every colony planet in this galaxy, squeezing them for resources and funneling wealth to a handful of rich governors. But they've never been able to touch Halcyon, and that really burns their buns.

Anyway, on that particular morning, my team was assigned to a planetary aid run on a farming colony called Susannah. There'd been an outbreak of some nasty strain of flu, and the Imperial-appointed governor was dragging his heels on sourcing a vaccine for the whole colony. (Of course, he'd gotten one himself months ago.) My team was supposed to land in a random town, vaccinate as many as we could, and then move on to the next town. Above all, we were supposed to avoid the governor's attention.

But when I noticed that the town's reservoir pump was malfunctioning, leaving the crops dry, I couldn't resist going to check it out. Needles aren't my forte, but machines are easy.

"It'll only take me a sec!" I called to my fellow Knights.

My buddy Chaz Rathun, a seven-foot, broad-shouldered feline-humanoid, yelled back, "That's what you always say!" But he didn't stop me.

Nor did any of the dozens of townspeople I passed on my way down to the edge of the reservoir. None of them even thought to yell out a warning, not even their machinist, who was newly missing a leg.

And that's how, when the Knights responded to my yell for help a few minutes later, they found me thrashing around in the reservoir, wrestling a saurian the size of a small elephant. The creature's underwater nest of twigs and mud piled against the intake pipes had caused the malfunction in the first place. The townspeople *totally knew about this*, because that very same lizard had chewed off Machinist Stewart's leg two weeks ago. Not that I found out about that until later.

I'm not still mad about that or anything.

Anyway, I managed to climb on the lizard's back—a risky maneuver 'cause of the razor-sharp scales and jagged spikes. It bucked like an angry bull, trying to fling me to shore or maybe drown me. I held on for a foolishly long time, until finally, Natalia Lantz pulled out one of her pink throwing knives (don't tell her I mentioned those—they're non-regulation, but they saved my life) and, like a badass, speared the creature right through its single eye.

"You could have hit me if it moved the wrong way," I panted, after I climbed out of the water.

"You'd have deserved it," Nat shot back. "What were you thinking? Your thrashing around made someone call emergency services, and they alerted the Authorities. The governor's enforcers are already on their way. Thanks to you, half this town doesn't get vaccinated today."

She collared me and dragged me onto the ship, which was actually a big help, since my knees were trembling so hard I could barely walk. I was pretty sure I pissed myself during the wild ride that saurian took me on. Luckily, my underlayer is super-absorbent.

"AND THEN CHIEF KNIGHT JOSTLIN GROUNDED ME," I FINISH, TRYING to ignore my brothers' snorts of laughter. "He knew I was already taking time off for Christo's wedding, so he just...extended it. I'm dirtside for a month."

He threatened to make it longer if I can't start thinking things through before I jump into them. Apparently, the local Authorities are now on high alert for unauthorized ships. The Knights won't be able to vaccinate any more Susannan people for months. Long enough for the disease to take out a chunk of the vulnerable population.

The guilt of knowing my screwup could cause hundreds to thousands of deaths is worse than being grounded. Plus, Jostlin threatened to make my grounding permanent if I fuck up again. Meaning, I'll be stuck sipping coffee with seventy-five-year-old veteran Knights while manning the emergency call center instead of being out in the field. I cringe at the thought.

"I didn't mean to disturb a gigantor-ass lizard," I mutter, addressing my shoes. "I just wanted to help them fix their pump."

"That's what makes it funny," Christo says, which doesn't make me feel better at all. "It's so *classic Leo.*"

"Rude...but accurate," I admit. I *try* to stay out of trouble, I swear I do. But it doesn't matter if there's just one pile of sheep dung in the whole field—I'm the one whose foot will find it. Every time.

Telling the story has weighed my mood down like a malfunctioning grav-sim. "Actually, you guys go ahead and play without me. The healer said I need to be careful with my neck. Whiplash."

"Aw, c'mon, Leo, we'll play gentle!" Wes calls. But I back out of the court before they can switch on the grav-sim.

Anyway, with my six older brothers and their six life partners, they've got even teams for flyball. I'd have been an unnecessary extra.

I take a seat halfway up the bleachers in the high-ceilinged viewing room. Through the glass, I watch as the grav-sim comes on and lifts everyone off their feet. Robbie palms the ball, his mouth moving as he calls to the rest of my blond, broad-shouldered brothers.

Their partners, who were huddled on the opposite side of the room formulating an attack plan, now hang onto the handles jutting from the wall to remain in formation. Where my brothers all look the same, no two of their sweethearts look alike. Robbie's Mariel is sweet-faced, petite, and pregnant; Jesse's Mai has sharp features, short black hair, and spikes in her ears; Christo's Julian is muscley and square-jawed.

My brothers chose well when adding to our family. They're all wonderful humans. Now that Christo is making it official with Julian, I know that Ma is going to start looking at me next. Wondering when I'll choose a nice person to keep our flyball teams on even numbers.

But I just don't look at people that way. Not ever.

Well, all right, hardly ever. There was that one time, when my heart felt like it was in zero-grav and I might float right up to the sun...

Then my wings melted and I fell. *Hard.*

I'm not in a hurry to do that again.

I'M SLINKING UP TO THE DINING HALL FOR LUNCH, HOPING TO GET IN line before my sweaty, ravenous brothers, when I bump into Clara Seranath.

My brothers have been teasing me since we were kids that I should date Clara. Yeah, no thanks. She *is* pretty, I guess, with long, smooth, pale hair that makes her look like an elf from a fantasy holo-vid. To be honest, she kinda looks like she could be our sister. But she acts like an annoying cheerleader from an Old Earth period drama. Over-the-top excited about *everything* yet can't seem to take anything seriously. I'm an energetic guy, but Clara makes me feel like I need to take a nap.

Oh, and she's bossy as fuck. When we were kids, she routinely forced me to dress up and play some side character in her never-ending pretend games. I sometimes have nightmares of Clara's high-pitched voice saying, "Now you're a dog. Sit, boy! Roll over!" and being powerless to stop myself from obeying.

That's the other thing about Clara—even when she annoys you to death, you somehow can't stop yourself from doing exactly what she wants. She knows exactly what buttons to push to keep you on her hook. It's like she can read minds or something.

"Leo!" she chirps. "*So* nice to see you again! Hey, c'mere, I've got a surprise for you."

Stars save me. Is she going to dress me up as a tree and make me perform in an impromptu pageant? If so, I hope my brothers don't see it. It's not like they're running low on reasons to make fun of me.

I step into the dining hall, sparing a quick glance over my shoulder to check if any of the Galway sibling flyball league has made it here yet. Clara tucks a hand into the crook of my arm and steers me past the cafeteria line to a table where—

I nearly trip over my own feet. The girl sitting at that table is the same one who rolled her eyes along with me at Clara's games, who bonded over our shared discomfort playing ladies-in-waiting to Clara's Empress. It's been, what, five years since I've seen her? But I'd know that face anywhere. Green-gold eyes, soft brown hair, and a faint splash of freckles across her suntanned nose.

Freckles I once kissed, right before I kissed her petal-soft mouth.

Miri.

CHAPTER THREE

Miri

I T'S LIKE MY BODY KNOWS HE'S CLOSE TO ME BEFORE I EVEN REGISTER his face. The warmth of his aura, yellow like sunshine, glows against my skin, pulling heat forward into my cheeks.

I'm going to kill Clara.

I can't believe she set me up like this. I asked her what time I should teleport over. Like chocolate wouldn't melt on her tongue, she said, "Oh, let's meet at lunchtime in the Newcastle dining hall! Can't wait to catch up!"

Apparently, when she can read minds and sees two people pining for each other, it feels like a moral imperative to shove them at each other.

But sometimes people have a good reason for not acting on their feelings. Sometimes they're trying to do the right thing by staying away.

Clara nudges Leo to sit across from me at the dining hall table. "Look who I found in the hallway!" she announces, as if it was purely accidental.

::*You're dead to me*,:: I say silently, knowing she'll be able to hear the words. Her smirk confirms it.

Leo looks like he's just been punched in the gut: shocked and slightly green. He trips over the bench seat, fumbling his grip on the table and thumping down sideways. His fair skin colors bright pink as he avoids my eyes.

He hasn't changed much, except maybe to build up more muscle. The rest of him is exactly how I remember. He's gangly and tall, pale eyelashes ringing wide, caramel-brown eyes. His features are objectively plain, so that if I didn't know him, my eyes might skate right across them, cataloging him as a bland everyguy. But nobody could ever be boring who has a smile like his, mischievous and crinkling, transforming his face into a thing of beauty and convincing whole rooms of people to laugh along with him.

That smile's absent now. I don't know if I'll ever see it again, after the way I treated him five years ago.

My eyes rove down his arms, clad in a navy blue jumpsuit. "You finished Knight training," I blurt. "Congratulations."

"You're a Devote," he replies. "Congratulations."

Discomfort twists at my insides. If only he knew how little I deserve to wear this robe.

"Do you like it?" I ask. "Being a Knight, I mean. Is it what you imagined?"

He shrugs and then nods. "It's great," he says. "Not right now, I mean. I got in trouble for riding a dinosaur. But other than that—"

I can't help the giggle that bubbles out of my throat. Stars, I forgot how he used to make me laugh. "Riding a what? *Leo!*"

"It was an accident." He's trying not to smile, but I can see the corner of his mouth twitching. The ice isn't totally broken, but there's a crack in it. A glimmer of the easy banter we used to share.

A rush of affection surges in my chest. My eyes prickle with the intensity of it. I missed this boy so, so much.

No, not boy anymore. *Man.*

"I think you're going to need to tell me that story," I say, leaning forward.

He finally flashes a smile. "Only if you tell me something juicy about being a Devote."

"Deal," I say. Out of the corner of my eye, I see Clara getting into the cafeteria line, smirking at us.

"I can't believe you did that!" I shriek later, as Clara and I clatter down the stairs toward the residential square. "What if he didn't want to talk to me? What if *I* didn't want to talk to *him*?"

"Well, you didn't," Clara points out. "But now that you have, you feel better, right?"

Depends on what *better* means. I'm no longer afraid of how he'll react, but my lungs are tight with regret. Every breath punishes me for a decision I made to protect him. A decision I'd make again, no matter how much it'd wreck me. It had to be done—it was a matter of hurting his feelings in the least cruel way possible.

I don't know if it's better to suffer the dull ache of distance, of not being part of his life, or dive headfirst into the sharp pangs that I feel being close to him. Each is its own special kind of torture.

"Hey," Clara says, nudging me. "If I knew it was going to make you all mopey, I wouldn't've done it."

I elbow her back. "Yeah, you would."

She shrugs, smirking. "Yeah, I probably would. Ugh, why didn't you want to take the zip-lift again? These stairs are killing my knees."

She knows I never choose the zip-lift if I can help it, not when the stairwell is lined with beautiful, brightly colored murals. Old paint peeks out from underneath the new scenes splashed on top; the art changes and expands with every new generation of artists. I'd spend hours admiring them if Clara let me.

I sigh in wonder as we exit the stairwell into the residential square. This level of the community is nine floors underground, but artificial sunlight fills the space with warmth. Sculptures made of wire twist from ground to ceiling, acting as ladders for clematis and wisteria. Fountains burble in the corners.

The floor is mostly carpeted in fake moss, but the walkways are tiled with a mosaic depicting the ancient Chinese *tianlong*—mythical creatures said to be the guardians of heaven. Dragons, they were called. And when strange, floating, transparent aliens appeared out of the sky to connect with humankind all those millennia ago, the ancient monks used *tianlong* as the aliens' namesake.

I walk along the belly of an ancient dragon, its white and green scales shimmering under the soft soles of my boots. I loved these dragons when I was younger. Used to lie down next to them, petting their tiled scales, until Mercy would catch me and scold me that lying on the floor is unsanitary.

We're heading toward Mercy Seranath's quarters, but our feet take us along a meandering path. As we pass one of the fountains that feed the underground stream, I say, "Remember when you pushed me in?"

"I did *not!*" Clara cries. "I just happened to gesture really forcefully and you were beside me."

"Suuure."

I can't help grinning at the memory. I always loved spending time at Newcastle Community. Not only did I get to see Clara, but it was also a reprieve from weeding fields and washing dishes by hand. Sure, I still had to do community service, but here the bots did all the hard labor. Clara and I were small enough that we got easy chores, like taking food to sick neighbors. And in our ample free time, we did nothing but play and run, the way we'd never been allowed to on Arrow Station.

Somehow Clara always roped Leo into our games. Her favorite was "Empress and Servants." One time, she pretended there was a lake monster and we were brave Knights who had to fight it off to save the community. I smile, remembering Leo and his brothers splashing and roaring, pretending to be the monster. Leo had argued that he wanted to be the Knight, not the bad guy, but he was overruled.

I heave a wistful sigh. Then I glance at Clara, hoping I'm not weighing down her mood with my melancholy.

Clara's aura, usually purply-pink, *has* gone a bit duller and more reserved. But when we stop at a red door wreathed in painted vines, I realize it's not me who's making her sad.

"We're here," Clara says softly and taps her keycuff against the lock, letting us into her adopted mother's quarters.

I follow her in, slipping off my boots in the entryway. Mercy's living space looks the same as when I last visited. The lounge room is upholstered in smooth baby-pink. The soft, squishy floor gives way in the middle to a circular sunken couch, full of soft throw pillows and handmade quilts. It used to be the coziest place to watch holos. Clara and I would curl up under one blanket, sharing a bowl of snacks. If Raoul was visiting, she would always try to talk him into unlocking holos that were above our age-appropriate rating. He actually did one time, but when we both proceeded to have awful nightmares about the horror holo he let us watch, Mercy made sure it would never happen again.

Past the lounge, there's a short hallway with three bedroom doors. I almost walk right past Mercy's and open Clara's before realizing my mistake. I'm not here for a sleepover.

"Mercy?" Clara says quietly. "How are you feeling? Miri came to see you."

"Miri?" Mercy's throaty voice carries out to the hallway. "Come on in."

I'm a little shy, entering her private space. When we were children, intruding on an adult's room was always a bit of an illicit adventure. Clara was bolder about it than me. She liked to steal Mercy's robes to play dress-up or borrow her cosmetics to make us look like Imperial courtesans. She didn't seem to mind the trouble we got into. I couldn't stand the way people's auras pulsed and spiked when they were angry, but for whatever reason, I usually went along with her schemes.

Mercy's room has changed the most since my last visit. Before, it was a tastefully decorated, impeccably neat space containing a bed, a wardrobe, a washroom, and a holo-projector. All that same furniture is still here, but it's disarrayed in a way that would have been unthinkable when Mercy was well. The bed is surrounded with monitors, wires, and a foldable table littered with medicine bottles. Used cleaning cloths sit in a pile near the washroom. The holo-projector is switched on, but even the serene meadow projected across the bed can't disguise how rumpled the covers are.

And how drastically its occupant has changed.

The Mercy Seranath in my memory is a brilliant, forceful woman. She was gray-haired even then, with blue eyes surrounded by fine lines. She didn't adopt Clara and Raoul until her mid-sixties. She was never partnered and had no biological children. But she was friendly with nearly every member of Newcastle Community—*thousands* of names and faces, and she remembered them all. As the community's Parliament representative, she'd spent a long career gaining their trust. Her job was to hear the issues brought to Parliament, collect arguments for and against, and educate her community on each topic before the people voted. It's a tough job to do well, and many Parliament reps serve for only a few years before handing over the position to someone else. But Mercy was dedicated to fostering a connection between the people of her community and the wider world they live in.

That straight-backed, blazing-eyed lady in my memory is hard to reconcile with the woman who lies in the bed before me.

She looks shrunken, more wrinkled than she used to be. Her gray hair is wispy and frazzled. I'm sure she hates that; she used to be embarrassed if anyone dropped by early in the morning before she had the chance to tame her flyaways.

There's a chair next to her bed. With a gesture, she invites me to take a seat. I see the onyx ring on her middle finger slip, sliding loose between her knuckles. Offering my hand to her, I step forward.

Her fingers, dry and cool, curl weakly around mine as I sit. "Miri, how wonderful to see you," she murmurs. "Thank you for coming."

"I'm sorry it's been so long."

She squeezes my hand. "You always come to visit Clara, not me. That's how it should be. You two girls need each other." Her eyes find Clara over my shoulder. "She'll need you more when I'm gone."

I shake my head. My instinct is to deny the inevitable, but the words sound false even in my head, so I don't voice them. We both know Mercy has precious little time left, and pretending she's immortal won't extend her life.

"Where's Raoul?" asks Clara with an edge of annoyance. "I thought he was going to stay with you."

"I didn't want to make him stay," Mercy says softly. "It makes him uncomfortable."

"To be with *our mother?*"

"I'm not really his mother," says Mercy, sorrow tugging at the lines around her mouth. "He was only under my care for a few months before he became a legal adult. He has little connection to this place, and my sickness upsets him."

"Oh, and the rest of us are fine with it?" Clara snaps.

"Clara..." I reach out without thinking to soothe the spikes of anger in her aura, but I pull back just in time.

Mercy sighs. "Everyone deals with mortality in different ways, darling. Some face it head-on and accept it, as I have. Others deny it and distance themselves from it, hoping to evade the same fate. Don't hold it against your brother that he is the latter kind."

Clara *hmphs*. "Well, I'm going to go find him. Miri, do your Devote thing while I'm gone." She stalks out but closes the door softly behind her.

I feel like a complete impostor, but telling Mercy I'm a fake Devote won't bring her comfort. "Is there anything that's been on your mind? Any lingering regrets or fears you want to talk through?"

My mind is whirling through every class I've ever taken on death counseling and grieving, but all Mercy says is, "I really could use some music. Would you tell the wallscreen to play that Irinova album I like?"

Startled, I stand up to tinker with the wallscreen's settings. A waterfall of gentle piano music pours through the hidden speakers.

"I've talked with Devotes enough," Mercy says, closing her eyes. "I know what's coming, and I don't fear it. All I want from you, Miri dear, is the company of a friend."

"I can do that," I say and clasp her bony fingers between mine.

I've been reading to Mercy for about thirty minutes—she asked for "a rip-roaring adventure, something with horses in it"—when the doorbell chimes.

"Another visitor," Mercy murmurs. She's getting sleepy. I should probably tell whoever it is to try another time. I put down the tablet and run to answer the door.

But my polite greeting stalls in my throat when I recognize the petite, curvy woman waiting there.

It's Leo's mother. *Stars above.*

"Hi there! Is Mercy up for one more visitor?"

Ana Galway has the same pale skin and brown eyes that she passed on to her sons, though she lacks their height. Her graying blonde hair is braided and coiled into a maze on top of her head.

"Hello," I choke out with an awkward little nod.

"Is that Ana? I want to see her," Mercy croaks from the bedroom. I stand aside to allow Miz Galway in, my palms sweating. How much does she know about my relationship with her son? At the time, we took care to keep it private, but I don't know what he's told his family since then.

"You're that playmate of Clara's, aren't you? You used to be such a shy little thing," Miz Galway says. "Lovely to see you grown up. And a Devote too!"

If she thinks of me as Clara's childhood friend, does that mean she doesn't know anything about the later years? Thank stars for small favors.

My voice sticking in my throat, I lead her into Mercy's room.

Miz Galway immediately perches on the end of Mercy's bed and starts chatting her ear off. I take the seat by Mercy's bedside, wondering if I should leave.

"...it's so wonderful to have all my kids in one place! Christo's wedding is this evening, so of course we're busy with preparations. But we'll have all week to enjoy each other's company. I came by to make sure you know you're invited, Mercy. The whole community is invited, of course, but I would particularly love to see you enjoying the celebration."

"Oh, thank you for thinking of me," Mercy says. "I wish I could."

"Why can't you?" I blurt. "We could borrow one of the community's hoverchairs."

Mercy shakes her head. "I'd be exhausted in minutes," she says. "You and Clara should go. Raoul too, if he's around."

"We'd be delighted to have them all!" Miz Galway gestures expansively with both hands, nearly dislodging the cord to one of Mercy's wrist monitors.

My heart thumps painfully in my chest at the sudden image of dancing with Leo. "Oh, that's so nice," I squeak, "but someone needs to be here for you, Mercy."

"You've entertained me all afternoon," Mercy says, waving a weak hand. "Go enjoy yourself. Stars know they probably don't let you have any fun at the Refuge." I open my mouth to protest, but she cuts me off. "I'll likely be asleep anyway. If I need anything, there's an alert button on my keycuff that I can press to summon a healer."

"But Mercy..."

"No buts. You and Clara go have fun. I'll go to bed early and dream I'm young."

Miz Galway squeezes Mercy's hand. "Got to go, lots of decorating left to do! Rest well, Mercy. And I hope I see you young ladies tonight!" Flashing another warm smile at me, she bustles out of the room. Distantly, I hear the front door swish open and closed.

Mercy's eyes are half-shut, but she still manages to look mischievous. "Miri, dear, you aren't going to wear that to a wedding, are you?"

I look down at my Devote robe, the front hanging open to reveal a sensible gray tunic and black leggings. "Is there dirt on it?"

Mercy chuckles. "I don't know how you and Clara manage to be so different. I've got just the thing for you to wear. I believe you and Clara used to play dress-up in my formal robes when you thought I didn't notice them missing?"

I grimace guiltily.

"How would you like to wear them tonight," Mercy offers, "with my blessing?"

"I don't know..." Truth be told, I never liked those robes. Not on me. They were gorgeous on Mercy, and even Clara had the swagger to pull off the style. But when I wore them, I never felt like myself.

"Don't you want to look pretty in case you run into that young man you like?"

My jaw drops, heat rushing to my cheeks. "How did you—no, don't tell me. Clara."

"Yes, she told me." The corner of Mercy's mouth curls into a little smirk. "Said you and that Galway boy had some sort of falling-out years ago, but she seemed to think it was water under the bridge. Is it?"

I pick at my thumbnail, unsure what to say. "He might still be angry with me." But there wasn't any red in his aura when I saw him at lunch. Just sunshine mixed with muddy discomfort and a tinge of rose pink.

Long-buried memories bubble up: *that pink color blooming around him as our eyes met, then our mouths.* I wince at the pang in my chest. "I'm not here to get back together with him," I say firmly.

And yet, I don't know how I'm supposed to keep my distance when seeing him again felt like light pouring into a dark room. It's one thing to tell myself I can't be with him, but it's a whole other battle to stop wanting to.

"Perfectly understandable." Mercy gives a solemn nod. "Still, it can't hurt to dress nice, can it? Just in case?"

I crack a smile. "I guess not."

CHAPTER FOUR

Leo

"What's with you?" Neena, my brother's wife, asks. We're in the recreation hall, getting the ballroom ready for the wedding tonight. To help decorate, Ma has recruited Robbie and Ward and their wives as well as my fifth-oldest brother, Jesse, and his partner, Mai.

Neena and Mai have managed to corral me into stringing flower garlands with them. They set me up at their table with baskets of brightly colored blooms fresh from the greenhouse. I've been watching them use sewing needles to thread the flowers on thin cords, interspersed with greenery and twisted with tiny twinkling lights. Their garlands look beautiful. Mine look...uh...somewhat crumpled.

"What's what?" I look up, needle half-stuck through a flower stem. "Are you maligning my flower stringing ability? Because I told you when we started that I wasn't going to be good at this."

"Not that." Neena waves her hand. "Your flowers are fine. Why are you so quiet? We usually can't get you to shut up."

I shrug. "Just thinking."

"All right." Mai reaches over to feel my forehead with the back of her hand. "Now I *know* there's something wrong."

I bat her hand away, wrinkling my nose at her. "Rude."

She laughs. "Love you, kiddo. You know I'm teasing. But Neena's right. You're acting a little...off."

I don't want to tell them about Miri. None of my family know about her; she's a secret I've kept like a note hidden in a pocket. At first it was too new, too scary, to tell anyone about. Then when it ended, it was too painful.

What is she even doing here? Isn't she supposed to be a Devote with important stuff to do?

I must've paused too long, because Neena huffs, "Fine, don't tell us."

"It'll be more fun to figure it out ourselves anyway," Mai says with a wink.

I'm vortexed.

FOUR HOURS LATER, THE GARLANDS ARE STRUNG, THE COOKBOTS HAVE delivered a tantalizing spread to the buffet table, and guests are starting to trickle in. Ma gushes over Christo and Julian's fancy, white-and-gold formal robes, to their shared embarrassment. Rhett, my fourth-oldest brother, is warming up on the ballroom's ancient piano module while a few other musicians from the community remove their instruments from timeworn cases.

Ward and Neena are dancing a silly, exaggerated courting dance, laughing harder the more annoyed Rhett gets at them. Wes, the second-oldest, and his wife, Ellie, join in.

"C'mon, Leo!" Neena shouts. "We need two more couples for a set! Get in here!"

I let them drag me in as Rhett starts up a livelier tune. Rhett's wife, Jolie, claims me as a dance partner. Her long, straight, wheat-gold hair matches Rhett's, which he's been growing out and wears in a ponytail. My oldest brother, Robbie, and his wife, Mariel, join us as the fourth couple, and we begin weaving in and out, hopping and twirling, our feet remembering the steps of the country dances passed down through countless centuries.

That's when I look up and see *her*. Miri. I both hoped and dreaded she'd find her way here tonight. My chest feels like it's been hit with a sledgehammer.

She's standing in the doorway, hesitant, looking around the room with those wide, golden eyes I remember so well. Stars, I even recognize that ornate red-purple robe she's wearing. It's one of Mercy Seranath's formal garments that Clara liked to play dress-up in. It's the exact color of the berry juice that stained our fingers when Clara talked us into raiding the greenhouse for an illicit snack. We had to be, what, twelve at the time? As I'm remembering the scolding we got from the head agriculture technician, she steps into the light, and the tiny beads all over her sleeves sparkle like gemstones.

She looks stunning. But she walks like she's afraid to move for fear she'll snag it on something, just as she used to when we played dress-up. Deep down, she's still that shy girl I first met when I was nine.

I drop out of the dance, leaving a confused Jolie to complete the steps with an invisible partner. My feet carry me across the room, eyes locked on Miri, my heart pounding painfully in my chest.

She sees me coming. Her eyes take up half her face, like an animal caught in headlights. My lungs feel like they're being squeezed.

"Hi," I say.

"Hi." Her voice is hoarse. She swallows, blinking fast. "Th-thank you for inviting me. I mean, tell your mother thank you. Everything is lovely."

"Thanks." *Say something else, you tongue-twisted fool.* "I made the garlands."

She scans the room, admiring the delicate fairy lights strung between fragrant blooms. "You did? They're beautiful."

I cough. "Uh...well...my vow-sisters did most of it, to be honest. I helped."

"Well, you all did a good job." She smiles, eyes locked on mine. I sort of forget what words are.

"You should ask her to dance," Clara butts in. I jump, because I honestly didn't notice until right now that Clara's standing right next to Miri. She's wearing another of Miz Seranath's robes, shiny lavender silk with pinwheels of turquoise embroidery.

I glance over my shoulder at the energetic spectacle of my family butchering a country set. "Oh, uh, that's just my brothers goofing off. The wedding ceremony's going to start soon. But definitely save me a dance later. If you want?"

Miri hesitates. Is she remembering what she said to me five years ago? *You have to stay away from me. I'm not good for you.*

Since then, those stinging words have echoed through my mind more times than I care to admit. I genuinely can't figure out what she meant, no matter how many times I've replayed the scene. It'd have made sense for her to say that if we fought all the time, or if she goaded me into doing more reckless shit than I already do. But it was the opposite. We never fought—the most we ever did was debate issues on which we disagreed. Her cautious nature pulled me back from the brink of several quarkbrained escapades. I trusted her judgment more than my own.

"One dance," she says softly. "It can't hurt."

But oh, yes it can. Because after that dance, I'll have to let her go again. And my heart has never truly understood why I should have to.

"Gather round, everybody!" my ma calls. "It's time for the ceremony!"

The crowd parts for Wes and Jesse, who are carrying the flower-festooned arbor into the middle of the room. Christo and Julian take their places underneath it, and the rest of the crowd forms a giant circle around them. A blue-robed Devote steps up to begin officiating the ceremony, and the jovial laughing and talking fade to a hush. Everyone reaches out to hold hands, symbolically connecting Christo and Julian's family and friends into one united whole.

Even though we're standing right next to each other, it still sends a jolt through me when Miri's hand slips into mine. She's holding Clara's on the other side, and I quickly take hands with the man next to me to prove this doesn't mean anything. We're just holding hands because that's what people do at weddings. Nothing to see here.

Stars, I'm going to dissolve into a puddle of sweat. I hope she can't smell me.

The Devote begins the ceremony, announcing, "Christian Galway and Julian Gutierrez have made a vow to each other privately. Today, they make that vow known to the world."

Across the room, I catch sight of my parents leaning against each other, beaming proudly. My ma wipes her eyes with Pa's absorbent pocket square. A few spots down, my brothers stand together. Jesse and Wes are grinning and elbowing each other. Robbie's kid yanks on his parents' hands, drawing them in closer.

In the center of our circle stand my brother and his partner along with the Devote who's officiating. Christo, as serious as I've ever seen him, takes Julian's hands. "Julian Gutierrez, I swear to support you in failure and success. Make my heart your home, for I will be your strength, your comfort, and your shield. May we never be parted until the end of this life."

Julian's vow is taken from an ancient religious poem: "Ask me not to leave you, nor turn back from following you. For where you go, I go; where you sleep, I sleep. Your family is my family, your prayers my prayers; when you die, let me be buried under the same tree. If you feel pain, let me feel it double. May our souls breathe the same aether when our bodies have gone to dust." His face glistens with moisture as he finishes reciting.

"They have vowed, and we have witnessed," the Devote announces. "Now the bond is sealed. May it never break."

Julian whispers something that makes Christo laugh. They kiss, and Christo reaches up to dab away his husband's tears.

The circle breaks into cheers as we press in to congratulate the two of them. I'm swept along, jostling against Neena, one of Julian's cousins bumping into my back. Everyone's hugging and crying and laughing.

Right, good, the mushy part is over. Time for the party to resume.

Rhett wastes no time getting back to the piano module. The other musicians take up guitars, flutes, and drums, and together they launch into a bouncy jig. Christo and Julian manage to extricate themselves from the group hug and begin the dancing. The rest of the wedding party joins right after them. Robbie dances with his son standing on his boots, while Mariel watches proudly, a protective hand curved around her belly. Ma and Pa dance a foursome with Julian's parents. My brothers leap in a frenzied circle, swapping partners on the spur of the moment but always returning to their sweethearts' arms. Neena and Ward, Jesse and Mai, Rhett and Jolie, Ellie and Wes.

A spike of longing stabs me in the chest. Most of the time, I don't sit around pining for a partner. Why would I need one? I've got my family and my Knight friends. I'm never lonely for long.

But every now and then, I get this feeling like...like I want someone to look at me the way Christo looks at Julian.

I'm pretty sure this feeling coming up again isn't random. It's because of a particular someone. The someone who's hovering by the buffet table, watching the dance with a sort of wistful smile that makes me wonder if she feels the same as I do.

To blazes with it. I need a drink.

The kitchbots are serving cherry-flavored punch, sweet and barely alcoholic. I drink half a cup in one gulp, then nearly spill the rest down my shirt when I see Miri closing the distance between us.

She doesn't make it, because a pair of broad shoulders cuts her off, back turned to me. All I can see is a short, brown ponytail and a midnight-blue robe in the Imperial style.

"Little Miri?" his deep voice rumbles. "Clara said you were here."

And then she's flinging her arms around his waist, my presence forgotten. "Raoul!" she squeals. "I'm so happy to see you!"

MIRI

In the instant I touch Raoul, a tremor rattles through me. Something's off. Something—

I step back and look him over. His aura is muted from the loud, rebellious burst of color it used to be. Something must be really bothering him to suppress his energy this much.

But to look at his face, I'd never know it. He's wearing a wide grin and a mouth-framing goatee, which somehow changes his whole face. It makes him look dashing, rather than the nervous, awkward, older brother I once knew. The well-tailored drape of his robe doesn't hurt either.

Over his shoulder, I see Leo slipping away, drink in hand, and a pang of disappointment twinges behind my ribs.

I refocus on Raoul. "How are you doing?" I ask. "What have you been up to these last few years?"

"Oh, I've been all over the place. Exploring the galaxy." He waves an airy hand.

He's avoiding the question. "You know," I blurt, "I saw Amy Ediya earlier. She said some of the Ediya Experiments are going missing—the ones who spend a lot of time offworld."

Raoul tenses, and something flickers in his aura before he forces it down. "Yeah?" he says carelessly. "Well, not me."

"You should be careful," I insist. "Clara too." Somehow I still haven't found a moment to tell her about Amy's warnings. I make a mental note to ensure I say something before the night's over.

But before I do that, I have to figure out why Raoul's lying to me.

CHAPTER FIVE

Leo

I *KNOW* RAOUL'S BASICALLY HER BROTHER. I *KNOW*. THAT'S WHY I FEEL so foolish and petty as jealousy smolders in my chest like a flame at the edge of a paper, licking char across my heart.

It doesn't matter anyway. It's been five years. More than enough time for the average person to get over their first love and move on...right?

Except I think there's something wrong with me. Ever since Miri, I haven't had feelings for *anybody*. It's not that I don't like people. I'd dive out an airlock for my Knight team, Chaz, Natalia, and Derek. We've gone through a ton of shit together, seen each other cry and puke, and any one of us would take a blast for the others. If that isn't love, I don't know what else the word is used for. But I don't get the tingles, the rush of euphoria, when any of them walk into a room. I don't lie awake at night imagining kissing them in various levels of undress. The idea of it sort of grosses me out.

My brothers tease me about high standards. My vow-sisters try to introduce me to their single friends. My fellow Knights roast me about being too awkward to get a date. But none of that is the problem. Shit, it's not even that I'm hung up on Miri. Up until this morning, I didn't really think about her *that* much. (Anymore.)

No, it's like, after our breakup, I literally *broke*. Like some ancient god decreed that I got only one shot at love. Screwed it up? Oops, sorry, better luck next life.

For a while I thought I was aromantic asexual, but that felt like the wrong label when I *had* felt attraction. But only toward one person, and only after we'd known each other for years. I guess that makes me demisexual. Does that label still fit if I've gotten emotionally close to a bunch of friends and still never felt a flicker of what I felt for Miri?

When I first met her, she was just some girl who hung out with Clara a lot. I figured she'd turn out to be just as bossy and annoying. But sometimes, when Clara wasn't looking, I'd catch her pulling faces or laughing silently. That was enough for my ten-year-old self to decide she was worth getting to know.

From there, we just sort of clicked. I invited her to watch my favorite shows with me in the holo-rooms, where she admitted in a whisper that she liked the adventure ones more than Clara's favorite high-drama tragedies. I taught her to play chess, hoping she'd be easier to beat than my brothers, but she quickly got good enough to smoke me. That led to us playing uniweb chess when she was back at the Refuge. She had to sneak into the dormitory and hide under the covers to play on her tablet, since tech was frowned upon there. In the chat, we'd banter back and forth, complaining about the various injustices of teen life and arguing over who had it better. (Secretly, I would've rather crashed my hovercycle a dozen times than live at the Refuge like she did. No tech? No thanks! But I pretended it sounded fun because I knew it'd make her feel better.)

One night, the Newcastle teen social group lit a bonfire by the abandoned greenhouse on the community's outskirts. I was eighteen and had just crashed my hovercycle in a spectacularly bad accident that got me banned from driving any of the community's heavy machinery for six months while I took a remedial safety course. My face was a bit bashed up and my arm was in a cast, but I went to the bonfire anyway, because I knew Miri was going to be there.

I saw her sitting by herself and couldn't help the way my steps turned toward her, like there were magnets in the toes of my shoes. I sat down next to her on an upturned planter box. "Where's Clara?"

She shrugged. Her smile seemed kind of sad. "Off making out with someone. I didn't catch their name."

"Didn't you just get here?" I raised my eyebrows. "She already left you by yourself?" My ma would've given me the tongue-lashing of a lifetime for being so rude to a guest.

Miri shrugged. "She said you were going to come hang out with me."

"How'd she know that though? She didn't talk to me first." I was annoyed on her behalf. "Not that I'm not happy to hang out, of course."

"It's just Clara being Clara." She sighed. "Hey, want to toast apples? Somebody brought a whole bag."

So we speared apple slices on long forks and held them over the fire. Crouching together in the face-reddening heat, we placed quiet bets on which couples would be next to disappear into the shadows. Then we laughed when we were right. As the night wore on, we played a virtual card game on my tablet, heads together, her floral scent mixing with woodsmoke. Close to midnight, Miri's eyelids started drooping. She rested her head on my shoulder and yawned, and without thinking, I tucked my uninjured arm around her, pulling her close to my side.

And that, right there, was when it hit me: the understanding that these warm feelings, the swooping in my stomach whenever she smiled, the heat in my skin that wasn't entirely from the fire...that was what people meant when they talked about romance. About wanting to sneak off beyond the glow of the fire. I'd never really got why some people could pick one single friend and decide that they wanted to smush their face on that friend's face...until then.

I realized you don't consciously pick which friend you want to kiss. Your body sort of does it *for* you.

Why then? Why not when we were twelve or fifteen? I honestly had no idea. All I knew was, after that moment when everything shifted, I couldn't see myself living without Miri. I knew I wanted to have a big family like the one I grew up in, but I could never picture the person who'd share it with me. Now, I saw my future kids with her brown hair and strange shiny gen-mod eyes.

Not that I said anything. There was part of me that was terrified to change anything, because what if I scared her away?

A valid worry, as it turned out.

Nursing my confusing cocktail of feelings, I watch as Raoul Seranath guides her onto the dance floor. He twirls her playfully before they fall into step with the other dancers. Is it my imagination or does she look uncomfortable?

"Aha!" Neena sidles up next to me. "I solved the mystery of Sad Leo. It's a *girl*."

"Shut up!" I choke. "She might hear—"

"She looks pretty busy to me." Neena squints. "Hey, that's Clara Seranath's little friend, isn't it? One of the other Ediya Experiments. Didn't you two used to hang out together a lot?" When I don't respond, she grins. "Stars, Leo, Ma Galway is going to die happy. She was glued to those Ediya Experiment specials when they aired. If she finds out she's going to have one of them for a vow-daughter—"

"Neena!" I wheel to face her. "Please don't spread anything around. There's nothing going on. Miri is a Devote now."

"So?" Neena shrugs. "That doesn't mean she's off-limits."

"It kinda does," I say miserably. "Devotes aren't supposed to get married."

"That's antiquated tradition. I've heard the Refuges are like one big polycule these days," Neena says matter-of-factly.

I put my hands over my ears. "Did NOT want to know that."

"Anyway, if you like her, you should just go for it," Neena says. "The worst she can say is no."

No, the worst she can say is, *I'm not good for you. Stay away from me.* And she already said it five years ago. Even now, the memory stabs like a dinosaur's dorsal spike.

Neena pats me on the shoulder. "Why don't you start with asking for a dance?" She gives me a light shove in the direction of the dance floor.

The music's winding down. Rhett and his band draw out the last few notes of the song as sweating dancers fall out of formation, laughing and clapping. The momentum from Neena's shove carries me across the worn wooden floor. Raoul's the first to see me, and his smile widens as his eyes flick between Miri and me.

She sees him notice me and turns, a flush rising on her cheeks—or was it already there from dancing? "Hi," she gasps, flustered.

"Want to dance?" I blurt. Might as well get this humiliation over with. I can feel Neena's eyes burning into the back of my head. The rest of my siblings are going to know all about this by the end of the night, and I'll never hear the end of it.

She glances back at Raoul, who's giving me the stink-eye while pretending to smile. For a second, I'm terrified she'll say no, but then she turns back to me and gives me a small smile. "I believe I promised," she says, putting her hand in mine. A thrill of magnetic energy zips up my arm.

The music starts up again, and she leads me into the line of dancers, confident in her steps. Though I've been learning these dances for longer, she performs them with more grace. I look like an awkward grasshopper, but I can't take my eyes off the way she glides. She's got the hem of her robe caught up in her left hand, the fabric sparkling, as she reaches for mine with her right to begin.

Rhett chose a slower, measured number for this dance, to let dancers rest from the frenetic pace of the last one. Ironically, these slow dances make it harder for me to not trip over my feet.

"How's Raoul doing?" I ask. Do I sound jealous? I hope she can't tell.

She frowns. "I can't figure him out. He's obviously trying to pretend the thing with Mercy isn't bothering him."

"Yeah?" I lead her in a sedate promenade walk, one hand clasping hers, one arm at her back. "Is it bothering *you* that he's not bothered?"

"Maybe a little," she admits. "He and Clara were arguing earlier. I know it upsets Mercy to have them fight, especially right now, when they should be making the most of the time they have left with her."

She's dodging the question. "What about you? Forget about Mercy. Does it bother *you?*"

It feels like a bold question to ask. But we used to be close enough to ask questions like this, and to answer them without feeling embarrassed or trying to hide. I'd like to think there's something of that trust left, even though we haven't spoken in years. I haven't changed *that* much.

She shrugs, turning away from me slightly as the dance leads her in a circle around the adjacent couple. When we face each other again, she says, "You want to know how I'm feeling? I'm sad for Mercy. I'm sad for Clara, who's in a lot of pain that I don't know how to protect her from. I'm worried about Raoul. Something's not right with him, and he won't let me ask questions about it. And I..." Her eyes flash to mine, and I'm momentarily dazzled by the illusion of depth when the light reflects just so. "I...miss you."

I don't know what to say to that. "I miss you too" seems inadequate. It definitely doesn't cover that first year of agonized longing with a hole in my life where she used to be. She was the only person I trusted enough to talk about that pain, but she was no longer there to talk to.

It got better. Slowly. But even though I'm so happy to see her again, I know I'm just ripping open old wounds that are going to hurt all over again when she leaves. I'd rather have her in my life in some capacity, even if it's at arm's length.

"Can we...try to stay in touch a little?" I blurt. "I want to try to be friends again, if we can."

A relieved smile warms up her features. "I'd like that too." Her hand slips from my shoulder to briefly brush my cheek, where blond stubble already prickles. "You've matured," she says, a note of discovery in her tone. I guess she's right. Past Leo would've been too heartsore to ask for friendship.

"Thanks." Grasping desperately for a way to lighten the mood, I fake-flex my arm. "Been workin' out too."

That gets a smile out of her...and...did her eyes just flick down my body in an appreciative once-over? My heart thumps.

I've never been the most handsome guy. Even if I was, I already have six older brothers with broader shoulders and beefier muscles. I was the scrawny kid no one looked at twice. No matter how much combat training I do with the Knights, I'm still what Mai likes to call "a bundle of toothpicks held together with sass."

Miri's the only girl who's ever taken me seriously. I thought she'd never look at me again the way she looks at me now.

She weaves under my arm, exchanging hands with the dancer to my left before returning to her space across from me. It's lucky she knows this dance because I'm not leading very well. Mostly I'm copying what she does.

The song winds down. The crowd applauds Rhett's piano skills, but Miri just stands there looking up at me, her fingers still hooked in mine. Both our hands are sweaty and warm, but I don't want to let go.

"It's been nice to see you again," I say. If *nice* is a synonym for *a tornado ripping through my insides.* "Do you want to go find a quiet corner and talk some more? I want to hear all about the Refuge."

Her hand drops from mine. "I don't know. I'm..."

She tenses up, whipping toward the door like she's seen a ghost. Her foot catches on the hem of her robe, and she trips. I grab her wrist to steady her, intending to make a teasing joke out of it, until I see her face. She's frozen, her eyes fixed on the door, fear evident in her wide eyes and parted lips.

"What? What is it?"

She shakes her head, looking up at me as if she forgot I'm here. "I just...felt something odd."

"Are you well? Do you need to sit down?"

"Yes," she says, moving out of the way of the dancers. "Or...no. I'm all right. I'm not sick."

"You just *felt* sick?"

"Not exactly." She bites her lip, seemingly warring with herself over what to say. "I need to go...check something."

"I'll come with you then." I'm worried she's going to go out in the hallway and suddenly faint.

Outside the ballroom, the rec level is busy. The party has drawn most of the community, but there are plenty of kids down here socializing in other areas while their parents attend the party. Through the viewing window of the zero-grav flyball court, I can see there's a rowdy game in progress. Social groups are clustered around tables playing games or chatting, and all of the holo-rooms are in use, with signs on the door indicating which drama is playing.

"Is everything all right?" Blast it, Raoul Seranath has followed us out of the ballroom. He leans down and peers into Miri's face, frowning. "Miri, you don't look so good."

Miri barely registers his presence. She glances around wildly, her breath coming fast and panicky. She leans heavily against a holo-room door advertising that, inside, a fifth-season rerun of *Bikini Vampires of Black Sand Beach* is playing.

"I'm going to call a healer," I say.

She shakes her head. "I'm all right." But her eyes don't focus on me. She's looking *up*, into the ceiling, like it's going to cave in at any second.

"Something bad is happening," she whispers and then sprints for the zip-lift.

Cursing, I follow hard on her heels.

CHAPTER SIX

Miri

I'VE NEVER FELT ANYTHING LIKE THIS BEFORE. I WASN'T EVEN USING my aether-sight. I had it closed off because the pulses of jealousy and longing in Leo's aura were almost overwhelming. I shouldn't know things like that anyway. He'd be embarrassed if he knew I could see.

But this crashing wave of *emptiness* can't be ignored.

Whatever's causing the horrible sensation is on a higher level of the community. It gnaws at my chest like a hungry parasite. I'm almost glad Leo seems dead set on following me around, because as we climb into the zip-lift I nearly collapse. Only his quick reflexes save me from a hard fall on my ass.

He's *really* concerned now, muttering to Raoul again about calling a healer.

"Here," says Raoul, tucking an arm around my shoulders. "Give her to me. I'll get her to the infirmary."

But Leo doesn't let go of me, and I'm irrationally glad. His aura is familiar and safe, even when muddied with jealousy and concern. Raoul used to feel comfortable too, but he hasn't been fulfilling the role of older brother in a long time. My body instinctively anchors to Leo's side, and I shrug off Raoul's arm.

"I don't want to go to the infirmary," I say. "There's something going on upstairs. I need to see what's happening."

"Upstairs?" Leo raises his eyebrows. "And you know this...how?"

I groan. The benefit of going with Raoul would be not having to explain my extrasensory abilities. I can't tell Leo the truth without betraying my promise to Amy.

"Sometimes I get hunches," I grit out. That's the excuse I've used at the Refuge before, when I slip up and forget I'm not supposed to know people's innermost feelings. "I'm just...sensitive."

Understanding dawns on his face. "Was the party too much for you? My vow-sister Jolie gets like that. She can only do, like, an hour of noise before she has to go sit somewhere quiet."

"No, no." The party, while it lasted, was the kind of energy I thrive on, bubbling over with love and excitement. "Something happening upstairs. Something—really bad."

Leo tenses and reaches for his toolbelt. When he's on duty as a Knight, that's where his stunner would go—but it's empty now. "Blast it," he curses softly. "Do you know what kind of bad thing? Is somebody in a fight?"

I shrug. "I...I'm not sure. It just felt like *nothing*."

He looks confused.

"Not *nothing* nothing." I struggle to explain. "Like a black hole. A dark void where nothing can exist." Not even aether. And life energy is supposed to be *everywhere*, as long as there's matter for it to move through. Only the empty expanse between stars should feel this bleak.

Leo grimaces. "Do you get death premonitions or something?"

I shake my head. I've been present for a death before, and this is not what it feels like. When a spirit rejoins the aether, it's not lost to darkness. It simply changes form and rejoins the energy that binds the universe. A void where aether dissipates would be *worse* than death.

But I can't explain any of that without telling him how I know.

"Let's just go look around," I insist.

Once again Leo's hand rests on his toolbelt. I don't want to break it to him that weapons will probably be useless against something this powerful. I'm not sure why I'm even running toward it. I should be *fleeing* as fast as I can.

Raoul's concern is different. He keeps flashing glances at Leo, then subtly shaking his head. I know he's trying to tell me that I'm saying too much, that I need to stop. I wish I had the telepathy that some of our siblings have so I could assure him that I trust Leo, but I'm not going to betray our secrets.

The zip-lift pauses at the next level, but I shake my head. "Up," I say, punching the button to close the door. Is it my imagination or is the empty feeling receding? Moving farther away, perhaps, or dissipating as if it never existed...

I stumble off the lift at the next level. With Leo at my shoulder, supporting me with a hand at my elbow, I chase the remnants of darkness, giving over to my aethersight. I still can't see anything out of the ordinary. The level is almost entirely vacant, with most of its inhabitants downstairs enjoying the party.

It's only when I arrive at a closed door that, in shock, I recognize where I am.

This is Mercy's home.

My hand trembles as I tap my keycuff against the scanner. Raoul stops me before I open the door, pulling my wrist away. "Is she in trouble?" he asks quietly.

"I..." I want to say no, but I can't. "I think she is."

Raoul sucks in a breath.

The door begins to slide open. Impatient, Leo fits his hand into the crack and wrenches it aside the rest of the way. All three of us rush in.

Everything is dark inside. Not evil dark, but the calm, soft dark of a house in night mode, with small glowing lights along the edges of the floor that keep it from true blackness. The adrenaline surging through my veins urges me to run, but I keep my steps slow and steady, approaching Mercy's bedroom door.

"I don't want to wake her," I whisper.

"Too bad." Raoul shoves the door open. "We have to check on her."

"Wait—" But he's already switching on the daylights in Mercy's room. I wince at the sudden assault on my eyes.

Mercy is nothing more than a long lump under the coverlet. I rush to her bedside, apologizing for the rude awakening, I just was so worried, wanted to make sure she was all right—

She doesn't move.

I peel back the covers and tap her arm. Mercy lies on her back, her face relaxed and peaceful, eyes closed.

I shake her shoulder, but she is limp and still. Not even a breath. Choking back a sob, I place two fingers against the pulse point in her neck, registering her cooling skin.

"Not responding!" Leo surges forward. "We have to start chest compressions."

Tears blur my vision. "We're already too late."

"She's gone?" Raoul murmurs.

I turn away from the empty shell that isn't Mercy anymore and bury my face in Raoul's shoulder.

Leo calls for the healer straight away. He doesn't tell her about the black hole thing, thank stars. He only tells her that I was too worried about Mercy to enjoy the party and that I wanted to check on her.

Deception is against a Devote's code of conduct. But I'm grateful for it nonetheless. Explaining how I knew that Mercy passed before I'd even seen her would have been difficult.

Besides, most of my brainspace is taken up with trying to figure out what just happened. If it was Mercy's death I felt, why was it so empty and dark? She seems to have passed peacefully in her sleep. Why should that create such a horrible aura? When I spoke to her earlier, Mercy didn't seem the type to fight against death or try to linger close to life, as it's said some unrestful spirits do.

There's no sign of the dire *nothingness* I felt before. It's dissipated as if it were never there—and there's only me to swear it ever was. It's got me worried that I'm imagining things.

The healers fold Mercy's body up in the bedsheet and carry her out on a hoverslab. They'll take her to the community's med center, where she'll be prepared for the funeral.

"Will you stay?" Raoul asks quietly, standing at my side as the hoverslab floats past us. "Her funeral will be the day after tomorrow. She had everything in place. Clara knows what to do."

"Of course I'll stay." I glance at my keycuff. I need to call Amy, tell her what happened. "I was going to sleep here in Mercy's suite...but it feels wrong now." Plus, I should find Clara before she comes home to an empty room. She's not answering my messages—she's probably still dancing at the wedding party, oblivious.

"Why would it be wrong to sleep here?" Raoul asks.

"It's just...too many memories." Mercy is gone, but there's a weighty, cold space where she ought to be. Another kind of void.

"I can show you the community's guest quarters," Leo offers, abandoning his conversation with the healers to join ours. "I'm staying there myself. There should be plenty of room for one more."

I flash him a relieved smile. "Thanks." Guilt rolls through me, and I add, "Sorry for ruining your evening. I hope this doesn't sour your brother's wedding."

Leo groans. "I should probably go back. I need to tell Ma. She'll be really upset—she and Mercy are good friends. Were. *Ugh*."

"Clara needs to know too." The heightened emotions of the last hour have worn off, leaving me drained. I'm suddenly desperate for sleep, but I can't rest, not when Clara's out there partying and doesn't know about Mercy.

So, instead of the guest dormitory, we head back downstairs to where the wedding party is still in full swing. Raoul stays behind to talk to the healers, leaving Leo and me alone.

There's an awkward silence between us in the zip-lift, the only sound the whirring of the pod along its tracks. Finally, Leo gestures at the shimmery creation Mercy insisted on lending me. "That robe is..."

"Oh stars." I move to shrug it off. "It's Mercy's. I need to return it."

"I don't think Mercy needs it back," he says with a sad smile. "I was going to say...it's the same one Clara used to make you wear, isn't it?"

"Oh...yeah. It is."

"It looks nice on you," Leo says. "But I can tell you don't like it."

I run my fingers over the silky fabric. "It's beautiful. But I'm not a princess."

"No, you aren't," he says, voice low and rough. It could have been an insult, but the way he says it makes it feel like a compliment.

I've been trying not to spy on his aura, truly, but it's hard to ignore the brilliant halo of light that surrounds him. It lends his plain face a dimension of magnetic beauty.

"I've been meaning to ask you," he says, and my stomach drops in mixed anticipation and dread. "When we spoke last time...why did you say you weren't good for me? I've thought about it a lot, but it still doesn't make sense. Even if it was just an excuse...you could've picked an excuse that was *true*."

The zip-lift dings, and both of us unstrap our safety belts, but we don't get out. We stand there inside the close confines of the pod, eyes locked. My heart is in my throat.

"Is that what I said?" I whisper. "I'd forgotten."

All I remember about that night is pure disgust. Not with him— with myself. It's a memory I've kept locked tightly away. Even glancing at the space where it's kept in the back of my mind makes me nauseous.

That night, after *years* of thinking my embarrassing little crush on Leo Galway was one-sided, he'd confessed the opposite. I'd met him in an empty holo-room, but instead of starting the shoot 'em up pioneer drama we were supposed to be watching, he pulled me down into an empty chair in the dark room.

"I want to tell you something," he said in a low voice. I couldn't see his face clearly, but the glow of his aura swirled sick-orange with nerves. Was it bad news? Were the Knights deploying him early and I wouldn't see him for six months?

"Yeah?" I said, my fingers reaching for his sleeve. "Whatever it is, don't worry. It'll be fine."

He laughed shakily. "I...Miri, I..."

The words seemed to get stuck in his throat. I could feel him shaking. It broke my heart to see him this distraught, and with unthinking ease I gently siphoned away some of his terror, letting the rest of his energy breathe.

Then he kissed me.

I wasn't prepared for it. His expression was a bare outline in the dim light from the waiting holo-projector, and his aura was clouded with anxiety. So, when his warm hands cupped my face, his lips brushing against mine, I gasped and jumped back in shock.

"Stars, I'm so sorry," he said, his nerves turning instantly to rust-brown humiliation and rejection. "I shouldn't have done that. I meant to do a speech thing first, and I was going to ask permission and everything..."

"No, no." I grabbed his flailing hands. "I just wasn't expecting it, that's all. Can we...try again?"

Some of his usual sunniness emerged through the clouds. I felt more than saw him smile. He leaned close, one hand anchored on my cheek, his thumb at the corner of my mouth.

Warmth bloomed in my stomach. My pulse fluttered in my throat. I closed my eyes and let the sensation take over. Soft, slippery kisses, hands gliding down shoulders, pleasure and desire as bright as a candle flame between us. Without quite meaning to, I found myself sitting astride his lap, pressing closer.

Clara had described several of her trysts in gory detail, but I'd always found them a bit hard to believe. Exchanging fluids, mouths exploring bodies, all fueled by a bright-burning desire that overrode rational thought...I couldn't imagine feeling that way about anybody.

But if there was anybody I wanted to try it with, it was Leo. Leo, who'd taught me to swim when I was nine. Who'd taken his first defeat at chess, when I was thirteen, with good-natured grace and only a little grumbling. Who crashed his hovercycle and insisted a broken arm was "not that bad," who laughed until coffee came out his nose when I made a silly pun at breakfast, whose happy-dog energy brightened every room he walked into. Leo, who had lately taken to messaging me "good night" and "good morning" every day, which gave me something to look forward to when I snuggled under my handmade quilt in the Refuge dormitory.

What I felt for him wasn't the fiery flames of lust that Clara seemed to think were natural. I didn't know if I was wired to feel things that way. But I knew there was something special about Leo, something that drew my eyes to him in a crowd. Something that made me trust him above anyone else I'd ever met, outside of my siblings.

And I knew that the kisses felt good. His hands on me felt *right*. In his arms, I was safe.

He pulled back momentarily, brushing my hair away from my face with gentle fingers. "Is this too much?" he asked. "I have a speech I was supposed to...it's about how I really like you and want to know if you'd be interested in officially..."

"Yes," I said, kissing him again.

"Yes to the courting, or yes it's too much?"

Yes to both, if I was honest with myself. I needed to slow down. My energy was getting too mixed up with his. I was feeling things that weren't mine to feel. I was—

Cold shivers ran down my spine.

I was letting my feelings bleed into his.

How long had I been doing this without meaning to? Was that why he'd suddenly started showing interest? Had my crush subconsciously manipulated him into reciprocating? How could I ever be sure that what he felt was his alone, when even just now, while he was trying to work up the nerve to confess, *I'd interfered?*

I pushed myself off his lap, stumbling backward.

"Hey..." He reached out for me. "Miri, it's fine if you want to take it slow. We don't have to rush anything. We have all the time—"

"You have to stay away from me," I choked. "I'm not good for you."

He froze. "What?"

"I'm not good for you," I repeated. "I'm sorry, Leo. I..." My instinct was to confess everything, but I bit my tongue against the urge. "Stay away." It came out a half-sob.

I let myself out of the holo-room, slamming the door shut behind me so he couldn't follow. I told Clara I was feeling sick and needed to teleport back to the Refuge. I buried my tablet deep in my clothes locker and let the battery die, so I wouldn't see Leo's confused messages asking me what was wrong. I didn't look at them for weeks, until they slowed and finally stopped coming.

And that was the last time I visited Newcastle Community for five whole years.

Now Leo's in front of me, a little more muscled and a little less baby-faced, but still the same guy I loved back then. Time has only made him *more* himself, and it'd be easier than ever to fall into his orbit.

Why did I tell him I wasn't good for him? Because he deserved better than to be forced to love me. But how do I explain that?

"I'm sorry," I say instead. Because that's all the truth I can give him.

He shakes his head. We're still inside the zip-lift, close enough that I can feel his breath brush my cheek. "I just don't get it," he says. "You know you could have told me if you didn't like me, right? You didn't have to make something up."

"I couldn't have told you that," I say, "because it wasn't true."

He actually flinches. "I don't understand," he says, the agony clear in his voice. "All this time, I thought you must hate me. If you cared, why would you push me away?"

I'm torn between my Devote training—which deplores deception of any kind, including lies of omission—and my imperative to keep my abilities secret. In the end, all I can give him is an anguished, "I wish I could tell you."

Then I rush out of the zip-lift and lose myself in the crowd, pretending I'm looking for Clara. No matter where I run, I can feel his eyes on me, full of hurt, questioning why, after all this time, I still don't trust him.

PART THREE

Newcastle Community, Halcyon

Year 3745, Week 12,

Daythree

CHAPTER SEVEN

Leo

WHEN I SHAMBLE INTO THE DINING HALL AT TENTH HOUR THE NEXT morning, I'm desperately groggy. I head for the coffee dispenser, ready to pour caffeine down my throat while it's still scalding hot.

Then again, maybe I should stay asleep. As my brain boots up, memories of yesterday keep flashing in front of my eyes like an outtake reel. Stars, it really couldn't have gone worse, could it? The woman who got away shows up for my brother's wedding. Should've been a recipe for a reunion straight out of a rom-dram. I mean, she even admitted she has feelings for me. I didn't dream that, right?

But it doesn't mean a blasted thing if she won't *talk* to me. I can't solve whatever went wrong between us if I don't know what it was.

"Excuse me, are you Leo Galway?"

"Hmm? Yeah. Hi. Who are you?"

"My name is Elane Annis. I'm a healer."

I rub crust out of the corner of my eye. Miz Annis is middle-aged with a narrow face that dimples when she smiles. Her curly gray hair is parted into two thick braids. She looks entirely too perky and awake.

"Hold on. Coffee, then talk." I fill a mug to the brim, drink half of it, whimper at the sensation of my taste buds burning off, and then turn back to Miz Annis. "What can I do for you?"

"If you wouldn't mind following me to the infirmary, please?"

"Uh, sure." She's already started walking, so I have to move fast to keep up. My coffee's going to spill.

However, when I step through the door of the infirmary and see who's waiting for me there, caffeine drops to the bottom of my priority list. Miri sits in one of the waiting room chairs, once again wearing her Devote robe and dressed plainly beneath it, the way she's always preferred. Raoul paces the middle of the room. And standing beyond them is an older man in a Knight uniform, his brown hair shot through with gray streaks. I recognize that square-jawed face. It's Monte Lawry, the senior Knight who leads the planetside emergency response team.

Also known as my future boss, if I get stuck on dirtside duty.

Lawry holds up his wrist. Because he's deaf, his keycuff adapter translates all spoken words into glowing text, projected into a hand-sized square just above his cuff. He can type his own words into it too. I move closer to read what he's written.

<Hello, Galway. Let's step into a private room for a chat.>

Miz Annis follows him into the room, and I trail after her. As I pass Miri, I notice she's biting her thumbnail. She looks up at me, eyes wide, but doesn't say anything.

Something's wrong.

I slide the door closed behind us. Lawry faces me, his expression neutral as Miz Annis comes to stand at his elbow. They look at each other, each waiting for the other to speak.

Finally, Miz Annis says, "You want to tell him or should I?"

Lawry taps out, <Be my guest.>

"Tell me what?" My heart is pounding. Everyone's acting weird. Am I in trouble?

Miz Annis sighs. "When we received Miz Seranath's body last night, we had no reason to suspect her death was anything but the result of her illness. However, it's routine to run an autopsy scan to finalize our medical records. And the scannerbot *did* find something. It highlighted bruise patterns on her neck. We double- and triple-checked, but it's not a mistake. Miz Seranath's cause of death was strangulation."

"She..." My heart starts pounding. "Someone killed her?"

"That's certainly how it appears."

"What did the dragons—"

"Of course, we asked them right away," says Miz Annis. "But that's the strange part about all of this. They saw nothing. None of them."

"That's impossible." Anytime someone even *thinks* of murder on Halcyon, a dragon immediately shows up to report it to the Knights. Other planets might have to search for evidence or question suspects, but here, all we ever need to do is call a dragon. They monitor this planet and its people so closely that very little slips by without their notice.

That's the way Halcyon has always been. Protected. Peaceful. Safe.

"At the moment," says Miz Annis, "we have no other explanation. Someone killed Miz Seranath and hid it from the dragons."

<And now,> Lawry taps, <there's a killer loose in your community.>

I'm going to need more than the dregs in my mug to make sense of this.

"Who'd want to hurt Mercy? Everyone likes her." I wince. "*Liked.*"

<The healers informed me that you, Leo, were among the first to discover the scene of the crime,> Lawry says. <Did you notice anything unusual?>

The memory of last night blinds me for a moment. Miri, pale under her freckles, rushing away from the party. *It felt like nothing. A void.* That's what she told me.

Is that what *murder* feels like to her?

Haltingly, I explain what I saw, which doesn't amount to much. Even saying it out loud sounds ridiculous. The woman I was dancing with suddenly felt ill and led me straight to the scene of a murder? Yeah, that's suspicious as blazes.

"She and Clara were the last ones to see Mercy Seranath alive, as far as we know," says Miz Annis.

I'm starting to get defensive. "Are they suspects? Is that why Miri and Raoul are both in the waiting room? Where's Clara?"

<We questioned them already,> says Lawry. <You are a late riser. It seems Clara is even tardier.>

Ah. "Well, I *know* they're not guilty," I say. "Even before Miri became a Devote, I saw her carry bugs up four flights of stairs to let them outside. She'd never hurt anyone. Raoul...I guess I don't know him that well, but it couldn't have been him. He was dancing with Miri at the wedding, and he was with us when we went upstairs. I never saw him leave the ballroom. He didn't have any opportunity to sneak off."

<That's consistent with what they told us,> Lawry says. <Since the three of you can vouch for each other, I'm inclined to believe you. But that doesn't shrink our suspect pool by much.>

I grimace, thinking about how many people were here last night. Newcastle is fairly large—its population has to be over a thousand. And that's assuming no uninvited strangers teleported in, although I think the dragons would notice if they teleported someone who was planning a murder.

A big chunk of the population was at Christo's wedding party during Mercy's time of death, and with luck, there'll be a few vids of people enjoying themselves to provide alibis. But it's still an astronomical number of suspects to comb through.

"I don't envy you the job," I say.

Lawry raises his eyebrows. <Funny you should say that...>

"Oh no..."

<You're familiar with this community and its inhabitants, so you are the natural choice to help with the investigation. Going around and asking some casual questions shouldn't raise any suspicion, particularly while you are known to be relieved of active duty.>

"Raise suspicion?" I repeat.

"Lawry believes we need to keep Mercy's cause of death a secret for the time being," says Miz Annis. "I know this runs counter to the dragons' usual guidance against deception, as well as Halcyon's leadership transparency mandates. But in this case, we feel that public knowledge of the murder will only cause people to panic and become suspicious of each other. It will be best to work quickly to catch the killer, *then* inform the community of the circumstances."

This was not how I was expecting my week to go. "So...are you saying I'm in charge now?"

<No,> Lawry taps sternly. <You report to me. I am simply trusting your knowledge of this community to help me investigate.>

"Got it."

Yeah, I'm definitely going to need more coffee.

MIRI

<Clara, where are you?>

My messages have been going unanswered all morning, but I can't stop trying. They're saying Mercy was *murdered,* and Clara still doesn't even know she's dead.

I combed through the entire ballroom last night, but no one knew where Clara was. A few people told me they thought she'd taken someone back to her room—but she's staying in Mercy's suite, and if she was there, we would have seen her. Eventually, I went to bed in the guest quarters, planning to check Mercy's suite first thing in the morning to see if Clara came home.

But so far, she hasn't.

<This is the worst time ever for you to disappear on a hookup,> I type. Then I delete it instead of sending. This is already going to be a horrible enough day for her when she resurfaces.

A door slides open behind me. Leo's coming out—I guess they're done questioning him. I could've saved them the time. Leo's the last person in the world who would hurt Mercy.

Honestly, up until this morning, I would've said the same for everyone in Newcastle, even those I don't know well. Communities are built on trust. When disagreements arise and personalities clash, everyone has to believe their neighbors have their back. Even as the healers took my fingerprints to rule me out as a suspect, their faces ashen with worry, I still couldn't bring myself to believe this is real. Why would someone kill an old lady who already had a handful of weeks left to live?

And more importantly, how could they have done it without the dragons sensing their violent intent? We've always lived under the belief that dragons are omniscient. They're telepathically linked, so what one of them knows, they all know. Plus, there are more dragons per square meter on Halcyon than any other planet in the universe. (Anecdotally, at least. Dragons aren't very cooperative when humans try to take a census.)

Leo excuses himself to the other Knight, then crosses the room and drops into the chair next to me. He's paler than normal and clutching an empty mug like it's his emotional support.

I don't know where we stand after last night. I thought I'd dread seeing him again, but now that he's next to me, I'm relieved. *Finally, someone who will understand how I feel.*

"Hey," I say.

"Hey."

We look at each other for a long moment, saying nothing. His hand brushes mine on the armrest of the waiting room chair. I slip my fingers between his and let my head fall onto his shoulder.

It's so easy to lean on him. So natural. A feeling of well-being suffuses my whole body as our energies mingle. It feels just the same as when we were younger. His hugs always made me feel like my blood was replaced with honey: thick, sweet, and sunshine-golden.

But it's that exact quality that makes me so dangerous to him. When I let my guard down, when I stop controlling the boundaries of my energy, emotions start to slip through. From there, I'm only a thoughtless wish away from nudging his feelings to match mine. If I have that much power, how easy would it be to change the course of his desires, thoughts, and actions?

Guilt curdles in my stomach. I lift my head, though he holds my hand too tight to pull away.

"This is bad," he says. "Did they tell you everything?"

I nod.

"Lawry wants me to help him investigate." Leo runs a thumb across the stubble on his chin, absentmindedly rubbing his other thumb against the side of my index finger. "Where do I even start? Who had issues with Mercy? No one."

"There's something else," I say softly. "Clara is miss—"

My tablet buzzes with a message. I rush to open it.

<Sorry. Sorry. Overslept. What's going on? Something has to be wrong. You never message more than twice in a row.>

My breath rushes out. "Thank stars." To Leo, I say, "Never mind. She must've stayed the night with someone." With a groan, I add, "Now I have to break the news to her."

<Where are you?> I message her.

<On my way back to Mercy's. Are you at breakfast?>

Shit. <No, don't go there,> I type in a panic. <Meet me in the square by the fountain. Some stuff happened last night. I'll fill you in.>

"Ask her if she saw anything. Maybe she knows who had a problem with Mercy. Or she's seen some out of the ordinary visitors." Leo bites his lip. His aura has a strange, wild tinge to it. "Will you have dinner with me tonight so we can compare notes?"

My heart leaps. Having dinner isn't necessarily a romantic proposition, like in holo-dramas. When a meal is eaten in a communal cafeteria setting, it's hard to get any privacy, let alone set a dateish mood. If he'd asked me to go somewhere private, I would've said no...probably. It would be the only right thing to do. But if all he's asking is a meal shared with a friend, to trade information on Mercy's mysterious death... it should be safe.

It'd be safer if I could tamp down on the blasted butterflies in my stomach.

"It's a plan," I say. *Not a date.*

I've just arrived in the residential square when I get another message from Clara. <Meet you at the fountain in five minutes. I gotta change really quick.>

I slap a palm to my forehead. *Why does she never listen to me?*

Tucking my scroll-tablet into my pocket, I jog toward Mercy's suite, hoping I can catch Clara before she goes in. But I'm too late. The door slides closed behind her as I shout her name from across the square.

There's no other option but to enter the passcode and dash in after her.

Already it feels lonely and bare in here, despite the clutter of medical equipment and crumpled rags littering the floor of Mercy's bedroom.

Clara's still in the ankle-length, violet skirt she wore to the wedding, although she's discarded the formal robe she wore over it. Her skirt is badly wrinkled and has a liquid stain splashed down the thigh. Was it from the punch they served at the reception, or something stronger she imbibed after she left with her lover?

One look at her aura, dark with grief and guilt, is enough to tell me she's figured out what the empty sickbed means. I open my arms, and she stumbles into them, burying her face in my shoulder.

"I'm here," I murmur as she shakes with sobs. "Shh, I'm here."

She mumbles something indistinct.

"What?"

"I wasn't," Clara says. She pulls back from me, finding a seat on the lounge chair and curling her knees up to her chest. "I wasn't here. She said she'd call for us if anything was wrong, but...I don't even remember half of last night, Miri. I wanted to let loose for a while, and I guess I got a little too blissed... She died alone. I wasn't there for her."

"Clara..." Stars, what do I say? Technically, Mercy *didn't* die alone, but the truth is worse.

As soon as the thought flickers through my mind, I wince. But it's too late. Clara's seen it. I may as well have spoken aloud.

Her face goes so pale, I'm afraid she's about to faint. "Miri," she says in a deathly quiet voice, "what happened?"

I don't have to tell her. The memories push forward unbidden. Nothing more than quick flashes, a highlight reel rather than a fully detailed timeline, but it's enough for Clara to get the gist.

Her fingers go to her mouth, trembling. Suddenly, she bolts to her feet and sprints for the washroom. The door slides automatically closed behind her, but I can still hear the muffled sounds of retching.

I wait until I hear a flush, then tap on the door. "Can I get you anything?"

Clara just moans.

"Is it all right if I come in?"

Another moan.

I slide the door open, edge in, and flip the medicine cupboard open. Clara's on her knees, her cheek resting on the seat of the waste receptacle. I thumb through the first-aid kit and find a hangover neutralizer tablet. I fill a cup with water and hand both down to her.

She swishes her mouth out, spits into the waster, then sips the water cautiously. Tears track down her face, but she isn't sobbing. She just lies against the seat, her head pillowed on a limp arm, crying silently.

Stars, I want to help her. If I could just dull the pain...

My aura is already pressing in on hers. I take a step backward, hoping the physical distance will help me create emotional space. It's not my job to feel everything she feels. My job—well, technically not my job anymore—is to help her understand her feelings and figure out what to do with them.

"No, I want you to," Clara whispers. It's so soft, I almost miss it. "Please make it hurt less. Just for a little while."

She's one of very few people who understand what I can do. She's seen everything in my mind, even though I've never said any of it out loud. That means she's maybe the only person in the galaxy who can consent to the manipulation I'm capable of.

"I don't know if it's a good idea..."

"Just do it," she grits out.

So I move closer again and allow my aura to mingle with hers. I gently suppress the overwhelming guilt that burns her up from inside. I can't take it away entirely—but I can make it bearable.

She sits upright. "Thank you," she groans, pressing the heels of her hands to her eyes. Then she drinks the water, swallows the hangover tablet, and pulls herself upright. "We've got a lot to get done today," she says. "Let's get to work."

CLARA AND I SPEND ALL MORNING CLEANING MERCY'S APARTMENT. It's customary for personal belongings to be shared among the community when a member passes away. Sentimental tokens are kept separate for family, but practical items such as clothing and household supplies are put into communal supply storage so that they won't go to waste.

Much of the work was already done before Mercy died. She knew time was short, so she'd been making lists with Clara. Personal gifts are already labeled, leaving the majority of her things for the community. All that's left to do is the disinfecting, folding, sorting, and hauling. We take about six trips to communal storage before lunchtime.

By the time all the rooms are cleared out, we're left with only Clara's travel case and a small memento box of things Clara put aside.

It occurs to me to ask, "Was there anything Raoul wanted to take?"

Clara frowns. "If there was something he wanted, he'd be here to claim it."

"Yes, where *is* Raoul?" He seems to have vanished into the aether after our morning interrogation in the infirmary. Where's he been all day? I don't think he has any friends in Newcastle.

"He's been the absolute worst lately," Clara complains. "Distant, glitchy, and he didn't help with any of Mercy's care. I mean, the healers did most of it, but we could've used the moral support."

"He was acting odd at the wedding last night too," I say. "Do you know what he's been up to the last few years?"

"Nope." Clara shrugs. "He's always like that. Gets annoyed if I poke into his business."

That reminds me of the other part of my conversation with Raoul. "I saw Amy Ediya right before I came here. She said some of the other Ediya Experiments are going missing, and it tends to be the ones who spend time offworld. Maybe you and Raoul should stay on Halcyon for a while longer?"

Clara rolls her eyes. "Amy's so paranoid sometimes. She gets worried if one person stops answering her messages. News flash—I just think she's annoying. The others probably got busy and forgot to call her back, and she's being dramatic about it."

"I don't know," I hedge. "It was more than just a missed message or two."

But Clara doesn't seem inclined to discuss it further. I'm surprised she's taking this so lightly. I was expecting concern, dismay...not utter disregard.

What if tampering with Clara's emotions earlier made it so she can't properly react to other things? My guts cramp with guilt. I shouldn't have done it, even though she asked me to. Playing with people's feelings is dangerous. The dragons already warned me.

Once the apartment is cleaned out and ready for a new occupant, Clara's focus turns to preparing the funeral tomorrow. We've already sent out invitations to everyone on the list Mercy left in her files. Mercy had most of the plans in place already; all we have to do is carry them out.

"Chef Riley messaged me about the memorial luncheon," Clara chatters as we make our way back from our last visit to community storage. "He wants to know if we should serve it outside in the garden or invite all the guests inside to the dining hall."

"Wouldn't inside be easier? Less setup," I offer. But my input isn't really important. I haven't felt like much help at all, other than emotional support for Clara, who's been zipping around all day in high-efficiency mode. The more she throws herself into the work, the more I worry. I think she's keeping herself busy to put off the moment her grief catches up with her.

"Let's go ask Chef Riley what he prefers," Clara suggests.

I check the time on my keycuff. "I'm supposed to meet Leo in the dining hall soon." I still haven't asked Clara if she saw anything strange last night. But she said she doesn't remember half of it. I feel like that's our answer.

"Leo, huh?" She wiggles her eyebrows at me. "How's that been going?"

I groan. "Don't ask."

As we're climbing the final flight of stairs toward the communal dining area, a wave of dizziness makes my knees buckle. I pause to lean against the wall.

"Whoa, hey!" Clara cries. "What's wrong?"

"I don't know..." Except, as she weaves my arm over her shoulder to hold me up, I suddenly do know. It's my aether energy. It's been trickling away all day, keeping Clara calm. I didn't even realize it was draining me. That's never happened before...

Because I've never consciously altered someone for this amount of time before.

I press my hand to my forehead. "It's just...been a long day. I think I need to sit down." I know she can read the lie in my mind, but neither of us want me to yank my energy back all at once. It'll wreck her. I have to slowly reel myself back, giving her time to adjust as the full weight of her grief settles back down on her.

She guides me up the rest of the stairs. "Let's go get you a cup of tea," she says. "I guess I'm about to need one too."

It's well past lunchtime, but not quite dinner hour yet. The dining hall is virtually empty. Next to the cafeteria line, there's a drink station that dispenses hot and cold water, coffee, fruit juices, and several kinds of tea. I choose calming chamomile, and Clara sends me to sit down at a table while she fills cups for both of us.

I hold the ceramic mug between my hands, admiring its design as I wait for the contents to cool. It's handmade, glazed in a pretty, red-and-blue stripe pattern. It never ceases to amaze me when I see all the little artisanal details that bring light and beauty to each community. When I was a newcomer, brought here from a cold and sterile space station, these loving touches were a constant joy to discover. Secret murals hidden behind leaves in gardens, handprints on centuries-old floor tiles, chests of hand-sewn cultural garb in styles dating back to Old Earth... each new find filled me with a sense of connection to thousands of generations of Halcyonites. Each new generation honors what came before, learns the secrets of old trades and masters old art styles, then builds them to new heights. It makes me want to cry thinking about it.

Oh stars. I *am* crying, salty tears dripping into chamomile steam. As I start to pull my energy back from Clara, the full impact of the last few days is hitting me hard. Mercy's really gone. And worse than that...the implicit trust we all had in this community, not to mention the dragons' rule, will soon be gone too.

Nothing's ever going to be the same after today.

CHAPTER EIGHT

Leo

"WELL, THAT WAS A BUST," I SIGH AS WE HEAD TOWARD THE DINING hall on our dinner break.

<It helped us shorten our list,> Lawry flashes. The man's determined not to accept defeat.

It's been a long afternoon of hunting through evidence that will narrow down our suspect pool. There were plenty of people taking vids and photos at the party. Ma was happy to send me everything the family captured—which was a lot—after I fibbed that I was going to edit the footage to a highlight reel as a wedding gift to Christo and Julian.

One of Julian's hovering cambots caught the moment Miri rushed out of the ballroom: precisely 20:03. The healers confirmed that the estimated time of death was around twentieth hour. That means we can rule out anyone who was in the ballroom at that time. I downloaded Ma's guest list so we could start crossing names off.

But even after hours of scrubbing through the footage, we've still only whittled the list down by half. There were just so many people in that room. Even if I could remember all of the names that go with their faces—which, yeah, not as easy as it sounds—they aren't all facing the vid-capture. I can recognize my brothers and vow-siblings by the backs of their heads, but I'm not that familiar with everyone else in the community, let alone Julian's extended family, whom I just met last night.

<This might take a few days,> Lawry taps out. <We have to keep at it.>

"We don't *have* days," I reply. "Not if you want us to solve this before rumors leak out." I'm getting more and more uncomfortable with Lawry's decision to conceal the truth about Mercy's death. If it comes out that the Knights are trying to hide an unsolved murder...yeah, that's not a good look for us.

My shoulders slump. Who the blazes am I to take this on? If we don't fix this, the equilibrium of Halcyon's society is at stake. And the guy Lawry's asking to solve it is *me*? A rookie Knight who's one more dinosaur rodeo away from losing his job? Lawry should've gotten one of my brothers instead. Wes has way more experience than me. Maybe I should bow out while I still have some pride left to lose.

My thoughts must be written all over my face. Lawry pats my shoulder in a bracing sort of way. <Why don't we call it a day?> he types. <We can get back to work tomorrow morning.>

"But there's so much to..."

<I could use some time off too,> he says firmly. <My mind is a ball of eels.>

I laugh at the thrashing motion he makes to illustrate the point. But stars, do I ever know the feeling. "All right. I'll take a break and get back at it tomorrow."

<Bright and early,> Lawry promises, laughing when I pull a face.

We're a bit early for the evening meal. The cookbots have everything prepared, but the cafeteria line is still short and the tables sparsely filled. As I join the line, I scan for Miri, and yes, there she is. She and Clara are seated together, mugs between hands, expressions identically morose as they stare into their drinks.

Looks like I'm not the only one feeling hopeless.

The cookbots fill my tray with fresh garden salad, shredded synthmeat in a smoky-sweet sauce, and bread rolls still warm from the oven. My mouth waters as I carry my food over to join the two women. The food on the space station isn't bad—we grow fresh vegetables in aquaponic tanks—but there's something special about dinners at home.

"Hey," I say, sliding into a seat across from them. "Bad day?"

"The worst," Clara moans. Her eyes are red-rimmed. Of course—she lost her mother. Why did I say it like that, all flippant? I'm such a glitch.

She glances between Miri and me, then says, "I'm gonna go get some food. Hold my seat!" She swings her legs over the bench and trots over to join the lengthening cafeteria line.

Miri still hasn't looked at me. She's clutching her tea mug like it's an anchor, her hair wisping out of its braid to hang in front of her eyes.

"Miri," I say softly.

Her eyes snap up to meet mine. She's been crying too, her face blotchy and nose swollen. Her eyes have gone more yellow than green. The intensity of her gaze sends a zip of some electric feeling through me. Is it attraction, or is it fear? Kind of both, if I'm being honest.

"Tell me you found something," she says in a low voice.

I twist my mouth in an apologetic sideways smile. "Wish I could. We combed through vids all day. I can give you a list of who it's *not*."

She covers her eyes, a half-sigh, half-sob breaking out of her throat. "I'm sorry," she says. "It's hitting me now. How bad this is."

"I'm right there with you." I reach across the table and rest my hand on her forearm. "So I'm guessing you didn't find anything either?"

"There wasn't anything out of place in Mercy's rooms," she says. "We cleaned them top to bottom. And Clara doesn't even remember last night. So that's no help."

I frown. "Does she at least remember who she left with, so we can rule them out?" Clara's pale blonde hair would've stood out in my intensive combing of the wedding vids. But now that I think of it, I never saw her once. She's still on the list of potential suspects.

Miri shakes her head. "She wasn't forthcoming. I'll ask again later."

She looks so much like I feel—exhausted and despairing—that my heart breaks a little. Even if I have to feel like this, I don't want her to.

"Lawry said I could have the rest of the night off," I say. "Do you want to get out of here?"

"Get out?" She wrinkles her eyebrows at me. "And go where?"

"Hovercycling," I say.

She huffs a small laugh. Back when we were teens, I'd try to convince her to come hovercycling with me almost every week, and she'd always come up with some excuse. Turned out the real reason she wouldn't do it was because my brothers told her I drive like a batmoth sitting on a whirly seed.

They're total liars. I'm the best pilot ever.

"Going fast can cure any bad mood," I tell her. "Seriously. Works every time."

"So does dying in a crash," she counters.

"Ouch, Miri, that's dark. You know me. I don't crash."

"You've been in four hovercycle accidents since I met you."

That's unfair. Several of those were more breakdowns than actual wrecks.

"Come on," I press. "I promise I'll drive extra safe. Don't you want to get out and breathe the fresh air?"

She rolls her eyes, but I've got her smiling, albeit sadly. "Can I get some dinner first? Or will my stomach regret having food in it?"

"I highly recommend dinner," I say grandly. Something about her makes me want to show off. I'm being a goof, but it's improving my mood. Hopefully, hers as well. "This synthmeat sauce will make you want to kiss the chef."

She laughs. "I saw Clara talking to the chef a few minutes ago. He's too old for me." But she gets up and joins the line.

I sink my teeth into my shredded synthmeat sandwich. Already I feel so much better. Is it because I skipped lunch and really needed some food, or is it because teasing Miri is fun?

I smirk to myself. *Probably both.*

WHILE MIRI FINISHES DINNER, I HEAD OUT TO THE GARAGE TO CHECK if the community's hovercycles are in good working order.

Newcastle Community shares ownership of all its bots and vehicles. Anyone who lives here can borrow communal tech for their personal use.

There's a screen just inside the wide retractable door that lists current bookings; I check the hovercycles and see that my favorite one is available. It's underlined in red, which means the automated diagnostic system noted there are "repairs advised." Good thing I came early then.

The garage's solar-paneled roof shelters several vertical carousels, each with dozens of charging stalls for bots and machinery. Most of the equipment in this garage is domestic or agriculture tech, but there are some for recreation: a fleet of hovercars, a few boats for the lake, vid-capture drones, and, of course, the hovercycles.

I find an empty workstation and guide my borrowed hovercycle into it. The vintage Cyclone has been in the community for three generations already. Hardly any of its parts are original, thanks to the vigorous beatings my younger self put it through while learning to drive it.

But I was also the one who put it back together. I know every tiny coil and curve of its sleek, paint-flaking form. And I've been *dying* to take it out for a flight since I got here.

"Wondered how long it'd take you to sneak in here." It's my brother Ward. He lives in this community full-time, and he spends a good chunk of his days in the garage. I learned all my mechanical skills from watching him fix up broken kitchbots and scrape dirt out of harvesters.

"Hey, Ward." I roll up my sleeves. "Y'all have been treating my baby bad again. She needs repairs."

"She needs a whole rebuild at this point," Ward says. "Maybe you can kiss her better."

I roll my eyes at him. He keeps going with the bit. "I know you've had a crush on her for a while. I heard you moaning one time when you were tinkering with her innards. Didn't want to say anything. Neena tells me you got a sweetheart, so I wouldn't want to make her jealous..."

I throw a bolt at him. Ward ducks, laughing. "You should invite your lady out for a spin. You can whisper 'Hey, sexy' in her ear, and she'll never know you're talking to the Cyclone..."

"Oh, that's it!" I lunge, tackling Ward. My brothers have been trying to find an excuse to get me to wrestle ever since I got back—their weird way of showing affection.

Ward flips me onto my back. I'm struggling to get a good hold on him when I hear the scuff of footsteps from the open garage door. Neena stands there with raised eyebrows. "What'd I tell you? Wrestling instead of getting work done. Galway brothers are all the same..."

Trying to catch my breath, I lift my head in time to see Neena step forward, revealing Miri standing just behind her. She shoots a side glance at Neena, and the two of them start giggling.

Ward lets me up, and I scramble to my feet, trying to pretend I have some dignity left. "Um...welcome to the garage."

"You didn't think I'd show up, did you?" she teases. "Found another way to occupy yourself?"

"No, I just had to make sure the Cyclone was—" Blast. I still haven't diagnosed the problem. I beckon her over. "Have a seat. This might take a minute."

Ward makes what he probably imagines is a sexy moan sound. *Note to self: kick his ass later.*

Miri shrugs off her Devote robe and lays it over the workbench before sitting cross-legged on top of it. Ugh, stars, I wish she hadn't taken it off. With the shapeless robe framing her body in Devote blue, it's easier to keep in mind how much has changed. How distant we are from each other's world.

When the robe's off, she looks just like she used to. Dressed for comfort in black leggings and an earth-tone tunic. Hair braided to the side. Her face is as round and cute as it ever was—she complains about having a chronic case of baby face, but the freckles and wide eyes are nothing more than a misdirection. Her green-gold eyes are always watching everybody, decoding them. She was a quiet kid, but when she spoke up, I could tell she'd been paying attention.

"Clara went to bed early," she tells me. "Wasn't feeling well. The funeral's tomorrow morning. Will you come?"

"I dunno." The diagnostic scanner turns up a loose belt in the cycle's interior. I grab my screwdriver and begin loosening the bolts, prying the cycle's exoskeleton open to examine the guts inside. "I didn't know Mercy that well, but..."

But seeing her dead, then getting put in charge of solving her murder, has linked us in a way I never expected.

"I'd like it if you did," Miri says, fidgeting with a loose thread on her knee. She's not looking at me. "You don't have to, of course."

"I'll try," I say. "Lawry wanted to start working again first thing...but I might be able to take a break for an hour."

She gives me a small smile. "Thanks."

We fall into a companionable silence as I work. At one point I look up and notice that her eyes are closed. She's meditating.

A memory flashes through me. Us as teenagers, attending the neighborhood prayer meeting. I used to close my eyes, and instead of thinking about the mysteries of the universe, I'd listen to her soft, even breathing.

She was always the more spiritual one. Honestly, I'm not much for praying. I put up with the meditation lessons as a child because those techniques were necessary for learning how to understand dragon-speech. If I wanted to be a Knight, I had to pay attention.

But Miri seems to get the *point* of meditation in a way I don't. She loves those prayer meetings, where people share their struggles and hold space for each other. Where, in silence, they find connection. Watching her meditate gives me an uncomfortable awareness that there's always more going on under the surface than she shows anyone. Even me. I'm an open book to her, but she keeps her own cover shut tight.

I go back to tinkering on the hovercycle. I'm finishing up, just about ready to screw the top panel back into place, when Miri says, "Leo?"

"Yeah?"

"What's that ship over there?" She points to the docking carousel where several of the community's hovercars are parked. Between the ranks of utilitarian vehicles, sleek and silver but not particularly fashionable, I notice a slim, cherry-red, two-seater starship. *That's new.* It looks like a classic model, needle-nosed with trim wings. Sexy as blazes, if I'm being honest.

"Hey, Ward!" I call.

Ward and Neena have been talking in low voices on the other side of the garage, but they both come jogging over. "What's up?"

"When did the community get such a fancy starship?" I ask, pointing.

"Oh, that's Raoul Seranath's," Ward says. "He and Clara flew in together last week. He asked if they could park it in here. We had a spare space, and it's small enough to fit, so..."

"They flew in together?" Miri frowns. "Clara told me she came directly from her Monroe school, and Raoul implied they haven't been in contact for a while before this."

"They probably got in contact when they heard their ma was dying," Neena says. "That's what I'd do anyway."

Miri's still staring at the ship, brow furrowed. "I'll ask Clara later."

I brush my hands off. "I'm just about done. You mind if I wash up really quick before we head out?"

"We'll take care of her," says Neena, grinning. By which she probably means, *We'll tell her lots of embarrassing Leo stories.*

Grimacing, I sprint to the garage's washroom, which has an industrial-strength cleanser to get the grease out of my fingernails. I peer into the grimy mirror; my hair looks rumpled and extra fluffy today. Probably all those hours I spent clawing my hands through it while examining wedding vids. Taming it will take at least one "shitting my pants as a four-year-old" story, so I decide to leave it.

I exit the washroom just in time to hear Miri telling Neena about how I wrecked this very same hovercycle when I was fifteen. Oh blazes. Now they're sharing ammunition.

"You're a braver woman than I am," Neena says. "I've seen how Leo drives."

Miri smirks. "Maybe I like going fast."

Stars. If there was a *How to Seduce Leo* guide, that smirk and the phrase "I like going fast" would be on the front page. *Fuck, I'm in so much trouble. This isn't "being friends" and you know it, Leo.*

I know we can't move forward with so much left unresolved between us. But there's a hopeful little voice in the back of my brain whispering that maybe it's not too late to clear the air. To make this work.

I try to act casual as I saunter up. "Ready to go?"

"It looks like it might rain," Neena points out. "You sure you want to go out tonight? The sunset will happen tomorrow too."

I wave my hand. "It'll be fine. The Cyclone has a built-in rain shield— I added it myself."

"Which means it works about forty percent of the time," says Ward.

I glare at him, but Miri laughs. I grab the hovercycle's starter ring from the peg next to the workbench and fit it into the groove between the handgrips. With a rusty cough, the Cyclone wakes from its dormant mode.

"That's what I'm talkin' about!" I grin and pass a helmet to Miri. Is that grease under my fingernails? The cleanser was supposed to—ah blazes.

"You sure you don't want to back out while you still can?" Neena teases Miri. "Blink twice for *help*."

Miri jams the helmet over her head. "I need a distraction," she says firmly.

"Your funera—I mean—" Neena seems to realize that might be the wrong word choice. "Uh, have a safe trip."

I straddle the hovercycle and run the safety belt around myself. Miri seems tentative about touching me at first, but then has to lean her full weight on me as she swings her leg over. Her body presses against mine, warming my back, and I have to take a few seconds to think about unsexy things. A whole twenty-minute ride with her arms locked around my waist... I don't know if I'll survive.

"Belt secured? All right then. Hold on to me." And I throw the Cyclone in reverse.

CHAPTER NINE

Miri

I CLAMP MY ARMS AROUND LEO'S MIDDLE, RIGHT HAND GRIPPING MY left wrist white-knuckled. Leo's brother cranks the garage door wide open. Wind ruffles my tunic as we exit the garage and pick up speed. My heart races, adrenaline bubbling through my veins like sparkling wine.

The hovercycle lifts higher off the ground. Below us, the community's farmlands sprawl across the rolling hills like a patchwork quilt over a lumpy mattress. We buzz across the top of a biodome, an artificial environment for crops alien to this climate. We pass close enough that I could reach out and touch the side of the shimmery bubble.

Leo veers away from the farm. We're heading toward a steep rock formation on the horizon. When we reach it—at much higher speeds than I'm used to—Leo barely slows down before driving the cycle straight up the rock face. Gravity slides me backward on the seat, the safety belt tugging at my middle.

And then I feel the sudden give as the old, frayed belt tears, sliding me farther back.

I tighten my arms around Leo, holding on so hard that I'm probably squeezing the breath out of him. I dig my heels into the stirrups on the sides of the hovercycle, trying to regain some security. My thigh muscles cramp from holding my butt to the seat.

Leo finally notices something's wrong. "Are you all right?" he yells, his voice crackling through my helmet's com.

And then we're summiting the mesa. The hovercycle levels out, and I'm able to scoot forward. We're on a relatively flat table of land, high above the surrounding plains. Spiky native plants jut out of cracks in the rocky ground.

"My safety belt snapped," I say. It feels strange to talk into the muffled closeness of the helmet. "I'm fine now, but I almost fell off."

He jams on the brakes, which almost sends me flying again. He shuts down the Cyclone and dismounts before helping me off.

My knees buckle. I find a flat space to sit, feeling the shakes rattle through me now that I'm safe.

Leo's found the frayed edge of the strap. I hear him curse quietly. He's got his helmet off now, blond spikes of hair pointing every which way. He leaves the cycle and kneels next to me, picking up one of my shaking hands with an expression of consternation.

"I'm really sorry," he says, folding my hand between his. "That didn't show up on the system diagnostic scan, but I should have double-checked the safety gear before we left. Are you going to be all right? Do you want to walk home?"

"Not yet." I need to stop shaking first. I take a few deep breaths, hugging my knees. Well, I *was* hoping the danger would help me forget about the rest of this awful day—and I was right. I'm suddenly crystal-focused on the present.

The sky above us is clouded gray, tinges of violet peeking through. It's late in the day, but not quite sunset. In the distance, the clouds mist into rain, graying out the horizon on one side. On the opposite horizon, the sky is beginning to clear.

"Is there anything I can do to help?" Leo asks anxiously.

I shake my head. "Can we stay here? Just for a minute. It's not raining yet, and the view is gorgeous."

It really is. We're close enough to the edge of the mesa that I can see the land spread out below us. Leo's community is easy to spot, with its mirroresque lake and patchwork of farmland. Way off in the other direction, I can see glints of solar panels that must mean another community.

"Well...I was going to show you this lookout spot on the other side of the mesa," Leo says. "But this place works."

He's sitting just a handsbreadth away. All I want is to lean my head onto his shoulder and bask in the Leo-ness of him. But I shouldn't drop my guard.

"When we get back," I say, "I think we should check out Clara and Raoul's ship. There's something about it that keeps bugging me."

"A weird feeling?" he suggests. "Like you got the other night?"

I nod. It wasn't quite as dark and disturbing, but the way the aether moved around that ship...something felt off. I noticed it as soon as I closed my eyes to meditate. Aether moves around inanimate objects sort of like wind. The spirit-energy can move straight through them, unimpeded, but it likes to swirl around the shape of things, defining and examining them. Nothing in the universe is ever fully, completely dead. All particles, even metal and rock, hold some amount of energy. It's not enough for most substances to become fully aware, like humans, animals, or plants can...but it's enough for me to sense the shape of them through my aethersight.

But there was a dead space inside that ship. According to the aether, the inside of that ship didn't *exist*.

Leo shifts next to me. When he speaks, his words are precise, carefully considered. "Being able to feel a murder from several floors down is pretty unusual, isn't it?"

My pulse pounds thick in my throat. "I guess it is." *Don't ask. Don't ask. I don't want to lie.*

So tell the truth, my mind whispers.

Up until now, I haven't even considered it. But why not? Amy's command to keep our powers secret was given when we were children. I'm a grown adult now. I'd like to think I have a better sense of who to trust. There's no one who feels safer to me than Leo. He deserves to know, given our history. And I'm sure he's already pieced together the outline of my abilities after the incident at the wedding. If he knows the full truth, I can help him get justice for Mercy. What could it hurt to tell one person?

What could it hurt...except both our feelings? Because when I tell him why I ran away from him five years ago, he'll never want to speak to me again. And I'll deserve it.

"There were rumors about the Ediya Experiments when you first came here." He lets out a soft exhale. "I didn't believe them. But I think I'm starting to. All that stuff about mutant superpowers...how much was true?"

"Some of it," I admit. It comes out sounding too casual. Surely, there should be a crack of thunder afterward?

"So, what, you can see the future?"

I laugh. "No. I can see how people's personalities and feelings color their energy output. Auras, if you want to call them that."

"Can you see mine?" He looks down at himself, like he just found out he's been splashed in paint.

Reluctantly, I nod. "But I try to shut it off when I'm talking to people. It feels intrusive if I know too much about how people feel about me."

A red flush creeps into his cheeks. "How long have you been able to—"

"My whole life."

Oh stars, he's rethinking our entire friendship now. I knew this would end badly.

A drop of moisture hits my forehead. And another on my cheek, and another on the back of my hand...

"Uh-oh," I say. "I think it's going to start—"

The sky opens up. We scramble to get back to the hovercycle, but we're soaked in moments.

"Climb on!" Leo calls over the noise of rain pelting down. "There's a shelter I can—oh blazes!" The safety belt is still broken. "Listen, I'm going to have you use my belt, and I'll sit behind you and help you steer. Is that all right?"

"You want me to *drive?*"

"I'll have my hands on yours the whole time. I promise."

I relent. "If you think it's safe." Climbing on, I wait for him to pull himself up behind me, adrenaline spiking in my veins.

Leo fires up the hovercycle, activating its rain shield to protect us from the elements as we accelerate. It flickers and dies almost immediately, causing him to curse and smack between the handlebars, trying to coax a few more minutes of life out of it. No luck. The rain slices down, a loud patter against my helmet.

"Lean your head to the side," he says. "My helmet keeps clunking into yours." I tilt my head, surrendering to the circle of his arms around me.

We circle around and head for the edge of the mesa. Beyond the ceiling of clouds, the brilliant colors of a red sunset spill across the horizon.

I'm soaked to the skin and shivering, still tense with fear that the second strap will break too. But as the sunset fills my vision, I begin to feel odd, magical, as if nothing is real. As if anything could happen.

We dive for a greenhouse on the outskirts of Newcastle farmland. "It's a spare," Leo says into the helmet-com. "Usually empty. Great place to wait out the storm."

I remember it well. It was infamous among Newcastle Community teens as a place to go for clandestine hookups. Sometimes the teen group had bonfires in the field next to it, burning old planter boxes or dried up branches. Some of the best nights of my life were spent here. Watching firelight cast shadows against Leo's flushed skin. Laughing, teasing, playing games, falling asleep on shoulders. We were never the couple sneaking into the darkness to be alone—we were too unsure with each other then. But that didn't make it any less thrilling to my young self, who kept every casual touch folded up in my mind like a secret treasure. I'd take them out every now and then, relive them, feel an echo of his ebullient energy rubbing off on mine. At some point, those memories got too creased and worn to be taken out often, but as we park in front of the greenhouse, Leo leaping down to slide the creaky old door wide open, my heart pounds in recognition.

Did he plan this? I'd have to be blind not to recognize the flame-red flickers of attraction that lick up and down his aura. He's trying to keep it contained, but he can't hide it altogether. The resonance between us is as strong as ever. I can't deny that I feel it too, though my experience of attraction is different than his. Less intense, less physical. I've always been more interested in the color of a person's energy than the shape of their body.

My stomach flutters with nerves as I dismount from the hovercycle and help Leo push it through the open door.

The greenhouse's interior is dim and musty, planter boxes lined up in neat rows with aisles between. No cultivated crops fill the waiting tubs of earth, but over in the corner, there's a lone berry vine clinging to life, feelers creeping out of its planter box to inch along the floor. White flowers bud between its leaves. I pick up a stray pot that's been placed under one of the roof leaks, catching rainwater, and empty it into the vine's roots. Might as well give the intrepid plant a fighting chance.

I turn around in time to watch Leo's aura flare with warm-pink affection. *Oh no,* I think. *I'm in trouble.*

But I don't stop him when he steps closer. He brushes a strand of hair out of my face—the ends have gone all rumpled and frizzy from the helmet. "Are you all right?" he asks. "The seat belt held up?"

I nod, unable to look away from the startling intensity of his eyes. They narrow as he says, "You're shivering."

"So are you," I say.

"C'mere." He opens his arms and envelops me in them. "I'll keep you warm."

"Are you sure you're not trying to make *me* keep *you* warm?" I tease, trying desperately to cling to the pretense that this isn't romantic. Yeah. Embracing in an abandoned greenhouse while a rainstorm crashes against the roof in cozy percussion, with a blood-red sunset glowing against the edge of the clouds...that's totally what happens in rom-drams right before the two main characters slap a high five and go off to eat pizza.

He doesn't say anything, just pulls me closer. Then, very quietly, he says, "You could've told me earlier."

My face is squashed somewhere in the vicinity of his heartbeat, so I can't read his expression *or* his aura. Is he angry with me? Embarrassed that I've seen too much?

"Amy made us swear not to," I say. "She thought it would put us at risk. That people would try to study us or use our abilities somehow. She wanted us to live like we were normal."

I feel him nodding. His thoughtful "hmm" vibrates under my cheek. "I get it," he says. "But it would've helped me understand, I think. That's why you broke it off, wasn't it? Because I was in too deep, and you could tell and you weren't ready for it."

I pull back, brows furrowing. "That's not true at all!" I exclaim. "Leo...I had a crush on you *way* before you liked me back."

He laughs. A lightning flash of surprised pink flattery zips across his aura. "Then why...?"

We're back to this. Why did I break it off? Why did I push him away?

I have to be honest.

Deep breath in. "Please know that I would never, ever intentionally hurt you." I squeeze my eyes shut, wondering if the words will choke me on their way out. "It's not just aura sight. I can sometimes manipulate the energy I see coming out of people. If they're sad, I can suppress it so they feel happy. If they're upset, I can make them calm." I swallow against the lump in my throat. "If...if they're best friends with me, really close, and I like them a lot...I could maybe accidentally make them fall in love with me."

My hands are braced against the small of his back, so I can feel the moment his body goes rigid. The moment he understands.

"I don't know if I did it," I whisper. "I didn't do it on purpose, if I did. But I realized I was letting too much of my energy leak into yours. I was afraid I was making you do something you didn't want."

He pulls away, his breath coming fast. His aura muddles with brownish hurt and confusion. "I...that can't be..." His hands drop away from me, and he turns to the side.

My heart is crumbling into dust. It's exactly as I feared. He can't even look at me.

"We should go," I say hollowly. "The rain is slacking off. It's only five minutes to the garage from here."

He hesitates, and I see the echo of flame amid the muddle of colors swamping him. He *did* bring me here in hopes of rekindling something between us.

Now I've ruined it. But at least I hurt him with honesty this time, not with secrets. There's a tinge of satisfaction in that, even though most of me is aching.

"You're right," he says. "We should go back."

The whole return flight, I'm counting the minutes until I can go back to the dormitory, close myself into a sleep pod, and cry into my borrowed pillow. Leo stays low to the ground, driving slow, a complete change from his joyous, soaring speed on our way out. I know it's not just the rain or the broken safety belt that's slowing him down.

I wish I'd never come back here.

Up ahead, the garage structure looms through the rain-mist, sheets of water rolling off its solar-paneled roof. The door stands open a crack, and Leo doesn't even bother stopping to widen it before he maneuvers us inside. He screeches to a stop and anchors the hovercycle with a jolt.

And that's when it slams into me, roiling my stomach and dizzying my head. I clench my fist in the shoulder of Leo's jumpsuit, afraid I might faint before I can climb down from the seat. The same dark aura from last night hovers like a cloud over the garage.

And we've just flown straight into the middle of it.

CHAPTER TEN

Leo

OVER THE YEARS, I'VE COME UP WITH A LOT OF DIFFERENT explanations for why Miri ran away. Everything from "she didn't really like me, she was just being nice" to "she wanted to take a vow of chastity before she joined the Devotes." Some of them made more sense than others, but none quite explained why she would disappear without just *telling* me what the problem was. I liked to think we had the kind of friendship where we could be honest with each other, even with difficult topics.

Supernatural powers weren't even on my list of theories until last night. And even then, I never would've guessed she thought I'd fallen in love with her because of *mind control.*

When she first said it, for an instant, I wanted to laugh. If she'd accidentally influenced me into liking her, then why did I linger in the indecision stage for so long? Why was it just me, my fantasies, and my hand every night for almost a year before I spoke up? Why did those feelings remain unbearably strong even when she was far away at the Refuge?

But then a little voice in the back of my mind whispered, *This explains why I never had feelings for anyone else, before or since. This is why it's only ever been her.*

The thought scared me into silence. I know I'm being rude—she probably thinks I hate her now, that I believe the worst of her. Truthfully, I don't know *what* I believe. I need some time alone to think.

But when I dismount from the hovercycle and turn to help her off, I'm jolted out of my thoughts. Her hands are shaking as she pulls her helmet off. Her face is the same sick-pale as it was last night, right before we found Mercy.

"Do you feel something weird again?" I ask.

She nods, glancing around the interior of the garage, her eyes unfocused. "I don't know what it is. Some*thing* or some*one*. But it's concentrated in here."

"You said that ship was bothering you before." I glance toward where it's parked. It hasn't been moved from its stall.

"That might be where it's coming from," Miri says haltingly. "I can't —it's so—I can't tell."

"Wait here," I say. "I'll go check it out."

As I move toward the ship, I half expect to start feeling something odd myself. But all I sense is the regular old garage smells: oil, metal, cleaners. Off in the back corner there's a soft clank of tools and a murmur of voices that keep it from being eerily quiet. Nothing here feels out of place to me, but a cold chill prickles at the back of my neck. The ordinariness of this place is suddenly creepy. I climb up onto the landing platform and do a circuit around the red two-seater. I can't resist running my fingers along the shiny-smooth paint. This thing has been lovingly maintained, even though it's decades old. It would've been an expensive ship when it first came out, and its value would have only increased since its manufacturer moved on to new models. I check the make and model detail on the fin: it's a Lightstreak Ultra. A quick search on my scroll confirms it's the 3701 model, which makes it over forty years old.

I wonder what job Raoul got offworld to afford this.

As I duck under the wing, my foot kicks against something soft. There's a crumpled wad of fabric on the ground. I pick it up, and it unfolds in my hands, silk-shiny and intensely colorful. Violet and turquoise.

"What's that?" Miri's voice trembles. Despite me telling her to stay put, she's right outside the carousel. She's still drastically pale, her freckles standing out. Her eyes have gone more gold than usual.

I shake out the garment to show her. "It's a fancy robe."

She moves closer to examine the silky material. "That's Clara's robe from last night," she whispers. "I thought she left it at someone's apartment when she went to hook up with them."

"Did you ever get that person's name?"

Miri shakes her head.

"And she doesn't remember *anything* from last night?"

"Well, she..." Miri sighs. "She was really upset about Mercy this morning. I didn't have the heart to ask her too many questions."

I press my lips together. "Well, I think we're going to have to."

"Does..." Her voice wobbles again. "Does this garage have security cams? I think...I don't know...we need to see what happened before we judge anything."

I couldn't agree more. "The booking screen has a visual log," I say. "Let me try to pull it up."

It takes me a few minutes to convince the garage's wallscreen to cough up the evidence. The device was manufactured offworld, so it came with a camera that records who walks past it and when. But because Halcyon doesn't usually need security cams, its surveillance recordings are buried under privacy locks.

Luckily, I once had to help Ward fix this wallscreen when it was on the blink, and I watched him type in the passcode for admin mode. I remember needling him because he used "121212." My brother obviously isn't that worried about security, since he hasn't bothered to change it. The vid archives open under my fingers, showing an up-close shot of my own frowning face.

"Twentieth hour last night," Miri says breathlessly. I watch her lips move in the image, a fraction of a second behind her real-life voice.

I type in the timestamp.

For several minutes, the cam shows nothing but an empty garage. A scalemouse skitters across the floor and climbs a support pillar, heading for its nest in the rafters. A kitchbot, sent for repair, wheels itself over to a charging port.

And then Clara appears in the middle of the floor, seemingly out of thin air. I glance at the time ticking up in the corner of the screen: she arrived here at 20:05. Minutes before we found Mercy's body.

She's wearing the robe, but it's hanging off one shoulder. She stands there a moment, her arms slack. Her face is strangely blank, yellow eyes flashing uncannily in the dim light. She turns around in a circle. When she catches sight of the red starship, she heads straight for it, the robe trailing on the dirty floor behind her. She keys in the unlock code and climbs up on the wing to get into the cockpit, the robe finally slipping off as she does so. Once the hatch closes, its mirrored windows hide her presence. No one would ever know she's in there.

I fast-forward through the rest of the footage, but she doesn't emerge until the following morning.

"She let me believe it was a one-night stand," Miri says softly. "Why would she hide in here all night?"

"What I want to know is how she randomly appeared in here," I say. "And why it happened to be minutes after the murder."

"She dragon-'ported, obviously. The dragons don't show up on cam."

"Yes," I say slowly, "but I don't think the dragons would teleport a killer."

Miri's face falls. "Are you saying you think she did it?"

"It's not proof," I say, "But this feels like the biggest lead we have so far. I need to show this to Lawry, and we're going to have to investigate Clara's movements that night. Miri, until we sort this out, I need you to be really careful around her. Don't meet away from public places."

"I know," she snaps. Then she rubs a hand over her face. "Sorry, I...I think I'm just tired. Tonight's been..."

It's been a lot. I know.

"Let's get back." I log out of admin mode, returning the wallscreen to its normal passive function. Then I follow Miri down the path toward the community entrance, our feet lit from below with glow-in-the-dark stones. The sky has settled into deep dusk, the rain tapering off to a sprinkle, and I'm feeling the weight of today's emotional rollercoaster settle onto me too. But I can't help the foreboding sense that I'm not going to sleep at all tonight.

PART FOUR

Newcastle Community, Halcyon

Year 3745, Week 12,

Dayfour

CHAPTER ELEVEN

Miri

I NEED TO TALK TO CLARA, BUT I DON'T KNOW WHAT TO SAY. WHERE would I even begin? Part of me wants to walk straight up to her and *ask* what she was doing teleporting into the garage minutes after Mercy's murder. When I suppressed all that guilt and shame for her yesterday, was I helping her hide from the truth that *she* was responsible? But my career as a Devote tells me that the head-on approach would be a mistake. Confronting someone always goes better if I ease into it, getting them to open up to me first.

With that in mind, I pull on my Devote robe, plait my hair, and head out of the community toward the lakeshore, where Clara should be busy preparing for Mercy's memorial.

Mourners are already teleporting in by the dozen. Many are wearing shades of green, Mercy's favorite color. She'd made that request in the funeral plan she drafted in her last days. I don't have anything green to wear, but there's a basket of green fabric scraps that the community's tailor donated. I tie one around my wrist and scan the crowd for faces I recognize. Mostly I'm looking for Clara, but if I'm being entirely honest, my eyes keep snagging on tall men with blond hair.

Leo said he'd try to be here...but he said it before everything else that happened last night. Is he too busy to come now?

Does he even want to see me at all?

Close to the water, I spot a flurry of activity. The community's gardeners are winding vines and flowers around a wooden arbor that looks to be borrowed from the garden. I think it's the same one from Christo Galway's wedding. The flowers are new ones, shades of white and blue instead of the bright orange, yellow, and purple that crowned the wedding.

Under the arch, a holo-projector stands, beaming a life-size image of Mercy into the space. She looks the way she did before her illness: strong posture, lively eyes, whitening hair. She smiles gently at the people who've gathered in her honor. My throat tightens with emotion. I can't stop comparing this image to recent memory—her body lying prone in her bed...

"Miri!"

I turn and spot the blue-robed Devote waving at me as she approaches. "Tierza! I didn't know you were coming."

Sister Tierza is a feline-humanoid Paotherrian. She's built both taller and broader than me, with a neatly braided black mane complementing the fine white fur that covers her face and hands. Her ears are long and pointed, but her eyes have blue irises not unlike an Earth Classic human. Her hugs are the best thing about her: soft, warm, and motherly. She envelops me in one briefly, then steps back to examine my expression.

"I got to know Mercy very well over the years, all those times we teleported here and back so you could visit your friend Clara." Sister Tierza takes both my hands and squeezes them. "How are you holding up?"

I swallow, tears suddenly welling. "It's been hard," I mumble. I want to tell someone how I'm feeling, but how do I explain any of it? It's not just the wrenching grief of being the last to see Mercy before she passed and the first to find her afterward. It's also the guilt of acceding to Clara's demands yesterday, suspending her grief even after the dragons told me it was wrong to meddle. It's the way my eyes are constantly drawn to Leo whenever he's in the room, my arms aching for the comfort of his embrace, and my terror that I could hurt him. It's the look in his eyes when I told him my fears, my deepest shame—for a moment, there was doubt in his aura. I don't know where we stand anymore.

Even the robe I'm wearing feels like a lie...

Tierza drops my hands and pulls me into another hug. "Oh, Miri, losing a supplicant is always difficult."

"She wasn't a supplicant," I say, my voice muffled in her shoulder. "Mercy was a friend. She didn't see me as a Devote."

I don't want to be seen as a Devote.

The bare naked truth of that thought shocks me, but I know it's been sneaking up on me for days. It's not just the shame of the dragons' admonishment. I think it was a mistake throwing myself into a job that gave me so much sway over other people's well-being. And with the dragons' omniscience suddenly in doubt, it's not just myself I'm questioning—it's the whole system.

How the blazes am I supposed to say any of this to Tierza? She'll never understand.

Over my mentor's shoulder, I catch sight of another familiar face. Amy is here. She's dressed in a flowing green-floral skirt with a white sleeveless top. Her wife trails along at her side, carrying one of their toddler twins on her hip.

If there's anyone who'll get what I'm going through, it's Amy. I break out of Sister Tierza's grip and wave to her.

"Miri!" Amy exclaims, but her smile is sad. "I'm so glad you were here for Mercy in her last days..."

"I need to talk to you," I whisper.

Something on my face must show the absolute chaos tearing through my insides, because Amy looks startled. "Of course. After the memorial?"

I want to say, "No, now," but people are already starting to gather in a semicircle, facing the arch where the holo of Mercy stands. "Sure," I say. I still haven't seen Clara anywhere.

There's another Devote here, one who must have been Mercy's regular counselor. He takes his place by the arch, closing his eyes for a short moment of silent meditation to prepare for leading the ceremony.

The size of the crowd is a poignant reminder of how many lives

Mercy touched. The auras around me are cloudy with a combination of sorrow and nostalgia for times past. I try to close off my aether-sight. Observing others' grief feels intrusive.

The new Devote introduces himself as Brother Raleigh. He reaches his arms out to either side, palms up. It's our cue to join hands. A stranger's sweaty palm slips into my left hand, and when I reach to my right, the hand that finds mine is ice cold. I glance over and see Clara, smiling at me almost serenely. Something ugly and fear-shaped leaps in my chest.

We're almost a complete circle, with Mercy's holo remaining still and smiling as Raleigh keeps an open space for her under the arch.

To start the memorial, Raleigh invites Miz Galway to sing. Leo's ma has a strong and steady voice, and once again I scan the circle for his familiar shape. A few of his brothers are there, but he's absent.

The rest of the circle begins to join in with the singing. The words are about the wonder of the universe, the miracle of consciousness, and the gift of life. The bittersweet melody swells in my throat. My voice cracks and wavers, but I sing as loud as I can, knowing that Mercy, who adored music, would've loved this.

When the song ends, Raleigh calls for a moment of silent remembrance. He breaks it by saying, "We invite Mercy's friends and family to share memories of her life."

A neighbor speaks first, telling a story of the time she hurt her leg in an accident with a farming bot. "Miz Seranath brought my meals every day, even though she was already sick. She was completely selfless in her dedication to her community. That is how I will remember her."

One by one, the crowd adds to the story of Mercy Seranath's life. They tell stories about her childhood and her adulthood, her everyday wisdoms, her love and generosity.

My favorite memory of Miz Seranath is kind of embarrassing. I'd been visiting Newcastle Community when I started my first menstrual cycle. I was behind on my Galactic Standard education, like all the Ediya kids were. Our AI tutors were frantically trying to catch us up to our age groups on math and reading, and somehow mine must have skipped the requisite sexual education that was supposed to begin at age nine. When I ran to Mercy, terrified that the bleeding meant I must be dying, she was so calm and gentle. She explained what my cycle was, gave me a frank, no-nonsense overview of the changes my body was about to go through, then took me to the healers for a birth control implant, "which you can activate later, when you need it."

I don't tell that story out loud. I keep my comments short, something about always feeling welcome in Mercy's home. Clara's hand tightens on mine, and I squeeze back.

The ceremony winds down, and I wonder when Clara is going to speak. But even after Tierza gives the last call, Clara says nothing. She just stares at the sky beyond the lake, hand loose and cold against mine.

I haven't been to many memorials, but I'm pretty sure it's uncommon for the family of the deceased not to speak of them at all. Raoul didn't say anything either—and when I scan the crowd for him, I realize he's missing. I would have thought he'd at least make it to the funeral! What's going on with those two right now?

Raleigh announces that it's time for the procession to the funerary grove. With volunteers discreetly handing out small, pungent cloth bundles, we move toward a small woodland, around a kilometer away, overlooking the lakeshore. There are all kinds of trees there: pines, fruit trees, even some plants native to Halcyon. As we walk, someone begins singing—a song of farewell, of hoping to meet again someday—and I join in. This time, my voice is stronger. I pray wordlessly as the hymn pours through me.

Deep into the funerary grove, near the edge of the lake, a fresh hole in the earth gapes open. Inside rests a biodegradable egg-shaped pod containing Mercy's remains.

Our cloth bundles contain fertilizer, which we take turns emptying around the pod. We sing through that too. Then, Mercy's closest neighbors take up the shovels provided. With efficient, quick strokes, they cover the pod with earth.

Once buried, the seed embedded in the pod will begin to grow and a tree will sprout, a lasting memorial to the life Mercy had lived. She'll join the forest of all the others who died in Newcastle Community before her, gone, even in time forgotten...but forever revered as a building block in the community's legacy.

Some of the mourners are already drifting back toward the community, where a special luncheon has been arranged. I linger behind to watch the burial ceremony as it wraps up. Leo's ma is one of the last few working on the burial, but despite the presence of his burly, blond brothers, Leo himself is nowhere to be seen.

I spot Amy heading toward me, but before she gets close, Clara intercepts me, linking her arm through mine.

"Miri. Hey. We have to talk."

"Yeah, we do." My throat cracks dryly when I swallow. "Leo and I were investigating last night, and we..."

Stars, what happened to easing her into it? *Pull it together, Miri.*

Clara pulls me away from the burial—and from Amy too—meandering deeper into the trees. "You what?" she asks, cool as anything.

"We found your robe by Raoul's ship in the garage." I frown. "Clara, what were you doing out there? You weren't actually with anybody that night, were you?"

She laughs, a strangely brittle sound. "I was with Raoul. He found me drunk and took me to the ship for a hangover remedy that he keeps in the first-aid kit. That must be how my robe got there."

She doesn't know I've seen the recording. Clara's been known to take dramatic license with the truth, but this is the first time I've ever caught her in an outright lie.

"But Raoul was with us," I say, "when we found Mercy. He came upstairs from the ballroom with us. He couldn't have been with you."

"No, of course, I meant after that," she says a little too quickly. "He found me afterward."

"And didn't tell you Mercy was dead?" I *know* she didn't find out until yesterday morning. The shock on her face was too genuine.

She shrugs. "I guess he didn't. He took me to the ship, and we rested there all night. That's where I woke up in the morning."

"Clara." Inexplicably, my eyes fill with tears. "Tell me the truth. You don't remember anything, do you?"

Her eyes narrow, and there's a sort of hardness in the set of her mouth. "Why don't you believe me?"

"There's a security cam," I say. "I saw you teleport into the garage alone. Raoul was never there." I'm surprised she hasn't already seen it all in my head. She usually has no reservations about peeking through my thoughts.

Her mouth firms into a line, and she grips my upper arm. I can feel the chill of her cold fingers through the fabric of my robe.

"Ouch!" I try to pull away. "Stop it. That hurts."

Clara closes her eyes, as if meditating. As a reflex, I check her aura.

Oh shit.

She doesn't have one.

How long has her aura been missing? I've been trying to block my aura-sight since the memorial started, trying not to let the grief from the crowd overwhelm me. Was she aura-less all along?

Now that I'm paying attention, the full impact hits me like a brick to the face. It's the same dark feeling I got on the night Mercy died—the same sensation that crawled over my skin last night in the garage. Worse than death: nothingness. Emptiness.

Nausea rises at the back of my throat. No. It can't be true. Clara can't be the murderer.

My first instinct is to call a dragon, the way we're taught when we're little, preparing for emergencies. The dragons will send Knights to save the day. They'll make sure the innocent are safe and the guilty are rehabilitated. Call a dragon and everything will be fixed.

But when I reach out into the aether, I can't make the connection. Every other time in my life, a dragon has been instantly ready to answer when I call. But this time, they're far beyond me.

Dragons couldn't see the murderer. And right now, they can't see *me*. Because I'm standing right next to someone who, to them, shows up as a blank space. They eat and breathe aether energy. Any place without it is a place they simply cannot go, like water-dwellers who can't breathe air. Like humans who can't spacewalk in their skin alone.

That's when the world disappears around us. I'm suspended in a dark nowhere place, like I'm being teleported.

But if dragons can't see us, then they aren't the ones teleporting us... Clara is.

CHAPTER TWELVE

Leo

I CHECK THE TIME ON MY KEYCUFF. BLAST IT, THE FUNERAL'S ALMOST over. I told Miri I was going to go, and I really wanted to keep that promise. But Lawry won't stop pacing in front of the garage's wallscreen, playing the footage from the night of the murder over and over, like he thinks the forty-seventh viewing will reveal something new.

It's mega-suspicious that Clara teleported into the garage minutes after the murder and proceeded to hide out in her brother's starship all night. But without further evidence, suspicious is *all* it is. It's not like she teleported in with blood dripping from her hands.

I wanted to arrest her first thing this morning so that we could question her. But Lawry thought we should build up our case against her first. I sigh and look down at my scroll, where I've been keeping a list of the evidence we have against her so far.

One: my family's wedding vids caught Clara slipping out of the ballroom, looking like she was about to get extremely cozy with her dance partner, somewhere around the time Raoul showed up to ask Miri to dance. That gave her ample time to go upstairs and kill Mercy...but it also took her out of sight of the cambots.

Two: we found Clara's dance and possible hookup partner. It turned out to be Julian's cousin, who was too embarrassed to tell us much. "We kissed a little," she said, red-faced. "She went off to get us drinks, but she didn't come back. I guess that was an excuse."

Three: we asked the dragons which one of them teleported her last night. They claimed it was none of them. We asked if any of them spied on what she was doing. They responded that, due to human privacy concerns, it would not be ethical to answer that. Fair enough, although I suspect they don't want to answer so they aren't forced to admit they saw nothing.

Four: we scoured the vid from the garage. If none of the dragons teleported Clara, how'd she teleport? And why go to Raoul's ship in particular? That's a super weird place to sleep off the effects of too many drinks.

Five: we need to search Raoul's ship???? Four question marks, underlined twice. That piece of evidence is missing because we can't break into the blazing thing. Raoul's security system is too good for even my mechanic skills to hack. I already tried enhancing the security vid where Clara keys in the passcode to climb into the ship, but the wing was at just the right angle to obscure her hand against the pad.

Until we can track down Raoul—who's disappeared again—or get the code from Clara herself, we're at an impasse. All we're doing in here is banging our heads against a wall. Metaphorically. Although I'm about to start doing it literally if Lawry won't let me leave soon.

<Stop your pacing,> Lawry types out. <You're distracting me.>

"You're pacing too," I point out.

He frowns. <Then go somewhere else.>

"Is that permission to leave?"

<No.>

Groaning, I meander back toward Raoul's ship, circling it for the ninetieth time. I'm bending down to examine the locking mechanism again when I hear a burst of chatter on the other side of the ship.

"How did you just *do* that? Did you just teleport without a dragon? Let go of me!"

I know that voice. That high note creeps in when she's agitated. *Miri*.

I'm stuck between the wall and the side of the ship. When I crouch, I can see Miri's blue-robed hem and one other pair of feet. Clara's, I'd bet my life. No one in Newcastle would wear those fashionable red boots with pointed toes. They're way too impractical, and they make a *click-click* sound whenever the wearer moves.

Which means Miri's right. They must have teleported in. No other way they could have snuck up on me.

But what's this about *without a dragon?*

Clara doesn't respond to Miri's questions. She's opening the ship now. There's a soft *beep* as the lock disengages. I crane to try to see Lawry through the space between their feet, but he's still engrossed in the wallscreen.

Oh no. They didn't walk in through the door—he didn't see them come in. Wishing I had Miri's powers, I try to beam a mental message: *look up and see us.* When he turns back to the wallscreen instead, I mouth a string of curses and frantically search for his call code on my keycuff. *Blast it, why don't I have it saved?*

The ship's cockpit door whirs open. "Get in," Clara grunts. Her usual chirp has gone flat.

The way Miri's feet are planted suggests she's trying to pull away. Her robe sways with the effort, brushing the tops of her flat-soled brown boots.

"C'mon. Talk to me, Clara. What's going on? Did you figure out how to teleport? Amy's going to be so—"

"Amy doesn't need to know," Clara interrupts. "Just get in."

"Where are you taking me? Clara, seriously, what is this? Are you...are you *kidnapping* me?" She laughs in disbelief. "Am I going to disappear like Saray and Harris and all the others?"

That's when another set of boots appears, climbing down from the starship's cockpit. A black, gold-embellished robe slithers down behind.

Raoul. He's part of this too. I don't want to say, "I knew it," because I still can't figure out how. He was with us during Mercy's murder after all. But Miri said he was acting strangely...

"Raoul?" Miri's voice wavers between hope and apprehension. "Help me out here? Something strange has gotten into Clara. She's...*ugh.*"

She makes a sound as though the wind has been knocked out of her. Her knees give way, and she drops to the ground.

"Get in," Raoul says to Clara, whose feet disappear as she climbs up onto the wing to swing into the cockpit. Then Raoul stoops, his arms going under Miri's backside like he's going to pick her up.

"No," she wheezes. "Stop."

And that's what unfreezes me. That breathy, barely there "stop." I know I'm a quarkbrain going against one, possibly two, murderers—but if I don't do something, I'm going to lie awake at night for the rest of my life remembering the woman I love begging for mercy as she's kidnapped.

I roll under the ship, arms folded against my chest. It dizzies me a little, but I shake it off. Raoul's already upright with Miri in his arms, trying to hand her up to Clara. He nearly drops her when he sees me.

I take advantage of his surprise and surge forward, ramming into him like a flyball star trying to stop the other team from scoring a winning goal. Miri flails in his arms. For a second, the only thing supporting her is my chest crushed against her on one side, with Raoul falling back against the starship on her other side.

I brace her as she kicks her feet free of Raoul's arms. She falls heavily into me, which gives Raoul a moment to recover as I stagger back. He narrows his eyes.

::Sleep.::

Out of nowhere, a dizzy spell hits me. I stumble and fall, banging my head hard on the wing of the ship. The instant headache bonks some sense into me, and I regain some of my balance. I scramble to get up off my ass.

But Miri's back on her feet already, standing in front of me like a loyal guard dog. I'd love to see her take a chunk out of Raoul's leg.

"C'mon, Raoul," she says, her voice dipping low. "I don't want to fight you."

He's trying to burn a hole in her with his eyes. But she stares back at him, unflinching.

"I'm stronger now," Raoul says, a corner of his mouth ticking up.

"Good for you," says Miri. "But I'm not eight years old anymore."

She narrows her eyes, and Raoul rocks back on his heels, as if she's hit him.

Some part of me still thought she was exaggerating when she told me all that stuff last night. I was holding onto hope that it was all sensational newsie chatter, that she's not really some supernatural wizard.

This leaves me in no doubt. Whatever power she has...it's real.

And Raoul has it too.

MIRI

SOMETHING'S WRONG WITH RAOUL'S AURA. I NOTICED IT BEFORE, BUT now that I've tried to use my ability on him, I'm sure of it.

It's like his energy is stunted, subdued. Clara still has none at all, but Raoul...I thought I would be able to stop him, push him back. But he was always better at mind control than me, and he *has* become stronger. I used to be able to brush aside his attempts at manipulating me like they were nothing. Now...I can still resist him, but it takes all my concentration.

He's been practicing the power.

Is he using it on himself? Hiding his ill intent from the dragons so it's invisible even to me?

I don't know how that's possible. But I don't know anyone else who's able to manipulate aether the way the two of us can. Clara could only ever read minds, not influence them.

I realized it as soon as I saw him, as soon as he commanded Clara to get into the ship. Raoul's been controlling Clara for some time. Maybe not constantly, but often enough that it's almost second nature to him. Like she's a puppet he's accustomed to wearing on his hand.

If Clara was the one who murdered Mercy, then I'm almost certain she didn't do it of her own volition.

I redouble my focus, determined to overpower him. Leo's leaning against the ship's wing behind me, swaying with a hand to his head. I have to keep Raoul from hurting him again.

But this mental stalemate is draining my energy fast.

"Why are you doing this?" I grit out, desperate to distract Raoul.

"Was it you who kidnapped the others? Raoul, *why*? Please, I just want to know. If you have a good reason, I'll come with you." It'd have to be a *really* good reason to convince me, but I need to get him talking to shake his concentration.

He opens his mouth to say something, and my heart thumps as I feel the mental pressure weaken...

Leo staggers to his feet and throws something. A loose screw he found on the ground maybe. I hear it clinking and rolling against the cement floor.

Not the most effective weapon in the world. And he didn't even throw it at Raoul. He threw it the other way, over by the door.

"Leo, run!" I cry.

"Not without you," he says firmly.

And that's when Leo's boss charges in with a stunner drawn. I'm shocked to see him wielding it in a civilian space on Halcyon soil, but I guess I shouldn't be. A murderer is on the loose.

Then Lawry's face goes blank, and his aura disappears. I see the exact moment it happens. As his energy leaves him, Raoul's flashes in a chaotic solar flare. That sick, wrong feeling punches me in the gut.

Lawry turns the stunner on Leo.

"Whoa!" Leo lunges at Lawry and manages to grab the wrist holding the stunner, directing its discharge away from himself. "Snap out of it, sir!"

As the two of them grapple, I shove against Raoul's consciousness with my own. That's when I notice Clara poking her head back out of the ship's open cockpit, blinking, one hand holding her head. "Miri? Is that you? Where am I? What's happening?"

"Clara!" She's got her aura back. Raoul's control is slipping. He can't hold three people at once, not while we're resisting him. "Help me distract Raoul."

She sways. "My head hurts."

And then she's blank again, falling back into the pilot's seat, head lolling back. The nauseous wrongness hits me again. Is it the aether reacting when Raoul uses his own energy to negate someone else's? I imagine it's hard to do without making the laws of the universe angry.

Leo's managed to wrestle the stunner away from his boss. He's begging, "Don't make me stun you." I can hear the tinge of panic he's trying to suppress. If he incapacitates Lawry, will Raoul try to take over his mind next?

"Just stop this!" I yell. "Get on your ship and go. Leave us alone."

"You're coming with me," Raoul grits. "Don't make me knock you out first."

"Try it," I snap. The "go to sleep" trick was his old favorite—he used it on us kids about every night. But it didn't work on me. At the most, it got me yawning.

He takes a few steps forward, and I realize he didn't mean he would knock me out with his mind—he's going to literally strike me. A sharp spike of fear bolts through my limbs. This is my big brother. He'd never...

Wouldn't he?

I stumble backward and trip right into Lawry's path. The Knight tries to grab me, but my elbow hits him in the nose. *Blast it!* The distraction gives Leo a chance to aim the stunner at Raoul. He cracks off a shot, but it doesn't quite hit Raoul square-on. It paralyzes one of his arms though. Raoul growls in frustration, reaching across his body to try to punch feeling back into the twitching limb.

Behind me, I hear shouts. Some of the garage mechanics heard the *zzzt* of the stunner and came to investigate. If Raoul can't control three of us, he definitely can't hypnotize a whole bunch of mechanics who might be carrying sharp, heavy tools.

Hoisting himself up with his good arm, Raoul scrambles into the cockpit, shoving Clara out of the pilot's seat. She fumbles with the passenger side seatbelt, eyes dead. Raoul casts me one last frustrated look, then yanks the cockpit hatch closed and revs the engine. Leo grabs the back of my robe and drags me out of the way as the parking ramp whirs out, allowing the ship to accelerate toward the open double doors.

We stand there, stunned, as the sporty red starship blazes out of the garage and vanishes into the aether.

I turn to Leo. "Are you all right?"

He pulls me to him in a desperate hug, tucking my head under his chin. I close my eyes and sink into his embrace, suddenly close to tears. Now he's seen it all. The absolute worst my power is capable of. He's seen me trying to use it to hurt someone. And yet all I sense from him is relief that we're safe.

Maybe I should have told him the truth all those years ago instead of running away.

A tap on Leo's shoulder breaks us apart. It's Lawry, sporting a nice red mark on his nose that's likely to turn into a bruise. *Oh no, I hope I didn't break it.*

He types into his keycuff adapter, which displays in bold, glowing letters, <What the fuck just happened?>

Leo looks at me, and I know from that quick glance that he won't say a word about my secret if I don't want him to. He'll keep quiet, even if it flares off his boss and gets him in trouble.

But I don't think I *can* keep quiet anymore. Not about this.

"Let's find Amy," I say. "I think this is a conversation she needs to be part of."

CHAPTER THIRTEEN

Miri

I MESSAGE AMY TO MEET US IN THE COMMUNITY GARDEN. MOST OF the crowd from the memorial has trickled down into the dining hall to demolish the feast Chef Riley prepared. Still, I make sure we don't choose a space too close to the main paths for our conversation. I forge deep into the shelter of overhanging trees and fat hedgebushes, seeking a quiet corner where we won't be disturbed. I found lots of these little spaces back in the old days. Clara's presence, much as I love her, wasn't conducive to peaceful meditation.

There's an old, forgotten stone bench at the back of the garden near a wall with peeling artists' graffiti all over it. None of us actually sit on the bench; we stand around it in a circle. It feels like some kind of secret ritual, and maybe it is. We're inducting Leo and Lawry into the full truth of the Ediya Experiments and what they did to us.

Amy listens gravely as we explain what's been happening the last two days.

"I thought Raoul was among the missing," she admits when we finish. "He was one of the first I lost contact with. It's been over five years since I heard from him."

I grimace. "I should have contacted you the second all of this started happening. I'm sorry."

"Don't apologize," Amy says sharply. "None of this is your fault."

"It might be though." I duck my head. "I don't know why Raoul and Clara came here in the first place—maybe they really *did* want to be here for Mercy. But my theory is, when I showed up, they changed the plan. I think Raoul's responsible for kidnapping the others, and I was supposed to be next."

Amy tilts her head as she considers that. "Did he ever say *where* he wanted to take you?"

"No..." I scour my memory. "He never actually asked me to go anywhere with him. He kept trying to get me alone that night. But Leo insisted on staying with us."

Leo's aura blazes with fierce warmth. I'm tempted to hug him again. He really did save my life, didn't he? So many times, over the last few days.

"I don't think Raoul had control of Clara yesterday," I say. "I'm not sure she even remembers what happens while he's in control. She might not have any idea he's using her. He might be erasing her memory after it's done."

Amy gives me a pitying look. "I know you want her to be innocent, Miri, but..."

"I want to rescue her," I blurt. "I want to get her away from Raoul. We can do that, right? Track their ship? At the very least, we should make them stand trial for Mercy's murder. We can't assume they're guilty until all the evidence has been examined. That's how it worked before dragons, right?"

<I agree we should go after them,> Lawry puts in. He's been quiet, watching his keycuff as it transcribes our words. I imagine this is the strangest case of his career. <However, it's not as simple as tracking the ship.>

"We would've needed to put a tracking device on it before they left," Leo explains. "And I'm kicking myself that I didn't think of that."

Folding her arms, Amy says, "Well, there can't be an infinite number of that model of ship in the galaxy. Is there a registry?"

"Good idea!" Leo unrolls his scroll to start searching.

While he and Lawry fill out a form requesting access to Imperial records, I pull Amy aside and say, "There's more I need to talk to you about."

When I told my side of the story to Lawry, I glossed over the part where I tried to mind control Raoul in return. But I confess it all now—the dark fear that's been eating me up inside. "Am I the same as Raoul?"

What I desperately need is for her to reassure me that, no, I'm not. That Raoul is a monster and I'm a good person—as loath as I am to believe the worst of my brother.

But instead, Amy sighs and says, "I was afraid this would happen."

I blink. "W-what?"

"You've probably wondered, over the years, why you got placed in a Refuge rather than an adoptive home," Amy says softly. "I regret to say that was my fault. I told Sister Tierza you would need special guidance and care to ensure your abilities didn't become dangerous. She was the only one I told—I made her swear to keep it private, even from you. What you may not know is that I wanted to send Raoul too, but he refused to live at a Refuge. I compromised and sent him to live with Mercy. I interviewed her as a foster parent myself. She was a strong-willed woman, hard to mentally control, but she had a heart of gold. I hoped she would be a good influence on him—and on you, since you visited so often."

My pulse pounds in my ears. *Amy* is the reason I never had parents? I can't breathe. I never would have expected such a betrayal from the woman I admire most.

"So you wanted them to train me as a Devote to channel my abilities?" I whisper. "Did you think it was better if I used them to help people instead of...whatever Raoul does?"

Amy's brow wrinkles. "Oh, Miri, no. I suggested you be raised in a Refuge because I thought the extra meditation and counseling would help you learn control. But when you went into training...I cautioned them against letting you become a Devote." She sighs. "They went against my advice, and ultimately, it was your decision to make. Not theirs or mine. Only you can choose your path, and only you can know when it is or isn't safe for you to use your abilities. I had to trust that you'd step away if it became a problem."

I'm shaking now, my hands clammy. All these years, as my secret weighed me down with guilt...Amy knew.

And she was afraid of me enough that she isolated me from any potential family I could have had.

I don't know whether I'm more angry or embarrassed. It burns that she thinks I'd ever hurt anyone or let power blind me. It burns hotter when I'm forced to admit her concerns are valid.

I wasn't born any kinder, wiser, or more mature than any other human being in the universe. Even if I had been, my ability to manipulate people's energy makes me dangerous. I could still choose to control anyone, anytime. What would I do if backed into a corner again? No one can be totally sure what they'll do in dire circumstances when instincts take over.

Amy was right to fear me becoming a Devote. It's been so easy to fix people's problems for them. Tweak their emotions. Nudge them into taking the actions I deem best. Once I've started doing that, where does it stop? How can I know where the line between helping and harming lies?

I can't. Because that line doesn't exist. It's all a blurry gray fog between help and control. I understood that even when I was little— that's why I stopped shushing babies that way. I was so determined to be "normal." But then somewhere along the line, I started rearranging the boundaries of where "normal" was.

I can never go back to being a Devote. If I do, I'm going to turn into Raoul.

LEO

Lightstreak made just a couple thousand starships in the year 3701. They're well-made and popular enough that a good three-quarters of them are still flying forty-plus years later. Good news for the owners. Bad for us because we have a long list of registrations to sort through.

Lawry starts by searching for any Ultra owners named Raoul. No luck. We try "Seranath" and several misspellings of it, but that's a bust too.

So we take out our scrolls, start at opposite ends of the list, and begin manually searching each name in the Knights' background-checking database, scanning for any connection to the Seranaths.

Miri and Amy have their heads together across the room, muttering about something I can't hear. My heart twists when I see that Miri is crying. This ordeal must be tearing her up. Her best friend and a man she considers a brother just tried to kidnap her. I'd be upset too.

Eventually, Miri goes off a little way to compose herself, and Amy comes to peer over my shoulder at my progress.

"There's just too many of the same model out there," I complain. "It'll take us days to go through all these names."

"Search the name *Ediya*," Amy suggests.

I type it in. One result.

"Well, well!" Amy looks smug as blazes. "Oberon Ediya bought one twenty years ago. Still listed as the registered owner. Color me shocked."

"You think the Ediyas have something to do with this?" I ask. "Didn't they get sent to a penal colony ages ago?"

"I have my suspicions." Amy braces her hands on her hips, the smirk fading into something like pensive worry. "My aunt and uncle are two of the most intelligent people in this galaxy. I doubt they've let imprisonment stop them from sticking their nose into galactic affairs. And I'll eat my boots if they've given up on monitoring their precious little experiment babies."

"Miri mentioned something about some of her siblings disappearing..."

Amy nods. "I checked up on Uncle O and Auntie Mel when those kids started going missing. They denied everything, of course. I couldn't *prove* they were kidnapping the kids back, and the Knights won't do jack diddly when all you've got to go on is a hunch. But *this*...this is my first piece of solid evidence. Raoul Seranath caught in the act of kidnapping one of his siblings while piloting Oberon's old ship." She rolls her shoulders, then cracks her knuckles. "I'm *very* curious what he'll say when I confront him with facts. Unlike Auntie Mel, Uncle O never was very good at acting."

<You believe they'll tell us where Raoul and Clara have gone?> Lawry types.

"Well, no," Amy says. "But I *do* think they know. So we'll have to trick them into giving something away."

AMY'S ALL FIRED UP TO LEAVE RIGHT NOW, BUT LAWRY HITS THE brakes. <We shouldn't rush into anything,> he says. <Let's take the evening to prepare. I have to make a report to the Chief Knight, and he might want to add to our security team.>

Amy wrinkles her nose and sighs. But she doesn't bother arguing when Lawry points out that waiting until morning will give everyone a chance to rest up. Miri in particular looks dead on her feet. A long day of almost getting kidnapped will do that to you, I guess.

I linger long enough to make sure Lawry isn't planning to leave me behind tomorrow. My grounding is technically still in effect, but since I'm the only other person who knows the details of the case, Lawry promises to tell Jostlin in his report that I'm essential to the team.

Then I head to the dormitory, change into my pajamas, and run my uniform through the cleaning press. But I don't jump into my sleep pod right away; my mind is still churning through the day's revelations. I wander out of the dorm and sit on the floor right outside the door, leaning against the brightly painted mural on the wall. The residential level sprawls in front of me, crowded with citizens coming home from their various days' work. Dusty agriculture overseers complain about malfunctioning bots to grease-stained mechanics. Weavers and knitters pore over fashion newsies with tailors. Old folks cup mugs of hot cocoa between their hands, praising the chef, who's making the rounds with a kitchbot carrying a plate of cookies for bedtime snacks. Teenagers walk their dogs. Toddlers splash in the fountains while their older siblings swing from the lower branches of the trees that reach toward the artificial sun. The light grows dim and red-gold as the dusk phase sets in.

This is home. Everything about it, the rhythms of its day cycle, the faces of its denizens, the tastes and smells and sounds, are all as familiar as the back of my hand. I love being a Knight and traveling the galaxy, but on some level, all my courage and sense of adventure wells up from this place. From the knowledge that, here in Newcastle Community, there is complete and utter safety.

That safety has never been challenged in my entire life. Nor in the whole history of Halcyon.

Until today.

Stars, I wonder what Lawry's thinking right now. Surely, he can't be as calm as he seems. We've discovered today that the universe contains a man whom the dragons can't see. A man who means to do harm, and there is absolutely no one to warn us what he'll do. No watchful mind-reading spirit to swoop in and whisper, *::He's planning to kidnap someone,::* then lead us right to him so we can complete the arrest.

It's completely up to us to stop Raoul.

And given what I saw the man do today, I don't fucking know how we're going to manage it.

I rest my forehead on my up-bent knees, breathing deep, trying to soothe the worried churning of my mind. Weariness tugs at me. I should get into my sleep pod, but I just can't stand being so alone right now. The bustle of the community saying goodnight, retreating into their rooms, is a comfort blanket.

The dormitory door swishes open. I don't pay it much attention until Miri's voice exclaims, "Leo! Are you all right?"

I lift my head. She and Amy are standing just outside the door, Amy dressed in black leggings and a dark green sweater. I scramble to my feet. "You two were going to sneak off without us!"

"Of course not," Amy says, rolling her eyes.

At the same time, Miri drops her shoulders and admits, "Maybe."

Amy folds her arms across her chest. "Are you out here guarding the door?"

"No." Why do I sound defensive? They're the ones trying to go behind Lawry's back. "But maybe I should be."

"We weren't going to go battle Raoul or anything," Miri bursts out.

"We were just thinking it'd be better to approach Oberon and Melanie Ediya with fewer people first. Like, just us."

"You can still do that! But don't you think it'd be better to have the Knights waiting around the corner, just in case things go south?"

Amy huffs.

"C'mon," I say. "It'll be better if we all wait 'til morning and go together, like the plan."

Amy heads back into the dorm, but Miri lingers. She's looking at me in this particular way she has, the expression I used to think of as her "good listener face." Calm and open, attentive, with understanding eyes shining gold in the dim light. It's the way she's been trained by the Devotes to engage people. It's how she gets me to spill my guts every time.

And it works really well, blast it.

"What's bothering you?" she asks softly.

"It's that obvious?"

"You're usually bright yellow, like sunlight," she whispers. "You're sort of muddy brown right now. Are you afraid?"

"No—"

"Because it's fine if you are," she adds hastily. "I am too. You can be both a brave Knight and a scared one."

"It's not that," I groan. "Well, not *only* that. It's...do you realize this changes everything? If Raoul can do whatever he wants and even the dragons can't stop him, then Halcyon is no different from any other planet in the galaxy. We're going to lose the peace we've had here for thousands of years."

"Raoul is just one man," Miri says.

"He's not though." I meet her gaze. "There are twenty of you."

Guilt nettles my stomach as her face falls. It's a low blow to insinuate she's the same as Raoul, but I have to say it, because I know she knows it's true. If both she and Raoul can control people, how many more of the Ediya Experiments could learn to do the same? How many of them would make the high-road decision to resist manipulating others? We can't count on it being all of them.

And what if the Ediya Experiments aren't disappearing? What if they're hiding from the dragons while they plot?

"Amy always said," Miri whispers, "that when we grow up and have children, we're going to change the human race."

Another punch to the gut. I dreamed of having children with her, years ago, but the knowledge that those imaginary children could have Raoul's dangerous abilities...that's a horrible possibility I hadn't ever conceived.

"What are we going to do?" she murmurs.

"I don't think we *can* do anything," I say. "It's been out of our control since the Ediyas started that experiment. Halcyon is going to change. We have to prepare for it."

She's quiet for a long while. We stand there, leaning against the wall side by side, as the overhead lights dim into night mode. Voices fade, doors close. Newcastle Community is asleep for the night.

Miri leans into me. Just my shoulder at first, but then she's stepping into my arms, hands sliding around my waist. My palm traces a meandering line down her back. I hope she's not looking at my aura right now. If she is, she'll see hopeless adoration splashed across me, a stain I'll never get out.

"Leo," says Miri very quietly.

My voice catches. "Yeah?"

She tiptoes up to kiss me before I'm quite ready for it. A strand of her hair catches between our lips. I gasp and almost inhale it.

"I thought you were keeping away from me," I whisper.

"Do you want me to?" Her small hands slide up my spine, from waist to shoulder blades. A shiver snakes down, sending blood to my groin.

"No," I breathe and slant my mouth over hers.

CHAPTER FOURTEEN

Miri

I'M DETERMINED TO KEEP MY EMOTIONS TO MYSELF THIS TIME. Nothing is allowed to ruin this.

Leo backs me up against the flowery mural. His kisses are hungry, desperate—I'm not the only one who's craving comfort right now.

His hands on me, after so long missing him, fill me with a giddy warm sensation. It's like stepping into a hot shower after hours in the rain: a skin-shivering, all-over pleasure. His blond stubble rasps against my skin. He smells so, so good, like sweat and sun and machine oil, with a hint of spicy soap. Until now, I wouldn't have imagined those smells could add up to something sensually compelling, but suddenly I want to roll in it. I press into him, grabbing handfuls of the back of his shirt.

I wind my arms around his neck, pulling him down to me. He responds by lifting me up, bracing me against the wall. My legs wrap around his hips. He gives a low, groaning laugh against my mouth, and the sound thrills me to my core. The thought of his pleasure turns me on more than any sensation in my own body.

His lips trail down my jawline to the tender patch of skin right behind my ear. I didn't know anything could make me tingle like this.

"Sleep pod," he mumbles into my neck.

I glance around, remembering that we're still in a very public place. Almost everyone is in bed, but if some late straggler were to walk by...

Oh my stars. I'm still wearing my Devote robe. Sister Tierza would want to strangle me if she saw me disrespecting the solemnity of my position like this.

"Sleep pod," I agree, sliding back to the floor. My legs are so shaky I can barely stand, but for once it's not exhaustion or fear.

I always figured I'd try sex at some point. After all, it came highly recommended. It just...never topped my priority list. My drive was always low, and while I could appreciate the aesthetic appeal of lots of people of various genders, none of them particularly made me want to take my clothes off.

With Leo, the attraction isn't quite physical either. Touching him is just a new way to express how his presence overwhelms me. How his voice resonates in my mind long after he's gone. How his smiles make me feel special. It's not about getting naked—it's about how I trust him with my naked soul. I'm not afraid to bare anything else.

The sleep pods in the guest quarters are mostly for singles. But there are a few double-width sleep pods in the far back corner. Hand in hand, we stumble down the row of pods, giggling at our own haste. We find an empty double pod and climb inside, closing the lid over us.

I grew up sleeping in pods—it's just as common as bed sleeping, particularly for people who live on space stations or do a lot of ship travel. Some find the close, coffin-shaped space unnerving, but for me it's a comfort. However, this is the first time I've ever shared one with someone else.

Leo switches the dim lights so we can see each other's faces. Even made for two, the pod feels smaller than usual. We're pressed together knee to chest, his arm under my neck, his hand trailing across my shoulders.

"Hi," he whispers.

"Hi," I say back, running a thumb across his stubbly chin.

He leans in for another kiss. This one is slow, soft, lingering. "What do you want?" he asks against my lips.

"Hmm?"

"Tell me what you want." He draws back a little, eyes searching mine. "Do you want to just kiss and then sleep? Because we can do that. This is…I don't have any expectations."

My heart swells. "I don't either," I say. "I just want to explore."

He huffs out a breath. "Stars, Miri." I feel my pulse skip at the way my name sounds on his lips. "I've never done anything like this before. You know that, right? This isn't casual for me."

"It's not for me either." My words are barely above a whisper.

His pupils widen, and he kisses me again. Deliberate. Meaningful. "Don't break my heart again," he says, and the husky tremble in his voice twists my gut like taffy.

"I'll…try." I turn my head away, staring at the cushioned inside of the sleep pod's lid. "I'm afraid too, Leo. I'm trying my hardest not to do anything that could hurt you." We both know what I can't bring myself to say.

"Miri," he says again. Will my name on his tongue ever stop making my insides leap? "I've been thinking about that. If you'd been forcing me to love you, wouldn't I have stopped when you left?" His eyes flit shyly away. "I thought about you every day for *years*, even when you wouldn't come near me. Isn't that proof it was real?"

This time, I'm the one who leans in for a kiss.

His hand roams down my side, gripping my hip. I let my own hands trace the outline of him, down the warm wrinkles of his shirt, and then under. His skin is softer than I expected. I push his shirt hem higher.

Undressing in the confines of the sleep pod turns what could have been an awkward, anxious moment into a tangled mess of laughter. His bare skin on mine feels like a joyous homecoming. Emboldened, I reach lower, seeking the hard bulge in the front of his trousers.

"Can I touch?" I ask breathlessly.

"Oh yes." It's almost a gasp, but then his voice drops low. "Can I touch you?"

I hold his gaze when I say, "Yes."

His fingers slip into the waistband of my leggings, pushing them and my unders down below my hips. I wriggle them farther down, letting them bunch at my knees. The elastic band resists as I try to part my thighs, granting him access to the places I've previously only explored alone.

He kisses me again, and this time his tongue darts between my lips. I flick my tongue along his, and he groans softly, his hand dipping between my legs. I startle myself with a sharp gasp when his exploring thumb brushes my sweet spot.

He gets this feral glint in his eye and nips my bottom lip, then breaks away to kiss my shoulder as his fingers continue to work their magic. He may be as new to this as I am, but he definitely spent some time reading those cringey "How to Make Sure Your Partner Has a Good Time" sex ed manuals we got in our last year of education.

He's not the only one who did.

The fastening of his trousers comes undone with a flick of my fingers. His member fills my hand, stiff and velvety soft. I stroke him, listening to his breathing hitch. "Is that good?" I ask. "Tell me what you like."

"Like that—that's—oh *yes*."

His fingers are doing magic to my nerve endings. Knowing how good I'm making him feel right now causes a wave of deep, primal satisfaction to roll through me, golden as his aura. I wasn't aroused when we first started kissing, but I'm definitely wet now. He's playing me like a piano, pushing me toward crescendo. I breathe in his scent in gasps as urgency builds between us, my muscles tightening.

His fingers falter, and he closes his eyes. "I'm gonna—" The warning isn't all the way out before he's spurting wetness over the back of my hand. The way his aura flares bright is maybe the most beautiful thing I've ever seen in my life.

He resumes his efforts, and I realize I'm nearly there as well. I can't control my whimpers, my sighs, the way my hips push forward demanding more.

"You're killing me," he growls against my neck.

The sound of his voice is what sends me over. Pleasure tears through me like an earthquake. I've brought myself to orgasm before, alone in my bunk in the dark, but sharing this moment with him feels so intimate and transcendent. It feels...sexy. That's the only word I can think of.

Soaked in pleasure, heart pounding, wrapped safe in the shelter of his arms and his aura.

I nestle my head on his shoulder and let everything go. The world feels so distant right now. He and I are the only two real things in this universe, cradled here in this sleep pod.

Tangled in our clothes, we drift off to sleep.

LEO

I'M CONVINCED IT'S ALL A NICE DREAM UNTIL I WAKE UP, STICKY AND way too hot, to find Miri curled in the crook of my arm. Which went numb in the night because I couldn't bear to move it and disturb her.

I ease the arm out from under her and start to wriggle back into my various items of clothing. It's still very early, and I want to let her sleep, but I figure it's better to go back to my own pod before everyone else wakes. This thing between us is so new, I still don't know how to explain it. I'd rather keep it private until we've explored the shape of our newfound intimacy a little more.

Or a *lot* more.

My movements rouse her though. She mumbles something incoherent and then, with an intake of breath, says, "Leo?"

"Yeah." I reach over to stroke her hair. "It's just after fourth hour. I was gonna move to another pod so folks don't tease us when we get up in the morning."

"Mmm. Good idea." She doesn't move though. Probably still half-dreaming. I drop a kiss on her forehead before exiting the pod on my own.

In the washroom, I shower and run my clothes through the cleaning press. The whole time, I can't stop remembering little moments from last night. Sounds she made. Her hands on me, shy but curious. The way her voice trembled when she said she'd try not to break my heart.

I've never felt so utterly blissed out in my life, but there's a cold weight of fear lurking in the back of my mind. *What if she changes her mind again? I don't think I could stand to lose her this time.*

I'll have to make the most of this offworld trip to convince her that this tender, newborn thing between us is worth a fair shot.

MIRI

WHEN I WAKE AGAIN, LEO IS GONE. WHILE I'M GRATEFUL THAT HE thought to make a discreet exit—I certainly don't want everyone gawking at us getting out of the same sleep pod in the morning—I already miss the weight of him next to me. Now that I've been lulled to sleep by the slow rhythm of his breathing, my single pod is going to feel empty without him.

I rush through my morning cleansing routine, then make my way up to breakfast. Leo's already there, spooning down oatmeal next to Lawry. When he looks up and meets my gaze, I'm sure the whole room can feel the connection between us. It's not visible in the aether—I keep obsessively checking, making sure my energy isn't bleeding too much into his—but it's palpable, this intimacy we share now.

If Clara was here, she'd elbow me and say, "He's giving you bedroom eyes," hoping to fluster me. My throat tightens, remembering that Clara's in thrall to Raoul right now. No time for flirty gazes over breakfast. Saving Clara has to be my number one priority.

PART FIVE

Hawking Penitentiary Planet

Year 3745, Week 12,

Dayfive

CHAPTER FIFTEEN

Miri

OUR PILOT IS A KNIGHT CALLED PRINCE, WHO HAS A PARTNERED dragon he introduces as Fairy. His maroon hair and sleeves of neon tattoos make him unmissable in a crowd. He and Amy tackle-hug each other, laughing and shoving like old buddies. Fairy glides through the cluster of our group. Zir curious attention brushes against my mind, but I shy away.

"I already spoke to the Hawking Penitentiary warden," Prince tells Lawry, as soon as Amy's done putting him in a jokey headlock. "They agreed to give us a brief interview with each of the Ediyas, but no more than three of us can go in the landing party."

Lawry nods. <I will go, of course. Amy too.>

"I want to go," I blurt.

They all turn to look at me. I blush but stand firm.

"I need to face them," I explain. "I...I need to..." Honestly, I don't exactly know *why* I need to see them. Maybe it's to reassure myself that they can't hurt me anymore.

"She should go," Leo says. I smile at him gratefully.

Lawry tilts his head to consider. <I'll allow it. They will respond better to people they feel they can control.>

We strap in for the flight. My heart pounds, my fingers trembling as I adjust my safety belt. This is my first offplanet flight in fifteen years. The last time was also the first flight I ever took. The one that took me from Arrow Station—where I was incubator-born and nannybot-raised—and crash-landed me on Halcyon. I've stayed here ever since, convinced this life was my destiny. Why would I ever choose to leave?

But rescuing Clara isn't a choice. Not in any meaningful way. To stay put when she's in danger—and when Raoul's actions put the whole planet in danger—is against the very core of my values.

I realize I haven't told the Devotes of Evergreen Refuge where I'm going. My instinct is to reach for my keycuff and dial Sister Tierza. But I still my fingers before they touch skin-warm metal. I don't know what to say to Sister Tierza right now. Not right after I've discovered she knew about my abilities all along.

I'll message her when I get home.

Gravity presses me into the seat as Prince lifts the ship off the ground. I brace for teleportation, holding my mind in the calm meditation space where thoughts drift by like leaves in a brook. I'm used to the sensation of my body disappearing around me, floating in that aetherspace outside of time. But I'm not used to teleporting as a group. Sensing other minds in the aether around me can be awkward. It's easy to see too much.

For example, I can instantly feel that Leo—sitting two seats to my left—is still thinking about last night. I blush and try to focus my attention elsewhere, but I accidentally get a faceful of Amy's emotions instead.

She's angry, but mostly at herself. I can't see the exact cause, but I can guess. She thinks she should have stopped Raoul before it came to this.

But how would she have known? None of us ever thought him capable of real harm. He was our big brother. He could be short with us, could sometimes use his power to quiet us when we were being annoying. But he never seriously tried to hurt us. Perhaps it was naïve of us to assume all twenty Ediya Experiments would grow up to be kind people who would use their power for good. But why should we have thought otherwise? We were innocent children.

The dragon pushes us back into the physical realm. I shudder and let out a breath, reacclimating to the press of artificial gravity. Over the com, Prince is explaining how we're going to dock at a guard station that orbits the prison planet below. I half-listen, nerves scrambling my insides. I haven't seen Oberon and Melanie in fifteen years. I don't remember their faces much at all. I remember them as tall, imposing presences in white lab coats, always asking questions designed to trap us. Always poking me with needles, dressing me in thin gowns and lying me on hard cots in the freezing medbay so they could run scans on my brain. I haven't recalled these memories for so long, and now they're rushing back, knocking me off-kilter.

Amy squeezes my shoulder. "Breathe," she whispers. "There'll be guards with us the whole time."

My eyes flick to Leo, one seat beyond her. He's watching me too, and though things are still uncomfortable between us, I see sympathy in his gaze. I wish Lawry was bringing him with us. No, I'm glad he's staying here, so he won't see me fall apart. Or do I want him to be there...

Stars, I don't have a clue what I want. He must be so frustrated with me.

It's ten more minutes of sitting uncomfortably in silence before the guard station radios permission for us to dock. As soon as we're anchored, Lawry beckons me and Amy to disembark. He orders Leo and Prince to stay put, which seems a little unfair, forcing them to stay aboard the cramped ship for hours.

And yet, if you ask the nauseous churn of my stomach, my task is the worse one.

A team of guards in Imperial red show us to the shuttles that will take us dirtside. The head of security herself—Captain Ykros, an imposing lady with gray skin, a bat nose, pointed ears, and buzzed-short hair—arrives to debrief us with a long list of things we're not allowed to do while on the planet surface. We can't carry weapons, talk about galactic politics, touch any machinery or fences (they could be electrified), interfere with guardbots, give the prisoners contraband of any kind...on and on and on. I resolve to keep my hands clasped behind my back at all times and speak when spoken to. That was expected when

I was little. Eyes down, answer in yeses and nos. Dr. Ediya hated it when we talked back.

"Miri?" Amy's hand is warm on my elbow. "You're hyperventilating. Do you need a minute?"

"I'm fine," I whisper. I pull in a breath, hold it for five seconds, then let it out slowly. *Perfectly fine. I might cast up on the shuttle ride down, that's all.*

I find the spacesick bags and hold one in my lap just in case.

CAPTAIN YKROS ESCORTS US TO OBERON'S ALLOTMENT FIRST. MY stomach is still churning, but I forget my nerves a little in the curiosity of seeing a prison planet for the first time. We learned about them in gen ed. Some of them are awful—the prisoners are forced to drive mining drones all day, getting sick from bad air and malnutrition.

But not all prisons are created equal, and of course, the better ones are where wealthier prisoners end up. I suppose Oberon and Melanie must have been decently rich by the time they were captured by the Authorities, enough to bribe their way here instead of a noxious mining colony.

Ykros explains the system as we break through the atmosphere. Instead of a cell or a mine, the inmates here are given a block of land, sheltered under a force-shield dome that keeps them from leaving. Some of them are farming domes, where each prisoner cultivates a patch of rare flowers or valuable wine grapes. Others are given manufacturing work like lacemaking or embroidery. It's still hard labor, but they each have a small shack to themselves, a frequently replenished stock of rations, and there's sunlight and fresh air. It doesn't seem so different from the Refuge.

Ykros lands our shuttle just outside Oberon's dome and ushers us inside quickly. "Let's make this quick," she grumbles.

The air outside the dome is thin and chilly, like a mountain peak in the summer. The sun beats down unforgivingly on bare rocky ground, without a glimpse of plant life in sight. The dome sits solitary, a huge, shimmery half-orb covering at least a few acres of land. There are no other domes nearby. It gives me a strange, lonely ache in the pit of my stomach to think about being imprisoned here.

Entering the dome is like stepping through a portal to a different world. The air fills my lungs with the scent of growing plants in moist earth. A sprinkling mist rises up from what must be hidden irrigation pipes in the ground. Our boots make prints in the imported soil, thick with green shoots.

We find Oberon kneeling in the dirt, examining the petals of a white flower that has just opened to reveal vibrant red streaks inside. "Not quite right," he's muttering to himself. "Not what I wanted. I'll have to backtrack. Cross the original strain with the one from last time, yes, that'll—what do you want?"

His head used to be shaved. I remember that in a shock, as his face registers familiar. He's older now; his skin has grown sun-weathered, and his hair has grown out to reveal a bald patch at the top.

The memories wash over me in a tidal wave. Oberon didn't like children. His questions were always scientific and abrupt, and he never engaged with us outside of the lab. To him, we were nothing but specimens.

He doesn't quite meet my eyes, but he looks at me. Scans me up and down. I can tell he doesn't recognize me. Fifteen years have turned a shy, mousy eight-year-old into an adult he cannot touch.

When his gaze travels to Amy, he stands up abruptly and almost falls over. "Gaela!"

"No," Amy says.

He blinks hard, rubbing his eyes with the back of his wrist. "*Amethyst?*"

"How many times do I need to tell you?" she asks, voice hard and unforgiving. "It's Amy."

"You need to go," Oberon says. "You shouldn't be here."

"I'm here because Raoul Seranath just tried to kidnap another one of your experiments," Amy snaps. "Know anything about that?"

Oberon cringes. Then he crouches back down to inspect his flower, as if pretending we're not here might make us go away.

Amy stomps over and holds her booted foot above the flower. "I'll grind it into the dirt, Uncle, I swear I will. You don't get to play ignorant about this."

"Don't, don't," Oberon begs. "It's taken me three years of breeding to create this strain."

"Then fucking tell me what you know!"

This man used to have complete control over my life. He could have culled me from the subject pool without a second thought if I didn't prove scientifically interesting enough. Watching him kneel in the dirt, begging for the life of a flower, pulls an emotion out of me that's akin to pity. It doesn't feel good to see the roles reversed.

"I don't know anything," Oberon insists. "Melanie was the one who talked to him."

"Oh, she talked to him, did she? How the blazes would you know? You've been in solitary for, what, fifteen years?"

Oberon shakes his head. "Raoul visited me. Not for long. He said I wasn't going to be any help, and he left."

"What did Raoul say *exactly*?" Amy lowers her boot, backing down on her threat to stomp the flower. "What was Melanie helping him with?"

"He...he wanted...his power was getting stronger, and he wanted someone to teach him to use it." Oberon winces, presses his fist to his mouth. "I told him I couldn't do anything for him. Me and Melanie, we're on this planet for life. I've accepted that. But I guess Melanie told him something else."

I thought my heart was racing before; now it's pounding like it might leap out of my chest. Does Melanie know how to help us? Help *me*?

"Told him *what*? Stop dancing around it, Uncle."

"Promise you won't hurt her," Oberon begs.

"I can promise you I'll do everything in my power to make sure she stays right the fuck here, in a dome on this planet, like she's been for the past decade. I'm not going to torture her or anything—that's *her* wheelhouse. Is that good enough for you?"

Oberon sucks in a deep breath, then stands again. He and Amy are nearly the same height. Under his wrinkles, there's a strong family resemblance between them. Something about the way their mouths set in a line when they're agitated. "Melanie hasn't given up on our project," he says very softly. "She's found a way to communicate offplanet. She's working with a group called Haven. She sent Raoul to them. I have no idea what happened after that because he never came back. And that's all I know, I swear. Now please leave me alone."

"With pleasure," Amy snaps. She turns to Ykros. "I think we're done here."

Lawry doesn't argue. He follows Amy and Ykros back toward the ship, but I hang back a moment longer. Oberon has returned to examining his flower—his latest experiment—with the detached curiosity he once showed me and my siblings.

I take a step closer.

"Go away," he mutters.

"I just..." Words are sticking in my throat. His aura is green like the leaves of the flowers. Whole and content. When I was younger, I remember it being much dimmer, cowed by Melanie's. This may be a prison, but to him, this little patch of earth where he can crossbreed flowers...maybe it's the first time he's ever been free of the overbearing influence of his sister.

I wish he'd been able to break away sooner. It could have made such a huge difference. For both of us.

Oberon looks up at me, tilting his head to the side. "Your eyes," he says. "They're..."

"I wanted you to know," I choke out, "that I forgive you."

And I flee.

BEFORE WE VISIT MELANIE, AMY INSISTS WE TAKE A BREAK TO debrief. We troop back to the shuttle, growing short of breath as our lungs struggle to pull enough oxygen out of the thinner atmosphere.

However, Amy seems not to be bothered, because she's already plotting our next move. "If Melanie's communicating with this Haven group, she could warn Raoul and Clara we're coming," she's telling Lawry. "We have to approach this cautiously."

Captain Ykros frowns. "You can't believe everything Oberon tells you. I don't see how Melanie could possibly communicate with anyone. We do a thorough sweep for transmitting devices and other contraband for every prisoner."

Amy folds her arms. "And you've never, ever missed even one? Because you're *that* good?"

Ykros bristles, her pointed ears twitching. "I don't appreciate your tone, Miz Ediya."

"All I'm saying is, Auntie Mel is a literal genius. I don't think it's impossible that she's managed to sneak something past you."

Huffing out a breath, Ykros says, "Will it satisfy you if I do another sweep before we go in?"

"It'll help," says Amy.

So we return to the guard station while Ykros and a few of the other guards double-check Melanie's space. We offer to stay in the shuttle and save them the trip, but Ykros insists we can't linger unaccompanied on the planet's surface. "It's to protect you from escaped prisoners," she explains. But it feels an awful lot like she's more worried about keeping *us* from looking around.

As soon as the shuttle takes off, Amy turns to us with determination flaring red through her aura. "If she doesn't find anything, we need to be on our guard. Ykros won't like to hear this, but the only other possibility is that Melanie is bribing someone to help her."

I glance nervously at the guards in the shuttle's cockpit.

<I agree,> Lawry taps. <But I don't think Ykros will be pleased if we accuse her people of corruption.>

"My thoughts exactly," Amy says. "That's why I want to speak with Melanie alone."

Lawry makes a gesture of protest, but Amy stands firm. "I'm the only one who might be able to get her to slip up," she says. "Lawry, your presence will put her on guard. Me...well, she thinks she knows how to mess with me. Which is why she might not take as much care with what she says."

Lawry says, <I hope you're right. But I still want to see what's happening.> From his weapons belt, he unclips a small case and pops it open. Nestled inside is a pair of gold stud earrings. <I thought we might need these at some point. One is a regular audio earring, but much more sensitive. Rather than capturing only the wearer's voice, it captures and records everything being said within earshot of the wearer. I can connect it to your keycuff so that we can answer you and guide you as we listen to what's going on.> He touches the other earring. <This one has a hidden holo-capture inside. The quality is a bit fuzzy, but it works.>

I raise my eyebrows. "I didn't know the Knights had tech like this."

<It's for accountability purposes,> Lawry explains. <When a Knight approaches a situation alone, this ensures they maintain our code of ethics. Amy is an exemplary Knight, but this situation is a serious test of her ability to be impartial.>

"He's right," says Amy, "and I think this is a great idea. Evidence recorded for us to play back later." She removes her own earrings and clips in the new ones. "Don't lose these," she warns Lawry, handing him her gold hoops for safekeeping. "They were a present from my wife."

CHAPTER SIXTEEN

Leo

I SHAKE THE DICE IN MY CUPPED HANDS, THEN LET THEM FALL ONTO the floor of the passenger bay.

"Three. Ooooh." Prince grimaces, sucking air in through his teeth. "Your spell fizzles. The giant rodents close in for an attack."

We've been deep into this roleplaying game for about an hour now. As soon as Miri and Amy went off to interview the Ediyas, Prince pulled out a tabletop board and asked our guards if they've ever played Dungeon. It's a testament to the pilot's charm that they abandoned their posts outside the ship and sat down to play with us. To my surprise, we've been having a ton of fun. Lowe and Vance are pretty cool for Imperial guards—they're playing twin elf brothers with a penchant for setting things on fire. And my paladin character is kicking some serious ass.

Well, fine, I'm mostly getting my ass kicked by these dog-sized rodents we're pretend-fighting. But that's totally the dice's fault, not mine. I think Prince gave me weighted ones.

I'm so into the game, I almost don't notice when the landing party gets back. I look up between one turn and the next and Miri has suddenly appeared, legs folded into one of the passenger seats, watching us.

I shoot her a little smile, lifting my eyebrows in a silent question: *How did it go?*

She shrugs. Then she pushes out of the seat, kneels next to me at the edge of the Dungeon board, and slips her arms around my waist. Her cheek presses into my shoulder. I loop my arm around her and pull her in, breathing the smell of her hair. She smells like floral shampoo, sun-sweat, and the strange tang of another planet's air.

"I saw Oberon," she says softly.

"And?"

"I felt sorry for him. I didn't expect to. I don't think he deserves to be imprisoned."

I tighten the hug. "Did you see Melanie too?"

"Not yet. Amy's going to talk to her alone." Miri tilts her head toward the starship's open exit door. I hadn't even noticed Lawry arrive, but he's right next to the doorway, arms crossed, leaning against the doorframe. The angle lets him keep an eye on the guards outside as well as the ones inside.

"Is everything all right?" I ask in a whisper. "Lawry seems tense."

She leans very close, her breath tickling my ear. "Amy thinks Melanie has someone on this station working with her."

I'd be lying if I said the ear-whispering wasn't a turn-on, but now's really not the time. "What should we do?"

She nuzzles into my shoulder. I can barely hear the words she breathes. "Lawry gave Amy a listening device. We can watch the interrogation."

"Yeah?" I stand up so abruptly that the board gets jostled. Luckily, the game pieces are magnetic. Prince said that's an absolute necessity for playing in zero grav.

Prince looks up at me in confusion, interrupted mid-story. "Time to take a break?" he asks. "That's fine, we can finish later."

Sorry, I mouth at him as I follow Miri and Lawry to the cockpit. There's a door between the flight deck and the passenger area, which gives us a little privacy from the guards.

Lawry unrolls his scroll and lays it flat on the floor, allowing the device's holo-projector to display the scene. It blooms before us in miniature, the figures a little larger than my hand. Amy's strapped into the shuttle seat across from Ykros. The two of them couldn't be stiffer if they were carved from granite. Ykros has one hand on her gun, fingers moving in a nervous tic.

"Can we get sound?" I ask.

Lawry fiddles with the settings. Not only does he tap into the audio, but he also gets it to auto-generate subtitles, which hover in midair. They lag a few seconds behind the audio, and they struggle to render the minimal small talk over the hum of the shuttle engine, but the quality improves when the shuttle lands. By the time Ykros finishes going over the rules with Amy, we're receiving sound and subtitles loud and clear.

Amy and Ykros approach the bubble-like cell where Melanie Ediya has lived for the past decade. Amy's shoulders square up as she enters. Her throat moves as she swallows.

Miri's hand slips into mine. Her whole arm is tense as a bowstring. I squeeze her fingers as the two figures become three, and Melanie Ediya enters the holo-capture frame.

"Amethyst." Melanie's voice comes rich and droll through the scroll's speakers.

"Auntie Mel." Amy's no good at hiding her hostility. *"Your kids keep disappearing."*

"Oh? Another? Who was it this time?"

"Clara and Raoul Seranath."

Melanie's mouth quirks up in a faint smile. *"Raoul. Such a good boy."*

"Where is he, Auntie?"

"Amy, sweetest, I don't know why you keep showing up to shout at me every time one of your siblings isn't as chatty as you like. Does it look like I'm at liberty to go around kidnapping people?" She raises her hands, indicating the vineyard growing behind her. *"I'm stuck here. Just ask the captain."*

Amy looks over her shoulder at Captain Ykros, who's glowering. Her hand remains on her holster.

"How did Raoul Seranath get hold of Oberon's ship?" Amy asks.

Melanie laughs. *"Did he? Interesting."*

"I know you must have had something to do with it," Amy presses. *"Where would Raoul take Clara? Where are the rest of them? You're getting bolder to try*

to snatch the ones who live on Halcyon. I bet you're furious your plan to grab Miri didn't work."

"*Little Miri?*" Melanie hums thoughtfully. "*A very interesting subject, that one. How's she doing these days?*"

"*I'm asking the questions, Auntie Mel.*"

But Amy's losing control of this interrogation. Melanie's not the type for villain monologues. She's a sphinx who spins out riddles until her opponent trips up, then devours them whole.

Lawry pulls at my sleeve. <Look at Ykros's hand.>

"What about it?"

<She's tapping on her gun.> Lawry squints at the holo. <I think it's a code.>

"Are you sure?" That seems a bit paranoid to me. I tap my feet all the time. It probably spells out absolute gibberish if you translate it into code.

<Positive.> He gives me an exasperated look. <If anyone knows nonverbal communication when they see it, I do.> He points at Melanie. <I think she's tapping something in her hand to respond.>

Now it's my turn to examine the holo closely. Melanie has her hands behind her back, so it's hard to tell. I shuffle clockwise around the image to see it from another angle. Melanie has a pink-banded keycuff around her wrist. Her other hand is clasped just above the band, her fingernail tapping against the tiny blank screen. Easy to write off as a nervous fidget, but this is Melanie we're talking about.

"What are they saying?" I ask.

He waits a moment to answer me, tapping the sequence onto his own hand as he watches Melanie. His frown deepens.

"What?"

<She's saying, *Get my niece out of here. Don't tell her anything.* And...>

"Yes?"

<She asked if Miri is here on the station. Ykros said yes. Melanie told her to take Miri to Haven.>

"Haven again." I snap my fingers. "That's where all the answers are."

Lawry goes back to watching the feed for more clues, but it seems Ykros has received the message and is ready to end the charade. She steps in and places a hand on Amy's shoulder. *"That's enough,"* she says. *"You're getting heated. Let's take a break."*

"I'm not done with her," Amy spits.

"Later," Ykros assures her, and the two of them retreat out of Melanie's dome.

Miri looks up from the holo. "So this means Ykros is the one helping Melanie? But she's in charge of this entire station?"

"Yeah." I cast a side glance at the door, behind which Lowe and Vance are presumably still trying to kill giant rats with Prince. I hope the flight deck door is soundproof. If not, we're screwed. "If the boss is corrupt, then this whole place is. We need to get out of here. Now."

<Wait,> flashes Lawry's keycuff.

Is he out of his mind? "What is there to wait for? They want to take Miri. We have to get her to safety. We can come back for Amy." It doesn't feel great, suggesting we leave her here, but I don't see any alternative.

<What if...> Lawry gives Miri an appraising look. <Maybe we should let them take her.>

I lunge at him without a second thought, halfway to throwing a punch before I even register the movement of my arm.

Lawry blocks it easily, grabbing my wrist and twisting it down. <CALM,> he signs emphatically with his free hand. <LISTEN.>

I breathe deeply, trying to dissipate the red haze across my vision. "What?" It comes out a cross between a huff and a growl.

Lawry releases me. I rub my wrist, which still twinges with pain. Lawry didn't get to be a senior Knight for nothing—he's strong.

<We hide a recording device on her, like we just did with Amy,> Lawry says. <They take her to the hideout of these people Melanie's working with. We sit back and listen as they reveal their plans and location.>

"And Miri?" I glance at her, fear coursing through me in the wake of anger. "How do we ensure she doesn't get hurt? We don't know why they want her or what they'll do."

Miri takes a deep breath, holds it, releases it. "I can take care of myself. I think it's a good idea. It might give me a chance to help Clara."

"Miri," I say softly. "No. You don't have to sacrifice yourself for anyone."

She meets my eyes. "I know I don't have to. I'm *choosing* to."

I want to argue. I want to demand that she stay here. Send Amy. Send anyone else.

But I also know she'd never forgive me if I overrode her wishes.

"I survived the Ediyas when I was little," she says. "I can take whatever they have in store for me this time. I really don't think they want to kill me. I think they want to study me, and that means the other missing Ediya Experiments may still be alive."

I swallow, my mouth suddenly dry. The only reply I can muster is a quick, curt nod.

<I have another set of holo-capture earrings,> Lawry types. <Let me go get them.>

As soon as he's out of the room, Miri lunges at me in a desperate embrace. "I'm sorry, Leo," she says against my shoulder. "Please don't be angry. I need to do this."

"I know you do." I crush her to me, wondering if she can see the fear flooding through me. What color is it? It feels black as the void, swallowing me up until all I am is sensation: racing heart, sweaty palms, the pressure of her arms holding me together. "I don't want you to leave again," I admit into the floral scent of her hair.

"This time," she says, "I fully intend to come back."

IT'S TEN MINUTES—A SHORT ETERNITY—UNTIL THE AIRLOCK ALARM goes off, warning us that Captain Ykros's shuttle is about to dock.

Prince pauses as he packs away the game board. The guards, Vance and Lowe, got some communication from the captain and hustled off the ship, leaving us free to explain the plan to our pilot. "Genius," was his assessment, "but the tricky part is going to be letting her get kidnapped while convincing them we don't want them to take her. It's tough to lose a fight on purpose."

"Bold of you to assume we're stronger than a space station full of

Imperial guards," was my response. I'm honestly worried about our chances of getting off this space station at all, with Miri or without her. Our window of opportunity to get gone has closed. We're going to have to fight our way out.

"Brace yourselves," Prince says now. "This is gonna get ugly." He tucks the Dungeon box under the pilot seat and removes a sleek black case instead, which he opens to reveal a blaster.

<That's not standard Knight issue,> Lawry observes.

"Nope," Prince says without a trace of guilt. "And I don't use it often. But I've needed it enough times that I don't see any sense in getting rid of it."

I pat the stunner at my waist. Its electrical pulse paralyzes temporarily but is nonlethal in most cases, which is why it's the favored weapon of the Knights. The Imperial Authorities aren't nearly as careful about taking lives. They'll be using real blasters. Adrenaline zings through me. *Yeah, we'll be lucky to get out of this one.*

<Remember, we're not supposed to know they want Miri,> says Lawry. <Act normal.>

"Should we pretend to still be playing Dungeon?" I ask.

Prince snorts. "I ain't risking my game board in the middle of a battle."

Miri nudges me. "Shh. They're coming."

Through the open passenger door, we watch as Ykros and Amy cross the hangar bay toward Prince's ship. I don't miss the nod Ykros gives to the two guards, who are once more at their posts outside our ship.

Prince is the one who greets them in the doorway. "What'd Melanie say? Did she tell you anything?"

Amy's shoulders slump. "I couldn't get anything out of her. I'm sorry, Lawry. I'm afraid I wasn't very professional." She folds her arms. "The captain brought me back here to take a break, but I want to try again. I'm not giving up. She does know something, if I can just—"

Her words choke off into a gasp as Captain Ykros swiftly presses her blaster to Amy's temple.

"Don't try anything stupid," she says smoothly, seeing all of us flinch toward our holsters. "Vance! Lowe! You know what to do."

She pulls Amy backward, and the two guards shoulder their way back into the passenger bay of Prince's ship, brandishing their own guns.

"Seriously, Vance?" Prince groans, holding up his hands in surrender. "I thought we were having a good time."

"Orders are orders," says the guard gruffly. "Get down on the floor, all of you. Hands above your head."

I obey, first kneeling, then lying flat when Vance shoves my shoulders down. The other guard, Lowe, secures my wrists with a painfully tight band. I try to flex my hands as much as I can, giving myself some wiggle room to get out of the binding, but I'm not sure I'll be able to break free on my own. I'd better pray they don't decide to kill us all, because if they do, we've just forfeited our chances of fighting back.

I hate that I was right and Prince was wrong. It *is* unfortunately easy to lose a fight. Especially when the baddies have a gun to your friend's head.

They tie Miri too, but they don't force her flat like me, Lawry, and Prince. I guess she doesn't look like much of a threat to them. I mean, fair, she barely comes up to my collarbone, but it's obvious they don't know *why* Melanie Ediya wants her. If they knew about her powers, they'd be a lot more careful how they treat her.

I turn my head, trying to keep my eyes on her as long as possible. They drag her to her feet and shove her toward Captain Ykros. The gold studs glint against her earlobes. Hopefully, Ykros won't remember that she arrived wearing a well-worn silver earcuff instead.

"Please don't hurt us," Miri begs. The break in her voice is pretty convincing. "You can do what you want to me. Just let the Knights go."

"Quiet," says Captain Ykros. "Lowe, take the lady to my private cruiser. No matter what she tells you, don't let her go. If you loose her restraints, I'll fire you out an airlock." Ah. Maybe the captain *does* have some idea what she's dealing with.

Amy struggles against Captain Ykros's tight hold. "What the fuck? Where are you taking us? Did Melanie set this up somehow? Oh, I'm going to kill that gli—"

"Dr. Ediya just wants your friend," says Captain Ykros. "You, she doesn't care about." She shoves Amy forward and fires.

I scream, flopping around like a fish in a futile effort to intervene. I'm terrified I'll turn and see Amy with her head blown off. But the captain aimed for her leg. Amy's collapsed on her side, bleeding badly from a wound in the back of her thigh, but her chest is heaving. She's not dead.

Thank stars.

"Hold them here for twenty-five hours, then let them go," the captain says to Vance. "If they make trouble, they take a spacewalk. I don't want to see any of them following my wake. If I do, *you* take a spacewalk. Understand?"

"Crystal clear, sir."

"Good." Ykros points at Amy. "Get a medic in here for the bleeding. Dr. Ediya doesn't want her dead, just out of the game."

Then she leaves.

CHAPTER SEVENTEEN

Leo

IT'S A DEEPLY SHITTY FEW MINUTES OF THE FOUR OF US CURSING AND writing on the floor of the ship's passenger bay. Lawry is closest to Amy and able to roll into position to put pressure on her wound. It's bleeding a lot, but not spurting blood, which I'm hoping means Ykros didn't hit any super important arteries. Amy's passed out from the shock and doesn't wake up right away—that worries me.

Vance finally comes back with a medic, who cleans out the wound and injects Amy with a small dose of healing-stimulant nanites. "She can't walk on it for at least three days," the medic orders. "No sitting either. Make sure she stays lying down. If she tries to get up, give her one of these knockout capsules and tell her it's a painkiller."

Then the medic leaves us. Vance shuts us inside the ship and goes to wait outside the door. Neither of them bothered to clean up the pool of blood or remove our wrist bindings.

"Well, this ain't great," says Prince gloomily. He's managed to prop himself up against one of the cushioned seats, wrists bound in his lap.

Lawry stares at his bloody hands, grimacing.

"Hey, Galway," Prince says after a minute. "Can you scoot over here and stick your hand in my rear pocket? I thought I'd be able to reach it if I stretched real hard, but I guess I'm gettin' old."

With my own hands stuck together in front of me, I shuffle over next to him and wriggle one hand awkwardly down the pocket. At the very bottom, almost too deep for my bound hands to reach, my fingertips brush a small, lipstick-sized case.

I pull it out and examine it. The side of it says, JOEL'S ∞-IN-1 LAZER SLICER.

"Old friend of mine invented it," says Prince. "It cuts shit real good. But, uh, you gotta be careful 'cause it cuts human body parts too."

I wince. "You first."

"Can't cut myself loose with my hands bound. You'll have to do it."

I curse under my breath. Prince holds his bound hands out in front of him and stretches his wrists apart as far as possible, the ties digging into his skin and leaving angry red marks. "Don't aim it toward anybody," he advises. "Point it right up against the ties and then back toward the seat. Yeah, just like that. Right, hold it steady...now click the button."

A red flash sears my eyeballs. Prince gives one last tug, and his bonds snap apart, the laser having sliced through all but a thin string of the material.

I realize I've been holding my breath. I drop the cutter and gasp for air. "You carry that thing around in your pocket? What if the clicker got pushed by accident?"

"Then I'd lose a leg or somethin'," says Prince. He snatches it up. "You wanna go next?"

"Give me a second to stop shitting myself."

"Can't change your unders without your hands to yourself," Prince points out.

I keep my eyes closed while he makes the cut. I don't watch when he frees Lawry either. But I do admit it might have been worth it once all of us have our hands back. We're able to clean up Amy's blood, run our clothes through the cleanser in the washroom, and cram down a nutrient bar each. We clean Amy up too, then lift her onto a row of cushioned seats with a rolled-up jacket under her head. She's still out cold. The nanite injection must have had a sedative in it.

Lawry types, <I've been recording everything that Miri's earrings send me. Ready to watch?>

"Why not," says Prince. "It's not like we're going anywhere."

We get comfy in the passenger chairs—too much sitting on the ground earlier means my butt's sore as blazes—and Lawry activates the holo-projector on his tablet.

MIRI

EVEN THOUGH THIS IS ALL ACCORDING TO PLAN—THE KNIGHTS subdued, me tied up in the passenger seat of Captain Ykros's small, four-seater personal vessel—I can't help the terror that courses through me.

Ykros isn't even paying attention to me. She got in, started the engine, and took off without sparing me a glance. I feel like a piece of cargo. At least I'm not blindfolded, so I can admire the stars around us. I can still see the green-brown expanse of the prison planet if I crane to look behind us. We haven't teleported yet—I'm surprised Ykros is waiting so long. Maybe she's planning to rendezvous with another ship.

I decide to push my luck and ask. "Where are you taking me?"

Silence. Is she really going to pretend I don't exist?

I keep pushing. "If Melanie put you up to this, wouldn't she want to study me back on the prison planet?"

That gets a *hmph* out of Ykros. "Unlike her brother, Dr. Ediya isn't obsessed with science for its own sake," she says. "She sees the bigger picture. And she's not alone."

"What's that supposed to mean? Are you talking about the people Melanie's sending messages to?"

"What messages?"

"Well, I just thought that—we talked earlier about someone helping Melanie communicate with the outside world, so I thought you must be taking her messages and sending them...somewhere?"

Ykros snorts. "Why would she need to get messages out when that boy visits her, like, once a week?"

"Raoul does?"

"Has been for years," Ykros confirms casually. "Getting tired of seeing him, I'll be honest. Little shit always demands special treatment like we're not doing *him* a favor. But he's funding my retirement, so..."

"So he's bribing you then. I was wondering how they got you to turn crooked. You seem like a good, upstanding Imperial soldier. Doesn't make sense that you'd decide to help a criminal kidnap people without a reason."

My words are calculated to prod at the murky-green guilt in her aura. I don't want to use my abilities to get her to talk, not if I can help it. But words are fair game.

"Melanie Ediya is not a criminal," Ykros snaps back. "She's a genius."

I wait, trying not to let my face show any interest.

"Raoul's an arrogant bastard, but he might be the only person in this galaxy who realizes how influential the Ediyas' work is," Ykros rants on. "There are going to be history books written a thousand years from now that cite their work as a turning point in human history. You're a fool if you haven't realized what's coming, now that there are humans with powers to equal the dragons."

A chill zips down my arms, raising creepflesh.

Ykros glances at me and smirks. "Oh yes, I know what you and your siblings are capable of. In fact, one of them should be arriving shortly to 'port us to Monroe. *Without* dragons."

So they *have* learned to teleport. Clara wouldn't confirm it, but I know what I felt when she 'ported me from the funeral grove to the garage. And Ykros is making it sound like it isn't *just* Clara...

"Is that where all the missing ones are?" I ask. "On Monroe?"

"They were never missing," says Ykros. "They're in training. And soon you'll join them." She looks over at me and actually smiles. "Haven't you always wanted to test the limits of what you can do? I know I would. You might think I've kidnapped you, but I'm actually setting you free from the rules of Halcyon and the dragons. You'll thank me once you realize what you were missing."

I hope these earrings are working. I hope, somewhere on the other end, Leo's listening. Because Ykros just told them exactly what they needed to hear.

What I wasn't prepared for is how much her words would resonate with me, how much *longing* they've unlocked. If this Haven group is where all my lost siblings have gone, and they're all learning to control their abilities there, then I'm suddenly desperate to join them. Maybe they can teach me to block my accidental tampering with people's minds. I could finally have a normal life. I could be with Leo without worrying I'm twisting his feelings.

If only I didn't have to submit to Melanie Ediya's experiments to do it.

LEO

"Monroe!" I yell triumphantly. "We have a lead."

"Yeah, great, we found the haystack," Prince groans. "Now we gotta find the needle. Monroe's an *entire planet*. Do you have any idea how many people live there?"

I vaguely remember learning about it in the Galactic Geography module I took in gen ed. "A couple billion?"

"Uh, yeah. Spread out across thousands of cities. We're gonna need more specific directions."

Groaning, I tune back into the recording.

Miri's asking who's supposed to come pick them up. *"Is it Clara or someone else?"*

"Who's Clara?" Ykros waves her hand. *"Never mind, I don't care. I sent notice that we needed a dragon-free pickup. They'll send who they send."*

"It's just that...I've been really worried about her," Miri continues, ignoring Ykros's annoyed sigh. *"Raoul seems way too controlling over her, and I'm just wondering if it's his fault she left her acting school."*

She emphasizes the last few words. I suck in a sharp breath. "I think she's trying to tell us something."

"Shh!" Prince slaps my arm.

"She went to Monroe Academy of Theater," Miri continues. *"Do you know if that's near where Haven is based?"*

"Don't know or care," Ykros snaps. *"Can we not tell our life stories here? I just want to get this done and go home."*

"It's in Hepburn City," Miri says helpfully. *"The academy. Is that close to where we're—"*

Ykros snaps, *"Haven's out in the slums, nowhere near the city center. Now will you shut up?"*

Prince, Lawry, and I share a triumphant glance. "Nice job, Miri," I whisper.

Lawry's already got his scroll out, typing in a uniweb search for the academy's address. <That's a decent lead,> he flashes on his keycuff adapter. <We can ask some questions at the academy. But I think we're going to need backup.>

PART SIX

Knight Headquarters, Halcyon

To

Hepburn City, Monroe

Year 3745, Week 12,

Daysix

CHAPTER EIGHTEEN

Leo

WHEN VANCE AND LOWE FINALLY UNLOCK OUR SHIP'S ANCHOR BOLTS an excruciating twenty-odd hours later—most of which we spend in fitful sleep on uncomfortable passenger-bay seat cushions—Lawry instructs Prince to teleport back to Knight headquarters on Halcyon. Even though there's no time to waste, Lawry still thinks it's necessary for us to report back to the Knight collective.

It's already afternoon, local time, when we land in the Knights' vast open airfield. The low rocky plateau is dotted with anchored starships and hovercars waiting for the next emergency to call them away. A row of bright white lights illuminates the path toward the elevator into the Knights' underground warren of offices, training gyms, and dormitories.

Prince stays at the ship to oversee a scan for tracking devices, because as Lawry puts it, <Ykros is too smart to let us go without one.> A team of healers arrives to transport Amy to the hospital, while Lawry goes off to consult with the other senior Knights. That leaves me to shuffle off to the dining hall for a quick coffee and some food.

It's between mealtimes, so the hall is dim and mostly empty. A kitchbot retrieves a packed-away portion of leftovers and warms the meal for me. After subsisting on nutrient bars for a day, even reheated protein-root mash tastes divine.

My insides warm and my blood zinging with recaffeinated energy, I head back to find Lawry. He's in his office on the top level, finishing up a debrief with our new backup team. I'm expecting a platoon of older Knights, broad-shouldered and scarred. The best-trained, the most-experienced, the strongest.

Instead, I peer through his office door and see...

Wait, what? Why are my friends here?

"Galway!"

"Rathurr!" I yell, launching myself across the room into a back-pounding hug with my best friend. As usual, I regret it instantly when he knocks the breath out of me.

Chaz Rathurr has gray-brindle fur all over his face and muscular arms, as well as pointed ears that are set rather higher on his head than an Earth Classic human's ears would be. His features are catlike, though his eyes look more humanoid: brown irises surrounded by whites.

Natalia Lantz and Derek Arbor are right behind him, and I pretend to choke as they jump into the hug.

Other than our navy blue jumpsuits, my team doesn't have much in common. Natalia's hair is violently orange. Her translucent, pale skin and magenta eyes betray a family history of genetic modification, while her power stance screams badass. She'll hit any target with just about any projectile—including the ship floor with vomit whenever she gets space-sick. Which is often.

Derek has a face for holo-vids: ponytailed black hair, brown eyes, sharp cheekbones and jawline. Too bad he's an "um, actually" guy. If we need someone to quote the rule book, Arbor's our go-to man. He's a genius for strategy, so we forgive him the pedantry.

Paired with Chaz's brawn and good humor, and my magnetism for trouble, we make a pretty well-balanced team. Albeit one Chief Knight Jostlin has seen in his office for disciplinary talks so many times that, whenever he sees us, he groans and says, "You again."

"What are you all doing here?" I exclaim.

Natalia snorts. "What do you think? We're joining your team. Lawry called Jostlin about an hour ago and told him to have us drop what we're doing. We just got briefed, and I think I speak for all of us when I say, *What the FUCKING BLAZES did you get us into this time?*"

"Seriously? I thought Jostlin was still mad at us. Well. Mostly me."

"Oh, he is," says Derek. "He said, direct quote, 'I can't believe that quarkbrain wormed his way into this case.' Told us that we're responsible for you, and if you fuck up, we're all out of a job."

Oh. Well, shit. No pressure at all.

"But, like, we're not going to fuck up though," Chaz adds bracingly. He slings an arm around my shoulder. "Jostlin even said you already have a lead."

"Right, yeah. The acting school." I grimace. "Feels like a long shot."

"I remember meeting that Clara girl one time," Chaz reminisces. "I was over to your community for your twentieth birthday, I think. Yeah. She was chatty, that one. Flirty too."

"So?"

"So she's not good at keeping her business to herself is what I'm sayin'." Chaz grins. "If she was going somewhere with her creepy brother, I bet she told someone at her school about it."

I fold my arms. "And you think her friends are equally chatty? What if they don't want to tell us anything?"

"They will if you're dressed like this."

That's Prince, returning from the direction of his ship with a heaping armful of colorful cloth. As I look closer, I realize they're crimson jackets with gold trim: a uniform only worn by Imperial Authorities.

"Why do you have these?" I ask. "Pretty sure it's illegal to impersonate an Imperial soldier."

Prince just winks. "Don't ask a magician to reveal his tricks."

Derek leans in and whispers, "His dad is the leader of the Greenjackets. They're probably dead men's uniforms."

I shiver. The Greenjackets are a rebel organization not unlike the Knights, except their leader is a pirate who, if rumors are true, has no problem killing Imperial soldiers and robbing merchant freighters. Their goals are pretty much the same as ours—help the poor and oppressed, stick it to the Authorities—but the Knights generally don't work with them because their "break a few eggs" mentality makes for bad optics on our end.

Lawry steps in. <This plan does involve a certain level of risk. We aren't sure what we're dealing with here—we could be walking into another trap, like we did on Hawking Penitentiary. I realize it's not standard procedure for Halcyon Knights to go undercover, but I think that's exactly what this situation calls for.>

Nat, Derek, Chaz, and I exchange glances with varying levels of discomfort. Lawry seems increasingly happy to bend the rules for this case. I'm not going to stop him—I want to find Miri as fast as possible—but it feels like now that the dragons have shown their weakness, even Lawry is starting to lose faith in their laws.

I take the jacket Prince hands me and push my arms through the sleeves. Its folds are crisp-pressed, the fabric cool. A bit wide in the shoulders and sleeves, but otherwise it fits well.

Miri, I think, almost a prayer, *I'm coming for you.*

MIRI

WHEN OUR PICKUP ARRIVES, I'M HALF-ASLEEP, DOZING WITH MY HEAD lolling against the headrest. Ykros seems content to drive straight into the void at sub-lightspeed, no dragon in sight. Flying too long in empty space makes me nervous—it's not advisable in a short-range ship like this one. Easy to run out of power, and shortly thereafter, out of air.

I'm jolted awake by Ykros speaking into the com. "Receiving transmission. Took you long enough, Seranath."

I don't hear the response, but when I scrunch down in my seat to peer up out of the viewport, I catch a glimpse of the sporty, vivid red ship I last saw hightailing it out of Newcastle Community's garage.

Raoul? Or is it Clara? Ykros hasn't specified which Seranath she's talking to.

There's a clank and a shudder as the red two-seater locks onto Ykros's ship with a tow cable. I suppose a magnetic field wouldn't cut it if we're going to teleport together. Co-teleportation requires physical contact.

At least, it does when dragons are involved. Who knows what it entails when gen-modded humans are doing the 'porting?

The weightless dark of the aetherworld surrounds me for the space of a breath, then releases me back into light and air. Gravity's back too. We're no longer in the void between stars—we're careening through an atmosphere above buildings as high as the clouds. It's a well-known skyline: Hepburn City, Monroe. An iconic location on the most high-profile planet in the Empire.

Ykros works the controls to slow our descent into the spaceport. The red starship releases the tow rope, which clanks loose against our ship's tail. But our escort doesn't leave us. Their shadow looms above the viewport, just barely out of sight.

As soon as we anchor, Ykros leans over to unbuckle my safety restraints. Then she releases the magcuffs around my wrists with a reluctant frown.

"Don't think you're free to run off, girl. I won't hesitate to shoot you in the leg just like I did your friend. You can walk to where we're going... or I can carry you over my shoulder, bleeding all over the train."

I swallow, my mouth feeling like it's full of cotton balls. I'm starving, thirsty, and dying for a pee.

"I'm not going to run," I croak. "I don't even know where we are."

That's not entirely true. I know we're in Hepburn City, a sprawling metropolis of which I've only ever seen panning shots in the opening credits of holo-dramas. Clara was so excited to move here—she thought it was a magical place that would make all her dreams come true. It makes me sick to think it might be her driving the red starship.

But when we disembark, it's not Clara waiting for me. My insides do a tiny, terrified flip as I see, backlit against the spaceport's cold floodlights, the tall, slim figure of my eldest brother.

My heart hammers behind my ribs. Is he going to try to control me like he did Clara?

"Here she is," Ykros says, pushing me forward.

Raoul looks me over, distant and detached, so different from how he acted at the wedding. I hate to think he was just pretending to be a fond brother the whole time. Surely, at least some of that was real?

"I have other business to deal with," he says shortly. "You have the address for Haven, don't you? Take her there."

Ykros glares. Obviously, hauling me around like a sack of potatoes for delivery wasn't part of her plan for the day. "Melanie said—"

Then her face goes blank, and that cold emptiness punches me in the gut again. Her aura all but disappears, suppressed by Raoul's control. "Come along," she says, tugging me away from Raoul with a firm grip on my upper arm.

"Raoul!" I call out, but he's already turning back toward his ship. Ykros's aura gradually returns as we march through the corridors toward the spaceport's main thoroughfare. As she regains control of herself, she seems mildly spaced-out and confused, which turns into a flared-off glower.

I'd rather not bother her when she's like this, but my bladder compels me to ask, "May I use the washroom?"

Ykros groans. "Fine." She alters her path to drag me into the spaceport's green-tiled, disinfectant-scented public facilities. She inspects the stall first, making sure there aren't any loose ceiling tiles or gaps under the sides where I could sneak out. She waits right outside the door while I take care of business, wash my hands, and try to fix myself a little in the mirror. There's just no hiding the fact that my armpits are damp with fear-sweat, my hair is a tangled mess, my neck is cricked from sleeping at a weird angle, and I haven't changed clothes in more than twenty-five hours.

Anyway, why should I care? I'm a prisoner. I should look like it. Or should I? I don't have a single clue how to behave. This is my first time in an offworld city.

I caught a glimpse of it from the air as we flew in. I woke just in time to see the clouds parting to reveal a breathtaking cityscape below. I'm used to hidden cities below the surface, with farmland and nature preserves aboveground. Hepburn City is the opposite of that. Spires and domes in a thousand colors, shapes, and textures vie for space like trees fighting to be the tallest. Ships whiz through the valleys between each building, sunlight flashing off sleek, curved wings and shiny tailfins. There could be as many people in this one city as there are in a whole Halcyonite province—or maybe they've simply made themselves so *visible*, so central to the landscape, in a way Halcyonites never have.

Clara once told me, "Once you see Monroe in all its glory, it's hard to imagine living anywhere else." But for me, it's difficult to see a place for myself in this bustle. How can anyone hear themselves think?

Ykros leads me out of the dim, chilly hangar, which resounds with metallic clanking and screeching, into the main corridor of the spaceport, following signs for the exit. Hoverbarrows and personal drones whiz along in their own dedicated lane, following the people whose luggage they carry.

The aether energy around me feels disturbed in a way I've never felt before. Too many lives intertwining and colliding. Too many people, agitated and stressed, some desperate to survive. On Halcyon, everyone lives in a carefully balanced harmony, each person's work bolstering the collective good. Here, it's like the holo-dramas: life is a constant struggle against the rest of the world. What another person gains is your loss, unless you reach out and take it back from them.

Stars, I hope I'm reading it wrong. Maybe we've just flown into a particularly dysfunctional part of the city.

"This way." Ykros steers us into a skybridge bathed in sunlight. Monroe's sun is a slightly different color than Halcyon's, and its sky is nearly the same blue as Old Earth's, rather than Halcyon's pale violet. I shrug my shoulders and bounce on my heels experimentally; gravity feels about the same as Halcyon's. I suppose it makes sense the two planets would feel similar. The early colonists chose planets that were nearly the same as Old Earth. Whatever wasn't quite right, they terraformed.

The skybridge is bustling with new arrivals. Families drag whiny children along, trunks levitating behind them. Everyone's dressed in the height of fashion, their dresses, tunics, and trousers concealed under long, loose outer robes that hang open at the front. I've seen these outfits in celebrity profiles and holo-dramas, but most people on Halcyon don't bother to dress so formally. Many people only have two or three changes of clothes and wear the same style every day. To have more is considered a waste of resources.

It's obvious that conspicuous consumption isn't considered a problem on Imperial planets like this one.

There also seems to be a higher percentage of gen-mod people here, plus a significant number of nonhumans or humanoid crosses. I've always been somewhat of an anomaly on Halcyon, where gen-mods are uncommon. Luckily, my reflective yellow-green eyes aren't terribly noticeable. They make me downright boring in this crowd, where I'm surrounded by a rainbow of hair, eye, and skin colors, as well as wings, horns, fur, scales, antennae, and other features I don't have names for.

Few of these people are true aliens. Only a handful of sentient species choose to blend with human society, and most of them are reserved to fringe planets, as their rights under Imperial law are somewhat in dispute. No, most of these people are descendants of folks who mixed their genes with animal or alien DNA long ago. Some of them, like the cat-people of Paotherr or others with Ykros's batlike features, did so to adapt to imperfectly terraformed planets. Others thought it looked cool. Still others did so for the purpose of creating ambassadors to hard to reach alien races. The practice has been hotly debated for the last several hundred years, but the descendants of former gen-mods are still thriving.

"Keep up," Ykros snaps, tugging me forward.

After the skybridge, we enter what seems to be a shopping center. Another thing I've only seen on holo-dramas. I keep my eyes forward, knowing from said dramas that sellers can be aggressive to anyone who acts like a tourist. Still, it's difficult not to gawk at the dizzying range of items on display: clothes, figurines, art prints, sex toys, food, sim downloads, mind-alts, keycuffs, musical instruments, and more.

We weave through the visual overload of it all, Ykros ignoring the sights as if she's seen them a thousand times. She shoulders between people, dragging me along until we reach the subtrain station. A quick scan of both our keycuffs and we're in the public transport queue, sandwiched between a black-robed man tutting at the time and a mother with her baby strapped to her bosom, rocking it as it wails softly.

Public trains are new to me too. I lived my first eight years on a space station with a dragon-blocking shield and the rest of my life on Halcyon, where children were taught how to call a dragon to teleport them at the same time they learned their alphabet.

But folks on other planets aren't as close to the dragons as Halcyonites are. People might go their whole lives never knowing how to call a dragon. Only pilots and random hobbyists ever bother to learn. The slow, inefficient public transport is a necessity here, whereas on Halcyon, driving a hovercar is an occasional sightseeing activity.

The subtrain arrives. We cram onto it, stuck standing because all the seats are full. I feel like I'm choking, pressed by people, bags, and strange smells from all sides. I focus on my breathing, trying to ground myself in the erratic rhythms of my overstressed, confused body.

Stops whiz by. The people crowded close to me stare into the middle distance, glazed looks on their faces, their auras a riot of clashing colors as each of them inhabits their own private world. It seems the only way people survive this bizarre experience is by pretending it's not happening.

A dozen stops and what feels like six thousand years later, Ykros says, "This is us. Follow me."

An escalator carries us to the exit. When we reach the street, I can see we've arrived in a less wealthy part of town. Buildings here are not as shiny as they were near the spaceport. Flashy paint peels on parked hovercars; glowing signs have missing letters where their lights have burnt out. I sidestep a vomit splotch on the pavement.

Uneasiness nips at my heels. I thought that once the crowd thinned out, I would breathe easier. But the vibes are off here. It's not the shabby surroundings—I've lived comfortably in much simpler places. Just because folks don't have time or money to care for their neighborhood doesn't mean they're bad people. No, what I'm feeling is akin to the *nothingness* Raoul's mind control gave off. It's not nearly that intense though. More like an itch in the back of my mind.

Ykros must feel it too. Her steps quicken, and her hand tightens on my arm.

A rickety escalator curls up and around the edge of a tall building. We step on and ride right to the top, to a door painted Imperial-flag red.

Ykros presses the buzzer. When the lock intones, "ID scan requested," she pulls my wrist forward and taps my keycuff against it.

There's a long pause.

"What if this isn't the right place?" I whisper.

The captain glares at me but doesn't respond.

Finally, an answering chime. The door slides open. A mouthwatering savory smell wafts out: bean stew and baking bread.

"Come in, come in!" trills a woman's voice from inside.

I glance at Ykros, but she shrugs. "My orders were to bring you," she says. "I'm done." She shoves me through the door, which swishes shut behind me with the finality of a prison cell, and I face a room full of strangers.

CHAPTER NINETEEN

Leo

I've always wanted to visit Monroe. It's the mythical glimmering planet in every holo-drama skyline shot. At any other time, I'd be desperate to see everything. Stroll the shopping center connected to the spaceport, smelling rare perfumes and sampling expensive candy I couldn't afford. I'd be begging my team leader for a day off so I could go see the tallest fountain in the galaxy. Or I'd buy one of the city's iconic ice treats at a street vendor, then eat it under the warming streetlamps while the city's almost year-round snowfall drifts gently from the sky.

But knowing Miri's in danger, all the bustle and glamor fades into a static noise around me. All I want is confirmation she's safe.

Our access to the earrings' recording cut out once Ykros and Miri teleported. We haven't been connected in almost a day. My mind can't stop inventing the horrible tortures she must be enduring, imprisoned by Melanie Ediya's minions. But Lawry wants us to wait to check the recording until we've found a safe base of operations.

"I hope you know where you're going," Nat grumbles. Our civvy robes aren't enough to keep the chill at bay as we hike block after block, hovercars whizzing overhead, scavenging hoppers darting between our feet in search of dropped morsels. Our warm Imperial jackets are folded in our packs; Lawry didn't want us drawing attention when we flew in.

Lawry pretends his wrist-adapter didn't pick up her words, although it totally did—I saw it.

We're headed away from the crowded, well-lit center of town, keeping to side streets and avoiding cambot patrols. All Lawry's told us is that he <knows a place> where we can set up without being watched. I think that's optimistic. I haven't stopped feeling eyes on me since we landed. Hepburn City is the sort of place where attention is worth more than credits and distributed more abundantly.

Finally, with another glance above our heads to check for cambots, Lawry turns down an alley and leads us down a poorly lit stairwell. The building above flashes with advertisements for various high-end fashion designers—it's a shopfront shared by several tailoring businesses. This basement looks like it's been forgotten by the cleanerbots that scrub the upstairs floors after each uber-rich patron tracks in slush.

However, Lawry rings the doorbell like he knows what he's doing, so I swallow my misgivings and wait patiently.

When the door slides open, my insides lurch like gravity's about to turn off. It's a young, brown-haired woman in a pale blue Devote robe.

Miri?

No. Not Miri. This woman is taller with regular brown eyes instead of gold. Her features are angular and thin, and there's mistrust in her gaze as the group of us crowd in from the cold.

"I haven't seen you here before," she prompts.

Lawry types quickly. <We are Knights. Important investigation to run. May we use one of your meditation rooms?>

He displays his credentials, and the Devote examines them carefully before nodding. "You may stay here, but not long," she says. "And we ask that you don't draw any unwelcome attention to our Refuge. We have gone undetected by the Authorities for six months so far, and it would be inconvenient to have to move again."

I exchange a raised-eyebrows look with Chaz. "This place is a Refuge?" I whisper.

The Devote overhears me. "It may not be as beautiful as the ones you are used to at home," she says. "We use technology here out of necessity, and we must remain hidden. But many have left Halcyon who did not wish to stop practicing the Halcyonite way of life. By keeping a sacred space open for them, we help them keep in touch with their roots."

"That's amazing," Chaz murmurs. "I never knew."

"We take pains to keep it that way," the Devote says sharply. "Nonapproved religious practice is outlawed under Imperial rule. The Authorities have shut down a dozen Refuges in this city in the last twenty years. Some Devotes have been imprisoned or sent to work camps."

I want to ask why she doesn't go home, why anyone would stay in this place that hates their very existence, but I keep my mouth shut. I know why. Wanting to help people, especially the ones who need it most, is a goal I can relate to. Sometimes you do quarkbrained stuff to try to give people a better life.

Stuff like fight a dinosaur because its nest was clogging some water pipes.

Stuff like impersonate a soldier in the galaxy's most powerful and unforgiving army, just so you can stop a murderer from upending your planet's whole society.

The Devote leads us through the basement—which, although dimly lit, is cleaner and warmer than it looked from the outside—to a private room that's doing double duty as a supply closet. She drags a curtain across the shelves of cleanerbot parts and cans of mysterious liquids, then pulls out a stack of cushions for us to sit on. The result is a small but semi-cozy office with just enough space for us to place Lawry's scroll in the middle.

"Thank you, Sister," Derek says. "We'll require some privacy now."

"Of course." The Devote backs out, sliding the closet door shut behind her. The space instantly feels stuffier.

<We're in range,> Lawry flashes with a quick grin.

And he begins to play back the recording.

MIRI

THE INSIDE OF THE APARTMENT BURSTS WITH GREEN. HANGING planters decorate every corner, dripping with moisture. The air is humid and smells faintly of sweat, but cooking odors are the strongest. An All-In-One BotPot steams next to the sink. Its display screen reads <SETTING: SOUP. 5 MIN.> As I watch, the "5" drops down to "4."

There are more people in here than I expected, reclining on threadbare couches and chatting at the large table. Beyond them, a dark hall stretches for longer than a typical single-family living unit. There's space for at least six bedrooms, maybe more. This must be a communal living space. It's built on a much smaller scale than Halcyon's communities, and it's aboveground rather than below, but otherwise it's not that dissimilar.

I stand there, awkwardly framed in the doorway, staring into the faces of the strangers whose living room I've just stumbled into. None of them say anything, and the silence stretches out to an uncomfortable length.

"Hi," I say at last. "I think this might be a mistake. I was kidnapped and brought here against my will—"

"Miri?"

I whip around. I know that voice, though it's been years since I heard it. "*Saray?*"

My fellow Ediya Experiment—one of my missing sisters—perches on the arm of the couch in a shimmery green robe that looks too expensive for the room, her eyes and lips dramatically lined. She's a tall, brown-skinned woman with hair that catches the light in shades of red and gold. Last time I saw her, she was a gawky teen with bad skin who was just figuring out that makeup can be fun.

As my eyes pan across the couch, I recognize more of my Ediya siblings. Rosa, a curvy brunette, sits next to Saray with a mug of tea between her hands. Ian, the youngest of us, is grown now, nineteen and round-cheeked. The ends of his hair are tinted yellow, with brown roots showing underneath.

"You're all alive," I blurt out.

Ian gives me a funny look. "Did someone say we're not?"

"It's just...you all went missing." I need to sit down. My knees are about to give out. "Amy says she hasn't been able to contact you in—"

"Well, yeah," says Rosa. "Obviously we're not answering Amy's messages. She means well, but you know what she told us about our powers. 'Keep them secret, don't ever use them.' We didn't want her coming here because, when she figures out we're in training, she'd take it the wrong way."

"But...but your uniweb profiles didn't have any updates either, and I thought..." I sit down hard on the nearest surface, a red and purple ottoman that clashes with all the other furniture. "You're training? To use your powers?" I cast another glance around the room. None of the rest of these people are familiar. Just in case, I drop my voice to a whisper. "They all know about it?"

Saray stands up and goes over to the kitchenette, where she takes a mug out of the cupboard. "Hot tea or cold?" she asks. "You look like you could use it."

Oh stars, could I ever. "Hot," I say. "Do you have chamomile?"

As Saray steeps the tea for me, Rosa explains. "This place is called Haven. Well, not the building itself. More like the group of people *in* the building, if that makes sense? The people here helped fund our creation. If Amy hadn't interfered, we would have been sent here to be cared for once the experiments were concluded."

"They're working with the Ediyas then?"

"Melanie, Gaela, and Oberon were part of Haven, yes," says a woman I don't know, who's sitting at the table flipping through a newsie page on her tablet. She's in her forties, and now that I'm getting a good look at her, she resembles Saray to an uncanny degree. "Created by it, in fact. Our leader, Glenna Ediya, cobbled together *their* genes from the best scientific minds of the last century. She needed geniuses to push the research further than ever so we could achieve our goals."

"Goals?" I repeat.

"Mother," Saray cuts in. The word shocks me. This woman isn't Saray's Halcyonite adoptive parent—she was taken in by a bachelor ambassador named Alan Lake. I guess I wasn't wrong about the resemblance between her and this Haven woman. Did the Ediyas take our genetic material from people in this group?

My heart trips over itself and begins to race. Does that mean I might have family here too?

"Let's not dump everything on her at once," Saray gently suggests. "The soup's ready. Miri, would you like something to eat?"

She places the warm mug of chamomile tea in my hands. The first sip reminds my stomach that it's very empty.

"That sounds wonderful," I say.

Whatever I was expecting when Ykros kidnapped me, it wasn't *this*. Tea, a hearty bowl of bean and vegetable stew, and familiar faces. I wasn't expecting this prison to feel so much like *home*. Like there's an empty place they've been holding open all these years, just for me.

Yet I can't quite let go of my misgivings. What is Raoul up to? Where's Clara? And why do I still feel that irritating little itch in the back of my mind telling me that something unseen is *wrong*?

LEO

LAWRY MUTES THE RECORDING WHILE MIRI CONTINUES EATING. I tear my eyes from her tiny holo-figure to glance at my team's faces.

It takes a long minute before any of us say anything, which, believe me, is unusual. Nat can *always* find something to say.

"So this group knows about their powers," Derek muses at last. "Actively helped create them, from the sound of it. I wonder what that woman was about to say before she got cut off. Something about Haven's goals..."

"I think we can retrace their steps based on the subtrain station they got off on," I cut in. "We can find them and—"

Lawry makes a gesture to cut me off. <Let's not storm in yet.>

An hour ago, I would've revolted against that order. Now, seeing Miri reasonably safe, I grudgingly admit he's right. She's not in immediate danger, and we'll probably learn more if we sit tight and watch how things progress.

<The earrings' batteries should last at least three days,> Lawry adds. <Let's take that time to assess what we're dealing with. In the meantime, we can investigate that acting school to get additional context.>

"Should we leave someone to monitor the recording?" I ask. "We don't want to miss anything important."

Lawry leans over his scroll and opens a settings menu. <I can link the live audio feed so one of us will hear everything she's hearing at all times. If problems come up, that person can alert us. But it obviously can't be me.> He gestures at his ears with a sarcastic smirk.

"I'll do it," I volunteer, maybe too quickly.

Lawry looks around for other volunteers, but the rest of the team is happy to let me do it. Begrudgingly, he types in my call code, and the link connects. It feels like being on a call with someone who pocket-dialed me. Murmurs in the background, the clinking of dishes. It sounds like Miri is helping wash up.

<Inform me at once if anything interesting happens,> Lawry says. He retrieves his Imperial Authority jacket from his pack and shrugs it on. <Let's get ready to go. We shouldn't wear out our welcome here.>

It turns out that Prince is a much better actor than any of us.

"Puff out your chest more," he mutters to me. "Don't stare at shit. If you're gonna pretend to be an Authority, you gotta act like you're the gun-totin'-est badass on this planet. You think locals walk around gawking at all the light-up signs? They act like they don't give a fuck about anything. Like the city should be looking at *them*."

I try to follow his directions. At least I can somewhat concentrate on what I'm doing, rather than what's going on in my earpiece. Miri has asked for some quiet time to meditate, so nobody's talking.

But I guess my confident posture isn't convincing, because Prince groans and rolls his eyes. "Aaand we're going to a *theater* to try to trick them into telling us stuff. Yeah, this is gonna go greaaat."

The academy is built into the basement of a theater that's obviously been in place for centuries. The building itself is hard not to stare at: a three-story, classically inspired stone structure with, frankly, a few too many cherubs carved on the pillars in front of it. A huge wallscreen takes up much of the second story, scrolling an endless list of performances, dates, and actor names.

I can't help it if I'm a little dazzled. Prince elbows me, a reminder to snap out of it. I lead the way up the steps. The doors swish open and let out a warm wave of butter-scented air. They're really committed to the historical theater aesthetic, even down to the antique popcorn hoppers and packets of candies based on Old Earth delicacies. One bright red pouch brags that it tastes like rainbows, whatever that means.

"Excuse me," I ask the ticket taker. "Which way to the academy?"

The black-uniformed girl gives me a strange look, tells us to wait, and scampers off. As soon as her back is turned, Prince elbows me hard. "*Excuse me,*" he mimics in a high voice. "You might as well tell her you're foreign."

"Well, what am I supposed to say? *Fuck you?*"

"It'd be more realistic," Prince snorts. "Monroens don't bother being polite. They just issue orders and wait for people to jump."

I shrug. I'm not gonna be a glitch to some poor girl just 'cause it's realistic.

The girl comes back in a minute and beckons nervously. "This way, sir."

We follow her down a darkened hall and through a door labeled *Authorized Persons Only*. Behind the door, the dim theater lighting transforms to a bright, cheerful hallway carpeted in sapphire blue. We pass several dressing room doors labeled with actors' names inside star-shaped nameplates before we arrive at an office with PRINCIPAL painted on the door. It's cracked open. A voice calls, "Come in," before we even have a chance to knock.

The girl disappears back down the hall. I let Lawry enter first and follow him in. The others wait outside.

The principal sits at an old-fashioned writing desk, on which are artfully stacked a number of printed books that I'm ninety-nine percent sure are for decoration, not for reading. A little sign at the front of the desk is engraved with the name *RODAN QUELL* and the pronouns *E/EM/EIR*. The principal sits at a side angle to the desk, legs crossed, hands clasped over eir top knee. E's wearing a black robe with subtle, silver moon-and-stars embroidery along the sleeve hem. A masculine style of robe, though eir makeup is minimal and androgynous. Eir head is shaved shiny-smooth. E's about fifty, I'd guess. Maybe older, but e's not showing it if so.

"Welcome," says the principal in a rich, throaty voice that I immediately know *must* belong to a singer. "I am Principal Quell. How may I assist?"

Lawry types quickly into his keycuff. <We are here to ask about one of your students. Clara Seranath.>

"Of course," says Principal Quell. "I'm encouraged to see the Authorities taking her disappearance seriously. I reported her absence two weeks ago, but the dispatcher told me, 'She probably just ran home to Mummy.' I've been in this business a long time, and I would know if one of my students was showing signs of burning out. Miz Seranath was thriving here. She would not have quit without a word."

"What do you think happened then?" I ask.

"I can only tell you what I suspect based on my conversations with her classmates. Have a seat."

The chairs are oddly squishy, upholstered with brown pleather and old brass rivets. The smell that poofs out when I sit down is a cocktail of sweat, perfume, and makeup oils.

Principal Quell recrosses eir legs and leans back in eir own plush armchair. "Miz Seranath was midway through a starring role in the academy's second-quarter production. *Elspeth and the Ghost.* Clara was perfect for the ghost role—the hair and the eyes! It's like she was gen-modded for the part. I could tell she was relishing it."

Lawry makes a *go on* motion. Or maybe, *get to the point.*

Clearing eir throat, Quell says, "Usually, she comes off stage hyped up and giddy. That night, she came back to the common room looking like…well, not to be too on the nose, like she'd seen a ghost. When Jana asked her what was wrong, she said she'd seen her brother in the audience and that she didn't know he was coming. However, her brother visits often, so I don't see why that should have shaken her. She went outside to talk to him. As far as I know, Jana was the last to see her. I noted her absence during breakfast the next morning, but all of her things were still in her room, and she hadn't told any of her friends she was planning to leave. We waited a few hours to see if she'd come back, thinking maybe she and her brother had stayed out late partying. But she never returned."

"Did anyone get a description of her brother?" Natalia asks.

"Tall, white, dark hair in a ponytail. Yellow eyes."

It sure sounds like Raoul to me.

<If you have any security recordings from that night, I'd like to look at them,> Lawry types.

"Certainly. I went through the footage myself after I made the report. There's not much there, but I'll show you what I've got."

As Principal Quell pulls up the security-cam recordings on the wallscreen behind em, I hear a quiet voice in my right ear. Miri's been silent this whole time—I almost forgot my earpiece was tuned in to hers.

"It sounds like she was afraid of Raoul," she murmurs. "I need to figure out what he's up to."

My hand flies to my ear. I turn away and whisper, "You can hear me?"

A soft laugh. "Why do you think I told them I needed to meditate? I actually wanted to eavesdrop on your investigation."

There's a whole catalog of things I want to say. "Later," is all I whisper before turning my attention back to Principal Quell's footage.

Not that there's much of it. A shot of the crowd leaving the theater, two dark figures swept along in their midst. It's hard to be certain they're Clara and Raoul. Could be someone else with long, platinum blonde hair, arm in arm with a different black-clad man. Quell follows them in clips from different cambots all the way to the subtrain station on the corner, where they're lost to the public transport system.

Lawry nods, disappointment etched in the lines around his mouth. <Thank you for your assistance, Mx Quell. Would you allow us to speak

to any students who know Clara well? I'd like to get their perspective on her disappearance.>

"I'll bring them right away," Principal Quell says. "Do you mind waiting here?"

<Not at all.>

Principal Quell wafts out of the room, leaving a cloud of perfume in eir wake. We sit in silence for a few moments, staring awkwardly at each other, crisp crimson uniforms sinking like quicksand into squishy brown armchairs.

"Do you really think the students are going to tell us anything?" Derek says at last. "This is a waste of time. We were getting more information when we were listening to—"

Lawry cuts him off with a sharp motion of his hand. He gestures to Principal Quell's wallscreen, which is still active. Easy for it to log our every move and play it back later, just as the garage screen did.

"Anyway, this is a waste of time," Derek concludes, somewhat petulantly.

"I agree," says Prince, to my surprise. He hasn't taken an active part in the investigation thus far—he's stuck to the role of chauffeur-slash-tour guide. I wonder if he's getting tired of being dragged along for the ride. "I think we should go." And then he makes a series of motions that I recognize as pirate sign language. I saw it in a holo-drama once: when pirates know their conversation can be overheard, they'll start an insult battle out loud while subtly signing their true business. Or at least that's how it worked in the drama.

Lawry recognizes it too. He frowns at Prince and makes the smallest twitch of a gesture in return. Prince repeats whatever he signed, eyes fixed on Lawry, dead serious. His dragon partner shimmers into visibility right above his shoulder. Ze seems to be telling him something the rest of us can't hear.

<Let's go,> Lawry flashes abruptly. <Now.>

The rest of us scramble to push ourselves out of these cursedly comfortable chairs. I open my mouth to ask what's going on, but Prince catches my eye and shakes his head.

Lawry hustles us down the same hallway we came in, out toward the public theater entrance. The tempting, burnt-buttery smell of popcorn whooshes into our faces as he wrenches the door aside and charges through.

We make it through the lobby and down the front steps before a voice calls out, "By Imperial Authority, you're commanded to halt!"

Shit. They have us surrounded, red jackets pushing pedestrians back to create a ring around us. I look to Prince, our best actor. Surely, he can bluff us out of this?

To his credit, he does try. "What's all this about?" he throws out, falsely jovial. "Something happening in there? Can we help?"

"No," says another voice, one that runs my blood cold. Captain Ykros steps into the ring, her arms folded. "I think you've done enough."

Oh fuck.

We're in trouble.

CHAPTER TWENTY

Leo

"I HAD A HUNCH IT MIGHT BE YOU," CAPTAIN YKROS SAYS, A SMIRK ON her black-tinted lips. "When my comrades here got the call from Principal Quell about a suspicious group impersonating Authorities, I said to Captain Armery, 'I bet I know who it is.' Imperial subjects aren't foolish enough to pull a stunt like this. It had to be Halcyonites."

The Authorities close the circle. One soldier grabs my arms, cuffing my wrists behind me while another woman rummages through my utility belt. She takes my stunner and scroll-tablet, then scans my keycuff and logs my ID. I now officially have a criminal record. I can't decide if I'm proud or embarrassed.

Mostly I'm just worried. Because if we're in jail, Miri has no way out of Haven. If we get sentenced and shipped off to a work camp, she'll be trapped there. Who knows how long it'll take the Knights to rescue us? They might decide it's too much political trouble. In the meantime, Miri will have no one looking out for her. Once the spy-tech earrings are out of range or the batteries die, we won't even know if she's alive.

"Watch that one!" Captain Ykros points to Prince. "He's a pilot with a partnered dragon. We'll need to keep a dragon-repellent shield up."

Once my entire team is magcuffed and divested of weaponry, as well as stripped of our illegal red jackets, the Authorities herd us toward the hovercar they've parked across the sidewalk. Our arrest has drawn a large crowd, complete with newsie bots recording video. Captain Ykros pushes out in front, using her prison-guard voice to demand a clear path.

My team gets jostled along between two lines of soldiers. I keep looking for an opportunity to run, but even if my hands were free, there are too many people blocking us in every direction. I wish Miri were here. She could use her magic, or whatever it is, to get the crowd to back off. Maybe she could trick the guards into releasing our bonds.

Stars, if I had her power, I'd be a total megalomaniac. Imagine being able to tell Authorities to shove it whenever I wanted! It'd feel so good to be able to help people without having to run from their oppressors. I could force the Authorities to stay away from that city Refuge so their Devotes wouldn't have to hide in basements for fear of arrest. I could make the governor of Susannah feel bad about being too much of a tightwad to vaccinate his citizens. I'd convince every squalid work camp to free their prisoner-slaves and give them wages and health care.

Except I get the feeling Miri doesn't like doing things like that. She thinks she's hurting people. So maybe she wouldn't even if she could. I don't fully understand why yet...although I think I started to when I saw what Raoul did to Lawry. Making him go all zombie for a minute, like the lights were on but nobody was home. It was terrifying, seeing someone gone missing out of their own head. I wouldn't want that done to me.

I still kinda wish I could try it on these Authorities. Just for a minute, long enough to get away. *Does that make me a bad person?*

The Authorities push us into the bench seats that line the back of the hovercar, but they don't belt us in. They remain standing, hanging onto the handlebars protruding from the walls and roof. There's only one door, a large sliding hatch on the right side of the vehicle. When the Authorities have all piled in, someone hauls the hatch closed, and the floor vibrates as the hovercar lifts into the air.

I've been planted in a seat close to the front, which gives me a great view of the city whizzing by underneath us. Other cars slow and drop down a lane to allow the Authorities' vehicle to pass. If I wasn't literally on my way to jail right now, I'd be enjoying this high-speed tour a lot more. Up ahead, the sunset glints off the tourist attraction I was most excited to see: the Diamond Drop Fountain. With bragging rights as the tallest in the galaxy, water cascades from the top of a skyscraper in a glittering spray that crashes into the moat at the building's base. The moat is kept cordoned off for safety reasons, but it's said to be as deep as the building is tall. According to legend, there's a secret city underneath for water-dwelling species. They say if you lean over the railing after dark, sometimes you can see the bioluminescent lights twinkling in the depths.

Our driver curses, veering around a snarl of traffic. We're on course to fly right over the moat, the water spray from the fountain arcing straight for us.

An idea forms in my head. I turn to Chaz, catching his eye and grinning. We've obviously been friends for too long, because he knows what I'm thinking. He lifts his brows in a silent *Are you sure?*

I shrug. This could go really badly for me...but so will getting thrown in jail. This might be my last shot to try *something*.

We're nearly even with the moat. I gauge the distance between myself and the hovercar's door handle, then I surge out of my seat. My hands are still cuffed behind me, but I hook the handle with my elbow, pushing it down and back so that the door jerks open.

Ykros shouts and jumps for me. I let my weight pull her with me, the two of us toppling out of the open door and into thin air toward the moat below.

Ykros cartwheels through the air, screaming. I concentrate on keeping my feet pointed downward. No matter how deep the water is, I don't think it's a good idea to land on my head when falling from more than two stories up.

The water rushes up to meet me, hitting me in the face like it's out for vengeance. Icy liquid shoots straight up my nostrils, going down the back of my throat. I gag, kicking hard for the surface and praying I won't black out. My knees and spine are screaming with pain. *Shit, I hope I didn't break anything.*

I cough and hack, struggling to stay afloat. As my lungs clear and I'm able to breathe again, I kick toward a shadowy area where I'm less likely to be spotted. I'm underneath the fairy-light-strung bridge where people come to take pics with the majestic spray of the Diamond Drop behind them.

No sign of Ykros. I cringe, hoping her comrades were able to rescue her.

And I sure hope *my* comrades took advantage of the distraction I handed to them. They wouldn't have been able to jump out in time to hit the moat, but I'm hoping my own exit was enough to throw the Authorities into a panic, allowing the others to somehow escape. Worse comes to worst, I'm free and I'll be able to mount a rescue operation.

That is, if I can get myself out of this blazin' moat. The walls are steep and slick, and I'm still bound. I've gotta get these blasted magcuffs off. Ykros will have had a release key on her when she fell in. If she's still swimming around in here, maybe I can take it or—

Movement in the water next to me. A slick *something* brushes my leg. I flinch, biting back a scream. *Please be waterweed. Or garbage. Something that's not going to eat me.*

I kick out, trying to make contact with whatever it is. An old shopping bag floats sluggishly to the surface, and I gasp, laughing my relief.

And then I feel the click as the magcuffs unlock.

Stunned, I pull my wrists forward and massage the red marks left by the cuffs. "How—"

I jerk back. Not an arm's length away, a pair of green eyes, mounted on top of a head that's mostly underwater, blink at me. A flipper lifts out of the water, showing me the release tool for the cuffs. The rest of Ykros's utility belt sways underwater, dangling over the creature's flipper like a trophy.

"Th-thank you," I stammer. "Uh, you must not like the Authorities either, huh?"

No answer. But they saved me and stole from Ykros, so I'm betting that's a yes.

"Know a way out of here?" I ask. "Actually, do you even speak Galactic Standard? I guess I should start there..."

The eyes sink under, and the flipper takes hold of my utility belt.

Well, whatever. If they want it, I guess they can have it. The Authorities already took all my stuff anyhow.

But instead of stealing my belt, they use it to tow me into a hidden tunnel back in a shadowy corner between the bridge and the street. This spot would be pretty much invisible from above—there's a raft of people's trash down here that no one's bothered to clean out.

The tunnel is dark and half-full of water that's a little warmer than out in the middle where the waterfall hits. There must be some kind of warming pump keeping the water a livable temperature for whoever makes their home in here, as well as preventing the surface from freezing over in this city's snowy climate.

"This is a way out?" I ask nervously. "Are you sure? It looks pretty dark in there."

The flipper shoves me in the back. I'm gonna take that as *Stop being a coward and get your ass in there.*

This might be a trap. Maybe their whole family is waiting at the end of the tunnel, knives at the ready for me to get served up for dinner.

On the other hand, if I stay in this moat, I'm going to get dredged out of it by the Authorities, who are likely to kill me. I guess I'd rather feed this fish-friend's family than hand myself back in to the Redjackets.

I clamber into the tunnel. It's a tight fit for my long limbs, but the slick walls help me scoot along. It gets pitch-dark almost immediately, so I just keep wade-crawling forward and pray there isn't a fork in the tunnel that leads to the sewer. At least it doesn't stink too bad. Just smells kind of dank—a place that's been damp for too long without being cleaned.

Eventually, I come to an area where I'm able to stand up. Warm, shower-temperature water dumps down on me from another pipe above. I grope along the walls and find the rungs of a ladder. They're slick with some kind of fungus or mold or whatever grows down here. But my choice is to either risk slipping and falling or stay down here forever and get cozy with my aquatic pal, so I start climbing.

It's just a couple of meters before my head bonks into hollow metal. I hook one arm around the ladder and reach up with the other, groping for a latch. My cold, slimy fingers find a switch and push it. The hatch whirs open, dusky light pouring in.

I hoist myself out, feeling like I'm in one of those holo-dramas where the main character narrowly escapes drowning and crawls onto the beach, kissing the ground. Not gonna do that though. I've come out in a grimy back alley that smells of piss. I think I must be on the other side of the street from the Diamond Drop because I can still hear the distant splash of steadily falling water. My black trousers and white undershirt are soaked, sticking to my skin and making me shiver as the temperature drops with night coming on.

Stars, I hope my team is all right. I'm afraid to use my keycuff to contact them in case they're still with the Authorities and I'd be giving myself away.

"Miri?" I whisper.

Nothing. I haven't heard anything from her either—not even background breathing, not since I fell in the water. Shit, I guess my audio earring isn't waterproof.

Looks like I'm on my own until I can find my way back to my team.

My first thought is to head back to the basement Refuge, but I realize I can't do that. If the Authorities are able to track my movements, I can't have them discovering the Refuge because of me.

So I wait until full dark—and until my clothes are somewhat drier—before leaving the alley and diving into the nearest subtrain station. The people down here are single-minded, striding between train and surface without sparing a glance for anyone around them.

I clean up in the public washroom. There's even a cleaning press for my wet clothes. I'm suspicious about whether it actually disinfects, but it dries. At least I won't have to worry as much about freezing to death.

Somewhat clean and much warmer, I wander around until I find a dark corner down a service corridor. There's a cambot patrolling the corridor every five minutes, but it doesn't go all the way to the end. There's a man huddled in the corner who seems to have figured out the cambot's path too.

"Hey, friend," I say. "Can I share your spot for a bit?"

He grunts and shifts so his body is in front of his backpack of possessions.

I hold my hands up in front of me, palms out. "If you pretend not to notice me, I'll pretend not to notice you. Deal?"

"Mmmph."

That's good enough for me. I don't have anything left for him to steal, so I curl up in an adjacent corner and wait to see if the adrenaline will fade in favor of sleep.

It does eventually. But it takes a long, cold, anxious while.

PART SEVEN

Outer Hepburn City, Monroe

Year 3745, Week 12,

Dayseven

CHAPTER TWENTY-ONE

Miri

I JERK AWAKE, MY HEART RACING LIKE I'VE JUST RUN FOR KILOMETERS. What was I dreaming? It's slipping away from me even as I try to grasp hold of the memory. All I remember is a feeling: helplessness and dread. Knowing something terrible would happen and being powerless to stop it.

My throat is all sleep-croaky. "Leo?" I whisper. "Are you there?"

The connection between us went silent last night after a loud, indistinct scuffle. I lay awake praying long past the time I should have drifted off, fearing that Leo and the other Knights were hurt or in danger.

"Miri. I'm here." Hearing Leo's voice feels like being thrown a lifeline.

I let out a breath, relief flooding through me. "Why couldn't I hear you last night?"

"My audio earring got waterlogged. I was afraid it was ruined, but it started working again after it dried out."

"*Waterlogged?* What happened?"

He starts telling a wild tale of getting captured by Authorities and jumping out of a flying car into a fountain. I shiver at the thought of him in danger, but hearing the wry laughter in his voice as he describes his misadventure reassures me that he's fine. Safe. For now.

"Where are you?" I ask. "Where are the others?"

"I don't know where the rest of my team is." There's worry in his tone. "I'm hiding in a subtrain station. I'm gonna have to move soon, I think. The station's getting busy, and my homeless pal just got up and left."

"Your—what? Who? Oh, never mind." I don't want him to leave. I'm irrationally terrified to lose the comfort of his voice.

I won't lie, it's really nice when he's the first thing I hear in the morning. It's almost like we're together in this sleep pod. Like we're waking up next to each other, talking about our wild dreams with the ease of an old married couple.

"I want this every morning," I say before I can stop myself.

"Want what?"

"You. Here."

A soft chuckle. "I'm not there."

"But it *feels* like you are." I dig my knuckles into the corners of my eyes. "I had a bad dream."

"I know. I could hear you making sounds." His voice is husky, a little embarrassed. Is this too intimate? Maybe, but I think I like it.

"What kind of sounds?" Oh stars, do I snore? What if I kept him awake all night with my snoring?

"Little whimpers." He pauses. "It was...sexy. Sorry, I know that's a weird thing to say when you were having a nightmare but..."

A frisson of warmth and awareness zings through my limbs. "You can call me sexy," I say breathlessly. Without him physically close to me, I don't have to worry that I'm manipulating his emotions as mine intensify.

"Stars, I wish I were there with you..."

Then someone calls out his name on his side of the connection. There's a rustle as he moves. Then muffled cursing. "My team found me. Uh...to be continued?"

My face burns, remembering that the earrings are not only linking my audio to Leo's but also recording everything we say. Lawry did promise, when we were setting up the earrings, that he would fast-forward and delete any parts involving the washroom. I devoutly hope he's going to delete this bit as well.

LEO

"THERE YOU ARE!" NATALIA CRIES TRIUMPHANTLY AS MY TEAM ROUNDS the corner, Lawry with his scroll unrolled in his hands.

"W-were you listening?" I stammer. "Could you hear—"

"No, Lawry figured because we linked your audio to his scroll yesterday, he could use the *Find Lost or Stolen Tech* feature to lead us straight to you." Nat lifts an eyebrow. "Why? What were you talking about?"

I snatch the scroll from Lawry, ignoring his protest, and tap into the spy program to delete the last five minutes of footage. Miri will thank me later.

When I hand it back, I meet his eyes and get skewered with a full-force glare. His fingers fly over his keycuff's adapter, and I read the scrolling wall of text he's flashing at me.

<That was an unbelievably reckless stunt you pulled. We thought you were dead. Chief Knight Jostlin was right to have put you on probation. This is your absolute last warning, Galway. If you can't control your foolish impulses, not only will you be grounded, your status as a Knight will be in jeopardy.>

Shame curdles my stomach. "But it worked, didn't it? You're all free."

"Yeah," Chaz says, grinning. "It did work. Genius, Leo! When Ykros fell out, they did an emergency landing and half of the Authorities ran to fish her out of the water. There were only a couple left to guard us. Nat headbutted one of them and I kicked the other one in the jewels, and then Derek got our cuffs unlocked. We took our stuff back and made a run for it." He tosses me my scroll and stunner. "Here ya go. Grabbed your things too, just in case you weren't dead."

<The fact that it helped us escape is irrelevant,> Lawry types, still

fuming. <If I see you putting your harebrained plans ahead of the team's safety again, you are out of this investigation.>

I swallow hard. "Understood, sir." But even though my instinct is to apologize, I don't voice it. Because, quite honestly, I'm not sorry.

I just saved all of our asses.

MIRI

I can't hear what Leo's boss is saying to him, but I bet it's a blistering telling-off. Honestly, if I didn't know Leo, I'd be furious at him too for doing something so quarkbrained. But he's been a danger magnet ever since I can remember, so this is pretty much business as usual.

I stretch, then reach for the button that will release the sleep pod's lid. For Leo's ears only, I say, "Tell Lawry to delete the next ten minutes. I have to get up and use the washroom. And...I won't be able to talk much for the rest of the day. You'll just have to listen. Sorry."

"Don't be sorry," he says. "Be safe." The words feel like a hug.

I rush through my morning hygiene as quickly as possible, my face burning at the idea of the device recording me on the waster or getting naked to run my clothes through the cleaning press. I re-don my fresh tunic and leggings and brush my hair thoroughly before leaving the washroom.

I stayed last night in a room that Saray and Rosa share. Each of them has a sleep pod on opposite sides of the room, with the space split down the middle for each of them to decorate half. Saray's side is elegant and neatly organized. Trunks full of clothes double as benches with cushions laid across the top. The walls are draped with black and gold tapestries embroidered with intricate designs. Rosa's side of the room is an explosion of action hero posters, with a large amorphous red beanbag as her main furniture. She slept in it last night so I could have her pod—I can still see the indent of her body pressed into its squashy center. She swore it was more comfortable than the pod and that she actually sleeps in it a lot. I don't know if I believe her, but it was kind of her to offer me her pod.

I let myself out of their room and make my way back down the hall to the main communal area. The whole floor has congregated there for breakfast. I'm still struggling to put faces to names—my own siblings I can recognize, but the rest of Haven feel like strangers. To make it even more awkward, they all know everything about *me*. Every time I meet someone new, they exclaim how it's wonderful to see me grown up. I gather they've gotten most of their information from those horrible Ediya Experiment newsie segments, though my siblings must have shared updates when they joined Haven, since they know I was a Devote. In fact, several of them congratulate me on my exit from "that cult." Which is a two-pronged stab: one, I don't agree that it's a cult, and two, I didn't leave on purpose. I fucked up and got kicked out.

"Is Clara here?" I ask Rosa over fried tomatoes on toast. "I assume she's part of your group, but I haven't seen her yet."

Rosa frowns. "Clara's 'resting' again," she says, using finger quotes.

"Is she all right?"

Ian says, "Who knows? Every time she goes off back to that acting school, she's *weird* when she comes back."

"Weird how?"

"Like something bad's happened? I dunno. She gets all quiet and sleeps a lot."

I wonder if that has something to do with how Raoul keeps manipulating her. Which reminds me. "How about Raoul? Is he here?"

"Oh yeah, he's around. We might see him later," Rosa says. "He's been leading our training."

I tense. "Will he lead the training today?"

Rosa shrugs. "I dunno. I think Glenna wanted to meet you, so she might take over for today."

The way everybody talks about Glenna Ediya here, it's like she's some amazing hero they all look up to. I really don't know what to expect from the creator—mother?—of the Ediya triplets. Either something went really wrong when she was raising them...or they turned out exactly how she wanted: brilliant and ruthless. Either way, the idea of meeting her ties me in knots. I put down my toast and reach for my mug of coffee, which Saray tops up from the stay-hot pot in the middle of the table.

"Thanks," I murmur. Warmth spreads through my chest, not just because of the coffee burning its way down my throat. It's good to be back with my siblings. We haven't had a reunion with this many of us in, what, five years? But I still feel a sense of belonging with them that, frankly, I never got at the Refuge. Stars know I tried to make that place my home. Only now do I realize that it was always a forced imitation of this easy, casual affection, which my siblings show by instinct.

The door alert chimes. Saray's mother, Adina, stands to check the ID scanner, then taps the button to unlock and open the door. "Good morning, Glenna! Come in and meet our new arrival."

I realize I'm holding my breath as the woman enters. I'm caught off guard by how *old* she looks. Her wrinkles prove her to be in her eighties at least—and showing her age is in itself an oddity, when age-defying treatments are common on Imperial worlds. Halcyonites are more comfortable wearing their years freely, but it's rare to see an elder dressed in the height of Imperial fashion. The clothes imply status and wealth that nearly always go hand in hand with face enhancements or gen-mods. Glenna's indigo robe certainly has the drape of an expensive fabric, fluttering in a short train behind her. The color blends beautifully with her aura: deep, rich purple, the color of a woman who's used to being in charge. Her coiled, silver hair frames her face like a raincloud.

She doesn't look very much like Melanie...not in facial features at least. But they both have the same sharp edge to their smile. They both hold themselves like each disc in their spine is a crown they can't afford to drop.

She sweeps right up to me, raking me with an assessing gaze. Self-consciously, I swipe my thumb across the corner of my mouth, hoping I don't have crumbs all over my face.

"Well," says Glenna at last. "It's wonderful to finally meet you, Mireya Alabas."

The name jolts through me like a lightning strike. "What did you just call me?" The only given name I've ever known is Miri. Evergreen is my legal surname, as all foundlings raised by Refuges take on the name of the place that raised them. It's the closest we get to a family name, and it's rare for someone to carry it all the way to adulthood without finding some kind of family connection or adoptive bond to replace it.

"Mireya Alabas," Glenna repeats. "That is your true name, the one that was stolen from you."

A lump in my throat swells until I can barely breathe. "They—they looked for my parents," I gasp. "The records were destroyed..."

"You were lied to," says Glenna with pity, "though perhaps not intentionally. Melanie and Oberon were diligent in copying their records and sending them to me for safekeeping. You've never been parentless. Your parents have waited a long time to see you again."

She makes a beckoning gesture over her shoulder. Through the door, which still stands open, a man and a woman enter holding hands.

The man has freckled, sun-golden skin and gray-peppered brown hair. His partner is a woman with a Roman nose and pale green eyes. They're both in their forties, and they're staring at me, eyes wide and uncertain. I bolt to my feet, pulse thudding hard and thick.

"My name is Arric Alabas," says the man. "This is my wife, Miriam. We believe you are our child."

Instantly, without warning, tears flood down my cheeks. I sit back down, struggling to breathe.

Miriam rushes over to kneel at my side. She's crying too. "We donated our DNA to the Ediyas many years ago when we were a young couple," she tells me, her voice breaking. "We couldn't have children the usual way. We didn't have any credits to pay for surgeries or incubator babies either. The Ediyas promised they could make a baby from our combined DNA at no cost. Of course, we thought that when you were old enough, we'd get to raise you. But you were stolen, and there was no way to get you back."

There's too much blood rushing to my head. I brace my elbows on the table and cradle my temples, afraid I might pass out. "All this time," I croak, "I had *parents?*"

They told us, when we were all adopted out to various strangers, that every effort had been made to track down our biological parents. That the trail had gone cold because the Ediyas' records blew up with their space station.

But how hard did they actually look? Did they search at all? My mother and father were here all along, with their kind eyes and their soft crow's-feet smiles and their graying hair, a couple who desperately wanted a biological child and couldn't have one. And I'd been left to the cold comfort of the Refuge, nurtured and guided by the Devotes, but always aching for the love of a parent. They told me I was alone in the universe.

Did they know it was a lie?

CHAPTER TWENTY-TWO

Leo

"WHAT ARE THE ODDS THOSE ARE HER REAL PARENTS?" CHAZ ASKS quietly. We're back at the basement Refuge in our supply closet room, watching Miri's dramatic breakfast play out while we eat a nutritionally suspect meal of pastries and coffee that we acquired from a vendor in the subtrain station.

Lawry shrugs. <I wouldn't put it past this group to send in a couple of actors to manipulate her. But the story sounds plausible, and they do look a lot like her.>

"This complicates things," Natalia says. "The way she reacted, her parents are obviously a weak spot for her. I don't know if we can trust her to stay focused."

Prince puts down his paper cup of coffee and groans. "I think this might be my fault."

Chaz gives him a confused look. "*How?*"

"Because I was in charge of finding her parents," says Prince quietly. "Right after those kids were brought to Halcyon, we *did* try. The birth records all blew up with the station. We tried searching an Imperial genetic database, but they don't have data on everybody. Just people who go in for gen-mods as an adult or have samples taken for medical purposes. We also thought the parents might've been Greenjackets who were off the Imperial grid, but when we ran tests, none of the kids matched the known Greenjacket donors. That was our dead end."

"You couldn't be expected to track down this secret group that nobody's heard of and gene-test them all," Derek says matter-of-factly.

"No, but I could've thought to dig into Melanie Ediya's past connections. Maybe I would've found Haven sooner, and this wouldn't be happening right now."

"Dude," says Chaz, "respectfully, that's dog waste. You're not the reason these people are kidnapping and mind controlling folks."

Prince shakes his head. "I'd be lyin' if I said I didn't always feel a little guilty, y'know? I did my best to make sure those kids were placed with families who'd love them and take care of them. But I know what it's like to lose your bio family. You always wonder what happened, even if you have a pretty good substitute family."

Derek narrows his eyes. "Isn't your bio dad the Greenjacket general now?"

"Well, yeah," says Prince, the corners of his mouth turning up. "But, like, *before* that happened...oh, never mind."

I return my attention to the tablet sprawled open on the floor between us. Lawry has been ignoring our side conversation, raptly focused on Miri's reaction to her supposed parents. The tiny tableau shows them seated in Haven's communal kitchen. Arric Alabas reaches across the table to clasp his daughter's hands, while Miriam dabs at her eyes with the sleeve of her robe.

Tears run unchecked down Miri's face. She's asking them questions— if they saw her as a baby, if they had any pics or holo-captures of her early years. In all the years I've known her, she never acted like she missed that kind of thing. She did tell me a few times that she wished she'd been adopted by a family instead of a Refuge. But most of the time, she acted like she loved it there. She'd jump to the Devotes' defense if anyone ever questioned whether it was a good place to raise a child.

Sometimes I'd catch her staring, sort of wistfully, when my brothers would tease me or my ma would tell me to eat my vegetables at dinner. At the time, I took it for bemusement at our boisterous family dynamic. Now I wonder if she secretly envied me the whole time. Guilt bubbles up from the depths of my gut. Should I have done something different? Been more welcoming?

I don't know. Maybe nothing could have replaced her real parents.

Suddenly, I don't want to bust in there and break her out anymore. I want them to be genuinely kind and loving. I want her to have them in her life.

Even if it might mean I lose her.

MIRI

As the emotional high of meeting my parents starts to wear off, awkwardness sets in. How are we supposed to fill in the gap of twenty-three years apart? They at least have the advantage of knowing about my existence before this literal second. They watched those newsie specials about the Ediya Experiments and memorized my eight-year-old face. I didn't even have pictures or names. Just questions.

Those questions are starting to spill out, but not in any particular order, and some of them aren't polite to ask. "Do you have any more children?" Well, no, they don't, because they needed a geneticist to make me in the first place. *Thanks for picking the scab on their oldest wound, Miri.* My face heats, but I don't know how to be cool about this situation. I'm a child again.

Saray makes tea for my mother, who finally manages to stop crying once she inhales the soothing herbal scent.

"There's so much I want to hear about your life," Miriam says, her voice shaky. "I want to know all about the place where you've been living. Did you go to university? Do you have a sweetheart? Am I going to be a grandm—"

"That can wait," Glenna interrupts, sparing me another blush. "Miriam, I hate to take your daughter away so soon, but she needs to join today's training session. I'll bring her back at the end, I promise."

The word "training" evokes my past experience as a new Devote at the Refuge. Long hours of silent meditation, interspersed with reading lengthy books on psychology and emotional wellness. I fully expect to be taken into a dark room and told to practice mental shielding for five hours.

Instead, Glenna takes me to the public lounge down the street.

It's early in the day. When we arrive, the grimy booths and scratched tables are mostly empty. A security bot scans keycuffs for ID at the door, but there's a human working the server's counter. She smiles at Glenna and says, "Your usual booth is ready, Miz Ediya."

"Are the others here yet?" Glenna asks.

"Got here just before you."

Saray, Ian, and Rosa clearly know this place well. They surge ahead of me, striding confidently toward the booth in question. Three more familiar faces await us there: Harris, Fatima, and...

"Clara!" I rush past Ian to throw my arms around her. They said she was ill, but she looks all right to me. Her energy is back to its usual pinky-purple glow, her hair as smooth and perfectly straight as ever. She laughs into my shoulder, surprise flickering through her aura.

"Miri, what are you doing here? Raoul said you decided to stay on Halcyon."

I tense up at the mention of Raoul. He's nowhere to be seen, but with half my siblings here already, it feels as if he could show up at any moment.

"How much do you remember of what happened on Halcyon?" I ask carefully.

Clara pulls a confused grimace. "What do you mean?"

"Humor me. What did we do there?"

Her eyes turn up to the ceiling. I can't tell if she's genuinely thinking or rolling her eyes at me. "I hooked you up with Leo...then we went to that wedding party and it was pretty wild. I blacked out and then...we had to deal with all of Mercy's things." The corners of her mouth pull down. I think she might be fighting tears, but I don't know anymore. How good an actress is she? "After that, you disappeared on me to go off with your beau. Then, right after Mercy's funeral, Raoul brought me back here."

Stars, she really doesn't remember half the trip. Or doesn't want to admit she remembers. Mentally, I hurl curses at Raoul, wherever he is, for doing this to her.

Two short, sharp claps from Glenna draw our attention back to the rest of the group. "A couple of announcements before we get started today," she says briskly. "First, let's welcome Miri home." Grins and cheers all around. "Second, Raoul isn't going to join us today. He's...busy for the next few days."

I glance at Clara and mouth, *Doing what?*

She ignores me. Given how little she remembers, maybe she doesn't even know.

"We're going to start with a short meditation period," says Glenna. I'm put slightly more at ease as we settle into the booth, shoulder to shoulder with my siblings, sinking back into the meditation space that comes to me like breathing after all my years as a Devote.

But I can't shake the uneasiness that settles around my shoulders like an itchy wool blanket. Nobody will directly say what Raoul is up to. I can't figure out whether they actually *know* or if he's gone rogue. And then there's the low-level hum of not-rightness that just won't go away.

I open my eyes and look around at my siblings. They're each sitting comfortably, eyes closed, deep in the zone. Glenna's not though. She's watching me, and when she sees me looking around, she beckons me to stand. I'm at the edge of the booth, so I ease away from Clara to slide my legs out.

Glenna pulls me into an adjacent booth and enables the privacy shield, a nearly invisible barrier that soundproofs our conversation. "Something bothering you?" she asks, not unkindly.

"I just...something about this place feels off. I haven't felt this way since—" Something clicks in my brain. "Since Arrow Station, when I was little. It felt the same way there."

Glenna nods. Her expression is thoughtful, but her eyes don't leave mine. "Is it sort of a low-level repulsion you're feeling? Like something's telling you this place is bad?"

I nod. "That's exactly it."

A smile curves her lips. "My dear, I think you're sensing the dragon-repellent shield. Fascinating. None of the others have mentioned feeling anything out of the ordinary at all. You must be highly sensitive."

I laugh without meaning to. "Tell me about it!" Then I pause, unsure how much Glenna already knows. I came here to learn control—should I trust her with everything? My siblings seem to. But my instinct is to hold back.

She leans forward, hands clasped on the table. "Melanie noted that you have aura sight, but she was certain you would grow into more than that. Your brain scans—"

"I'd rather not talk about what they did to me as a child," I interrupt. Thinking about that time always comes with a wash of sense-memory, my body cold, my chest tight with nerves and something I would later name as loneliness. They never hurt me, not physically, but growing up like that...constantly being pulled away from my peers for tests, not knowing if they'd find me unworthy and make me disappear like some of my other siblings...it left a mark just as surely as a cut from a knife. The fact that this group works with Melanie is another reason to be cautious.

To deflect, I snag on a question that's still bothering me. "Why do you have dragon shields up? Are you trying to keep us from escaping?" That's what these shields are most often used for, to keep prisoners from talking a dragon into teleporting them away. I don't know exactly how they work, but they send out some kind of signal undetectable by humans that dragons find repulsive. No dragon will come within a few kilometers of the device. The prison planet probably had one planted near every inmate's dwelling. Maybe that explains why I felt nauseous there too.

Glenna reaches for my hand, as if to pat it reassuringly, but I pull away and ball my fists in my lap. "We aren't holding anyone prisoner here," she says earnestly. The shimmer of gold sincerity that washes through her aura makes me believe *she* believes that. I'd have to ask Saray to be certain, however. Saray's ability to taste the difference between a truth and a lie has never steered her wrong.

Glenna goes on. "My dear, I'm sorry for the way you were brought to us. Melanie has an unfortunate tendency to steamroll over other people's feelings in pursuit of progress. She knew you would bring value to Haven, and so she delivered you to us. She ought to have explained the situation and allowed you to make your own decisions. That's what I'm hoping to do while you're here with us. But always, *always,* you're free to leave."

I think she knows I won't. Not now that they've reeled me in with my siblings and parents, with good home-cooked food and the promise of control over my powers. Plus, if I'm going to help the Knights get justice for Mercy, I still need some solid evidence to prove Raoul killed her. If I could just talk to him, I could try to record a confession. Why does he keep disappearing?

But Glenna doesn't have to know I'm so eager to stay. "All right then," I say. "Convince me."

Glenna's smile widens. "I'm glad you're giving us a chance. You were raised in a Refuge, yes? Trained as a Devote?"

I nod.

"Some of this is going to be hard for you to hear then. I only ask that you hear me out with an open mind." She unclasps her hands, flattening them on the table.

"I'll try..."

Glenna takes time to think before she begins. "Groups similar to Haven have been around for a long time, in one form or another. Ever since the dragons swooped into humans' lives, there've been skeptics who didn't see their interference in human development as a good thing. Some of the groups before us were violent reactionaries who believed that dragons should be destroyed. When I got together with some friends to create this group sixty years ago, I wasn't interested in trying to *kill* dragons. Instead of fighting the dragons' hold on society, I believe we should elevate human abilities to become *equal* with the dragons. In short, if we eliminate our need for them, we diminish their power over us without causing them harm."

I blink. "So that's why Melanie and Oberon crossed dragon ancestors' DNA with ours?"

"Exactly," Glenna says with a smile. "We hoped that, if we showed the galaxy that humans can teleport, read minds, and control our own destinies, then people won't need dragons anymore. Humankind will be self-sufficient again, as we ought to be."

"What's wrong with relying on the dragons though?" I'm feeling a tad defensive. My Halcyonite upbringing taught me to revere the dragons almost as minor deities and accept their guidance. I've been encouraged from the second I set foot on Halcyon to believe that humankind's connection to the dragons is a mutually beneficial, transcendent gift from the universe. My education placed huge importance on logical thinking, asking questions, and basing arguments on evidence, but not once did it occur to me to question the presence of dragons. That aspect of our lives was sacred and separate.

"Why should we have to?" Glenna spreads out her fingers, tracing a ring-shaped mark on the table. "They help us out of the goodness of their hearts, or so they've always claimed. But their help comes with rules, caveats, and drawbacks. They refuse to teleport anyone whose energy is too chaotic. That can mean the sick and injured, but it can also mean 'anyone they don't like.' And how is it fair that most of the galaxy's starship pilots, for thousands of years, have been forced to take calming mind-alts in order for the dragons to allow them to teleport?

"The dragons also had an outsize influence in our decisions about which planets to colonize. There are some planets they simply refuse to teleport us to. They say it's because those places are dangerous, but what if those planets are hiding technologically advanced alien races, plants that could cure disease, or even important clues to our universe's history? What if the dragons are arbitrarily deciding what we can and cannot handle and making the unilateral decision not to show us certain things? Do you think that's right?" She's getting passionate now, hands curling into fists.

This is a new perspective I've never even thought of before, and it's blowing my mind. A week ago, I might have dismissed it as foolishness. But that was before I got thrown out of the Refuge, then witnessed the dragons unable to solve a murder.

"Do you know what my daughter Gaela discovered when she found the dragon ancestors on Atlantis?" Glenna asks, her voice lowering. "She learned that the dragon ancestors were exiled there from Halcyon. Because the dragons who ascended decided that the ones who didn't were 'unworthy' and didn't deserve to live on their precious homeworld. Is that the kind of being you'd trust to be an arbiter of justice?"

I draw in a breath. Somehow, in all Amy's stories about how she discovered the dragon ancestors and then followed the trail to rescue us from Arrow Station, she never mentioned that detail. I did briefly wonder why the dragon ancestors weren't on Halcyon, but my naïve child's brain rationalized that they must have wanted to go somewhere else to get a little peace and quiet after humans came to their planet. It never occurred to me that the dragons might have removed them by force.

Through the privacy shield, I can see that some of my siblings are done meditating and beginning to get restless, shooting Glenna annoyed glances for ignoring them.

"I'll let you observe today's training while you think things over," Glenna says. "I want you to have all the facts when you make a decision about your future. But to answer your previous question, that's why we have the dragon shields up. Because we have no reason to trust them, and every reason not to."

She lowers the privacy barrier and slides out of the booth to address my siblings again, leading them through a variety of mental exercises. I stay where I am, apart from the group, feeling my mind spin and waver like a dropped plate.

Glenna believed everything she said to me without a doubt. I could see the sincerity permeating her aura. That and the slow-burning anger she's harbored all these years at the injustice of it all.

What happens if I decide to believe her? My whole life is built on faith in the dragons, and it's already starting to crumble. If I accept all of this, it means I can never go back to the way things were, not even if I learn perfect control over my powers.

My future, which seemed so easy to predict a week ago, is a giant question mark now.

CHAPTER TWENTY-THREE

Miri

"Let your body relax, but be aware of every part of it."

Glenna's leading my siblings through another series of meditation exercises. I slide into the seat next to Clara and casually follow along, paying close attention for anything that strikes an "off" chord.

"Check in with each of your physical senses, one at a time," says Glenna. "What can you smell? Taste? Hear? Touch? See?"

So far, normal. Glenna might as well be a Devote leading a prayer and meditation session.

"Now let your attention drift to those other senses, the ones unique to you."

Ah. Here we go.

"Open to them. Drop your mental blocks. Tell me what you are sensing."

Saray is first to speak, eyes closed, lips parted. "I taste worry. Someone in here is nervous about losing their job."

I glance toward the host, who's out of earshot. I hope she's not in any trouble because of us.

Clara says, "Someone next door is thinking about sex."

Ian laughs. "Isn't everybody, always?"

"No." Clara glances at me, elbowing Ian. "Asexual people exist, you quarkbrain."

I hide a grin behind my hand.

The others sound off, stretching their senses like muscles. I let myself do the same, though I keep my observations quiet. I love watching my siblings' auras—they've always been much brighter to me than everyone else's.

"Now that your passive senses are awake," says Glenna, "I want you to push onward into active energy."

"What does that mean?" I whisper to Clara.

Glenna overhears. "Working with your siblings, we've discovered that there are two aspects to your abilities. Passive senses are things you notice about the world that others can't perceive. Active use of your power involves turning your energy outward to influence the world around you. Would anyone care to demonstrate?"

Clara raises her hand, eyes sparkling with mischief. She stands up and saunters four tables over, toward a young man who's sipping coffee, scroll unrolled on the table with a newsie page hovering over it in holo form. "I know you have happy patches," she murmurs. "Can I have one?"

"Listen, lady, I don't know what you're talking about—"

"Please?"

I watch as her vibrant, purple-magenta aura reaches tendrils into his weaker, dimmer one. He doesn't stand a chance. Shoving a hand into his pocket, he removes a pack of clear patches. "Take them all," he says. "I insist."

"Thanks, sweetie." Clara accepts the pack, tucking it into her own robe's pocket. She winks at me as she waltzes back to our table. "Too easy. I should pick someone with a bit of backbone next time."

My stomach churns. "I didn't know you could make people do things," I say quietly. "I thought it was only reading minds."

"Yeah, that's what it used to be." Clara waves the happy patches at Glenna, who takes them from her and walks nonchalantly past the man's table, dropping them next to his elbow as she passes. "Ever since I started visiting Haven and taking lessons with Raoul, I've been learning how to change people's minds. Once I figured out how to do it on purpose, I realized I've been doing it by accident for...well, probably since I was a little girl. Only now, I can *decide* when I do it."

Her words feel like a lifeline, a reprieve after so long fearing my own abilities and trying to suppress them.

And yet. "Isn't that...I don't know...not very ethical?" I venture, lowering my voice. "Practicing on people like that poor guy?"

"We're careful," Clara says with a wave of her hand. "Glenna watches us to make sure we don't hurt anyone. She's always harping on about the responsibility we have to use our abilities wisely. She says one day, with enough practice, we could be running this galaxy. So we don't want to do anything that'll give people reason to hate or fear us. We want to be a force for good."

My head is a muddle as I try to pick apart my shame and the dangerous streak of hope that I might be wanted, valued, for the very power the dragons rejected me for. But I can't shake the feeling that the dragons were right to stop me. Isn't interfering with others' autonomy a bad thing? What if that guy needed his happy patches? What if Glenna hadn't decided to give them back? How are we supposed to know what constitutes using our powers wisely, or what's good for other people?

"I can hear you spiraling," Clara whispers. "They really messed you up at that Refuge, huh?"

Did they? Honestly, I don't even know anymore.

Glenna returns to the table and smiles proudly at Clara. "Well done, Miz Seranath. Last week you only got him to give you one patch. Who'd like to try next?"

Saray takes a turn next. Her passive skill is tasting lies, so it makes sense that she can also use it to force the truth out of a reluctant secret-keeper. She gets the bartender to admit she's got a crush on Ian. Ian tries and fails not to look pleased with himself.

Then Rosa, whose passive ability is to feel sympathy pain when someone is sick or injured, finds a dancer with a broken toe and just walks over and *fixes it*.

I'm wildly impressed. As part of Devote training, I had to take a lot of healer courses. Modern medical tech can fix nearly anything in a fraction of the time a body takes to naturally heal. But the ability to *instantaneously* repair an injury would be so blazing useful. "Could I learn how to do that?"

"We're not sure yet," Glenna says with an indulgent smile. "So far, abilities seem unique to each individual, but that's not to say you couldn't refine your skills in a direction that interests you."

"We do impossible shit every day," Ian pipes up. "Nothing's impossible anymore, not for us."

Yeah, I'm definitely getting that feeling.

"Now, if anyone's up for a bit more showing off," Glenna says, "Mireya hasn't seen anyone teleport yet."

My jaw drops. "You can *all*…"

"Not that well," says Saray modestly. "I've only managed to go a couple of meters, max."

"I basically just flicker in place," Harris adds.

Glenna says, "The ability seems to correlate with how skillful you are in using your active ability. It exercises the same muscle, so to speak. Clara, why don't you give her a demonstration?"

I open my mouth to say that I've already seen Clara teleport but decide to swallow the words. Because that was while Clara was under Raoul's control. She isn't going to remember, is she? Or if she does, she won't admit it.

"Can you teleport me with you?" I ask instead. "I want to see how it works."

"Good idea!" Clara jumps out of the booth and holds out her hands for mine, her small, manicured fingers closing around my rough palms. "Now, close your eyes and think happy thoughts, just like you're dragon-'porting," she tells me.

I find myself holding my breath as I let my eyelids drift closed. It's not that I don't trust Clara…actually, it is. The last time she 'ported me, it was into Raoul's clutches.

Where *is* Raoul anyway?

I barely notice the weightless pause between heartbeats as we 'port. I'm too busy telling Clara, *::We need to talk. I have some questions::*

"I know you do," she says aloud. I open my eyes. We're outside on the street, in a shadowy spot behind a street vendor selling fried brown-sugar pastries. Clara drops one of my hands but keeps hold of the other, leading me out onto the sidewalk. Snow drifts down lazily around us, freckling her platinum hair. "You've been thinking loudly all morning. I know you're really stressed out about us messing with people's minds, but I promise you, we aren't hurting anybody. We're being really careful. And the dragons can't see what we do here, so you don't need to worry about them."

I frown. "It's not that," I say, though it's not *not* that. "Clara, how long have you been with Haven?"

"About a year, I think. I've been taking lessons from them whenever I can get away from the Academy."

"You *think?*"

She shrugs, her neck muscles tensing. "I've been having memory issues. Glenna says I slip too deep into other people's minds and forget I'm me. I try not to do it, but it just happens. I'm sorry I forgot some of the time we were together on Halcyon. I—"

"I don't think it's your fault," I interrupt in a rush. "I saw Raoul take control of you, back on Halcyon. I think he might be using you. And I'm worried you're not the only one." I turn so I can walk and face her at the same time. "Clara, does your memory loss ever happen when Raoul isn't here?"

She frowns. "Um...I'd have to think back..."

I change tack. "Can you read everyone's mind in Haven?"

"Not everybody," she says. "Not our siblings. Glenna has been teaching them to block mind control. And Raoul's been..." She chokes on the words a little. "Helping."

Not helping very well, if he still has so much control over Clara without her being aware of it. I wonder if he's been doing the opposite: worming through their mental barriers to establish control without them sensing it. "Can you read Glenna?"

"A little." Clara shrugs. "She's been practicing blocking us out, but she doesn't have the natural skill like we gen-mods do."

"And is there anything she's ever thought about in your presence that makes you think she's lying about all this? The dragons and—all of it?"

"No." Her response is immediate. "Saray agrees with me. We've talked about it, all of us, when Glenna's not there. It's all completely against what Halcyon taught us, but no, she's not lying. She has real reason to doubt the dragons. And she really thinks we might be able to improve things for humanity."

Much as I'm relieved we're not in danger from Glenna, part of me was hoping to hear that she's a liar. It would make it so much easier to choose a side. "One more question," I say. "Do you know where Raoul went? What he's up to right now?"

She shakes her head. "Glenna doesn't know either."

That surprises me. "I thought she was the leader. Wouldn't he tell her if he—"

"She's flared off about it," Clara says, her voice low. "She's trying to convince Haven that he left on her orders, but I heard her thoughts. He took off again with no warning. Actually, he wanted to take us with him, all the siblings, but she said no. I guess there was a bit of a fight about it. Glenna's trying to contact Melanie to ask what she put him up to."

"So she thinks Melanie has something to do with it?"

"She doesn't have any proof," Clara hastens to add. "But yeah, that's what Glenna thinks."

"And you? What do you think?"

Clara's eyes flick away. "I...don't know. It's not my business."

"It's very much your business if Raoul is making people do things they aren't aware of," I argue. "Because *people* includes you."

"Raoul wouldn't hurt us," Clara argues. "Never ever. He's our brother."

In her voice, I hear the child that she once was. That we both were. Sheltered and neglected by the adults who were in control of our lives, looking at our older siblings with near-blind devotion. Particularly Raoul, the oldest and strongest with his powers. If we needed something from Melanie and Oberon—medical treatment, new clothes, a special diet for a sibling with food allergies—he was the one who'd speak up on our behalf. He was the one who'd take the punishment if the Ediyas were displeased with us as a whole.

I hate to think that he'd ever exploit or mistreat us in any way. But I believe what she says is true, to some extent: he's not *hurting* us. He might be convincing himself that controlling us is in our best interest. He's wrong—and it is causing harm—but maybe he doesn't see it that way. Or is deliberately pretending not to see it.

In Clara's aura, however, my attention snags on something else. There's a maelstrom of confusion, snarled up right around her head. It's missable because the rest of her energy is as vivid and ebullient as ever. But something about the way it moves right underneath the snowflakes settling on her hair...

"Hey, Clara," I say, reaching for her arm. "Do I have your permission to try something with your aura? I just want to see if I can undo this little knot you have, right around here." I wave a hand over the crown of her head to demonstrate.

She shrugs. "Sure. I trust you. But it's probably just, I don't know, depression or...whatever. I'm like this whenever I get back from a trip. Travel is exhausting."

Yeah, that's what the others said too. But I'm wondering if she actually gets like this whenever she gets back because she's been hanging out one on one with Raoul. I think Raoul is the one tangling up her mind.

CHAPTER TWENTY-FOUR

Miri

WE DUCK UNDER THE AWNING OF AN APARTMENT BUILDING, MY BOOTS squishing in the slush that's dripping down to melt on the heated pavement. I let my eyes unfocus slightly, giving over to the aura-sight. I rest a hand against Clara's forehead and gently probe with my energy. I have to be careful. I only want to see if this is a deliberate muddlement that I can undo, not mess with her natural reactions to recent trauma. I won't be doing that again. It was draining on both of us, and all it did was postpone her pain, not heal it.

Clara sucks in a breath as I prod against the roiling, confused part of her aura.

"Tell me if I should stop," I murmur.

"It's not that," she says, her voice breathless and faraway. "I...I just remembered something."

Experimentally, I push into the tangle again. Clara's choked cry makes me draw back again.

"No, keep going." She grabs my palm and smacks it onto her forehead again. "I remember—Miri, I'm remembering what—fuck, I can't even— here." Her hand finds *my* forehead, and suddenly I'm seeing memories through her eyes.

"Congratulations on getting into the Monroe Academy of Theater," Raoul says, offering Clara a small, ribbon-wrapped box.

She accepts the gift with a thrill of excitement. Her older brother has been distant for so long, but now they both live offworld. Does this mean he's going to visit more often?

***

Clara runs up the stairs, excited to meet Raoul for another trip to Haven, his cozy group of friends who are secretly helping him expand his gen-mod abilities. She pauses at the top of the stairwell when she sees Principal Quell shaking Raoul's hand. "I admit, I was skeptical when you recommended your sister for admittance here," Principal Quell says, "but she's done remarkably well. She was born to act."

"I've always thought so," says Raoul. "It's worked out very nicely, her placement in this school. She's happy, she's close to Haven, and she's under your capable watch."

Clara is too far away to sense their thoughts clearly, but their words jangle a warning bell. Since when did Raoul know Principal Quell well enough to personally recommend her acceptance to this school? Why does it feel like they're arranging things neatly behind her back?

As she approaches, she feels both of them putting up mental shields against her thought-reading. She pastes on a smile, pretending she didn't hear.

***

Lately, it feels like Clara's days off drain her more than her school days. She spends all morning flexing her mental abilities with Glenna and the handful of other Ediya siblings that Haven has managed to recruit. Then, when she's already exhausted and ready to go home, Raoul takes her aside for intense private study.

"Think of teleporting like this," he's saying. They're sitting in a café down the street from Haven, the smell of coffee and incense as heavy as the thick velvet curtains draped across the booth to make their table private. "Your mind can travel to another place in an instant, can't it? In just a heartbeat, you can think of, say, your dormitory at the Academy, and in your mind, it's like you're there. Now just...imagine you're taking your body with you."

Clara sighs. It does sound nice to be at the dorm, safe in her sleep pod. But imagining herself there and teleporting there are two very different prospects.

"It doesn't have to be as far as that," Raoul presses. "Try just a meter or so. From your side of the table to mine. Try it."

She closes her eyes and humors him. Pictures herself becoming weightless as air, drifting through the table like a ghost to land on the cushion at Raoul's left. She puts the force of her will behind it, the way she would if she were trying to convince someone to hand over their scarf. Except the hapless mark is her own self.

When she opens her eyes, she sways with momentary disorientation. Raoul has reappeared at her side, and the curtains are draped a different way. It takes her a full twenty seconds to realize she's done it—swapped sides of the table. She's teleported.

"Tell me everything!" Raoul exclaims, clapping. "How did it feel? What did you think about?"

And as soon as she's done telling him, she hears his voice inside her mind.

::Do it again. This time, next booth over.::

She obeys without even intending to. It's easier the second time. But then panic sets in as she sits alone at the empty table. Why did it feel like my body did it without me?

Then Raoul is there, teleporting in next to her, his warm arm snaking around her shoulders.

::Forget,:: *he's saying.* ::Forget everything.::

And she does.

***

"Your brother's here," Jana whispers as Clara walks out of rehearsals. "He's in Principal Quell's office. Hope you're not in trouble."

Clara hopes so too. Raoul isn't supposed to come until Dayseven, and today's only Dayfive. Why's he talking to Principal Quell? Something in the back of her mind is bothering her about that. She almost feels like she's seen them talk before... but no, that didn't happen, she definitely would have remembered.

"Thanks, Jana," she says. "Save me a spot in the dining hall?"

Instead of heading down to dinner, her feet take her up the stairs toward the principal's office. If Raoul's here talking to Principal Quell behind her back, she has a right to know what they're discussing.

She's worked herself into a fume by the time she gets to the top floor. But she doesn't want to bust in and interrupt whatever they're talking about—she'd rather snoop.

Principal Quell's office is down a long hallway just underneath the theater, mostly taken up with dressing rooms and prop storage. There's an empty dressing room right next to the office, which makes a perfect dark space to hide in while she eavesdrops on their minds.

Raoul's guard is down, thinking she's downstairs and out of range. It takes the barest effort to slip into both their minds at once, balancing their perceptions and thoughts so she can get a clear picture of what's going on.

They're on a vid-chat call together. Principal Quell is silently stressing about whether eir wallscreen's secure connection is truly untraceable. Sticking my neck out for this arrogant little turd, *e's thinking.* This better be worth it.

But Raoul is laser-focused on the face projected from the screen. Because that face is Melanie Ediya.

Her voice sends shivers across Clara's skin, her hands immediately growing clammy with memories of long hours sitting bored on a cold exam table. Of fearing she might be next to disappear.

"I want to discuss strategy," Melanie is saying. "My contact has arranged this short window where we will not be monitored. I'm glad you took my suggestion to set up the call outside of Haven. My mother and her people don't have the stomach for the kind of discussion I want to have here."

Clara barely dares to breathe.

"I've had a lot of time to think about our next move," Melanie goes on. "Now that we've established that the experiments were successful—that the children are capable of learning teleportation as well as mind control—we're poised to take the galaxy by storm. I believe we could even take hold of the Empire with a well-placed infiltrator.

"The main obstacle, in my mind, is the Halcyonite religion. The dragons have their hooks more deeply into that population than anywhere else in the galaxy, and it's my blasted luck that's where the experiment children were sent. The Empire is already half-primed to discard the dragons—Glenna's run some very successful information campaigns to get newsies and court counsel on our side—but the way

the Halcyonites worship them is concerning. I fear our subjects will never embrace their power and stop relying on dragons unless Halcyon as a whole chooses to end the human-dragon relationship."

"That's inconvenient," Raoul says, "because Halcyon is basically untouchable. You can't so much as sneak out a fart on that planet without a dragon noticing."

Melanie nods. "I've thought long and hard about how to circumvent their attention. And I think your power, Raoul, might be the answer. You can convince people of anything, alter their perception to your will. And I wondered...could you alter your own energy to be just like the dragon-shields? Create something that makes you invisible or repellent to them?"

Raoul tilts his head, stroking the short hairs on the side of his jaw. "You know, I think it's possible. I'll have to test it."

"The real test will be if you can shield on others too. A small attack group, infiltrating Halcyon without the dragons noticing. Imagine how it would look to the sheep who hang on the dragons' every word if, one by one, all their Refuges go up in flames. As if the gods themselves have taken away the dragons' power and punished their chosen elite."

Principal Quell gasps at the suggestion. "You're talking about terror attacks," e breaks in. "Thousands of deaths."

At least someone in the room is saying something. Stars above. Clara wonders how the principal got dragged into this. But she can't dive deep into eir motivations without losing the thread of the conversation.

"An unavoidable necessity," Melanie says smoothly. "The Devotes are the most likely to resist our emancipation from the dragons. Once they are gone, the people of that planet will be looking for answers. Our experiments will be in the perfect position to step in and guide them forward. I consider that a much greater good to balance out the tragedy of lost lives."

Clara can't read Melanie since she's not physically present, but she knows the way the scientist thinks. The "tragedy" line is an appeasement, nothing more. Melanie won't feel even the slightest bit remorseful about killing thousands. This is war to her—a war for the future of humanity—and she's decided the Devotes are her enemies.

A chill shakes Clara as she remembers: Miri is a Devote. A faceless genocide is a hideous enough prospect, but one that takes the life of her best friend and sibling? Absolutely not. She won't let Raoul get away with this.

"I'm going to have to do a test run first," Raoul says thoughtfully. "Maybe take one of the trainees and see if we can do something against the dragon's code. Carry weapons...maybe beat someone up...lie to a bunch of people..."

"Nothing that leaves a trace," Melanie cautions. "We can't have any witnesses to report you to the Knights."

"Don't worry, I'll wipe their memories after," Raoul says with a wave of his hand. Then he grins. "You know what? I got a message not long ago. The old lady who adopted me and Clara is dying of some illness. It'd be completely normal and unsuspicious for us to visit our ma, right? And if she happens to kick off a little early...well...no one could say they didn't see it coming..."

Clara presses her fingers to her mouth, willing herself not to vomit. Raoul never told her that Mercy's so ill she's dying...

Or did she find out and he wiped her memory to keep her away?

"Perfect," says Melanie. "I'd like to see you test this as soon as possible. Report back when you get it done."

Raoul nods. "You can count on me."

And then he's leaving the office, his attention turning toward the next order of business...

Which is slamming open the door of the dressing room where she's hiding and grabbing her by the arm. "Sneaky little spy," he says, his voice casually teasing, which makes the intent in his mind so much more horrific. "That was more than you were meant to hear. Never mind. You and I are going on a little adventure together."

It's like ice water flushing through me, weakening my stomach and my knees.

Melanie has convinced Raoul that the Devotes need to die. If I hadn't been kicked out of my Refuge, was he prepared to kill *me*?

"He's been controlling me for so long," Clara whispers hollowly. "Hiding my own memories from me to keep me compliant." Her pale eyebrows come together in a determined glare. "I'm not going to let him do it again."

I didn't realize I was crying until she swipes the moisture away from my cheeks with the edge of her sleeve. All I can say is, "*We're* not going to let him."

CHAPTER TWENTY-FIVE

Miri

"I don't want to go back," Clara mumbles. We've been standing under the shelter of the awning for maybe ten minutes, leaning on each other in complete shock. It's hard to believe, even with the evidence of Clara's memory, that Raoul did all this. That he planned the whole time to kill Mercy and use Clara to do it. That he was prepared to destroy every last Devote, including me.

"We have to go back," I say, impressed at how firm and solid my voice sounds. I feel like I'm standing on jelly, the planet reeling underneath me. "We have to find out if Glenna knew about any of this. If she did..."

If she did, I don't care if she's right or wrong about the dragons. Haven can't be a home to me, can't teach me anything, if it houses people who are willing to destroy me and everyone I love. Not even if my parents are among them.

Clara's still surrounded by a riot of shifting colors. Dark green horror and disgust battle with fiery anger, almost blotting out her usual cheerful pinky-purple. I hate seeing my friend in so much distress, but this time it's easy for me to reel in the instinct to smooth out her aura. Meddling would make me no better than the man who tangled her mind up in the first place.

Interestingly, Clara doesn't need to calm her emotions before teleporting. That requirement must be something the dragons impose, because Clara's still steaming mad when she takes my hand and 'ports me back to the lounge.

We arrive in the back alley, where we find the rest of my siblings practicing 'porting a few meters at a time. Ian and Harris are trying to make a leapfrog game out of it, taking turns 'porting a few meters ahead of each other. I'm amazed at their skill, considering that a week ago I thought human teleportation was beyond our capacity to learn.

Saray materializes right next to us, making me jump. "You're back!" she exclaims. "You two took forever. Did Clara get blocked and couldn't get back or something?"

Clara and I look at each other. Saray will smell a lie before we're even done telling it.

::Can we trust her?:: I ask Clara.

She turns her gaze to Saray, giving her a long, thoughtful look before nodding.

"Miri noticed a tangle in my aura. Someone's been fucking with my memory." Clara folds her arms. "I think you might be able to guess who."

Saray sucks in a breath through her teeth. "Every time he took you for private lessons...that was when you came back tasting weird. He tried to convince us it was the acting school stressing you out. He's good at muddying my senses—it didn't smell like a straight-up lie, even though I knew something wasn't adding up."

Clara's shoulders slump with relief. "You believe me? You won't take his side?"

"Sis." Saray puts a hand on Clara's shoulder. "You're good at acting, but I know what the truth tastes like."

"Then help us," I butt in. "We need to know if Glenna's in on this."

Saray shakes her head. "Clara and I have already tested her."

"Some new things have come to light," Clara says, tight-lipped. "Miri's right. We need to confront Glenna, and it would help a lot if you'd be our witness."

"Confront me?"

I startle again. Clara's mind reading has let us down—Glenna's managed to sneak up behind us. *No, not sneak.* There's nothing surreptitious in her aura. She's cool as an icicle.

"Why don't we go back into the lounge?" Glenna suggests. "I'm assuming what you have to say is private?"

"No." Clara clenches her jaw. "Let's gather the whole group. I think they should hear this too."

IN THE END, WE GO BACK TO HAVEN'S COMMUNITY BUILDING AND convene on the roof. The building has a tentlike snow shelter stretched across its flat rooftop. The canvas blocks the cold wind and, except for a few holes dripping slush, repels precipitation quite well. Under it, the rooftop is a maze of growth pods and small potted trees. Warmth radiates from sun lamps mounted on the tent poles. The rooftop space is as big as a couple of Newcastle Community greenhouses put together, though it feels smaller when cluttered with so many plants. However, when Glenna calls a "family meeting," as she puts it, a startling number of people filter up from the building's living area to fill the spaces between planters. Haven isn't just one set of communal rooms—it's everybody in the whole blazing complex.

I gaze out at the crowd, impressed by the wide range of ages and cultures represented here. I see elders in hoverchairs who took the zip-lift, right next to mothers holding toddlers' chubby hands. How does Glenna recruit? Do people just come to her, led by whispers of a place where dragons won't watch their every move? Or does she seek people out and plant doubt in their ears?

Is this even all of Haven? Several times, I've heard people here reference their influence in the Imperial court. Are there more like Ykros out there, loners who follow their own agenda but report back to Glenna or Melanie?

Satisfied with the crowd, Clara begins to tell her story. How Raoul has been manipulating her for a long time, teaching her to be pliant to his "guidance," erasing her memory when she rebelled. Saray has her eyes closed, lips parted. Seeking a lie in what Clara says, no doubt.

When Clara gets to the part about Raoul and Melanie conspiring to destroy Halcyonite Refuges, a universal gasp goes up. "That is *not* what we stand for," a man in the front row shouts. "We didn't join this community to abet a genocide!"

Glenna has her hands over her face, head bowed as if in prayer. When she finally drops her hands to speak, there is a hint of wetness glimmering in the corners of her eyes. "My daughter," she says. "What have you done?"

Melanie. She's talking about Melanie. A child she created in a lab to usher in the new era of humanity she dreamed of. But that's the thing about children. No matter how much care one takes with the exact combination of their genes, no matter how much good faith and hope goes into their conception...children don't grow up to anyone's specifications. They are each their own person with their own choices to make. And sometimes, they choose wrong.

"Did you know?" Clara insists, her aura intense with anger and hope intermixed. "Have you been in contact with Melanie like Raoul has?"

Glenna shakes her head. "I...yes, I'm in contact with Melanie," she admits. "Though frankly, I have more productive conversations with Oberon. My daughter has repeatedly insisted that I free her from prison. But I refuse to endanger my people who could pull those kind of strings. I mourned when she and her brother were captured, but their methods represented a liability to our group and our goals. They were drawing unwanted attention. An escape would be much too high-profile, too carefully investigated."

"That's all true," Saray murmurs.

"Then she or Raoul didn't ask for your help in attacking Halcyon's Refuges? Or in murdering Mercy Seranath?"

"No," Glenna says. "I swear on my life, on the lives of all these people I love. I would never condone such actions. We are not terrorists. Haven is not about killing the past. It's about building the future and making it accessible to all."

Clara and I look to Saray, who nods once again. "No word of a lie."

"I believe you," Clara says, returning her attention to Glenna. "But

Glenna, if no one here is helping Raoul, where is he right now? You said he's gone off to do something important..."

Glenna gives a helpless shrug. "That was a lie. He disappeared as soon as he brought in Miri yesterday. He told no one where he was going. I chalked it up to him needing a break after his adoptive mother's passing...but before he left, he requested to take all of his siblings with him. He was angry when I denied him. He tried to use his influence on me to force me to agree, but I am not as easy to manipulate as he'd like."

"He's gone to do it," I say softly. They all turn to look at me, and I feel heat rising to my cheeks at the attention. "He's going to Halcyon to attack the Refuges." It's already been a whole day since Raoul left. Plenty of time for him to prepare whatever attack he has planned.

I excuse myself and make my way toward the stairs. There's no time to waste. I have to stop him.

LEO

"Leo?"

Miri's voice comes soft in my ear. Muffled, because she's got her hand over her mouth, talking into the hem of her sleeve. To the outside observer, she probably appears to be overcome with emotion or nausea, running to the nearest washroom. She dodges inside and closes the door, then leans against it with a half-sigh, half-sob.

"I'm here," I say aloud.

My team is still in shock from what we just heard. The drama unfolding on the tablet-sized holo display was nearly cinematic. People shouting over each other, questions mixed with outrage. Glenna was doing her best to control the scene, but it was obvious she, too, was rattled by what Clara revealed.

Now we're all huddled around Miri's small holo-figure as she rests against the sink. She's taking deep breaths, the sound ragged in my ears. She's either fighting a panic attack or trying not to cast up. Maybe both.

"Did you hear all that?" she asks.

I nod, then remember she can't see me. "We did. Do you need us to come rescue you?"

"Rescue *me*!" She laughs harshly. "Who cares about me? Raoul's out there, apparently planning to attack my home. Leo, I need you and the Knights to stop him *right now*."

"How?" I shake my head. "We don't know where he went. You don't either."

Miri makes a little squeak-scream of frustration. At any other time, I'd think it was cute as blazes, but right now my entire brain is consumed with trying to find a way to fix this for her. She's panicking, terrified, and I should *be there*. I should be able to protect her.

Then it hits me.

"You can sense him when he's trying to hurt people," I exclaim. "You're our best tool to find him. Miri, let us come get you. We'll go stop Raoul together."

<Now, hold on,> Lawry interrupts. <Let's be thoughtful about this. We can't rush after Raoul without backup. One woman is no replacement for a full strike team of Knights.>

"There's six of us," Chaz points out. "How many more do you want?"

<Raoul could control at least two to three people at a time,> says Lawry. <I don't want us to rush into a situation where half our team could be fighting the other half while he gets away. We need to return to Knight headquarters, explain the situation, and prep a new team.>

"But it'll take almost a full day to get another squad briefed," I argue. "That's time we don't have. Raoul's out there *now*, and he's not going to wait for orders."

Lawry gives me a look that could freeze a sun. <Do you think your idea is better? Run in with no plan or backup whatsoever?>

"I don't know, but the faster we act, the less likely that people will die!" I really shouldn't be challenging Lawry when he's already flared at me, but I can't help it when his idea of a plan is to get bogged down in regulations and wait for orders. "Miri was able to fight against Raoul's mind powers last time. I think she might make the difference now, even if he tries to control half our team. Besides, she knows him. She can *feel* when he starts doing evil shit. So we should—"

<Galway.> Lawry pauses, rubbing his forehead, before he keeps typing. <I knew bringing you into this investigation was a bad idea. You have a long record of flying by the seat of your pants, and you are emotionally involved with our most important witness. Your inside knowledge of the case was helpful for a time, but your attachment to Miri is getting out of hand when you prioritize her over the guidance of your senior.>

My jaw drops. "That's *not* what's happening here." I flash a glance at my teammates. "Tell him! I'm not making up some excuse to go get my girlfriend. My plan just makes more sense!"

They're making sympathy eyes at me, but none of them speak up. Derek makes a *quit while you're ahead* gesture behind Lawry's back, shaking his head while drawing his fingers across his neck.

<Pardon me if I don't trust the man who, last night, dove out of a moving vehicle into a fountain and left the rest of the team to fight our way out of Imperial custody,> Lawry says. His eyebrows are doing a lot of the talking for him; right now, they're nearly meeting in the middle, his frown lines starkly defined. <I will take suggestions from anyone else on the team, but Galway, one more belligerent word out of you, and you're welcome to return your Knight gear and catch a taxi home.>

The words feel like a blaster shot to the chest. He's threatening to kick me off the team—possibly out of the Knights entirely—just because I back-talked a little. Can he even do that? More importantly, do I have time to play this ridiculous little power game, when Raoul might already be in the middle of carrying out his murder plot?

No. The answer is no. And if Lawry's going to treat me like a fool for wanting to save lives, then I don't see any reason to trust his leadership anymore.

I stand up abruptly. "Miri," I say. "Are you there?"

There's a soft "mmm" in response.

"Glenna said you could leave anytime," I whisper. "So I need you to go catch the subtrain and meet me at the spaceport. We're going after Raoul, you and I."

"Got it," she whispers.

"Oh, and one more thing," I tell her. "Ditch the earrings."

Then I tap on my keycuff to sever the connection between Lawry's scroll and my audio input. He could still track me if he tried hard enough —my tech is very traceable—but at the moment, I don't really give a flying fuck. He knows where I'm going. I just don't want him to be able to watch us.

"It's been real," I tell him. I throw a casual salute at my friends, who are staring at me with the same jaw-dropped expression they were wearing when they found me on the buckin' back of a giant lizard in the Susannah reservoir. "See you later."

And then I walk out of the Refuge into the cold winter dusk of Hepburn City, completely and totally on my own.

I feel like I've just jumped out of another moving hovercar but I haven't yet splashed into the fountain. It's kinda like flying, but with an *uh-oh* rising swiftly toward me. This is definitely the dumbassest thing I've ever done...

Except, funnily enough, I don't regret it.

Yet.

CHAPTER TWENTY-SIX

Miri

THEY SAY HEPBURN CITY IS DANGEROUS TO WALK AT NIGHT. IF THE newsies are to be believed, there're a dozen muggings each time the sun goes down. Half of them are said to happen in the subtrain station, which is where I'm headed, bundled in a warm coat that Saray loaned me.

"You'd better bring it back," she said while I shoved my arms through the sleeves. "That's a designer piece."

She must have tasted the truth in my words when I promised I would return. Otherwise, she'd never have let me leave with it.

I leave the perimeter of the dragon shield as I descend the steps into the subtrain station. It's a tangible weight lifted off me. I draw in an inadvertent gasp, the snowy chill burning my lungs. The glare of the overhead light feels sharper, the steps beneath my feet sturdier. I'm impressed that my siblings have been practicing their abilities within the shield. Its repellent signal has been interfering with my perception more than I thought...

Though not enough, sadly, to write off the last few days as a disturbing dream. What I've seen and heard was all too real.

"Miri! Wait up!"

I turn to see Clara sprinting toward me, blonde hair in flyaway strands across her face. She clatters down the steps and leans against the handrail next to me, panting.

"I want to come with you," she gasps. "You're going after Raoul, aren't you? I need to be there. I need to face him."

"Is that a good idea? He *has* spent a lot of time learning how to control you."

Clara shakes her head. "Now that I know what he's doing, I'm going to resist. You can help me. If you see him tangling up my brain again, just undo it."

"That's not as easy as it sounds," I caution. "I might not be able to protect you and myself at the same time."

"Then I'll fight back," Clara says, squaring her shoulders. She reminds me of a ten-year-old who's about to get into their first fistfight. Kind of makes me want to go, *Ohhh honey, no.*

Except she's an adult, and it *is* her right to face Raoul if she wants to. If the tables were turned, I'd probably be squaring up for a fight too, no matter the odds. I don't even have to imagine how betrayed and furious she feels—it's splashed all over her aura in discolored splotches, like wine stains on a party dress.

I sigh and hold out my arm to her. She links hers through it, and we descend into the subtrain station together.

I'll admit, it does feel good to have a friend at my side on that long train ride. The crowds of strangers ebb and flow like tides as we approach the city center, swelling until the whole train is standing room only. By myself, I would have felt tiny and vulnerable. With Clara clinging to my arm, and Leo waiting for me at the station ahead, I feel like I'm wearing a shield generator—protected by an invisible force.

The names of stops are unfamiliar and almost lost to the murmur of the crowd. I'm grateful when Clara tugs my sleeve and says, "The spaceport stop is up next."

We prepare to exit, shoving our way closer to the train doors. A hand brushes my ass, maybe accidental, maybe on purpose. I drive an elbow backward toward the owner, turning just in time to chirp, "Oops, sorry, excuse me!" Their aura is tangled up with ember-red lust—not the candle-bright thrill between partners, but a secretive, cruel thing that delights in shame and control.

I don't even feel bad about letting my power slip its leash. Just a little. Just enough to damp that ember down to coals. It might not be strictly ethical, but I don't see myself losing a wink of sleep over suppressing that perv's enjoyment of assault.

Clara squeezes my arm with a wicked grin. "Nice."

The doors open, and we're swept out into the station by the surge of people behind us. I'm instantly scanning the platform for messy blond hair and a sunshiny aura, but nobody sticks out. It's hard to pick out individual auras in this muddle anyway.

The escalator carries us into the bustling interchange of the main station. The smell of food from stalls upstairs competes with body odor and the odor of damp floors as people track slush in from outside. I wish Leo had time to tell me where he wanted me to meet him. In this stew of people, I have no idea where to begin looking.

"Clara, can you hear Leo's mind?" I ask in an undertone.

She shoots me a sarcastic look. "With this many people around? If I try to listen for someone, I'll get clonked between the eyes with the galaxy's most massive headache."

"Fair enough." I scan the station again and spot an escalator across the way. "Let's go up a level. Might give us a better view."

Just before we reach the escalator's summit, I scan the next-level balcony. My heart thuds as I recognize a blond figure with its golden halo of energy, leaning over to wave frantically. I nearly trip when the escalator ends.

Clara's wearing a shit-eating grin when I turn to her. "Go," she laughs. "Go get him!"

I break into a stumbling run. Leo's dodging pedestrians, flaring people off as he moves against the traffic flow. When we collide, it's literal. He dances around an annoyed saurian-humanoid, muttering, "Sorry, sorry, excuse me," and I run face-first into his chest. He's halfway through apologizing before he realizes it's me.

When his arms come up around me, I breathe out a sigh of relief.

The pressure of his hug is a weight lifted off my shoulders, a deep breath after being underwater. "I missed you," I say into the front of his shirt.

He doesn't say anything, just pulls me tighter against him. He's breathing hard, his chest stuttering. It almost feels like he's...crying?

I lift my head to look at him. He won't meet my eyes, but his are red. "Leo," I say, "what's wrong?"

"How much did you hear before I ended the connection?" he asks, gesturing toward his ears. My earrings are gone. Not wanting to expose Haven to unnecessary surveillance, I threw them in a gutter down the street from the apartment complex.

"Not a lot," I confess. "There was stuff happening on my end too."

He closes his eyes, huffing out a breath. "I may have...uh...just gotten myself fired."

He starts explaining the whole saga from his end. I guess there was a lot I missed. Even when our audio sensors were connected, I could only hear his side of conversations—like most personal tech, his audio earrings are designed to filter out background noise.

I'm not surprised that Lawry was angry about him jumping out of the hovercar. It was a quarkbrained thing to do. But it's so quintessentially *Leo*. Doing brave, selfless, dumbass things on the faintest chance it'll save someone else. I can't help but love him for it.

Yet even if the stunt did save his team from imprisonment, it sounds like it torpedoed his chances of being taken seriously when he most needed Lawry to listen to him.

"I think you did the right thing," I say, brushing a thumb along Leo's blond stubble. He doesn't smell great—I guess falling into a fountain and drying out in a subtrain station will do that to a guy—but I can't seem to stop touching him.

"For now, sure. In this one situation." He closes his eyes and groans. "For my career though? I've probably just shot myself in the foot."

"Hey," I murmur. "This *one situation* is the survival of thousands of people all over Halcyon. I think the Knights will take that into account."

"And on that note, we probably shouldn't waste time." He glances behind me, noticing Clara standing there for the first time. "You brought *her*?"

"Fuck you too," Clara says sweetly.

I jump in before they trade any more insults. "She can help us find Raoul."

Leo starts walking, keeping one arm curved around my shoulders as he throws Clara a distrustful glance. "All right. We need to find a taxi ship that'll take us to Halcyon."

Clara says, "Taxis go through the Knights' checkpoint before they land on Halcyon. They'll send us to Knight headquarters. We don't have that kind of time to waste. Glenna has an old six-seater Vortex sitting in a hangar somewhere around here—she'll let us borrow it."

"Show us where then," Leo says.

As Clara leads us toward another escalator, taking us to the spaceport's upper levels, a newsie segment playing on a wallscreen catches my attention. I pause to read the scrolling subtitles, forcing Leo to stop with me. "What? What is—" He follows the direction of my gaze, and the flush drains from his cheeks.

<BREAKING: EXPLOSION AT HALCYON REFUGE LEAVES AT LEAST 104 PEOPLE DEAD. LOCAL OFFICIALS INVESTIGATING CAUSE. MACHINERY MALFUNCTION UNLIKELY, SAYS KNIGHT.>

"Unlikely?" I half-laugh, even though the image of a smoking black crater in a patch of idyllic farmland is anything but funny. "For a group of people who don't *use* machines? I'd say it's pretty blazing impossible."

"Do you recognize that place?" Leo asks me, squeezing my shoulder.

I start to tell him that just because I grew up in one Refuge doesn't mean I know them all, but then I recognize a distinctive misshapen boulder in one of the panning aerial shots the newsies captured. "That's the Refuge across the mountains from Evergreen. Lavender Valley." My breath catches in my throat. Raoul knows Evergreen Refuge well. I remember him coming with Clara and Mercy a few times to visit me there, back in the early days. "Do you think Evergreen might be next?"

Leo presses his mouth into a thin line. "He's not going to get a chance to hurt anyone else."

LEO'S THE ONE WHO PILOTS THE SHIP, BUT I'M THE ONE WHO CALLS the dragon to 'port us back to Halcyon. I have to tamp down the writhing ball of nerves in my gut so that the dragon doesn't get spooked.

I'm able to convince the dragon that we don't need to stop by a Knight waystation because we already have a Knight on board. The dragon is suspicious because ze knows Clara is suspect number one in the Knights' murder investigation—but ze can't find any trace of murderous intent in Clara's mind. So ze lets us go, although I'm certain ze's going to tattle on us to Lawry.

We decide to check Evergreen Refuge first. After the dragon drops us off, Leo brings the starship low to cruise over the treetops. The sun went down hours ago, leaving the forest a dark blur under us. I have all my senses open, seeking that dark aura that follows Raoul when he's messing with other people. Clara has her eyes closed tight as she searches for an echo of his thoughts.

"I don't think I can land at the Refuge," Leo says. "There's not enough open space. There's a community up ahead. I think that'd be the safest spot to bring the ship down."

The community is a few hours' walk from the Refuge. "I don't feel Raoul anywhere nearby," I say. "Do we have time to walk all the way there and back on a hunch?"

Leo shoots me a grin. "I'm not planning to walk."

As we're circling in for a landing on the flat landing pad right outside the community's garage, Clara gasps and points. "Isn't that—"

Leo's hands slip on the controls, wobbling the ship a little more than necessary. "The Lightstreak," he finishes. Sure enough, the cherry-red paint on the sleek starship is hard to mistake. "He's here."

The moment our landing gear touches down, Clara and I undo our safety straps and rush to disembark. If Raoul is inside the community, who knows what he's up to?

But the garage techs dash our hopes of finding him quickly. "The guy who brought that ship? Yeah, he just dropped it here and headed up to the Refuge without even a hello. Didn't bother to give me the starter ring so I could move it to a charging port inside. Bit rude, but I s'pose he had something urgent to do."

Clara pipes up. "I have the lock code. I'll help you move it."

"Clara—" I start, but she's already marching over to the ship, fingers flying over the keypad. The ship's cockpit slides open, smooth as silk. Leo's jaw drops.

"She's, uh, remembered a lot of stuff that Raoul tried to make her forget," I tell him quietly.

"I'll say." He starts toward the ship. "Clara, can you open the cargo hold?"

I'm about to ask why, but as soon as Leo pops the hatch open, my question dies on my lips. Inside the narrow belly of the ship, pallets are jammed together with barely any wiggle room. Pallets containing little fist-sized balls that I instantly recognize from the action holos I used to watch with Clara.

Bombs. Specifically, the type usually used on mining planets. They'll punch a kilometer-wide crater in the toughest rock. In one particularly dark holo-drama—which, looking back, was almost definitely Imperial propaganda—the Greenjackets used them to level a city.

Leo stumbles back with a yelp, then slams the hatch shut before any of the garage mechanics can peer inside. "There's enough firepower in there to shatter this entire planet into asteroids," he whispers.

"Well, I suppose that answers what happened to Lavender Valley Refuge," I say, my stomach rolling at the thought of it.

Leo looks over at the mechanics. "On second thought, I don't want anyone moving this ship. It stays right here." He gestures at Clara to lock it back up. "The guy who left it here...you say he went up to the Refuge? How long ago?"

One of the mechanics answers, "About three hours? Ish?"

That's more than enough time to get to the Refuge. We can't waste any time.

"Last question," says Leo. "Would you mind if we borrowed a couple of hovercycles?"

CHAPTER TWENTY-SEVEN

Miri

As soon as my borrowed helmet is secured under my chin, Leo guns the hovercycle's engine. Despite the fact that we double-checked this machine's safety belts, I cling to him with armpit-dampening nerves. Wind bites at my clothes, chilling my skin through the thin leggings and tunic. I find myself longing for the extra protection of my Devote robe.

When I was first sent away from the Refuge, I felt naked without it. Now the thought of putting it back on, even against the cold, is uncomfortable. It stands for a commitment to a way of life—a *religion*—I no longer feel able to wholeheartedly support. At least, not until I do a lot more learning and soul-searching.

These nerves aren't *just* because of our mission, or because I'm about to experience Leo's driving again. Returning to the Refuge, knowing all I know now, scares me shitless. I can't even completely explain why. Sister Tierza and the rest of the Devotes haven't changed. It's me. In just a week away, *I've* changed enough that I feel like I don't belong there anymore. I don't know *where* I belong. Having to explain that to Sister Tierza is going to be really blazing difficult. Particularly because she'll be so gentle and understanding about it. Her disappointment stabs worse than most people's fury.

The hovercycle angles upward, gravity pulling at us. I clench my thighs harder around the seat, my knuckles whitening from my grip around Leo's chest. Bright white headlights and a low hum, barely audible over the whipping wind, remind me that Clara's hovercycle rides close in our wake.

As the lamps of the Refuge glow brighter ahead of us, *nothingness* curls into my brain like fingernails digging in. Exactly the same as it felt the night Mercy died. Except now I know what it means. Somewhere close by, Raoul's using his mental powers to control somebody.

I slap Leo's shoulder. "Raoul's here. I feel it."

He brakes hard, bringing the hovercycle to a slow coast as we enter the Refuge's main cluster. "Any idea where?"

"Somewhere ahead. That's all I'm getting."

The dormitory cabin looms long to my right, the healing center to my left. In front of us, lamps illuminate the curve of the meetinghouse, currently empty.

Except there's a light on in the dining hall.

I squeeze Leo's arm, pointing. He pulls us to a halt, Clara coming in behind, and anchors the cycle so we can dismount.

The wooden door to the dining hall stands ajar. It swings aside easily under a tentative tap. This late—it's close to midnight local time—there should be barely a handful of people awake. One or two sleepless supplicants, and night owl Brother Arjun staying up late to pour them chamomile tea before ushering the last few stragglers to bed.

But when I step through the door, the first thing I see is Brother Arjun facedown on the table.

He's not alone. There are more people in here than I expected—a good dozen or more. It looks like they were in the middle of their evening snack, judging by the plates of sweets and mugs of tea scattered across the tabletops. But snacks usually get passed out around twenty-first hour. Have these people been lying here for hours?

I shake Brother Arjun's shoulder. He's still alive, at least, but all I get out of him is a groggy mumble. His aura is the rainbow muddle of a dreamer.

"Clara," I say, my voice almost a whisper. There's no need to be quiet here, but for some reason, I feel compelled to. "Can you see anything in their minds?" Where I see a cloud of emotions, Clara can get clear, articulated thoughts.

She sits down next to Brother Arjun, resting a hand on his forehead. Her eyes flicker closed, and she's still for a long moment.

Then she gasps, and grabbing my hand, she transfers what she saw to me.

The attack on the neighboring Refuge has everyone on edge tonight. Half the Devotes were weeping silently during evening meditation. The loss of so many innocent lives—friends—weighs heavily on everyone's hearts. But Brother Arjun maintains faith in the dragons. They will catch whoever's responsible and make sure they never endanger Halcyon's peace again.

His way of coping has always been taking care of others. If he can warm a body up with tea, put a smile on someone's face with fresh-baked cookies, then his own soul is at peace. He does so now with extra care, brewing his special calming blend, pouring out a cup for each anxious pair of hands. There are more folks here after bedtime than usual, and they stay up later, worried about missing friends, tortured by grief.

A new supplicant enters, a thin man with brown hair in a ponytail and a neatly kept beard. Brother Arjun is sure this man wasn't at any of the prayer meetings earlier—he'd remember that face, if only because of those golden eyes. He's only ever seen eyes like that on one other person: Sister Miri. Stars bless her. He hopes she's been doing well since she left abruptly last week...

"Welcome, friend," says Brother Arjun. "Would you care for some tea?"

And then the man's voice is worming into his mind, pulling his eyelids shut, whispering, ::Sleep, sleep, sleep...::

It wasn't hours ago. They were up late because of the attack—they've only been asleep half an hour at most.

Thank stars they're all alive. Knowing what he was sent here to do, I don't understand why Raoul spared them.

But no, that's not his style. Raoul didn't kill Mercy with his bare hands—he used Clara to do it. He doesn't want to watch people die. He'd rather let someone else do it for him. Or some*thing...*

Oh blazes. I know where he's gone.

"The waterfall," I blurt. "If the dam blows, the flood will wipe out the

Refuge. He's going to make it look like an accident, just like he tried to do at Lavender Valley and with Mercy."

"How far is the lookout point?" Leo asks.

"It's a hike. We might catch him if we gun it on the cycles."

"Let's go then." Leo already has the door open, rushing out to mount the hovercycle. He lends me his arm to help me climb up behind him. Right before I swing my leg over, he leans in and presses a kiss to the visor that shields my face. Then one on my hand, his lips warming the chilled skin of my knuckles.

It feels like he's saying goodbye.

Swallowing hard, I mount the hovercycle behind him as he jams his helmet back on. The hovercycle leaps forward, leaving my stomach behind. The bright white beams illuminate just enough of our path to anticipate upcoming curves. How many times did I stride up and down this dirt trail, dodging puddles and tree roots on my way to the lookout point? I almost always hiked it in the early morning when everything was damp with dew and the air was crisp. Never was this path dangerous or threatening. The predators stay in the high crags, and the dam holds back the worst of the river floods that used to wash through the valley before the Refuge was built.

But now, in the deep of night, with the aura of *wrongness* creeping tendrils down my spine...it feels like an entirely different world. Like everything that once was good and pleasant has been dipped in poison. Like we're careening toward death.

We very well might be.

The closer I get, the stronger I feel Raoul's influence. It must be costing him a lot of energy to keep the Devotes asleep from a distance like this. Maybe it's just enough of a distraction that I'll have a chance to interrupt whatever he's trying to pull off.

I'm so used to the walk taking longer that we nearly blast right past the lookout point before I remember to tap Leo's shoulder. "Stop! We're here!" He toes the brake, coming to an abrupt halt that jams the steerbars into his ribs. The hum of the engine quiets. My thighs cramp from tension as Leo helps me dismount from the cycle.

And there stands Raoul, limned in light reflecting from Halcyon's rings, a face both familiar and strange at once. My brother. My oldest protector. A childish part of me wants to run to him and throw my arms around his waist, trusting that he'll stand between me and Melanie as he always used to.

But he's Melanie's tool now. Maybe, in a way, he always was. Good Cop to her Bad Cop, kind where she was cruel, but always in service of getting us to obey.

"I heard the hovercycle and figured you were with that quarkbrained Knight," he says casually as I stride toward him. Like he's not surprised to see us at all.

Leo tugs my arm to hold me back, but I approach anyway. He stays in the shadow of the trees, drawing his stunner.

I join Raoul at the rail of the lookout, back to the view, facing him with arms crossed. "What the blazes are you thinking? Did Melanie really send you to blow up all the Refuges?"

He responds with another question. "What did you think of Haven?"

"It was...not what I was expecting," I admit. "Their perspective on the dragons surprised me."

Raoul leans forward. "When Clara told me you left the Refuge, I hoped that you could see reason and be saved from the cult."

I cringe at the word "cult." It's an accusation Imperials have thrown at Halcyon for years. "I really don't understand this the way you do," I say carefully. "Perhaps I don't believe the dragons always know best for humanity, the way I used to. But I don't see any reason to kill the Devotes. Why not let them believe what they believe? Who are they hurting?"

"Don't you see how dangerous Halcyon is for the galaxy?" Raoul leans toward me, his golden eyes intense enough to almost glow under the ringlight. "If the dragons control one planet, what's to stop them from expanding their control?"

I shake my head. "That's Imperialist thinking. The dragons don't want that."

"How do you know?" Raoul starts ranting about humans getting complacent in our reliance on dragons, ignoring opportunities for advancement and independence as a species because we're foolishly comfortable with being an alien race's cultivated pets.

"Genetic modification. That's what you mean, isn't it?" I ask. "You're talking about Glenna's idea that we should mod everybody to have dragon powers so that we don't need the actual dragons."

"Exactly!"

"Raoul, have you lost your mind? Humans can't be trusted with this kind of power." I shake my head. "I don't even think we—the Ediya Experiments—should have it. I've already witnessed some dangerous manipulation being done casually by the members of Haven."

"That's why Melanie's plan was to hand-raise the experiment kids with good values," Raoul insists. "The Halcyonites interrupted that—"

"No, they didn't." I plant my hands on my hips, wishing I wasn't so much shorter than him. "The Devotes helped me control my power as much as they could. They taught me it was immoral to take away anyone's free will. And Haven seems to be teaching the opposite. I'm sorry, but I just can't believe that's fine." Raoul opens his mouth to respond, but I talk over him. "If this plays out the way Glenna wants it to—if all the Ediya Experiments become experts at manipulating people and climb our way to the top of the Imperial government—we're going to become the worst dictators the galaxy has ever known. Yes, worse than the Emperor. At least he doesn't take away people's right to feel how they want about him. He doesn't erase people's memories of what he's done to them. He can control what people do with military force, but he can't crawl inside their mind and drive them like a blazing starship. And that's what we could do, Raoul. We could do all those things, and worse. *We're* the bad guys here. Our line of gen-mods should end with us."

Raoul stares at me. This is almost definitely the most I've ever spoken to him—certainly the loudest I've ever shouted.

"So you think—" He clears his throat. "You believe we are wrong. That *we're* the ones ruining humanity. Miri, can't you see how your upbringing has taught you self-loathing? Do you really want to trust the voices of your mentors who told you to hide yourself and be ashamed?"

The words pierce me. I do hate that part of my upbringing. That's why Haven felt so wonderful at first. They let me believe I wasn't a mistake of creation. That I was more than a time bomb waiting to explode.

Speaking of time bombs…

"Raoul, where did you plant the bomb?" I ask. "I know you're planning to blow the dam and flood the Refuge. Surely, you can see that's not the action of someone who cares about human lives."

The faintest flinch tells me I've struck home. His hand goes to a bulge in his robe pocket, and creepflesh ripples across my skin.

He hasn't planted the bomb. There's still time.

"Please," I beg, not caring how pathetic it makes me sound. "Don't hurt them. They're my family. This isn't a time for violence—we need to talk through this. Figure out how to navigate life being who we are. Not kill everybody who says we're wrong."

He shakes his head. "I'm sorry, Miri. Melanie laid it all out for me. Destroying the Refuges will undermine the dragons' authority on a large scale the way nothing else would. I have to do this."

He pulls out the bomb—so small, just a little black sphere the size of a teacup—and winds up to throw it at the dam.

CHAPTER TWENTY-EIGHT

Miri

I PANIC.

.:*DON'T!.:* I scream mentally. I take hold of his aura—his colors shot through with darkness from the knowledge of what he's about to do—and ruthlessly twist it to my will. Magnifying his guilt and fear. Poking holes in his conviction.

Raoul falls to his knees, the bomb still active in his hand. He's triggered it, blinking a slow red light between his fingers. How much time do I have until it goes off? If it blows right here in his hand, we're both dead. But the dam? Are we far enough away that it'll hold? Will the blast still level the Refuge?

"Miri!"

Leo and Clara are done waiting for me to talk Raoul down. They're both running toward us. Leo has his stunner aimed at Raoul. *Do it,* I urge him silently. *One blast and we can stop this!*

But he's not looking where he's going. His toe catches on one of the wooden steps. As he grabs for the lookout handrail to steady himself, the weapon goes flying over the edge.

I grit out a quick, "Stay back!" But it's too late. They've already distracted me enough to shake my concentration. Raoul gets back up, priming to throw the bomb again.

That is, until Leo jumps on his back like a gangly, blond marsupial baby, reaching for the bomb to wrest it away. Like this is a game of flyball, not a life and death struggle.

Raoul snarls, his face contorting into unrecognizable anger. Leo lets go way too quickly and thuds to the ground, eyes glassy. He gets to his feet, wavering like he's drunk, and moves toward the railing. Hooks one knee over. Hoists himself up.

"Don't be fucking evil!" Clara yells. "That's Miri's boyfriend! You can't throw him off!"

"Shut up," Raoul flares at her—and she does, too used to taking his orders. Leo's got his other leg over now, sitting precariously on the rail with nothing between him and a steep drop.

I grab his arm. "Leo, push him out of your mind. Please, fight him!" I'm still trying to clamp down on Raoul's feelings, forcing him to put down the bomb, but with my concentration split between him and Leo, I don't have enough mental power. The most I can do is hold them both in limbo as the bomb ticks closer to explosion, its lights flashing faster and faster.

Then Clara's between me and Raoul, her hand on the arm that's poised to throw. She reaches her other hand out to me, and I take it, keeping one hand in a tight grip on Leo's arm in case he falls.

I may need to build my "aggressive" skill set, but Clara's doing just fine. She digs into Raoul's memories, pulling me deeper into his mind than I've ever been able to go.

In here, he's the boy I remember, seventeen, scrawny, face pocked with acne. He's heartbreakingly lonely. No one has ever cared for him the way he cares for his younger siblings. He desperately craves Melanie and Oberon's approval, but Oberon is uninterested, and Melanie is manipulative enough to use his desire for motherly love to make him do anything she asks. Even if it's helping her separate a child from the rest, soothing the kid while she puts them through torturous tests to determine the strength of their power. Even if it's wiping the other kids' memories of the ones who disappeared, though he's never perfectly successful—his siblings can feel the empty space when someone's missing, even if they don't have words to put to it.

Some part of Raoul knows what he's doing is wrong. He pushes it deep down, tells himself he's doing what's best for everyone. The Ediyas will spare the others if he sacrifices this one. If he wipes that one's memory. If he keeps everyone compliant and quiet.

When offered a chance to escape, he takes it. Amy is strong-willed and capable of standing up to Melanie. For a short time, he clings to the hope she offers: a chance to see the outside world and a family built on kindness instead of fear.

But Amy doesn't have time to parent twenty younger siblings. All too soon, he's left with his family separated and a new mother who feels like a stranger. Mercy's kind attentions, her pride and approval, ring hollow because they're so easily won. Because he doesn't have to hurt to win them.

He seeks Melanie again, finds her imprisoned and bored. Worms his way into Ykros's good graces to make himself useful. Melanie sends him to establish contact with Haven. Having imagined them as a powerful Greenjacketesque freedom-fighting group, he's disappointed to discover a modest commune in a decrepit block of apartments. Glenna's idea of activism is occasionally writing letters to the Imperial Council. He latches onto her belief that the dragons are holding humanity back, but he challenges her to do more. Reclaim the lost children. Train them to be what they were born to be: rulers of the galaxy.

If he and his siblings take hold of the power given to them by birthright, they'll never have to feel small or afraid again. Or at least, that's what he tells himself, lying awake in a sleep pod shaking after the nightmares.

But Glenna hesitates. Her vision is nothing more than the community she lives in now, extended to the rest of humanity. A world where no one lives under anyone else's boot heel. A world where all of humanity is equal and none can seize power.

A world awfully similar to Halcyon, except instead of relying on dragons, humans teleport themselves. Rule themselves, individually and collectively, needing no dragon-prescribed law to keep the peace.

Actually, Glenna's vision of the world sounds fucking beautiful to me. But Raoul rejects it. I don't think he even believes it's possible. Inside, he's still that scared child. He believes he must control others to protect both them and himself. Only if he's in full control, with nothing and no one to warp his mind, will everything be put right. Only then will the nightmares cease.

That's when he went back to Melanie. That's when the plan took shape to eradicate everyone the dragons control, breaking the aliens' power over humans for good.

::Raoul,:: I say, hoping Clara can pass my words along. *::Listen to me. You don't need to do any of this. You're letting fear rule you.::*

::And your naïveté rules you, little sister.::

::You're wrong,:: I tell him. *::I've lived more than half my life with the fear that Amy instilled in us, that no one could be trusted with my secret. I felt abnormal and wrong. I tried so hard to be like everybody else. But those fears don't protect me anymore. They were holding me back from being my whole self with the people I love.*

::See, Melanie put conditions on loving you—on loving all of us. She told us we were only useful if we could teleport, or see auras, or hear thoughts. She was wrong. We loved you regardless of any of that. Me, Clara, Mercy...even Glenna. You don't have to gain power to be safe, to deserve love.::

Raoul wants to laugh in my face. He needs me to be wrong. Needs this to be the right thing to do. Otherwise, how can he ever face a mirror again, knowing that he murdered hundreds? No, shaking loose the dragons' hold on people's minds has to be the only solution.

::But who told you that?:: Clara interjects. *::Melanie? The same woman who still gives you nightmares? And you trust her?::*

A wave of self-loathing from Raoul, so strong it makes my knees buckle. He can't deny she's right. But then I must be lying about caring for him, because no one could possibly love such a monster.

::I do,:: says Clara. Her softness shocks me, given her vengeful anger just hours ago.

::I do too,:: I say, even more surprised to find myself meaning it. Raoul's not wrong about being a monster. He's done terrible, unforgivable things. But he's still my brother. And now that I've felt the emotions he's been bottling up, hidden under a false aura of calm, I know he's not an evil man. He can still change his mind. *::Please...you have to disarm the bomb.::*

And I let go of his emotions. I let him feel what his body is telling him to feel. Guilt, fear, rage, terror, remorse...I let it run through him without enhancing the emotions I deem correct, without suppressing the ones that seem wrong. Because he needs to come to this on his own terms.

We all do.

He lets go of Leo first. Waking up to see the yawning darkness below him, Leo yells and overbalances, falling backward off the railing into my arms. He knocks us both to the ground, and I just sit there holding him, breathing in his scent as my heart pounds. I almost lost him. We might be about to die anyway. I want the last thing I taste in this world to be the salt of his skin.

Then Clara gasps and lets go of Raoul. The bomb is flashing rapidly now, a high-pitched beep announcing it's nearly about to detonate.

"Raoul," she yells. "Throw it!"

"I can't," he says. "It won't go far enough." And then his eyes find mine. "Tell Glenna I hope she'll forgive me."

And he disappears.

Not a heartbeat later, the shockwave tears through us, flattening us all and making the lookout platform wobble dangerously. Leo tries to drag us to solid ground, but when the shock subsides, the platform has held. We're alive. Safe.

He and I stand, knees wobbling, but Clara stays down in a heap, shaking with sobs. "He teleported with it," she chokes out. "He didn't have time to throw it far enough. I was still connected to his mind. I felt him die."

I wrap my arms around her, shaking with her. I'm too numb to cry, but my teeth chatter with shock. "Come on," I hear myself say. "Let's go home." Meaning the Refuge.

But I already know it's not home anymore. Nowhere is. Not for me.

WE TAKE THE DOWNHILL DRIVE VERY SLOWLY. I'M NOT IN A HURRY TO put anyone in unnecessary danger. We've lost enough today.

The Devotes in the dining hall are slowly waking by the time we park our hovercycles out front. They wander out into the night, blinking in confusion, colliding with a group in their nightclothes venturing out of the dormitory to investigate the loud *boom* that woke them.

"Miri?" Sister Tierza has a blanket around her shoulders. Well-worn flannel pajama bottoms stick out underneath the blanket's hem. "What's going on? It's the middle of the night."

"It's a long story." I look to Brother Arjun. "Is there any tea left?"

"It's gone cold," he says, "but I can brew some more."

And so, in short order, half the Refuge crams into the dining hall as I explain what happened.

Leo must have alerted his Knight team, because they arrive a little later, stunners drawn as if they expect a fight. It takes them a moment to realize it's over and holster their weapons.

Part of the emergency response team heads down to the community to defuse the bombs in the Lightstreak's cargo. But Leo's three friends stay for a rehash of the last few hours...and so does Lawry. He's trying not to show how furious he is. It rolls off him in fiery waves, so strong that I have to move away from him or risk a headache.

<Why didn't you call me as soon as you found him?> he types out at last, his fingers jerky.

"With respect, sir," Leo says, "Last time I tried to tell you something, you fired me."

Lawry doesn't like that, but he doesn't have much of a response. His furious energy wanes a little, replaced by bitter-green regret. At last, he says, <I will note that in the report,> then turns on his heel and leaves.

"Miri. Do you have a minute?" Sister Tierza is at my elbow.

My stomach bubbles with leftover guilt. After being reprimanded by the dragons and disappearing for a week, I'm sure the Devotes were worried about me. It was cowardly of me not to tell them what was happening.

"I'm sorry we didn't have much time to talk at Mercy's funeral," Tierza says. "How are you holding up?"

Her energy is pastel with genuine concern. I feel like I'm more her supplicant now than her colleague.

"I don't know," I respond honestly.

"Do you want to talk about it?"

I might start crying if I unload everything on her. But I think I have to. I owe the Devotes an explanation before I leave again.

I know now that I can't in good conscience call myself a Devote, not until I work through the moral tangle of my powers—and not until I know for sure where I stand with the dragons. If they're allies or rivals.

So I sit Tierza down in a quiet corner and begin to talk. I hold nothing back. Not the dragons' rebuke, my guilt over my own actions, or the truth of my power. I tell her about reconnecting with Leo, about Mercy's death, about Haven and meeting my parents. And I tell her about Raoul. What he's done, and what his ability means for Halcyon.

She listens without interrupting, her aura a sympathetic pale blue. When my eyes spill over, she hands me her absorbent pocket square and puts an arm around me. And when I'm done telling it all, she says, "I think you're doing the right thing."

I expected her to be disappointed in me. Devotes aren't supposed to have a mid-career crisis. It's a lifelong commitment, a solemn vow to serve the people. A Devote can't just get bored and quit.

But Tierza says, "To be honest, Miri, I never doubted your passion for helping people, nor the kindness of your heart. But I had some concerns about what your particular situation would mean for your career. When we were appointed as your caretakers, we were told to watch over you, to give you all the tools you needed to control the power you were born with. We tried our best but..."

"But there are some things only I can choose for myself," I finish. "Thank you for giving me the space to figure that out, Tierza. I will be sorry to leave you."

"And we'll be very sorry to lose you." Tierza drops a kiss on my hair. "Come back and visit sometime, won't you? You're still very dear to us. Leaving won't change that one bit."

I squeeze her around the shoulders, then extricate myself and dry my face. My nose is definitely going to be swollen and red. I'd like nothing better than to disappear into the dormitory and sleep for ten hours straight.

But I can't vanish when Leo's sitting at the other end of the dining hall, his friends consoling him as he stares glumly into a steaming cup.

LEO

MY TABLET SCREEN IS TURNED OFF, BUT IT LIES IN FRONT OF ME, HALF-unrolled. If I activate the screen again, I'll see the message:

<Given recent reports of your conduct, you are relieved of duty as a Knight of Halcyon, effective immediately. Please collect any belongings you have left in any official dormitories and headquarters and return your Knight-issued equipment within one week. If you wish to discuss this decision, my door is open. However, frankly, Galway, you've been given a lot of second chances, and I'm not inclined to make that error again. Cordially, Chief Knight Jostlin.>

Well, I've officially done it. Flared off the Knights so bad that I've lost my job.

It's not as if I can't find something else to do with my time. Communities always need mechanics. It's just...being a Knight was my dream, ever since I was a tiny little wheatstraw. I built it up to be this fantastic adventure in my head, noble Knights saving people and making the galaxy a better place. You'd think the reality would've disappointed me, but it was even better. Because all the thrilling heroics came with an added bonus of the best friends I could ever ask for.

"Don't you dare start crying," Natalia growls. "I'm leaving if I see even one tear."

"She's just saying that because she's a sympathy crier," says Chaz confidentially.

Derek says, "Even though the myth prevails that crying makes you weak, evidence suggests that people who are comfortable expressing their emotions are often more resilient."

Chaz nods. "I think that means it's fine to cry if you want to."

"I'm not going to cry!" I protest. "Really, I'm not."

"Why the fuck not?" Natalia snaps. "I'd cry if I didn't get to work with me anymore."

Aw, man, why'd she have to say it like that? Now I actually might cry. I miss them already. When we got thrown together straight out of Knight training, I thought the senior Knights were out of their minds for putting together a group of wildly different personalities. But it turned out to work like a dream. Chaz was the muscle, Derek the brains, Nat the banter, and I was the audacity. Together, we kicked some serious ass.

Imagining the asses they'll kick without me...well, my heart's doing this funny little trick where it hurts like somebody's wringing it dry of blood.

"You should go to the Chief Knight," Derek says. "Appeal your firing. Tell them Lawry was under a lot of stress and got too heated."

"Yeah!" exclaims Chaz.

But I shake my head. It's not just Lawry. Every senior I've ever had has told me I'm too reckless. Maybe I'm just not cut out for this work, despite how much I love it.

I turn to the side so Natalia won't see the tears that spring to my eyes.

Prince says, "You got other options anyhow. If you want me to set you up for an interview with the Greenjackets, let me know. I got connections."

"The Greenjackets?" I never strongly considered them as an option. The Knights do a lot of the same things: helping people in famine-stricken, disaster-torn colonies, bringing food and medicine, helping them evacuate when necessary. The only difference is that the Greenjackets tend to secure funding by attacking Imperial freighter ships, stealing their goods, and selling them on the black market, whereas the Knights are funded by pooled donations from Halcyon's communities. The Greenjackets' activism always felt a tad too close to piracy for my comfort.

"Just think about it," Prince says with a wink. "For what it's worth, I mean it as a compliment when I say they could use a guy like you. Quick thinker. Fearless. Willing to do anything to help people. If the Knights don't value that kinda person, the Greenjackets certainly will."

"Pretty sure you're not supposed to say shit like that while wearing a

Knight uniform," Natalia says dryly. "People will start to wonder which side you're on."

"There ain't no sides," Prince shoots back. "Just people trying to make this galaxy a better place in all sorts of different ways."

Goes to show you how squishy I am inside right now, because that makes me tear up again.

"Leo..."

Oh shit, Miri's coming over. I dash a sleeve across my eyes. I thought she was busy talking to that Paotherrian Devote with the black-and-white fur.

She seems like she was coming over to talk, but takes one look at my face, closes her mouth, and slides her arms around my waist. I press her close. Her nose is red, and that means she's been crying too.

My friends exchange a glance, then back away slowly. Chaz grins and flashes me a sign of approval. I ignore him.

"Looks like we're both out of a job," Miri says into the front of my shirt.

"You too?"

"I just officially quit as a Devote." She pulls back to look up at me. "I'm going back to Haven. It's not a perfect organization, but it'll be a good start while I figure things out."

My heart sinks. The future has just opened up with a myriad of possibilities, but going back to Monroe wasn't one of them. No doubt there's a Wanted bulletin with my name on it. Even if there wasn't, what would I do there? Fix the bots that polish floors for rich folks? Drive the subtrain? A life without travel and adventure would kill me slowly.

"You aren't coming with me, are you?" she says quietly.

"I don't think Monroe is for me." I wince. "Is this it, then? Are we going to break up?" *Time to brace myself for the pain.*

"I don't want to," she says seriously. "I don't know how to make this work, and I know it's selfish to ask, but...I want to keep you in my life." She takes a deep breath. "You don't want to stay with Haven right now. That's fine. I was thinking...we could do something long-distance?"

A tiny lick of hope kindles in my chest. She thinks she's selfish wanting to be with me? Blazes, I'm the selfish one, because I'll take that deal.

"Long-distance is better than losing you," I say.

I don't know who leans in first, but suddenly we're kissing in full view of the crowded dining hall. I can hear my friends cheering in the background, and Nat loudly making fun of how Miri practically needs to stand on a chair to reach...but I don't care.

We're alive. We're together. And the uncertainty of the future can't stop me from wanting to dive into it headfirst.

AFTER

Hawking Penitentiary Planet

to

A rural Susannah village

Year 3748, Week 27,

Daythree

AFTER

Leo

THREE YEARS LATER...

"WATCH OUT!" CHAZ YELLS. "WE GOT INCOMING. GET OUT OF THERE, NOW!"

"We gotta go," I call to the prisoner. For someone who's spent almost two decades in this solitary dome, the guy isn't that eager to leave. He keeps trying to shove seed samples and vials of mysterious liquid in a bag made out of a pillowcase.

"If I leave this research behind, I'll be of no use to you," Oberon Ediya says calmly, shouldering his bundle.

"We're not freeing you 'cause you're useful," I scoff, herding him toward the exit.

"No? I'm aware the Greenjackets have changed leadership, but even so, I've always understood them to be motivated by their cause. This is not an easy prison to break into. They have to have a good reason."

"You assume I'm doing this for the Greenjackets." I shove him between the shoulder blades, urging him to run toward our getaway ship. "Why? Just 'cause I'm wearing their uniform?"

"Well...yes."

The incoming guard ships are starting to fire on us now. I dodge to the side, yanking Oberon out of the way as a blast narrowly misses us. "I'm here because you still have folks out there who care about you. And someone I care about is one of them."

"What?" Oberon yells over the sound of more blasts hitting the earth at our heels. "I don't even know who you are."

We rocket up the stairs into the ship's belly, the hatch folding closed behind us. "Yeah," I pant, turning to face him in the dim light of the passenger bay. "You don't know me. But I think you know my colleague."

He turns to follow my gaze. Amy Ediya stands in the flight deck doorway, making an uncertain attempt at a smile. She's not wearing her Knight uniform—this little rescue operation is unsanctioned, her participation a secret she's keeping from the Halcyon team—but she commands every bit as much respect in leggings and a leaf-embroidered tunic.

Oberon collapses into one of the passenger seats. "Amy? I thought you gave up on us."

Amy takes the seat next to her uncle. "I might've," she admits dryly. "But after Raoul led us to Haven, I suddenly had a grandmother to get to know. Glenna and I have had a lot of time to talk about the past. She regrets sending you and Auntie Mel into exile. And she never quite gave up on the idea of setting you free."

"She couldn't convince anyone it was a good idea to free Melanie though," I say. "Inciting Raoul to violence three years ago proved she was still dangerous. But Glenna made a good case for you. Said you'd served your time for your own past mistakes."

Oberon shakes his head. "I'm in for life according to Imperial sentencing."

"Yeah, well, that's why they hired a team of jailbreakers who aren't beholden to Imperial law." I pat him on the shoulder. "Buckle up. Our pilot's about to do a few evasive maneuvers."

Right on cue, the entire ship jolts to one side. Oberon scrambles for the safety belt, his expression panicked and slightly ill. Poor guy. This is his first starship flight in, like, twenty years, and his last one was a crash landing. I'd be a little rattled too.

But given my new line of work, this is an average Daythree for me.

Daring escapes and breaking the law are baked into the job description as a Greenjacket. With my team at my back, there's no dangerous situation we won't jump into.

Nat, Chaz, and Derek quit the Knights too, shortly after my firing. They saw the way Lawry and other senior Knights ended up lying to Halcyonite citizens about Mercy's murder and the Lavender Valley Refuge explosion, and they decided they were done. The Greenjacket general, Royal DeSanto, was all too pleased to take us in. A team of well-meaning troublemakers fit perfectly into the Greenjackets' space-pirate Robin Hood mission.

It's been a rough ride. Kind of awkward to explain my job to my ma at family gatherings. But I wouldn't change a thing, even if I could.

Oberon clutches the armrests, knuckles white. "Where are you taking me?" he chokes out.

I reach for a spacesick bag to hand him. "Somewhere safe."

He doesn't look like he believes me—but he doesn't have to take it on faith for long. Our safe haven is just a teleport-blink away.

MIRI

THE DRAGONS ARE DANCING IN MY LIVING ROOM AGAIN. THEY ARC back and forth above the heads of the two toddlers who are learning how to share the building blocks Machinist Stewart carved for them.

I step into the room and go to sit cross-legged on the floor next to my mother, who's minding the babies. "Hi," I say softly. "Looks like we're playing nice today."

"Mm-hmm." Mom smiles, eyes still fixed on her charges. "Gia only cried a little bit earlier. It was because she pinched her finger, though, not because they were fighting."

I glance up at the dragons. "How long have they been in here?"

Mom shrugs. "Oh, awhile. I don't really notice them anymore."

I can't help but feel like they're spying on me. Like they think I've moved to this backwater planet so I can concoct evil plots. It's strange—

I used to see dragons as a good omen. A sign that things would be all right. Lately, I'm only ever suspicious of their presence, even when it's innocuous.

Haven still has its hold on me, I suppose. I stayed with them for only six months, but what they taught me is hard to forget.

Not that I necessarily want to. Most of what I learned from them was good. And I got my parents out of the bargain. When I chose to leave, they asked if they could come too. Never mind that my destination was a poor village in a dusty, hot-as-blazes agricultural colony. They didn't even blink, just said they were looking forward to a change of scenery.

In some ways, it feels like I've been training for this life a long time. This middle-of-nowhere farming community, with precious few bots to do our labor and not much in the way of tech—that's all too familiar. It's what the Refuge taught me all those years.

"Miri!" Another foster child, thirteen-year-old Anja, wrenches the front door open and shouts down the hall. "They need you in the infirmary! Healer Alabas said hurry up and finish your lunch break!"

I've barely had time to check on the kids, let alone eat a meal, but duty calls. I run to the kitch, snag a nutrient bar, and cram it into my mouth as I climb the stairs out of our dugout house.

It stays remarkably cool in the sheltered underground space, but the desert sun above is a whole other story. My wide-brimmed hat keeps my face shaded as I cross the courtyard from our house to the long, boxy concrete building that is the village's infirmary.

Anja follows at my heels. She wanted to learn how to be a healer, so my father's been allowing her to shadow him as long as she doesn't get in the way. Mostly, he makes her run little errands like this one.

Anja is a plague orphan, one of five who live in the dugout house with me and my parents. I didn't set out to become a foster parent. But when the twins' parents succumbed to the deadly flu last year, leaving them orphaned, I saw my younger self in those wide-eyed faces and stepped up. After that, word got around that I have a soft spot for kids with no family. The townspeople, to their credit, haven't left me to provide for them alone. I'm always finding gifts of secondhand clothes and extra food outside my door.

It also helps that my father was a doctor back on Monroe. Setting up our own infirmary made us invaluable to a town still suffering the aftereffects of an epidemic, not to mention the physical dangers that come with farming in a harsh environment. When Leo first suggested this place, I thought he overestimated my ability to help. But the niche we fell into feels like it was made for us. Or maybe I've grown to fit it.

I'm taking off my sun hat and outside shoes in the infirmary's anteroom, stepping into sterile slippers, when Dad pokes his head out. "Miri, darling, we could really use you over in Room 6. I can't give Mas Turner any more painkillers, but he's—"

"I'm on my way." I stop only to wash my hands, then head into the room where a farmer lies recovering from the harvester-bot accident that mangled his right arm.

"Mas Turner, how are you doing?" I ask, even though the answer is clearly visible. The pain fills his aura with white, blood-streaked oblivion. It's not just physical pain either—the healers have tried to blunt the sharp edge of it with medication. No, it's the knowledge that he may never regain full use of his arm that's hurting him worse.

"Miri," he groans. "Please." That's all he needs to say.

My powers are an ill-kept secret in this village. They'd deny it to their last breath if an outsider asked any questions, but among the townsfolk, there are plenty of anecdotes. *My appendix burst, and Miri held me together as they were prepping me for surgery. She made the birth of my child go easy when the midwife was occupied. I was grieving my wife, and Miri gave me strength to go on.*

They don't know what it means, exactly, or how it's possible. But they know I am the one who takes away pain.

It was Rosa who showed me how. During my time at Haven, I made it my mission to learn how to heal the way she does. I never quite mastered her ability to stimulate physical healing in the body. That skill remains beyond me. But she helped me fine-tune my ability to manipulate auras until I was able to block pain, both emotional and physical. Not forever, of course. Just for a time, while the person regains the strength to heal on their own.

That time I lifted Clara's pain away, feeling terribly guilty the whole time, I had no idea that it would come to be my calling—the way in which I channel my power to remain in control of it.

These days, with the infirmary sucking away so much of my energy, I rarely find myself meddling in people's emotions, either accidentally or on purpose. It proves true what Glenna always told us: use your power, hone it, and control will come to you naturally.

Mas Turner's energy is weakened from his accident, but when I push through the cloud of agony, there's strength beneath. A will to live. I feed that strength while pressing the pain down, watching Mas Turner's face. His breaths begin to come slower and more even. His glassy eyes clear and focus. "Thank you," he sighs, eyelids flickering shut.

Anja peeks in. "Is he asleep?"

I hold a finger over my lips. "Not yet," I whisper. "Give him some space."

"Healer Alabas sent me to tell you there's a dust cloud rolling in."

A hopeful fizzing sensation tickles my insides. "Is it a storm or a visitor?"

"A visitor," says Anja, grinning.

I jump to my feet, heart hammering faster. Mas Turner is nearly asleep. He mumbles, "Don't go yet."

"You'll be fine," I murmur, patting his uninjured hand. "Just rest."

In the anteroom, I check myself in the mirror as I step into my outside shoes. My face is as freckled and tanned as ever, my hair braided into a crown to keep it out of my way while I work. I'm wearing an unglamorous set of scrubs dyed the same powder blue as my old Devote robe. Fleetingly, I wonder if I should put on some makeup or wear fancier clothes.

But Leo never asks for that. In fact, I think he'd probably laugh.

The cloud of dust precedes him as always. Like a storm blowing into town, only instead of destruction, it brings wild laughter, kisses, and a soft-simmering joy that fills my lungs to bursting.

When I run out into the street, there's a small group of villagers gathering. They've seen the cloud too. They cast me knowing glances, then pointedly go about their business. That's my unspoken contract with them. I heal their ills and ease their pain, and in return, they pretend not to notice that my sweetheart is an outlaw.

Joining the Greenjackets has been good for him, it really has, but it's complicated for *us*. He's wanted by the Authorities for an ever-growing list of civil disobediences, associations with criminals, and outright piracies. Living with me on Susannah would be too dangerous. And I couldn't see myself joining the Greenjacket army, not even to be close to the man I love. So we compromise, and he sneaks out to visit me once every couple of weeks, hiding his ship in the desert rocks and falling into my bed for a long weekend.

It's not what anyone would call a fairytale. But it's ours, and it's sweeter than any fantasy I could invent. A stolen happiness, kept safe and secret, full of promise and all the sweeter for its fleeting nature.

Anja tugs at my sleeve. "Is it Pa?" she whispers. The kids don't call me Ma—I don't let them—but Leo loves it when they play pretend that he's their dad. He agreed with me that having biological children is ethically shaky, given the burden of power I'd be passing down to them. But it didn't stop him wanting a big family; so when orphans started showing up on my doorstep, he embraced the chance to be a father figure with his whole warm heart. It's adorable, seeing him give "hovercycle rides" with the twins on his back, the three of them yelling "vroom vroom!" and tearing around the courtyard like a cyclone. He promises he'd never claim the space their biological family should take, but he'll give them love and pride and support as long as they need it from him.

The dust cloud rolls in and spins to a halt right outside the infirmary door. As the cloud settles, the shape of a lanky figure dismounting from a hovercycle fades into view. Anja rushes toward him just as he gets his helmet off. He picks her up and swings her around, exclaiming at her new hat and asking if she got taller in the last few weeks.

Then he puts her down, a determined glint appearing in his eyes. And the next minute, I'm the one in his arms, pressing my lips to every inch of his face I can reach. He finds my mouth with his and draws out a long, slow kiss that makes my heart flutter like a bird.

I frame his face with my hands. "You grew your hair longer."

He reaches up to muss it further—it's already helmet-shaped. "Yeah. I haven't had much chance to cut it lately. Besides, Nat says it makes me look dashing."

"I think you look handsome and badass." I kiss his bearded cheek again, then press my face into his shoulder. He smells like dust and sweat and...wait. There's the smell of another world on him.

That's when I see the second hovercycle behind him and the balding figure dismounting from it, his profile making my stomach lurch.

"Oberon?" I whisper, searching Leo's expression. He's smiling, so I relax a little.

"Remember when you told me how you thought Oberon deserved to be free?" he says softly. "Well, Glenna agreed with you. She helped me set this up. The Greenjackets provided the firepower, but she did all the planning." He glances over his shoulder before adding, "Melanie's still locked up. I don't want you to worry you're not safe...but if it makes you uncomfortable to have Oberon around, I'll take him somewhere else."

"No," I say after a moment's thought. "Susannah could use an experimental geneticist. The farmers are always trying to figure out how to make crops grow better. I think he could help."

A grin breaks across Leo's face. "Good. Then we'll get him settled this weekend." He slides a hand around the back of my neck, fingertips stroking the sensitive skin behind my ear. "Though let's leave plenty of time for..."

I pull him down for another kiss. I can feel his aura blending into mine, bright sunshine yellow, a cold drink of water in this blazing dry heat. I'm confident my energy won't overpower him—we're strong apart...and strong together.

The dragons come swooping in to investigate, unerringly drawn to hearts at peace. And because I'm feeling generous, I let them sip down some of my happiness.

They're children of this universe after all. Neither evil nor angelic. They're creatures who simply exist and deserve a chance to prove themselves.

Just like me.

Thank you for reading! Did you enjoy? Please add your review because nothing helps an author more and encourages readers to take a chance on a book than a review.

And don't miss more from Mindi Briar coming soon!
Until then try THE STARS IN THEIR EYES by City Owl Author, Kristy Gardner. Turn the page for a sneak peek!

Also be sure to sign up for the City Owl Press newsletter to receive notice of all book releases!

SNEAK PEEK OF THE STARS IN THEIR EYES

By Kristy Gardner

Calay was shattered.

She felt it. Everywhere. Deep within her heart. Her mind. Her spirit. Her left tibia.

Something wasn't right.

Every time she moved, a raw grinding forged its way through her leg. Bone against bone. And enough pain to make her wince long enough to contemplate...nothing. Nothing at all. It hurt. Everywhere.

Between stabbing torrents of full body agony, the cold of the concrete penetrated her soul. She pressed herself against the floor. The hardness of it a welcome retreat—and somewhat alien feeling—from the heat searing through every inch of her being. The recalescence of her broken body a brutal admonition of the misery that came with living. Of living, itself.

It was all that ever was. All that ever would be.

Breathe in. Breathe out. Just breathe. Do. Not. Panic.

With every inhale, small particles assaulted the back of her throat. She coughed. Each shudder sent ripples of pain through her chest. Her fingertips grazed the floor, coming to rest in a powdery substance. Granular and smelling sweetly of pine.

"Sawdust," she gasped and it gathered in the back of her throat. She coughed again.

"Sit up," she gasped.

Fighting against slowly choking to death on the dust, Calay pushed her body upright. She leaned back and surveyed her surroundings.

It was dark.

Her head ached.

Her eyes too.

It was like she'd downed three too many gin and sodas and was trying to make sense of her surroundings through the bottom of a shot glass.

Hell, it wasn't like she hadn't done that before; she could do this.

"Hello..." she called into the murky blur in front of her.

Nothing.

"Tess?" She waited. "Tess! Is anybody there?"

Silence.

She was alone.

A nondescript stickiness welded her eyes half-shut. Calay brought her hand to her head and felt a puffiness where her right temple should have been. Her hand traced the sticky substance across her forehead, down the flesh of her cheek, past the ridge of her collarbone, and into the large, dark puddle below. It was like she was sitting in a black hole brimming with sawdust, stars.

I'm lost in space.

Between labored gasps, she tried to focus her eyes. The black hole she was sitting in wasn't a black hole. It wasn't black at all. It was red.

Really red.

Only one thing was that shade of red. She'd seen enough of it over the last four years, that was for sure. Since The Change began.

Blood.

A funny thought occurred to her that it was her blood.

And then she had a more serious realization that wasn't funny at all.

It was everywhere.

Furiously, she wiped at herself, madly clearing the coagulated liquid from her face and eyes as best she could. It clung to her eyelashes, stained her lips, and matted her hair to her ear. Dried bits flaked off in chunks, creating a spectacle of falling paint chips.

If painting was self-discovery and every good artist paints what he is, Calay had painted a mess of her internal workings all over the damn place. That is, if twentieth-century Abstract Impressionist art meant anything anymore. But it didn't.

Don't think about that now. There's nothing you can do about that. No choices to be made. Focus on what you can control.

"So what *can* I control?"

She tried to open her eyes again. Clearer. An improvement.

Spots of red still garnished her vision, but she could see more now. Aside from the darkness, small rectangular windows splayed light across the floor in tidy, broken cross sections. Dust danced midair like woodland fairies lost—or trapped—in a maze. Through a thin door, she spied stacks of large crates littering a far wall and beside them, a plastic sheet dividing the doorway to what she assumed was another room. Before The Change, the wooden rafters in the ceiling would have been home to cooing pigeons and families of sweet mice. Now they were cold and barren, littered with abandoned cobwebs and dark shadows. Who knew what roosted up there? When The Change started, even rodents knew enough to get the hell out of Dodge. Or they were dead. Like everyone else.

And the room—it was big. Bigger than big. *It's fucking huge.*

A warehouse.

"Where am I?" She coughed. She recounted her last steps, trying to remember something. Anything. It seemed she'd spent half her life trying to recount why she was in the situations she found herself in. She was no angel, but she wasn't worse than anyone else, was she? In the small town where she'd spent most of her childhood, kids got into trouble all the time; there wasn't much else to do. A little too much to drink on a Friday night. Driving a little too fast on the backroads. Enjoying a little too many rendezvous in her twenties. And thirties. But she'd always found her way back, hadn't she? She'd always made it home. To her apartment. To herself. And eventually, to Tess.

Tess.

Calay's heart fluttered at the thought of her. She was happy and in love with Tess the morning of The Change. She'd had no idea the world was about to literally come crashing down around her. It had been a morning like any other Sunday morning—an ocean of cozy sheets and not nearly enough kisses. There were never enough kisses. Their breath had pooled on each other's necks while the sun wrapped their naked bodies in the warmth of a late Spring sunrise. The skin on Tess's thighs was warm. Tender. Familiar.

Tess released a gravelly moan as Calay's tongue plunged deeper. Her fingers, too. She took her time. There was no rush; she wanted to explore every inch of Tess. Every morning. For the rest of their lives.

The world would wait.

Calay looked up at Tess, her eyes shining. Tess took Calay's face in her hands.

"Come here, Cay," Tess smiled, bringing Calay up to meet her mouth. Their hair intertwined as they kissed in the sparkling morning light, their soft bellies pressed flat together.

The feeling of Tess wasn't new to Calay. When they had got together five years ago, Tess immediately felt like home. But her body had been foreign. It was the first time Calay had taken a woman to bed. Or rather, they'd taken each other to bed. Calay was nervous and awkward; Tess was confident and gentle. Until she wasn't. It didn't take long for their passion to rise and consume them that first night. And through every first since.

"You get all my remaining firsts." Calay beamed between kisses.

They were made to love each other, if you believed in that kind of thing. To save each other. From the obligations of life, and the expectations they'd never live up to. From their own vices—and Calay had many. She wasn't in denial that she tended to drink too much or that she'd faltered in her relationship with her parents.

Poor decision making was a habit for her, and she often relied on Tess's stability. She was impulsive, and Tess accepted that—Tess accepted *her*. They were two halves of a whole, a team, and had been for much of their adult lives. Once they'd left the rural community in which they'd grown up, they'd found a six-story walk-up in the city at the end of a tree-lined street with cobblestone sidewalks. It was new and exciting and quaint and absolutely charming.

It was a place to call their own.

It was also small and old. The cupboards were chipped and often bare, but their hearts were full. Over the years the linoleum floor peeled, and the curtains they'd foraged at the local thrift-store faded with sun, while their relationship fastened and grew into something less than perfect. Tess could be hard at times and Calay, stubborn. Their fights—

loud and sometimes lasting for days–embedded themselves in the foundation of the apartment. A chipped doorframe that had been slammed too strongly and a shattered mirror tucked behind the water heater were evidence of their passion. Once, the proof made its way out of the fridge, past Calay, and through their fourth-story window, landing at the feet of a neighbor below. That was the last time the freezer ever saw a container of Chunky Monkey.

But they always made up. Their love for each other pulled them back together as much as it drove them to argue. They were strong women and stronger together.

They liked their neighborhood. Here no one furrowed their brow at two women holding hands. Folks didn't gossip as they passed through the supermarket. Neighbors occasionally even invited them over for dinner parties, which they almost always attended, grateful for the company and a hot meal. Eventually, the dated apartment with the tattered orange sofa and clunky TV became not just a respite but a home. As much a home to them as they were to each other. It was all theirs.

"Make love to me," Calay gasped between breaths.

Tess rolled Calay onto her back and gathered her full breasts in her hands. Her teeth gently teased her nipples which rose to attention. Calay giggled breathlessly.

"I need you, T..."

Tess moaned back in response as her mouth made its way down Calay's stomach, her hands cupping her mound, fingers dancing over her clit.

"Yes, please," Calay moaned.

"Tell me you love me."

"I love you."

"Do you love me?" Tess grinned and cocked an eyebrow.

"I fucking love you!" Calay laughed.

Tess's fingers plunged inside Calay at the very moment the city exploded around them.

It sounded like a jet engine crashed through the wall of their apartment. It felt like it too. The room shook violently. Both women screamed, jerking backward, severing the physical connection between them. Their eyes widened in fear. Calay clamped her hands down over her ears. The entire building vibrated under the weight of the noise. Neither one of them knew what to do, so they crouched, cowering with the sheets tangled around them.

The noise stopped.

Tess looked at Calay, her eyes wide, "What the fuck was that?"

"I...I don't know," Calay stammered.

Moments passed. Then minutes. Neither one of them willing—or able—to move.

"It had to be...was it an earthquake?" Tess pressed.

Calay shook her head. Her legs trembled too.

"Calay, what the hell just happened?"

"I don't know Tess! I know as much as you do. Maybe we should turn on the televisi—"

The noise started again.

It was metal grating against metal and some kind of deep whirring like they were inside a car compactor. Only louder. So much louder. The building shook more violently this time, and the room seemed to tilt on its axis before righting itself, only to shift at an even more severe angle the other way.

Then it fell.

Calay shuddered. Shook off the memory. As she peered across the warehouse a chill wound its way around her spine. The cold, hard truth was unmistakable: she was no longer in her apartment; she never would be again. Still, Tess should be there with her. Where one went, the other followed. So why wasn't she? After The Change the stakes became clear: survive together or die. Calay couldn't bring herself to think about what their separation might mean. For her. For Tess.

Calay didn't think she'd be here. In this warehouse. At thirty-two. Broken, bloodied, and begging for her life. She didn't think she'd wake up one morning and have her entire life turned upside down. Or her apartment. But that was exactly what happened four years ago. She didn't think everything they'd built together would burn up in the Dumpster fire they had once called Seattle. Or Earth. She didn't think she'd lose everything—and everyone—she'd ever loved.

She didn't think, at thirty-two, she'd be utterly alone.

She had to find Tess.

Calay slowly–painfully–dragged her body to the far end of the warehouse and through the thin door. Every push and pull sent lightening rods of pain through her leg, threatening to overcome her consciousness. She looked at the mountain of crates in front of her. Getting up was going to be a fight, and fight she would. Like she'd always done.

She reached up from the hard floor and placed her hands on top of a box. It creaked beneath her palms. She leaned on the surface, taking some time to steady herself. It bent under her weight.

"Just breathe."

Her throat released a yelp of desperation as she rose. Her balance waivered on her good leg. She tensed her stomach muscles and pulled herself up. *You are strong. Steady, now.* There. Good. She was standing. Calay looked at the boxes. *Maybe there's something in one of these that will help me get out of here. Or mend my leg. Or both.* She tried to lift the lid off a crate. It wouldn't budge. She pressed her lips together and her body forward and tried another. It was locked tight. The same thing with the next five. No matter how she pried her fingers between the cracks, all she had to show for her effort was bloodied knuckles and scraped fingertips.

Eying the crates at the other end of the room, she knew she had to somehow make it over there and try them too. She leaned carefully on the injured leg and found the floor rising to meet her. Or rather, she was falling to meet it.

"Fuck!" she howled as she fell forward into another box. *Oh no.* If hell existed, this was it. Her ass hit the concrete with a loud *crack*. Whether it was the wood or her leg, she wasn't sure. Calay winced; this was a disaster. Her leg couldn't be broken. It just couldn't. If it was fractured, she was as good as dead. If it was sprained or the muscle or ligament was torn...well, she could work with that. She examined her body, running her hands over her joints. Her puffy eye. Her shivering limbs. Toes to tailbone to the top of her head, she was intact. *Mostly*.

"What the...?"

The box. The force of her body collapsing into the wooden crate knocked the lid

clean off. Inside, amongst the packing material and wrapping were bottles of water and bags of dehydrated food. She spied cans of beans, cellared potatoes, even some sacks of dried fruit.

"Small miracles..." She exhaled. She tore the top off a bag of dried mango and savored the explosion of sugar on her tongue. It railed into her bloodstream, giving her a burst of energy. Of hope. She cracked the top of a bottle of water and gulped down half of it. Took a breath, then drank the rest.

Rolled the dice on that one. But then again, she'd always made her own luck. When The Change happened, it was her resourcefulness that kept her and Tess alive as they made their way out of the city. It was also what made her such a pain in the ass to love. She'd never been one to compromise, let alone fail. Except for maybe where her family was concerned. Her mother always told her stubborn was her middle name. And she'd always replied she'd gotten it from someone.

Maybe that was part and parcel why their exchange had been so explosive when she'd come out. Her parents were stuck in their ways and she was stuck in hers. Stuck. Stuck in that town. In a life she didn't want. In relationships that didn't make her happy. How many years had she fought who she was in order to be who *they* needed her to be? All she'd ever wanted was to belong. To them. To Tess. To the truth of her identity. If they couldn't handle it, that was their issue. Not hers. Or so she told herself. And yet, her heart ached at the memory of her mother and father. She shook off the mental image. She'd survived then, and she would survive now.

Despite her resolve, the strain of the effort washed over her body. Her eyes grew heavy and her torso slouched against the wood. Time didn't pass. It merely faded between bouts of consciousness. Sometimes light shone through the fractured glass windows, sometimes it didn't. In those dark moments, a chill wound its way through Calay's mind and refused to let go. It threatened to steal the breath from her lungs. The life from her veins. The world—hope—ceased to exist. She did, too. As the light turned over, rising brighter and then fading to black, Calay would try to rise again. And again. And again. And then, one day, as the sun crept across the windows high above, she pushed herself from the bottle and plastic littered floor. And this time, she stayed up. She pressed her heel down and put a little weight on her injured leg, hobbling around the enclosed space. The pain was excruciating, but she could move. *Thank Christ, it wasn't broken.* The gratitude that flooded her body almost sent her off kilter, but she held her own. She had to. For herself. And for Tess.

On the morning of The Change, Calay had taken care of Tess. As books piled off shelves, and the meager amount of dishes they owned smashed onto the kitchen floor, sending shards of razor-sharp glass throughout the apartment, Calay had grasped for her. The bed rolled on its side, sending the two lovers onto the floor, clinging to each other with their eyes sealed tight. Furniture tumbled around them. They screamed, but beneath the noise of bursting pipes, breaking gas lines, and layers upon layers of crumbling drywall, their cries went unheard.

"Tess?" Calay choked out, her hands feeling their way through the chaos, "Tess!"

No reply. Panic rose in her throat once again.

"TESS!"

She slid from beneath fragments of their splintered dresser and pulled herself up on the plasterboard that used to be their bedroom wall.

"What the fuck is happening?"

Surveying the apartment that was no longer an apartment, she coughed and choked back a sob. Beams of morning light fought through the wreckage, casting shadows over what was left of their home and deep within her mind. *If anything has happened to Tess—*she pushed the thoughts out of her mind and blinked back tears. Tess had to be there somewhere. She didn't know much, but she knew at least the room had stopped moving.

"Tess!" she tried again. Silence. A whimper crawled up her throat.

"Cay...Cal...Calay," Tess stuttered from somewhere in the dust, "I...I'm stuck."

"Tess, where are you?" Calay's hands flew over the debris, desperate for any sign of movement. "Tess! Say something!"

"I'm over here." The sound of Tess's labored breathing filled Calay's ears, but she saw nothing.

"Where? I can't tell where you are. Keep talking!"

"I think...there's something on top of me. I think I'm under the mattress."

Her head dizzy from the fall, Calay spied the mattress across the room. She gripped what she could to keep herself upright—jagged pieces of the snapped bedframe, the edge of her sanity—and stumbled toward it.

"Tess! Tess, I'm here." Calay bent to find Tess pinned beneath what was left of their bed.

"You'll have to lift it, Cay. I can't."

"It won't budge!" Calay looked around, confused. "Why is it so fucking heavy?"

Then she realized the television and the rest of the dresser were on top of it.

"Um, hang on Tess, I gotta move this shit off to get ya out." Calay hesitated, swallowed hard. She was desperate to know but terrified to find out the answer, still, she asked, "Are you okay?"

"I think so. My arm hurts. I think I banged it."

"Is it broken?"

"No, I don't think it's broken."

"Are you bleeding?"

"No, no I don't think so. Are you okay?" Tess's voice raised several octaves. She reached for Calay's face, her fingers marred and covered with dirt. Calay grasped her fingers and held them to her cheek.

"Yeah. I hit my head, but I think I'm fine. It's a good thing the mattress is on you." She stopped short of what she was about to say as she peered at the sharp, splintered wood. She didn't want to think what would have happened to Tess if the mattress hadn't landed on her first.

Slowly, Calay pried enough of the weight off the mattress and Tess wiggled free.

They fell into each other's arms.

"My darling, are you alright?" Tess cooed.

"I'm fine. I'm fine. Are you?"

Tess's hands shot to Calay's face again, brushing her hair out of her eyes, examining her head.

"Seriously, I'm fine. Just a little concussed. I'm sure the hospital will fix me right up."

Tess's eyes pleaded with Calay, but Calay shook her head and forced a smile.

"What the hell just happened?" Calay asked, redirecting Tess's attention to the disaster in front of them.

"I don't know. I think...I think the building collapsed."

"We have to get out of here." Calay reached into the dresser, pulled out a couple t-shirts, and handed them to Tess.

"Here?"

Calay shrugged. "Where else?"

Tess nodded; her blue eyes sunken behind a curtain of shock. Calay knew the look well—she was feeling the same way herself.

"Right," she replied.

"Right," Calay agreed.

There, in the ruins of what had been their home, Calay and Tess got dressed together in their bedroom for the last time.

"You ready?"

Tess nodded, still shaking as she tried to tie the laces on her sneakers.

"Let me help you." Calay bent, finishing the loops for her. "There. Like new."

She looked up from Tess's feet, their gazes meeting. Calay tried to hide the fear behind her eyes but failed. They both did. Seeing Tess this way made Calay's heart ache. But there wasn't much she could do about it now. All she could do was try to get them to safety.

"Which way?" Tess asked.

Calay looked around, her lips pressed firmly together. She took Tess's trembling hand. They both swallowed hard. And began to make their way toward the light.

The warmth of the sunlight crawled across Calay's eyelids as it inched across the warehouse floor. She pulled herself from her reverie and the questions tumbled through her mind. *Where is Tess? Is she looking for me? Is she safe?* There was only one way she was going to get her questions answered. She had to move.

Calay sized up the plastic sheet leading to the other room. Before now, she'd been immobile. Trapped. But now the notion of freedom tugged at her limbs. She hadn't seen a doorway yet, and there had to be an exit somewhere. The contents of the boxes had kept her alive, but they wouldn't last forever. Now she'd have to save herself.

She limped toward the door, one unsteady step at a time. As she reached the opening, the plastic sheet rippled. *The wind?* The air was stale with the scent of old blood and sawdust. *What fucking wind?* A halo of light encompassed the frame and a loud bang echoed through the room. No—someone was there, just beyond the curtain of plastic.

Calay wasn't sure if she should duck and run, stand and fight, or hug whoever was on the other side.

"Look, if we're going to use this space for the mission, we need to dispose of the body. We can't have a corpse rotting in the middle of an operation."

Okay, no hugs.

Calay flailed more than ducked behind the closest crate. She squatted, pressing herself against the cold brick wall, hoping to God the trail she'd left in the sawdust and blood wouldn't lead them right to her. *Maybe they'll think I'm already gone.*

Two figures in military-green and black brushed through the slab of plastic only feet from where she crouched. They marched into the next room.

This is it. Now or not ever.

Calay mustered her strength and pushed through the plastic in the opposite direction. On the other side was pitch blackness. Nothing but an abyss of shadows. She stood, paralyzed by indecision and fear. Those men had come from somewhere; if she could just find a light. Shaking, she reached her hands forward, following the wall. Small nails and pointed edges poked the tips of her fingers. The weight of the darkness swam around her, threatening to pull her down. She had to keep moving. She placed one foot in front of the other, careful not to bump into anything and give away her location. As her eyes adjusted to the lack of light, ahead, something glinted. Something huge. Sharp metal glimmered through the darkness, nearly twice her height. It towered before her. Her breath caught in her throat; her hands flew to her mouth. She stifled a scream. *There's no such thing as monsters.* Except, there was. And they'd ended civilization as the world knew it. Calay edged closer to whatever it was in front of her, ignoring the feeling in her legs to flee the other way. She took a break, steeled herself, and placed a palm on the silver surface. *Do or do not.* A large steel door. This was the chance she was looking for. She threw herself against it, leaning on the metal for support. She turned the handle and pushed as hard as she could. It didn't grant her so much as a courteous nudge. She knew if she didn't move now, she never would. The body dumpers would see to that.

"Where the fuck did she go?" one voice boomed across the warehouse.

"She should be right here," said the other.

"Where could she go? She's dead."

"Well, she's supposed to be dead."

"What do you mean 'she's supposed to be dead?' Of course she's dead! I saw to it with my own hands."

"Dead people don't move."

Rapid footsteps circulated beyond the plastic sheet. It'd be moments before they were on her. And in this world, that could mean any number of things, even in her state. She'd seen enough to know a little blood and a few cracked ribs didn't stop the unthinkable from becoming doable.

Calay's vision swam and her mind drifted. The morning of The Change, she and Tess had learned that grim truth the hard way. Society—humanity—had crumbled like sheets of ice in spring. Swift, jagged, and without warning. Smoke stung their eyes and billowed from piles of bricks that had once been buildings. Electricity poles dangled over sidewalks. Electrical boxes shot sparks up into the dusty sky like birthday cake sparklers. And the smell—shit and piss flowed freely down gutters and into drain ducts.

"Don't look at it." Calay gagged, turning away from the street, resting her hands on Tess's shoulders. They faced what was left of their apartment building only to find that view not much better.

"We should have stayed inside." Tess had mourned as they stepped out of their apartment and into the street. "What the fuck happened?"

No words came to mind. Calay stared in disbelief.

The apartment complex didn't just collapse, it was literally flipped on its side. What was six stories was now less than one, stretching the length of the entire city block. The remains of other buildings were spread beneath it, shattering the lives of the people they'd called their neighbors. It was a cemetery of broken bricks and concrete. Calay squinted, fighting to see through the dense cloud of ash. Human limbs protruded through the wreckage, pale and at odd angels. Survivors clawed forward from beneath it all. Tortured sounds of pain and panic bled into the air.

"But...how?" Calay's eyes teared up, swollen with confusion and fear. *It's like a scene out of a war movie.* She pushed down the urge to cry. "We have to remain calm."

Tess's arm brushed against hers and she jumped despite herself.

"What's happening, Cay?" Tess begged.

"This wasn't an earthquake," she said, "was it...do you think it was terrorism?"

They looked at each other, their mouths agape. Calay's went dry. Since 9/11, and the Berlin and Paris attacks, terrorism was something you saw on the news or in movies. It was something that happened over "there," never to anyone you actually knew. Not in your own backyard. Not here, not now. That was the belief, anyhow. The false truth they all told themselves so they could sleep at night; so they could feel safe. The idea someone may have bombed their building turned Calay's stomach.

Her legs began to give way. Her vision turned woozy. *I have to remain strong, for Tess.*

"Hey!" A large man barrelled into them; two small children tucked under his arms. Calay hit the ground with enough force to rattle her teeth as he pushed past. The children were crying, their faces marked with soot and their clothes mangled and torn. Calay recognized the kids from down the street. She'd hopped their hopscotch only a week earlier.

"Look out!" the man growled.

Blood pooled in his dark beard, dripping in a steady stream onto his chest as he careened down the road. His eyes were dark, wide, and manic. The kid's frail arms waved in the air, jostling side to side as the man ran, his breath labored and heavy.

"Are you guys okay?" she called to them, dusting herself off, starting to rise, "hey wait—are you alright?"

"Help us!" the one child pleaded. Her dark curls waved to Calay from the motion as she bounced in the strange man's arms.

"Help us!" the small boy parroted. His body shook violently with each step the man took.

Calay spun to Tess. "Are they asking us?"

Tess stood, her mouth hanging open, at a loss. *Who is that man?* Calay turned back to the trio, bounding further away. *I have to do something.* The kids seemed to be asking for her help. *I have to do something.* Seconds later and they'd be gone. *I have to do something, now!*

"Stop! Hey you, stop!" She took several steps after them, only to watch all three disappear in a plume of red twenty feet in front of her. Calay's feet planted themselves firm where she stood.

"What...where did they...?"

"Oh my God." Tess's skin went pale.

"Where did they go?"

Tess looked at Calay, her eyes wild, desperate, and afraid.

"They were right here!"

"I feel nauseous."

"This is impossible, T! People don't just disappear."

Tess doubled over. Calay rushed to her side, crouched, and wrapped her arms around her shaking body as she heaved what was left of last night's dinner into the street.

"Where did they go?" Calay muttered to herself, more than anyone else.

Tess said nothing.

"People don't just disappear. Where did they...?"

Calay's eyes returned to where the threesome had been only moments before. Gone.

Just like Tess. Four years after that awful day, Calay now knew what happened to people when the blue lights hit them. Still, her mind couldn't reconcile the idea someone existed and then they didn't. Tess was gone, but she was out there somewhere. *She has to be.* So Calay firmed her resolve, focused on the door in front of her and decided: she, too, had to exist. She had to survive. She had to get out of that warehouse.

"Open! Please dear God, open!" She pulled, she pushed, she pleaded, she begged. The panic rose like a tsunami in her chest. Tears began to roll down her cheeks as she fought with the door handle.

And then she saw it: the pin. Like the walk-in freezers in the bar where she used to work. Before The Change. Before everything went to shit. *Pull the pin, you idiot! Pull the damn pin! Pull it now!*

She wrenched the pin out of the hole and the door popped open with a gentle click. She burst through it into fresh sunshine. It was warm, full of life, and best of all, not in that damned warehouse.

She looked around—and her heart sank.

The light shone through a skylight above her, stairs on either side. *Up or down?* Her heart thumped in her chest. *Up or down, damnit?* Down certainly meant out, right? But wouldn't that be the logical—and expected—thing to do? She leaned over the railing and peered over. There were a lot of flights below, more than she could count. The sun felt closer than the Earth. Calay considered her leg and wondered if her knee could handle the impact of all those stairs, one after the other. Would she just collapse in a heap at the first landing? *Oh please,* she prayed to a God she'd long since stopped believing in, *don't make me out to be the woman in a bad horror movie.*

"Up it is." She decided.

She climbed as fast as her leg would allow, hoping against hope the decision would buy her time to figure out a plan. A plan—the idea was laughable. *Plans are what fall apart when you're busy running for your life.*

Calay shook her head. The morning of The Change, all their plans went out the window when theirs exploded under the weight of their falling building. She could still smell the smoke and burning bodies that day. It was seared into her memory. Particulate matter hung in the air around them, settling to the ground in a fine dust. Voices floated amongst the ash.

"Place them in the street! Keep them clear of anything that might fall!" Someone shouted.

Calay watched her neighbors move the injured from the remains of buildings to the center of the road, gently placing them on the fractured concrete as to not exacerbate their pain.

"Wrap them up!" someone else ordered, "keep them warm!"

A woman was dragging sheets and blankets from wherever she could find to wrap them with until help could arrive. Another was wrestling water from a gushing fire hydrant into buckets and bowls. The initial shock seemed to be subsiding. People were rallying.

Whatever happened—whatever it was—seemed to be over.

"I got you." Calay pulled Tess closer. "It's okay. It's going to be okay. Help will be here soon."

"Shouldn't there be sirens?" Tess became rigid in Calay's arms.

Calay's breath caught in her throat. Tess was right. Where were the emergency responders? Surely, they'd hear them coming. Aside from the sounds of people shouting and crying, it was quiet. Too quiet. Something wasn't right. As the air cleared, every hair on Calay's body stood on end. A prickle curled down her spine; dread flooded her body.

"I was wrong," she gasped.

"What?"

"Something's off," she whispered to Tess.

"What's off?"

"I don't know." Calay's pulse quickened, her breathing shortened. "Something's wrong."

"What do you mean, Cay?"

"I don't think this is it."

"Why?" Tess pressed, "what are you talking about? Do you hear something?"

Calay shivered as she looked up.

"Oh my God!"

A hundred feet above them, something hovered.

It was large, round, smooth, and white. Bigger than the city block, it hung in the air like a balloon, weighing nothing, and at the same time, carried the weight of a planet. With the city buildings in rubble on the ground, it was the only thing in the sky, blocking out the sun, and emanating a pale blue aura. The glow filtered down through the smoke, illuminating an eerie glow through the street.

"What is that?" Calay gasped. She inhaled sharply but none of the air reached her lungs. She couldn't breathe. She couldn't move.

Tess raised her head from Calay's chest.

"Oh my God—Calay, what *is* it?" Tess echoed, scrambling away from Calay's embrace and against what was left of a wall. What was just moments before, their wall.

Calay shook her head, stunned with fear.

A flicker of movement pulled Calay's gaze from the floating orb. *What...?* As she tried to make sense of what she was seeing, people laying in the middle of the street started to disappear into clouds of red mist. The words evaporated from her tongue as pale dots littered the ground where their bodies had been. In some places, it oozed, thick and red down the broken pavement, seeping into the cracks and pooling far beneath their feet. Beneath what was left of the street, the city's sewers were slowly being paved in blood.

The realization of what was happening cascaded over Calay like an avalanche.

People—her neighbors—were being murdered and vaporized in front of her eyes.

"We have to go," Calay said too quietly for anyone to hear, "we have to *go* Tess!"

The strange silence that just moments before echoed through the city, ended abruptly as blood-curdling screams of terror washed over Calay. People cowered and ran, glass shattering underfoot. They trampled one another, young and old, in their flight to escape the danger. Many of them burst into fogs of red themselves.

Calay turned to Tess, who was standing behind her throwing up on her own shoes. Calay kneeled before her.

"I don't know what's happening, but we have to get out of here! Right now, okay?"

"I don't know if I can, Cay."

"You have to Tess." Calay dared a glance up and saw a woman trip over the curb and explode into red just before her head hit the ground. "Right fucking now! Or you're going to die. Like them."

Tess nodded, her eyes glazed and red from the smoke. Calay held Tess's face in her hands, forcing her to meet her gaze. She needed some kind of agreement from Tess. An acknowledgment of what she was saying.

"Got it? We run. We run now."

Calay grabbed Tess's hand, unsure if her lover had the wherewithal to follow her, and they ran. People poured out of cars and into streets. Around them, city blocks burst into chaotic nightmares of death. And red. So much red. New trails of smoke decorated the morning sky as cars were lit ablaze. Buildings crashed into each other, sending the people within them into a hailstorm of concrete and glass.

"Run!" they called to people frozen in the street, "you have to run!"

Those that did, followed close behind. They raced across the street, narrowly avoiding getting hit by a city bus. The people behind them were not so lucky, getting caught in the wheels and dragged along the undercarriage. Calay turned to look, regrettably. Their insides were smeared onto the pavement before her. The bus's horn blared.

Calay felt herself scream more than she heard it. Her voice rattled inside her chest like a freight train. She felt herself moving toward the mess of people that no longer were.

"Calay!" Tess called after her.

"Oh no, oh no!" Calay stammered, "I told them, I..."

"It's not your fault," Tess told her. She put her hand around Calay's arm and pulled her along, away from the carnage.

"I told them to run!" Calay wailed. Tess answered her, but Calay didn't hear her words. Instead, a deep whirring and grating sound filled the air, chasing away her reply. The screams and wails of people afraid to die or mourning the loss of someone who *did*, momentarily drowned out. As she stared at the mess in front of her, Calay caught fragments of Tess's words.

"Calay!" Tess snapped, herding Calay's attention.

"Huh?" Calay replied.

"We keep moving."

Calay nodded, her mouth twisted from shock.

"Stay with me," Tess urged. She leaned in, pressing her forehead against Calay's. Tess caressed Calay's face with one hand while lifting a gold pendant from around her neck with the other. Subtle gold ridges glinted in the shape of a crescent moon at the end of a delicate chain. "To the moon and back, remember?" Tess's eyes went to Calay's throat. Calay fingered the same shape around her own neck. It was the first gift they'd ever given each other. A reminder that no matter what happened or where they went, they'd belong to each other. It was destined in the stars. The feel of it between Calay's fingers brought her back from the darkness that threatened to overtake her.

"You and me, right?" Calay whispered.

"You and me." Tess nodded.

So that's how it was, until now. Tess was somewhere and Calay was going to find her, if she could just make it out of that damned building. As with that first morning, Calay put one foot in front of the other. *One flight at a time. Just take it one flight at a time. Don't think about how many there are. If you make it through this one...*she stopped short. She'd what—make it? She wasn't so sure. She wanted to tell herself it would all be alright, but she'd stopped believing in fairy tales long ago. Before The Change, fairy tales gave humanity hope. But now, fairy tales got you killed.

Calay reached the top of the staircase; there was another door. She reached for the handle and it opened rather easily; too easily. She stepped outside and found herself on the roof. Several smokestacks towered to her left; a shed sat to her right. And it was a long way down to the ground on either side. She was surprised to see other buildings on the block, spaced within only a few feet of each other. She'd assumed— wrongfully—they'd have dumped her somewhere more remote. This wasn't remote at all. She squinted at the busted skyline. She knew this area. It was in the core of the city.

I could scream. Maybe someone will hear me.

"Right," she scolded herself, shaking her head, "like the thugs who are trying to find and dispose of your corpse."

She ran her hand over the back of her neck, working out a kink while she worked out a plan. Shouting would be a stupid idea, at least in that moment. *Give them time to give up and get lost; hide. Then you can take your time making your way down the stairs.* But before Calay had the chance to move, the door to the roof swung open with a clang.

The two men regarded her, and she them. Their eyes a dangerous combination of confusion and anger. Hers were overflowing with fear. She was in no condition to defend herself and they knew it. What were they waiting for? Her eyes shifted between them and the door. She'd never get past them. She felt like a wounded bird being eyed up by a pair of foxes.

She looked around the cavernous expanse of sky and air and sunshine. She had nowhere to go. Never before had being free felt more like a prison.

The bigger one smirked. This was not going to end well for her.

Facing the consequences of her impetuous decision to climb rather than descend, she knew she had to make another quick decision. There was no way they were going to let her walk out of there. She was either going to be killed or would have to risk killing herself in her attempt to escape. She knew what she had to do. *I have to jump.* She wished she could fly. *Wingless little bird.*

She steeled herself against the pain she knew was to come and sprinted for the closest side of the building. The gravel crunched behind her under their heavy boots while every step she took felt like someone was wailing a sledgehammer against her knee —an incessant throbbing drummed along her bones, culminating as a monstrous symphony in the back of her head. Her knee may not be broken but it certainly wasn't in any kind of shape to run. Her vision wobbled; her lungs refused to cooperate.

She couldn't stop. She wouldn't stop.

Keep moving.

As she approached the ledge, a long, desperate, frenzied howl escaped Calay's mouth and she leapt into the abyss. Into the unknown. Into a total and complete chasm of air.

It was all that ever was. All that ever would be.

Don't stop now. Keep reading with your copy of THE STARS IN THEIR EYES by City Owl Author, Kristy Gardner.

And find more from Mindi Briar at www.mindibriar.com

Want to learn more about Mindi Briar? Find all the details of her upcoming books at www.mindibriar.com

And discover THE STARS IN THEIR EYES by City Owl Author, Kristy Gardner!

The stakes were clear after the Change— survive together, or die.

Calay and Tess's love has kept them alive four years after the aliens decimated Earth. But when Calay finds herself fighting for her life and Tess missing, she hears death knocking. Banging, really. She has nothing. Scraps for food, the clothes on her back, no safe place for respite. And yet, she is determined to risk it all to reunite with the one woman she has ever loved. She only has one choice: she must find Tess.

Reluctantly, Calay braves the new nightmares of a ravaged Pacific Northwest, alone. Thrust into the darkness, she is haunted by horrors beyond her imagination—alien executioners, a mysterious man, the rise of a sinister cult, and a shocking family secret that challenges everything she thinks she knows.

As the lines between good and evil blur, Calay's desperation threatens to destroy what's left of her humanity. Her heart smeared across her tattered sleeve, she is pulled deeper into the madness of a world that has become kill or be killed.

Calay must deny her feral instincts and resist becoming a monster herself. While confronting her demons, she stares down the barrel of a terrifying truth: she may be forever alone. Time is running out and she knows it. Her only hope is to become who she is truly meant to be and unify with the love of her life once and for all. But, at what cost?

To survive, Calay must choose between the unthinkable: give up, or give 'em hell.

Please sign up for the City Owl Press newsletter for chances to win special subscriber-only contests and giveaways as well as receiving information on upcoming releases and special excerpts.

All reviews are **welcome** and **appreciated**. Please consider leaving one on your favorite social media and book buying sites.

Escape Your World. Get Lost in Ours! City Owl Press at www.cityowlpress.com.

ACKNOWLEDGMENTS

This book was a hard one to write. For starters, it's based on characters that I've been playing with for literally over half my life. It inspired the creation of the Halcyon Universe, went through at least seven rewrites before it even got to this version, and then three more rewrites to become the book you're holding. It was the story that wouldn't let me go until I did it right.

Part of why this story has such a hold on me is because it's the story of a woman and her relationship with religion and spirituality. I started writing it long before I left the church I grew up in. Writing about a made-up religion in a fantasy/sci-fi world helped me process my complicated feelings about my faith, and I wrote version upon version of this book trying to understand what my characters (aka: me) truly believed about the universe.

At some point, my doubts built up to an insurmountable degree, and I left the Christian home church fellowship I was raised in. I was still searching for a spiritual understanding of the world, so for a while, I attended a different religious gathering, where I was welcomed warmly and taught a much more open-ended and joyous version of faith. Yet I found myself leaving that group, too.

This version of the story came together when I finally had sufficient distance, after not attending any organized church for a few years. But Miri is very much a reflection of my feelings and fears at the time when I was still reaching for some way to make sense of my spirituality.

This book has other deeply personal aspects to it—the main characters' experience of (a)sexuality, and the wish-fulfillment depiction of a future utopian society—but regardless of pouring so much of my own unique experience into this story, I hope that the reader finds something to relate to.

Over the course of writing a bajillion different drafts, I've had a LOT of beta readers. I would just like to put out a blanket "thank you" to anyone who read any of my previous drafts, and an apology that I can't remember how many of you there are.

To the amazing beta who helped me with the latest draft: Skye, you are an absolute BOSS for pinpointing all my little character inconsistencies. Thank you for helping me make this book shine.

My sincere gratitude to City Owl Press for giving the Halcyon Universe a chance to be seen by the world. Y'all have been nothing but stellar to work with. Lisa and Tina, you two in particular have been so helpful and just generally awesome.

Thanks are also in order to my IRL writing buddy, Chelsea, who helped keep me accountable as I put this draft on paper (screen?) over the course of countless weekend writing sessions in a local hippie coffee shop. I'm eagerly waiting to read your dragon book!

As always, thank you to my husband Joe for being the best sounding board and cheerleader through the process of writing. You always ask the hard worldbuilding questions, and you inspire me daily through your art and imagination.

And of course I can't forget to shout out all the wonderful ace authors who've paved the way and inspired me to write about my own experience. Asexuality is a spectrum, and I've found it valuable to read about ace and aro experiences that are different from my own. Here's a list of recent reads:

Adult:

- The Baker Thief by Claudie Arseneault
- Ace of Hearts by Lucy Mason
- The Romantic Agenda by Claire Kann
- Gender Queer by Maia Kobabe
- Common Bonds (anthology)
- ACE by Angela Chen (nonfiction)

Young Adult:

- Loveless by Alice Oseman
- Tarnished Are the Stars by Rosiee Thor

ABOUT THE AUTHOR

MINDI BRIAR'S favorite book as a
child was "Commander Toad in Space,"
an early sign that she was destined to
become a gigantic nerd. She lives in the
Seattle area with her husband and
three cats, two of whom are named
after punctuation marks. She will be
your friend if you offer tea, or if you
want to talk about Star Wars.

www.mindibriar.com

facebook.com/mindi.writes
twitter.com/mindi_writes
instagram.com/mindibriar

ABOUT THE PUBLISHER

City Owl Press is a cutting edge indie publishing company, bringing the world of romance and speculative fiction to discerning readers.

Escape Your World. Get Lost in Ours!

www.cityowlpress.com

facebook.com/CityOwlPress
twitter.com/cityowlpress
instagram.com/cityowlbooks
pinterest.com/cityowlpress
tiktok.com/@cityowlpress